A Royal Proposal

BARBARA HANNAY
JENNIFER FAYE
ELLIE DARKINS

MILLS & BOON

First Published in Great Britain 2019
by Mills & Boon, an imprint of HarperCollins*Publishers*
1 London Bridge Street, London, SE1 9GF

A ROYAL PROPOSAL © 2019 Harlequin Books S. A.

The Prince's Convenient Proposal © 2016 Barbara Hannay
The Millionaire's Royal Rescue © 2017 Jennifer F. Stroka
Falling for the Rebel Princess © 2017 Ellie Darkins

ISBN: 978-0-263-27484-4

0419

MIX
Paper from
responsible sources
FSC˙ C007454

Printed and bound in Spain
by CPI, Barcelona

THE PRINCE'S CONVENIENT PROPOSAL

BARBARA HANNAY

For Sophie and Milla.

CHAPTER ONE

WEDNESDAY MORNINGS WERE always quiet in the gallery, so any newcomer was bound to catch Charlie's eye as she sat patiently at the reception desk. This morning, her attention was certainly caught by the tall, dark-haired fellow who came striding through the arched doorway as if he owned the place. He was gobsmackingly handsome, but it was his commanding manner that made Charlie almost forget to offer him her customary, sunny and welcoming smile.

A serious mistake. The cut of this fellow's charcoal-grey suit suggested that he actually had the means to purchase one of the gallery's paintings.

And, boy, Charlie needed to sell a painting. Fast. Her father, Michael Morisset, was the artist most represented on these gallery walls and his finances were in dire straits. Again. Always.

Sadly, her charming and talented, but vague and impractical parent was hopeless with money. His finances had always been precarious, but until recently he and Charlie—actually, it had mostly been Charlie who'd struggled with this—had managed to make ends meet. Just. But now, her father had remarried and his new wife had produced a brand-new baby daughter, and his situation was even more desperate.

Charlie was thinking of Isla, her new, too fragile and tiny half-sister, as she flashed the newcomer a bright smile and lifted a catalogue brochure from the pile on the counter.

'Good morning,' she said warmly.

'Morning.' His response was cool, without any hint of an answering smile. His icy grey eyes narrowed as he stopped and stood very still, staring at Charlie.

She squeezed her facial muscles, forcing an even brighter smile as she held out a brochure. 'First time at the gallery, sir?'

Momentary surprise flashed in his eyes, but then he said, 'Of course.'

Charlie thought she caught the hint of an accent, and his gaze grew even chillier, which spoiled the handsome perfection of his cheekbones and jawline and thick, glossy dark hair.

'How are you, Olivia?' he asked.

Huh?

Charlie almost laughed. He looked so serious, but he was seriously deluded. 'I'm sorry. My name's not Olivia.'

The newcomer shook his head. 'Nice try.' He smiled this time, but the smile held no warmth. 'Don't play games. I've come a long way to find you, as you very well know.'

Now it was Charlie's turn to stare, while her mind raced. Was this fellow a loony? Should she call Security?

She glanced quickly around the gallery. A pair of elderly ladies were huddled at the far end of the large space, which had once been a warehouse. Their heads were together as they studied a Daphne Holden, a delicate water colour of a rose garden. The only other visitor, so far this morning, was the fellow in the chair by the window. He seemed to be asleep, most probably a homeless guy enjoying the air-conditioning.

At least no one was paying any attention to this weird conversation.

'I'm sorry,' Charlie said again. 'You're mistaken. My name is not Olivia. It's Charlie.'

His disbelief was instantly evident. In his eyes, in the curl of his lip.

'Charlotte, to be totally accurate,' she amended. 'Charlotte Morisset.' Again, she held out the catalogue. 'Would you like to see the gallery? We have some very fine—'

'No, I'm not interested in your paintings.' The man was clearly losing his patience. 'I haven't come to see the artwork. I don't know why you're doing this, Olivia, but whatever your reasons, the very least you owe me is an explanation.'

Charlie refused to apologise a second time. 'I told you, I'm not—' She stopped in mid-sentence. There was little to be gained by repeating her claim. She was tempted to reach for her handbag, to show this arrogant so and so her driver's licence and to prove she wasn't this Olivia chick. But she had no idea if she could trust this man. For all she knew, this could be some kind of trap. He could be trying to distract her while thieves crept in to steal the paintings.

Or perhaps she'd been watching too much television?

She was rather relieved when a middle-aged couple came into the gallery, all smiles. She always greeted gallery visitors warmly, and Grim Face had no choice but to wait his turn as she bestowed this couple with an extra-sunny smile and handed them each a catalogue.

'We're particularly interested in Michael Morisset,' the man said.

Wonderful! 'We have an excellent collection of his

paintings.' Charlie tried not to sound too pleased and eager. 'The Morrisets are mostly on this nearest wall.' She waved towards the collection of her father's bold, dramatic oils depicting so many facets of Sydney's inner-city landscape. 'You'll find them all listed in the catalogue.'

'And they're all for sale?' asked the woman.

'Except for the few samples of his earliest work from the nineteen-eighties. It's all explained in the catalogue, but if you have any questions, please don't hesitate to ask me. That's why I'm here.'

'Wonderful. Thank you.'

The couple continued to smile broadly and they looked rather excited as they moved away. Behind her back, Charlie crossed her fingers. Her father needed a big sale so badly.

Unfortunately Grim Face was still hanging around, and now he leaned towards her. 'You do an excellent Australian accent, but you can't keep it up. I've found you now, Olivia, and I won't be leaving until we have this sorted.'

'There's nothing to sort.' Charlie felt a stirring of panic. 'You've made a mistake and that's all there is to it. I don't even *know* anyone called Olivia.' She sent a frantic glance to the couple studying her father's paintings.

After she'd given them enough time to have a good look, she would approach them with her gentle sales pitch. Today she had to be extra careful to hit the right note— she mustn't be too cautious, or too pushy—and she really needed this guy out of her hair.

She cut her gaze from his, as if their conversation was ended, and made a show of tidying the brochures before turning to her computer screen.

'When do you get time off for lunch?' he asked.

Charlie stiffened. He was really annoying her. And

worrying her. Was he some kind of stalker? And anyway, she didn't take 'time off for lunch'. She ate a sandwich and made a cup of tea in the tiny office off this reception area, but she wasn't about to share that information with this jerk.

'I'm afraid I'm here all day,' she replied with an imperiousness that almost matched his.

'Then I'll see you at six when the gallery closes.'

Charlie opened her mouth to protest when he cut her off with a raised hand.

'And don't try anything foolish, like trying to slip away again. My men will be watching you.'

His *men*?

What the hell…?

Truly appalled, Charlie pulled her handbag from under the desk, dumped it on the counter, and ferociously yanked the zipper. 'Listen, mate, I'll prove to you that I'm not this Olivia person.' Pulling out her purse, she flipped it open to reveal her driver's licence. 'My name's Charlotte Morisset. Like it or lump it.'

Her pulse was racketing at a giddy pace as he leaned forward to inspect the proffered licence. There was something very not right about this. He had the outward appearance of a highly successful man. Handsome and well groomed, with that shiny dark hair and flashing grey eyes, he might have been a male model or a film star, or even a barrister. A federal politician. Someone used to being in the spotlight.

It made no sense that he would confuse her—ordinary, everyday Charlie Morisset from the wrong end of Bankstown—with anyone from his circle.

Unless he was a high-class criminal. Perhaps he'd heard the recent ripples in the art world. Perhaps he knew that her father was on the brink of finally garnering attention for his work.

My men will be watching you.

Charlie snapped her purse shut, hoping he hadn't had time to read her address and date of birth.

'So you've changed your name, but not your date of birth,' he said with just a hint of menace.

Charlie let out a huff—half sigh, half terror. 'Listen, mister. I want you to leave. Now. If you don't, I'm calling the police.' She reached for the phone.

As she did so Grim Face slipped a hand into the breast pocket of his coat.

White-hot fear strafed through Charlie. He was getting out his gun. Her hands were shaking as she pressed triple zero. But it was probably too late. She was about to die.

Instead of producing a gun, however, he slapped a photograph down on the counter. 'This is the girl I'm looking for.' He eyed Charlie with the steely but watchful gaze of a detective ready to pounce. 'Her name is Olivia Belaire.'

Once again, Charlie gasped.

It was the photo that shocked her this time. It was a head and shoulders photograph of herself.

There could be no doubt. That was her face. Those were her unruly blonde curls, her blue eyes, her too-wide mouth. Even the dimple in the girl's right cheek was the same shape as hers.

Charlie heard a voice speaking from her phone, asking whether she wanted the police, the ambulance or the fire brigade.

'Ah, no,' she said quickly. 'Sorry, I'm OK. It was a false alarm.'

As she disconnected, she stared at the photo. Every detail was exact, including the tilt of the girl's smile. Except no, wait a minute, this dimple was in the girl's left cheek.

Then again, Charlie supposed some cameras might reverse the image.

The girl, who looked exactly like her and was supposed to be Olivia Belaire, was even wearing a plain white T-shirt, just as Charlie was now, tucked into blue jeans. And there was a beach in the background, which could easily have been Sydney's Bondi Beach. Charlie tried to remember what she'd been wearing the last time she'd been to Bondi.

'Where'd you get this photo?'

For the first time, Grim Face almost smiled. 'I took it with my own camera, as you know very well. At Saint-Tropez.'

Charlie rubbed at her forehead, wishing that any part of this made sense. She swallowed, staring hard at the photo. 'Who is this girl? How do you know her?'

His jaw tightened with impatience. 'It's time to stop the games now, Olivia.'

'I'm not—' This was getting tedious. 'What's *your* name?' she asked instead. 'What's this all about?'

Now it was his turn to sigh, to give a weary, resigned shake of his head and to run a frustrated hand through his thick dark hair, ruffling it rather attractively.

Charlie found herself watching with inappropriate interest.

'My name's Rafe.' He sounded bored, as if he was repeating something she already knew. 'Short for Rafael. Rafael St Romain.'

'Sorry, that doesn't ring a bell. It sounds—maybe—French?'

'French is our national language,' the man called Rafe acceded. 'Although most of our citizens also speak English. I live in Montaigne.'

'That cute little country in the Alps?'

He continued to look bored, as if he was sure she was playing with him. 'Exactly.'

Charlie had heard about Montaigne, of course. It was very small and not especially important, as far as she could tell, but it was famous for skiing and—and for something else, something glamorous like jewellery.

She'd seen photos in magazines of celebrities, even royalty, holidaying there. 'Well, that's very interesting, Rafe, but it doesn't—'

Charlie paused. Damn. She couldn't afford to waste time with this distraction. She made a quick check around the gallery. The vagrant was still asleep in the window seat. The old ladies were having a good old chinwag. The other couple were also deep in discussion, still looking at her father's paintings and studying the catalogue.

She needed to speak to them. She had a feeling they were on the verge of making a purchase and she couldn't afford to let them slip away, to 'think things over'.

'I *really* don't have time for this,' she told Rafael St Romain.

Out of the corner of her eye, she was aware of the couple nodding together, as if they'd reached a decision. Ignoring his continuing grim expression, she skirted the counter and stepped out into the gallery, her soft-soled shoes silent on the tiles.

'What did you think of the Morissets?' she asked, directing her question to the couple.

They looked up and she sent them an encouraging smile.

'The paintings are wonderful,' the man said. 'So bold and original.'

'We'd love one for our lounge room,' added the woman.

Her husband nodded. 'We're just trying to make a decision.'

'We need to go home and take another look at our wall space,' the woman said quickly.

Charlie's heart sank. She knew from experience that the chances of this couple returning to make an actual purchase were slim. Most true art lovers knew exactly what they wanted as soon as they saw it.

This couple were more interested in interior décor. Already they were walking away.

The woman's smile was almost apologetic, as she looked back over her shoulder, as if she'd guessed that they'd disappointed Charlie. 'We'll see you soon,' she called.

Charlie smiled and nodded, but as they disappeared through the doorway her shoulders drooped.

She wished this weren't her problem, but, even though she'd moved out of home into a tiny shoebox studio flat when her father remarried, she still looked after her father's finances. It was a task she'd assumed at the age of fourteen, making sure that the rent and the bills were paid while she did her best to discourage her dad from throwing too many overly extravagant parties, or from taking expensive holidays to 'fire up his muse'.

Unfortunately, her new stepmother, Skye, was as unworldly and carefree as her dad, so she'd been happy to leave this task in Charlie's hands. The bills all came to the gallery and Charlie was already trying to figure out how she'd pay the electricity bills for this month, as well as providing the funds for nourishing meals.

Skye would need plenty of nourishment while she cared for Isla, *tiny* little Isla who'd taken a scarily long time to start breathing after she was born. Despite her small size, Charlie's baby sister had looked perfect, though, with the sweetest cap of dark hair, a neat nose and darling little mouth like a rosebud. Perfect tiny fingers and toes.

But the doctors were running some tests on Isla. Charlie wasn't sure what they were looking for, but the thought that something might be wrong with her baby sister was terrifying. Since Isla's birth, her father had more or less lived at the hospital, camping by Skye's bed.

Charlie was dragged from these gloomy thoughts by the phone ringing. She turned back to the counter, annoyed to see that Rafael St Romain in his expensive grey suit hadn't budged an inch. And he was still watching her.

Deliberately not meeting his distrustful grey gaze, she picked up the phone.

'Charlie?'

She knew immediately from the tone of her father's voice that he was worried. A chill shimmied through her. 'Hi.' She turned her back on the exquisitely suited Rafael.

'We've had some bad news about Isla,' her father said. 'There's a problem with her heart.'

Horrified, Charlie sank forward, elbows supporting her on the counter. *Her heart.* 'How—how bad is it?'

'Bad.'

Sickening dizziness swept over Charlie. 'What can they do?'

There was silence on the other end of the phone.

'Dad?'

'The doctors here can't do anything. Her problem is very rare and complicated. You should see her, Charlie. She's in isolation, with tubes everywhere and all these monitors.' Her father's voice was ragged and Charlie knew he was only just holding himself together.

'Surely they can do *something*?'

'It doesn't sound like it, but there's a cardiologist in Boston who's had some success with surgery.'

'Boston!' Charlie bit back a groan. Her mind raced. A surgeon in Boston meant serious money. Mountains of it. Poor little Isla. What could they do?

Charlie knew only too well that her father had little chance of raising a quick loan for this vital operation. He'd never even been able to raise a mortgage. His income flow was so erratic, the banks wouldn't take the risk.

Poor Isla. What on earth could they do? Charlie looked again at the paintings hanging on the walls. She knew they were good. And since her father had married Skye, there'd been a new confidence in his work, a new daring. His latest stuff had shown a touch of genius.

Charlie was sure Michael Morisset was on the very edge of being discovered by the world and becoming famous. But it would be too late for Isla.

'I'm going to ring around,' her father said. 'To see what help I can get. You never know…'

'Yes, that's a good idea,' Charlie told him fervently. 'Good luck. I'll make some calls too and see what I can do. Even if I can get some advice, anything that might help.'

'That would be great, love. Thanks.'

'I'll call again later.'

'OK.'

'Give Skye a hug from me.'

Charlie disconnected, set the phone down, and let her head sink into her hands as she wrestled with the unbearable thought of her newborn baby sister's tiny damaged heart, the poor, precious creature struggling to hold on to her fragile new life.

'Excuse me.'

She jumped as the deep masculine voice intruded into her misery. She'd forgotten all about Rafael St Romain and his stupid photo. Swiping at tears, she turned to him.

'I'm sorry. I don't have time to deal with this Olivia business.'

'Yes, I can see that.'

To her surprise he seemed less formidable. Perhaps he'd overheard her end of the conversation. He almost looked concerned.

'You were speaking with your father,' he said.

Charlie's chin lifted. 'Yes.' Not that it was any of his business.

'Then clearly I am in the wrong. I apologise. The woman I'm searching for has no father.'

'Right. Good.' At least he would leave her in peace now.

'But the likeness is uncanny,' he said.

'It is.' Charlie couldn't deny this. The photo that had supposedly been taken in Saint-Tropez showed a mirror image of herself, and, despite her new worries about Isla, she couldn't help being curious. 'How do you know this Olivia?' she found herself asking. 'Who is she?'

Rafael regarded her steadily and he took a nerve-racking age before he answered. Trapped in his powerful gaze, Charlie flashed hot and cold. The man was ridiculously attractive. Under different circumstances she might have been quite helplessly smitten.

Instead, she merely felt discomfited. And annoyed.

'Olivia Belaire is my fiancée,' he said at last. 'And for the sake of my country's future, I have to find her.'

For the sake of his country's future?

Charlie's jaw was already gaping and couldn't drop any further. This surprise, coming on top of her father's bombshell, was almost too much to take in.

How was it possible that a girl who looked *exactly* the same as herself could live on the other side of the

world and somehow be responsible for an entire country's future?

Who was Olivia?

Charlie had heard of doppelgängers, but she'd never
really believed they existed in real life.

But what other explanation could there be?

A twin sister?

This thought was barely formed before fine hairs lifted
on Charlie's skin. And before she could call a halt to her
thoughts, they galloped on at a reckless pace.

This girl, Olivia, had no father, while to all intents and
purposes she, Charlie, had no mother.

Charlie's father had always been vague about her
mother. Her parents had divorced when Charlie was a
baby and her mother had taken off for Europe, never
to be heard from or seen again. Over the years, Charlie
had sometimes fretted over her mother's absence, but
she and her dad had been so close, he'd made up for the
loss. Money worries aside, he'd been a wonderful dad.

The two of them had enjoyed many fabulous adventures together, sailing in the South Pacific, hiking in
Nepal, living in the middle of rice fields in Bali while her
father taught English during the day and painted at night.
They'd also had a few very exciting months in New York.

When her father had married Skye, Charlie had been
happy to see him so settled at last, and she'd been thrilled
when Skye became pregnant. She liked the idea of being
part of a bigger family. Now, though, she couldn't help
thinking back and wondering why her father had limited
his travels to Asia, strictly avoiding Europe. Had he actually been avoiding her mother?

Charlie gulped at the next thought. Had he been afraid
that she'd discover her twin sister?

Surely not.

CHAPTER TWO

RAFE WAS REELING as he watched the play of emotions on the girl's face. He was still coming to terms with the frustrating reality that this wasn't Olivia, but her exact double, Charlotte.

Charlie.

The likeness to his missing fiancée was incredible. No wonder his detectives had been fooled. The resemblance went beyond superficial features such as Charlie Morisset's golden curls and blue eyes and her neatly curving figure. It was there in the way she moved, in the tilt of her chin, in the spirited flash in her eyes.

Take away her blue jeans and sneakers and put her in an *haute couture* gown and, apart from her Australian accent, which wasn't too terribly broad, no one in Montaigne would ever tell the difference.

The possibilities presented by this resemblance were so tempting.

Rafe, Crown Prince of Montaigne, needed a fiancée.

He'd been engaged for barely a fortnight before Olivia Belaire took flight. Admittedly, his arrangement with Olivia had been one of hasty convenience rather than romance. They'd struck a business deal in fact, and Rafe understood that Olivia might well have panicked when she'd come to terms with the realities of being married to a prince with enormous responsibilities.

Rafe had come close to panicking, too. One minute he'd been an AWOL playboy prince, travelling the world, enjoying a delightful and endless series of parties…in Los Angeles, London, Dubai, Monaco…with an endless stream of girls to match…redheads, brunettes, blondes… all long-legged and glamorous and willing.

For years, especially in the years since his mother's death, Rafe had been flying high. He and Sheikh Faysal Daood Taariq, his best friend from university, had been A-list invitees at all the most glittering celebrity parties. As was their custom, they'd made quite a hit when they arrived at the wild party in Saint-Tropez.

Just a few short weeks ago.

Such a shock it had been that night, in the midst of the glitz and glamour, for Rafe to receive a phone call from home.

He'd been flirting outrageously with Olivia Belaire, and the girl was dancing barefoot while Rafe drank champagne from one of her shoes, when a white-coated waiter had tugged at his elbow.

'Excuse me, Your Highness, you're needed on the phone.'

'Not now,' Rafe had responded, waving the fellow off with the champagne-filled shoe. 'I'm busy.'

'I'm sorry, sir, but it's a phone call from Montaigne. From the castle. They said it's urgent.'

'No, no, no,' Rafe had insisted rather tipsily. 'Nothing's so important that it can't wait till morning.'

'It's urgent news about your father, Your Highness.'

In an instant Rafe had sobered. In fact, his veins had turned to ice as he'd walked stiff-backed to the phone to receive the news that his father, the robust and popu-

lar ruling Prince of Montaigne, had died suddenly of a
heart attack.

Rafe's memories of the rest of that dreadful night were
a blur. He'd been shocked and grief-stricken and filled
with remorse, and he'd spent half of the night on the
phone, talking to castle staff, to his country's Chancellor, to Montaigne's Chief of Intelligence, to his father's
secretary, his father's publicist—who were now Rafe's
secretary and publicist.

There'd been so much that he'd had to come to terms
with in a matter of hours, including the horrifying, ines-
capable fact that he needed to find a fiancée in a hurry.

An ancient clause in Montaigne's constitution required
a crown prince to be married, or at least betrothed, within
two days of a ruling prince's death. The subsequent marriage must take place within two months of this date.

Such a disaster!

The prospect of a sudden marriage had appalled Rafe.
He'd been free for so long, he'd never considered settling
down with one woman. Or at least, no single woman had
ever sufficiently snagged his attention to the point that
he'd considered a permanent relationship.

Suddenly, however, his country's future was at stake.

Looking back on the past couple of weeks, Rafe was
ashamed to admit that he'd been only dimly aware of the
mining company that threatened Montaigne. But on that
harrowing night he'd been forced to pay attention.

The message was clear. Without a fiancée, Rafe St
Romain would be deposed as Prince of Montaigne, the
Chancellor would take control and the mongrels intent
on his country's ruin would have their way. In a blink
they would tie up the rights to the mineral wealth hidden
deep within Montaigne's Alps.

Among the many briefings Rafe had received that

night, he'd been given an alarming warning from Montaigne's Chief of Intelligence.

'You cannot trust your Chancellor, Claude Pontier. We are certain he's corrupt, but we're still working on ways to prove it. We don't have enough information yet, but Pontier has links to the Leroy Mining Company.'

In other words…if Rafe wasn't married within the required time frame, he would be deposed and the Chancellor could take control, allowing the greedy pack of miners to cause irreparable damage to Montaigne. Given free rein, they would heartlessly tear the mountains apart, wreaking havoc on his country's beautiful landscape and totally destroying the economy based on centuries-old traditions.

With only two days to produce a fiancée, Rafe had turned to the nearest available girl, who had happened to be the extraordinarily pretty, but slightly vacuous, Olivia Belaire. Unfortunately, less than two weeks after their spectacular and very public engagement ball, Olivia had done a runner.

To an extent, Rafe could sympathise with Olivia. The night she'd agreed to step up as his fiancée had been a crazy whirlwind, and she certainly hadn't had time to fully take in the deeper ramifications of marriage to a ruling prince. But Rafe had paid her an exceedingly generous amount, and the terms for their eventual divorce were unstinting, so he found it hard to remain sympathetic now, when his country's problems were so dire.

Despite his wayward playboy history, Rafe loved his country with all his heart and he loved the people of Montaigne, who were almost as famous for the exquisite jewellery they made from locally sourced gemstones as they were for their wonderful alpine cuisine. With the addition of the country's world-class ski slopes, Montaigne offered an exclusive tourist package that had been his country's lifeblood since the eighteenth century.

Montaigne could never survive the invasion of these miners.

Regrettably, his police still hadn't enough evidence to pin Pontier down. They needed more time. And Rafe desperately needed a fiancée.

Damn it, if Charlie Morisset hadn't just received a phone call from her father that had clearly distressed her, Rafe would have proposed that she fly straight home with him. She would be the perfect foil, a lifesaving stand-in until Olivia was unearthed and placated, and reinstated as his fiancée. He would pay Charlie handsomely, of course.

It seemed, however, that Charlie was dealing with some kind of family crisis of her own, so this probably wasn't the choice moment to crassly wave money in her face in the hope that he could whisk her away.

'How on earth did you manage to lose Olivia?'

Rafe frowned at Charlie's sudden, cheekily posed question.

'Did you frighten her off?' she asked, blue eyes blazing. 'You didn't hurt her, did you?'

Rafe was almost too affronted to answer. 'Of course I didn't hurt her.' In truth, he'd barely touched her.

Instantly sobered by the news of his father's death, he had dropped his playboy persona the very moment he and Olivia had left the party in Saint-Tropez. As they'd hurried back to Montaigne, Rafe had reverted to the perfect gentlemanly Prince. Apart from the few tipsy kisses they'd exchanged while they'd danced at the party, he'd barely laid a hand on the girl.

Of course, he'd been grateful to Olivia for agreeing to a hasty marriage of convenience, but since then he'd been busy dealing with formalities and his father's funeral and his own sudden responsibilities.

'I'm sorry to have troubled you,' he told Charlie now with icy politeness.

She gave a distracted nod.

He took a step back, loath to let go of this lifeline, but fearing he had little choice. Charlie Morisset was clearly absorbed by her own worries.

'I think Olivia might be my sister,' she said.

Rafe stilled. 'Is there a chance?'

She nodded. 'I know that my mother lives somewhere in Europe. I—I've never met her. Well, not that I remember—'

Her lower lip trembled ever so slightly, and the tough, don't-mess-with-me edge that Rafe had sensed in Charlie from the outset disappeared. Now she looked suddenly vulnerable, almost childlike.

To his dismay, he felt his heart twist.

'I've met Olivia's mother,' he said. 'Her name is Vivian. Vivian Belaire.'

'Oh.' Charlie looked as suddenly pale and upset as she had when she was speaking to her father on the phone. She seemed to sag in the middle, as if her knees were in danger of giving way. 'That was my mother's name,' she said faintly. 'Vivian.'

Rafe had been on the point of departure, but now, as Charlie sank onto a stool and let out a heavy sigh, he stood his ground.

'I didn't know she had another daugh—' Charlie swallowed. 'What's she like? My mother?'

Rafe was remembering the suntanned, platinum blonde with the hard eyes and the paunchy billionaire husband, who'd had way too many drinks at the engagement ball.

'She has fair hair, like yours,' he said. 'She's—attractive. I'm afraid I don't know her very well.'

'I had no idea I had a sister. I knew nothing about Olivia.'

He wondered if this was an opening. Was there still a chance to state his case?

'I can't believe my father never told me about her.' Charlie closed her eyes and pressed her fingers to her temples as if a headache was starting.

Then she straightened suddenly, opened her eyes and flashed him a guilty grimace. 'I can't deal with this now. I have other problems, way more important.'

Disappointed, Rafe accepted this with a dignified bow. 'Thanks for your time,' he said politely. 'I hope your other problems are quickly sorted.'

'Thank you.' Charlie dropped her gaze to her phone and began to scroll through numbers.

Rafe turned to leave. This dash to the southern hemisphere had been a fruitless exercise, a waste of precious time. His detectives would have to work doubly hard now to find Olivia.

'But maybe I *could* see you this evening.'

Charlie's voice brought him whirling round.

She looked rather forlorn and very *alone* as she stood at the counter, phone in hand. To Rafe's dismay her eyes were glittering with tears.

So different from the tough little terrier who'd barked at him when he first arrived in her gallery.

Maybe I could see you this evening.

He wasn't planning to hang around here till this evening. If Charlie couldn't help him, he would leave Sydney as soon as his private jet was available for take-off.

But the news of her mother and sister had clearly rocked her, and it had come on top of a distressing phone call from her father. With some reluctance, Rafe couldn't deny that he was part-way responsible for Charlie's pain. And he couldn't stifle a small skerrick of hope.

He was running out of time. If this was a dead end, he needed to hurry home, but if there was even a slight chance that she could help…

'I've got the gallery to run and some important family business to sort out,' Charlie said self-importantly. 'But I'd like to know more about Olivia. Maybe we could grab a very quick coffee?'

Was it worth the bother of wasting precious hours for a very quick coffee? The chances of persuading this girl to take off with him were microscopic.

But what other options did he have? Olivia had well and truly gone to ground.

Rafe heard himself saying, 'I could come back here at six.'

Charlie nodded. 'Right, then. Let's do that.'

By the end of the day, Charlie was feeling quite desperate. Her phone calls hadn't produced promising results. Apart from launching a *Save Isla* charity fund, she didn't have too many options. When she called her father she learned that he hadn't fared any better.

After her very quick meeting with Rafe, she and her father planned to meet to discuss strategies, and Charlie knew she would be up all night, setting up a website and a special Facebook page, and responding to the media outlets she'd contacted during the day.

Unfortunately, there would be no time to challenge her father about Olivia. Charlie was deeply hurt that he'd never told her about her twin sister, but right now she had another sister to worry about, and she knew her dad was beside himself with worry. It was totally the wrong time to pester him about Olivia Belaire.

* * *

Promptly at six, Rafe was waiting at the gallery's front door. To Charlie's surprise, he'd changed into a black T-shirt and jeans, and the casual look, complete with a five o'clock shadow and windblown hair, made him look less like a corporate raider and more like—

Gulp.

The man of her dreams.

She quickly knocked that thought on the head. She was already regretting her impulsive request to see him again. There was little she could learn about Olivia over a quick cup of coffee. But Charlie needed to understand why her sister might have agreed to marry such a compellingly attractive guy and then run away from him.

It was bad enough having one sister to worry about. She needed Rafe to set her mind at rest, so she could channel all her attention to Isla's cause.

Suddenly having two sisters, both of them in trouble, was hard to wrap her head around. As for her emotions, she'd have to sort them out later. Right now, she was running on pure adrenaline.

In no time, Charlie and Rafe were seated in a booth in the café around the corner, which was now packed with the after-work crowd. The smell of coffee and Greek pastry filled the small but popular space and they had to lean close to be heard above the noisy chatter.

'We should have gone back to my hotel,' Rafe said, scowling at the crowded booths.

'No,' Charlie responded quite definitely.

'It would have been quieter.'

'But it would have taken time. Time I don't have.'

His eyes narrowed as he watched her, but he'd lost the hawk-eyed detective look. Now he just looked extraordinarily *hot*, and she found herself fighting the tingles and flashes his proximity caused.

Their coffees arrived. A tiny cup of espresso for Rafe and a mug of frothy cappuccino for Charlie, as well as a serving of baklava. Charlie's tummy rumbled at the sight of the flaky filo pastry layered with cinnamon-spiced nut filling. Rafe had declared that he wasn't hungry, but she wasn't prepared to hold back. This would probably be the only meal she'd have time for this evening.

She scooped a creamy dollop of froth from the top of her mug. 'So, the thing I need to know, Rafe, is why my sister ran away from you.'

He smiled. It was only a faint smile, but enough to light up his grey eyes in ways that made Charlie feel slightly breathless. 'I'm afraid I can't answer that,' he said. 'She didn't leave an explanation.'

'But something must have happened. Did you have a row?'

'Not at all. Our relationship was very—' He paused as if he was searching for the right word. 'Very civilised.'

Charlie thought this was a strange word to describe a romantic liaison. Where was the soppiness? The passion? She imagined that getting engaged to a man like Rafe would involve a truckload of passion.

Even so, she found herself believing him when he said he hadn't hurt Olivia. 'So you've heard nothing,' she said. 'You must be terribly worried.'

'I have received a postcard,' said Rafe. 'There were no postage marks. The card was hand delivered, but unfortunately no one realised the significance until it was too late. It simply said that Olivia was fine and she was sorry.'

'Oh.' Charlie offered him an awkward smile of sympathy. No matter what reasons Olivia had for wanting to get out of the engagement, she'd been flaky to just take off, without facing up to Rafe with a proper explanation.

'My mother ran away,' she told him, overlooking the hurt this admission made.

Rafe lifted one dark eyebrow. 'Do you think Olivia might have inherited an escapee gene?'

Charlie was sure he hadn't meant this seriously, but the mere mention of inheritance and genes reminded her of Isla. She had to make this conversation quick, so she could get on with more important matters. 'Look,' she said, frowning, to let him know she was serious. 'I'd really like to know a little more about my sister. Where did you meet her?'

'In Saint-Tropez. At a party.'

'So, she's—well off?'

'Her father—her mother's husband,' Rafe corrected, 'is an extremely wealthy businessman. They have a house in the French Riviera and another in Switzerland, and I think there might also be a holiday house in America.'

'Wow.' *And my father can't even afford to buy one house.* Charlie tried to imagine her sister's life. 'Does she have a job?'

'None that I know of.'

'So, how does she spend her days?'

'Her days?' Rafe's lip curled in a slightly bitter smile. 'Olivia's not exactly a daytime sort of person. She's more of a night owl.'

Charlie blinked at this. She only had the vaguest notions of life on the French Riviera. She supposed Olivia was part of the jet-set who spent their time partying and shopping for clothes. If she emerged in the daylight, it was probably to lie in the sun, working hard on her suntan. Just the same, it bothered her that Rafe wasn't speaking about her sister with any sense of deep fondness. 'And what sort of work do you do?' she asked.

'That's a complicated question.'

She felt a burst of impatience. 'I don't have much time.'

'Then I'll cut to the chase. I'm my country's ruler.'

Charlie stared at him, mouth gaping, as she struggled to take this in. 'A ruler? Like—like a king?'

'Montaigne's only a small principality, but yes.' His voice dropped as if he didn't wish to be overheard. 'I'm the Prince of Montaigne. Prince Rafael the Third, to be exact.'

'Holy—' Just in time, Charlie cut off a swear word. She couldn't believe she'd met a real live prince and was sitting in her local café with him. Couldn't believe that her sister had actually scored a prince as a fiancé. 'You mean I should be calling you Sir, or Your Highness, or something?'

Rafe smiled. 'Please, no. Rafe's fine.'

Almost immediately, another thought struck Charlie. 'Olivia might have been abducted, mightn't she? That postcard might have been a—a hoax.'

Rafe shook his head. 'Security footage in the castle shows her leaving of her own volition. We know she drove her car towards Grenoble. After that—?' He frowned. 'She disappeared.'

'She might have been kidnapped.'

'There's been no request for a ransom.'

'Right.' Charlie gave a helpless shrug. 'And you've had your people searching everywhere? Even down here in Australia?'

'Yes.'

As Charlie sipped her coffee, she tried to put herself in Olivia Belaire's shoes. What would it be like to be engaged to this good-looking Prince? To be marrying into royalty? Would Olivia have been expected to undertake a host of public duties? Would she be required to chair meetings? Run charities? Visit the children's hospital?

At the very thought of a children's hospital, she shivered. *Poor little Isla.*

Fascinating though this conversation was, she'd have to cut it short.

But, as she speared a piece of baklava with her fork, she couldn't help asking, 'Do you think Olivia might have got cold feet? Could she have been worried about the whole royalty thing? All the responsibilities?'

'It's possible.'

'That's hard on you, Rafe. I—I'm sorry.' Lowering the enticing pastry to her plate, Charlie picked up her phone instead. She needed to check the time. She had to meet her father. She really should leave.

As if he sensed this, Rafe said, 'Before you go, I have a proposition.'

'No way,' Charlie said quickly, suddenly nervous. Prince or not, she'd only just met the man and she wasn't about to become embroiled in his troubles. She had enough of her own.

'You could earn a great deal of money,' he said.

Now he had her attention.

CHAPTER THREE

CHARLIE CERTAINLY BRIGHTENED at the mention of money, and Rafe was surprised by his stab of disappointment. After all, her reaction was exactly what he'd expected.

Now, however, caution also showed in Charlie's expressive face, and that was also to be expected.

'Why would you offer me money?' she asked.

'To entice you to stand in as your sister.'

She stared at him as if he'd grown an extra head. 'You've got to be joking.'

'I'm perfectly serious.'

Leaning back, she continued to watch him with obvious distrust. 'You want me to pretend to be your fiancée?'

'Yes.'

'Oh, for heaven's sake, that's ridiculous. Why?'

At least, she listened without interrupting while he explained. She leaned forward again, elbows on the table, chin resting in one hand, blue eyes intent, listening as if transfixed. Rafe told her about the inconvenient clause in Montaigne's constitution, about the country's mineral wealth and the very real threat of a takeover, and the possibility of ruin for the people who meant so much to him.

Charlie didn't speak when he finished. She sat for a minute or two, staring first at him and then into space with a small furrow between her neatly arched brows. Then she picked up her phone.

'Excuse me,' she said without looking up from the small screen. 'I'm just researching you.'

Rafe smiled. 'Of course.' He drained his coffee and sat back, waiting with barely restrained patience. But despite his tension, he thought how pleasant it was to be in a country where almost nobody knew him. Of course, his bodyguards were positioned just outside the café, but in every other way he was just an ordinary customer in a small Sydney coffee shop, chatting with a very pretty girl. The anonymity was a luxury he rarely enjoyed.

'Wow,' Charlie said, looking up from her phone. 'You're the real deal.'

Rafe's moment of fantasy was over. 'So,' he said. 'Would you consider my proposal?'

She grimaced. 'I hate to sound mercenary, but how much money are we talking about?'

'Two hundred and fifty thousand dollars US.'

Charlie's eyes almost popped out of her head. Her first instinct was to say no, she couldn't possibly consider accepting such a sum. But then she remembered Isla.

Fanning her face with her hand, she took several deep breaths before she answered. 'Crikey, Rafe, you sure know how to tempt a girl.'

Wow—not only would she be able to help Isla, she would be a step closer to finding out about Olivia as well. How could she pass up such an opportunity to meet her long-lost sister and maybe get some answers?

But even as she played with these beguiling possibilities Charlie gave Rafe a rueful smile. 'It wouldn't work, though, would it? I'd give the game away as soon as I arrived in Montaigne and opened my mouth.'

Yes, her Aussie accent *was* a problem. 'Do you speak French?'

'Oui.'

'You learnt French here in Australia?' Rafe asked in French.

'I went to school in New Caledonia,' Charlie replied with quite a passable French accent. 'I lived there for a few years with my father. Our teacher was a proper Frenchwoman. Mademoiselle Picard.'

Rafe smiled with relief. Charlie's French might be limited, but she could probably get by. 'I think you would manage well enough. Olivia isn't a native French speaker.'

'As long as I dropped the crikeys?'

His smile deepened. 'That would certainly help, but we would try to limit the amount of time you needed to speak in public. It's all about appearances, really. And when it comes to how you look, you certainly had me and my detectives fooled.'

'But I haven't agreed to this,' Charlie said quickly. 'It's so risky. I mean, there's so much room for things to go wrong. What will happen, for example, if Olivia doesn't turn up before your cut-off date? *I* couldn't possibly marry you.'

She went bright pink as she said this.

Rafe watched the rosy tide with fascination. This girl was such a beguiling mix of innocence and worldliness. But now wasn't the time to be distracted.

'I'm confident we'll find Olivia,' he assured her. 'But whatever happens, you have my word. If you come to Montaigne with me, you'll be free to leave at the end of the month, if not sooner.'

'Hmm… What about—?' Charlie looked embarrassed. 'You—you wouldn't expect me to actually behave like a fiancée, would you? In private, I mean?'

This time Rafe manfully held back his urge to smile. 'Are you worried that I'd expect to ravish you on a nightly basis?'

'No, of course not.' She dropped her gaze to the half-eaten baklava on her plate. 'Well, yes…perhaps. I guess…'

'There's no need to worry,' he said more gently. 'Again, you have my word, Charlie. If you agreed to this, I would proudly escort you to public appearances as my fiancée, but in both public and in private I'd be a total gentleman. You'd have your own suite of rooms in the castle.'

Just the same, the thought of taking Charlie to bed was tempting. Extremely so. Despite her innocent, cautious façade, Rafe sensed an exciting wildness in her, an essential spark he'd found lacking in her sister.

But, sadly, his years as a playboy prince were behind him. Now responsibility for his country weighed heavily. If Charlie agreed to return with him to Montaigne, the engagement would be a purely political, diplomatic exercise, just as it had been with Olivia.

Charlie was very quiet now, as if she was giving his proposal serious thought.

'So what do you think?' he couldn't help prompting, while trying desperately to keep the impatience from his voice.

Charlie looked up at him, all big blue eyes and dark lashes, and he could see her internal battle as she weighed up the pros and cons.

Rafe wished he understood those cons. Was she worried about leaving her job at short notice? Were there family commitments? Did this involve the phone call from her father? A jealous lover?

He frowned at this last possibility. But surely, if there

was a serious boyfriend on the scene, Charlie would have
mentioned him by now.

'I can't pretend I'm not interested, Rafe,' she said suddenly. 'But I need to talk to—to someone.'

So…perhaps there was a boyfriend, after all. Rafe tried
not to frown.

'When do you need a decision?' she asked.

'As soon as possible. I hoped to fly out tonight.'

'Tonight? Can you book a flight that quickly?'

'I don't need to book. I have a private jet.'

'Of course you do,' Charlie said softly and she rolled
her eyes to the ceiling. 'You're a prince.' She gave a slow,
disbelieving shake of her head, but then her gaze was
direct as she met his. 'What time do you want to leave,
then?' she asked.

Now. 'Ten o'clock? Eleven at the latest.' He pulled a
chequebook from his pocket and filled in the necessary
details, including his scrawled signature. 'Take this with
you,' he said as he tore off the cheque.

Charlie took it gingerly, almost as if it were a time
bomb. She swallowed as she stared at it. 'You'd hand
over that amount of money? Just like that? You trust me?'

Rafe didn't like to point out that his men would be
tailing her, so he simply nodded.

She folded the cheque and slipped it into her handbag
and she looked pale as she rose from her seat. 'I'll be as
quick as I can,' she said. 'Give me your phone number
and I'll text you.'

CHAPTER FOUR

MICHAEL MORISSET, WHO had the same curls and clear blue eyes that Charlie had inherited, looked as if he'd aged ten years when she met him at the hospital.

It was frightening to see her normally upbeat and care-free father looking so haggard and worn.

Skye looked even worse. Only a few short days ago, the happy mother had been glowing as she proudly showed off her sweet newborn daughter. Now Skye looked pale and gaunt, with huge dark circles under her eyes. Her shoulders were stooped and even her normally glossy auburn hair hung in limp strands to her shoulders.

Charlie's eyes stung as she hugged her stepmother. She couldn't imagine how terrified Skye must be to know that her sweet little daughter had only the most tenuous hold on life.

'Would you like to see Isla?' Skye asked.

Charlie nodded, but her throat closed over as her father and Skye took her down the hospital corridor, and she had to breathe in deeply through her nose in an attempt to stay calm.

The baby was in a Humidicrib in a special isolation ward and they could only look at her through a glass window.

Isla was naked except for a disposable nappy, and she

was lying on her side with her wrinkled hands folded together and tucked under her little chin. A tube had been inserted into her nose and was taped across her cheek to hold it in place. Monitor wires were taped to her tummy and her feet. Such a sad and scary sight.

'Oh, poor darling.' The cry burst from Charlie. She couldn't help it. Her heart was breaking.

She tried to imagine a doctor operating on such a tiny wee thing. Thank heavens she had found the money for the very best surgeon possible. She suppressed a nervous shiver. This was hardly the time to dwell on the details of what earning that money entailed. Her baby sister was her focus.

As she watched, Isla gave a little stretch. One hand opened, tiny fingers fluttering, bumping herself on the chin so that she frowned, making deep furrows across her forehead. Now she looked like a little old lady.

'Oh,' Charlie cried again. 'She's so sweet. She's gorgeous.'

She turned to her father and Skye, who were holding hands and gazing almost fearfully at their daughter.

'I've found a way to raise the money,' Charlie told them quickly.

Skye gasped. 'Not enough to take her to Boston, surely?'

'Yes.'

Skye gave a dazed shake of her head. 'With a special nurse to accompany her?'

'Yes, there's money to cover all those costs.'

'Oh, my God.'

Skye went white and clutched at her husband's arm, looking as if she might faint.

'Are you sure about this, Charlie?' her father demanded tensely. 'I don't want Skye to get her hopes up and then be disappointed.'

Charlie nodded. 'I have the cheque in my handbag.' Nervously, she drew out the slim, astonishing slip of paper. 'It might take a few days before the money's deposited into your bank account, but it's a proper bank cheque. It's all above board.'

'Good heavens.' Her father stared at the cheque and then stared at his daughter in disbelief. 'How on earth did you manage this? What's this House of St Romain? Some kind of church group? Who could be so generous?'

This was the awkward bit. Charlie had no intention of telling her dad and Skye about Rafe and the fact that she'd agreed to be a stand-in as a European prince's pretend fiancée. For starters, they wouldn't believe her—they would think she'd taken drugs, or had been hit on the head and was hallucinating.

But also, telling them about Rafe would involve telling them about Olivia, and this wasn't the right moment to bring up that particular can of worms. Charlie was angry about her father's silence over such an important matter as her sister. On the way to the hospital she'd allowed herself a little weep about her absent mother and unknown twin sister, but she'd consoled herself that by accepting the role of fake fiancée she was actually taking a step closer to finding the truth.

For now, though, they had to stay focused on Isla.

'Dad, you have my word this money is from a legitimate source and there's nothing to worry about. But it's complicated, I'll admit that. You'll have to trust me for now. You've got enough to worry about with Isla. Let me take care of the money side of things.'

'I hope you haven't gone into debt, Charlie. You know I won't be able to pay this back.'

'You don't have to worry about that either. The only issue will be finding someone to run the gallery while I'm—' Charlie quickly changed tack. 'I'll be—busy organising everything. Do you think Amy Thornton might be available?'

'I'm pretty sure Amy's free. But for heaven's sake, Charlie—' For a long moment her father stared at her. 'If you don't want to tell me, I'm not going to press you,' he said finally. 'I do trust you, darling. I know you won't be breaking any laws.'

'Of course not. I've managed to find a generous—' Charlie swallowed. 'A generous benefactor, who wishes to remain anonymous.'

'How amazing. That's—that's wonderful.'

Charlie forced a bright smile. 'So now your job is to get busy with talking to doctors and airlines and everything that's involved with getting Isla well.'

'I don't know what to say.' Tears glistened in her father's eyes. 'Thank you, Charlie.' His voice was ragged and rough with emotion. 'Not every girl would be so caring about a half-sister.'

The three of them hugged, and Skye was weeping, but to Charlie's relief her father quickly broke away to find a nursing sister. In no time he and the nurse were making the necessary arrangements. Her dad was stepping up to the mark and adopting full responsibility.

She was free to go.

She'd never realised how scary that could be.

A frenetic hour later Charlie had rung Amy Thornton and secured her services at the gallery for the next month. She'd showered, changed into jeans and a sweater for the long flight, and had taken her cat, Dolly, next door to be minded by Edna, a kind and very accommodating elderly neighbour.

As she frantically packed, she couldn't believe she was actually doing this. She didn't dare to stop and think too hard about her sudden whirlwind decision—she knew she'd have second, third and fourth thoughts about the craziness of it all. The only safe way to keep her swirling emotions under control was to keep busy.

Finally, she was packed and ready with her passport, which was, fortunately, up to date.

Rafe arrived just as Charlie was sitting on her suitcase trying to get it closed. He shot a curious and approving glance around her tiny flat with its bright red walls and black and white furnishings, which she was quietly rather proud of, and which normally included her rather beautiful black and white cat.

Then he eyed her bulging luggage and frowned.

'I know it's winter in Montaigne,' Charlie offered as her excuse. 'So I threw in every warm thing I have. But I'm not sure that any of my stuff is really suitable for snowy weather.'

Or for an aspiring princess, she added silently.

Rafe passed this off with a shrug. 'You can always buy new warm clothes when you get there.'

Yes, she could do that if she hadn't already reallocated his generous payment. She felt a tad guilty as she snapped the locks on her suitcase shut.

Rafe picked it up. 'I have a taxi waiting.'

'Right.' Charlie stifled a nervous ripple. This was going to work out. And it wasn't a completely foolish thing to do. It was worthwhile. Really, it was. She would provide a front for Rafe while he got things sorted with Olivia and saved his country from some kind of economic ruin. And little Isla was getting a very important chance to have a healthy life.

Straightening her shoulders, she pinned on a brave smile. 'Let's get this show on the road,' she told Rafe.

To her surprise, he didn't immediately turn to head for the door. He took a step forward, leaned in and kissed her on both cheeks. She caught a whiff of expensive after-shave, felt the warm brush of his lips on her skin.

'Thank you for doing this, Charlie.' His eyes blazed with surprising emotion and warmth. 'It means a lot to me.'

Charlie wasn't sure what to say. When people did un-expectedly nice things she had a bad habit of crying. But she couldn't allow herself to cry now, so she nod-ded brusquely. Then she followed him out, shut the door, and slipped the key under the mat outside Edna's door, as they'd arranged.

As she did so, Edna's door opened to reveal the old lady with Dolly in her arms.

'We thought we'd wave you off,' Edna said, beaming a jolly smile as she lifted one of Dolly's white paws and waggled it. But then Edna saw Rafe and she forgot to wave or to smile. Instead she stood there, like a statue, eyes agog.

Great.

Charlie suppressed a groan. When she'd told her neigh-bour about her hastily arranged flight, she hadn't men-tioned a male companion. Now *everyone* in their block of flats would know that Charlie Morisset had taken off on reckless impulse with a tall, dark and extremely hand-some stranger.

Conversation was limited as the taxi whizzed across Syd-ney, although Rafe did comment on the beauty of the harbour and the magnificent Opera House. In no time, they arrived at a private airport terminal that Charlie hadn't even known existed.

There was no queue, no waiting, no taking her shoes off for Security, not even tickets to be checked. Her passport was carefully examined though, by a round little Customs man with a moustache, who did a lot of bowing and scraping and calling Rafe 'Your Highness'. Then their luggage was trundled away and there was no more to do.

Rafe's plane was ready and waiting.

Oh, boy. Charlie had been expecting a smallish aircraft that would probably need to make many stops between Australia and Europe. This plane was enormous.

'Do you own this?' she couldn't help asking Rafe.

He chuckled. 'I don't need to *own* a jet. They're very easy to charter, and I have a priority listing.'

'I'm sure you do,' she muttered under her breath.

At that point, she might have felt very nervous about flying off into the unknown with a man she'd only just met, but Rafe took her arm as they crossed the tarmac, tucking it companionably under his, and somehow everything felt a little better and safer. And he kept a firm steadying hand at her elbow as they mounted the steps and entered the plane.

Then Charlie forgot to be nervous. She was too busy being impressed. And overawed.

The interior of Rafe's chartered jet was like no other plane she'd ever seen or imagined. It was more like a hotel suite—with padded armchairs and sofas, and a beautiful dining table.

Everything was exquisite, glamorous and tasteful, decorated in restful blues and golds. As they went deeper into the plane, there were wonderful double beds—two of them, Charlie was relieved to see—complete with banks of pillows, soft wall lamps, and beautiful gold quilts.

The only things to remind her that this was a jet were the narrowness of the space and the lines of porthole windows down each side.

'OK,' she said, sending Rafe a bright grin. 'I'm impressed.'

'I hope you have a comfortable flight.'

'There'd have to be something wrong with me if I didn't.'

He looked amused as he smiled. 'Come and take a seat ready for take-off.'

Rafe's bodyguards had boarded the plane as well, but they disappeared into a section behind closed doors, leaving Rafe and Charlie in total privacy as they strapped themselves into stupendously luxurious white leather chairs. An excessively polite, young female flight attendant appeared, dressed demurely in powder blue and carrying a tray with glasses of champagne, complete with strawberries and a platter with cheese and grapes and nuts.

Oh, my. Until now, Charlie had been too busy and preoccupied to give much thought to what being a prince's fiancée involved, but it seemed this gig might be a ton of fun. Despite her worries about Isla and about all the unknowns that lay ahead of her, she should try to relax and enjoy it.

The flight was a breeze. First there was a scrumptious meal of roasted leek soup, followed by slow-cooked lamb and a tiny mousse made from white chocolate and cherries, and to drink there was wonderful French champagne.

Charlie gave Rafe a blissful smile as she patted her

lips with the napkin. 'This is so delicious,' she said, for perhaps the third or fourth time.

He looked slightly bemused and she wondered if she'd gone a bit too far with her praise.

Of course, she'd been out with guys who'd fed her beautiful meals before this, but it was still an experience she could never get tired of. At home, she'd done most of the cooking before her father's marriage, and she now cooked for herself in the flat, but she'd never seemed to have time to learn more than the basics. Fancy gourmet food was a treat.

After dinner, Rafe said he had business to attend to and was soon busy frowning at his laptop. Charlie, yawning and replete, changed into pyjamas and climbed into an incredibly comfortable bed.

She expected to lie awake for ages mulling over the amazing and slightly scary turn her life had taken in one short day, but with a full tummy, an awesomely comfy bed, and the pleasant, deep, throbbing drone of the plane's engines, she fell asleep quickly.

Rafe suppressed a sigh as he watched Charlie fall asleep with almost childlike speed. Was that the sleep of innocence? He hadn't slept well for weeks—since the night of his father's death. There always seemed to be too much to worry about. First his guilt and despair that he'd been so caught up in his good-time life that he'd missed any chance to bid his father farewell. And then the weighty realities of assuming his sudden new responsibilities.

Now he scanned the emails he'd downloaded before boarding the plane, but there was still no good news about Olivia, or about the intelligence surveillance on Claude Pontier.

Rafe was confident that it wouldn't be long now, before they caught Pontier out. Montaigne's Head of Police, Chief Dameron, was a wise, grey-haired fellow, approaching retirement, so he had a wealth of experience. He'd come up through the ranks, earning his promotions through hard work and diligence, but he'd also been trained by the FBI.

Consequently, his combination of old-school police procedures with the latest technical surveillance savvy was invaluable. Rafe had every faith in him.

Now Rafe looked again towards the bed where Charlie slept, curled on her side with golden curls tumbling on the pillow, and he was surprised by the tenderness he felt towards this girl who'd so readily stepped into her sister's shoes. He wondered if their similarities were more than skin deep.

He suspected that the two girls' personalities were quite different, found himself hoping for this, in fact. And that made no sense at all.

When Charlie woke, the flight attendant was offering her a tray with orange juice and a pot of coffee.

'We'll be landing in Dubai in less than an hour,' she was told.

Really?

A glance through the doorway showed Rafe, already up and dressed and sitting on one of the lounges, working on his computer again. Or perhaps he'd been working all night? Charlie downed her orange juice and hurried to her private bathroom to change out of her pyjamas and wash her face.

She took her tray with the coffee through to the lounge.

'Good morning.' Once again, Rafe's smile held a hint of amusement. 'You slept well?'

'Unbelievably well,' Charlie agreed.

She settled into a lounge and took a sip of coffee. 'I didn't realise we'd be landing in Dubai. I guess we need to refuel?'

'It's not a long stop,' he said. 'But yes, we need to refuel and my good friend, Sheikh Faysal Daood Taariq, wants to give us breakfast.'

'Did you say a—a sheikh?'

'That's right.'

Charlie stared at Rafe in dismay. The thought of breakfast with a sheikh was even more confronting than stepping onto a private jet with a prince. She took a deeper sip of her coffee, as if it might somehow clear her head. 'Are you sure I should come to this breakfast?'

'Well, yes, of course,' said Rafe. 'You're my fiancée.'

'Oh, yes.' This demanded more coffee. 'Yes, of course.' Charlie's hand shook ever so slightly as she refilled her cup from the silver pot. The deeper ramifications of becoming her sister Olivia were only just sinking in.

This, now, was her reality check. When she stepped off this plane, she would no longer be Charlie Morisset.

'You'll like Faysal,' Rafe told her with a reassuring smile. 'I've known him for years. We met when we were both at Oxford.'

'I—I see. And he's a proper sheikh, but you just call him Faysal?'

'Yes, and you can call him Faysal, too. He's very relaxed and used to westerners.'

'But will I need to wear a headscarf, or curtsy or anything?'

Rafe grinned. 'Not today. Not in his home.'

'What about shaking hands? Is that OK?'

'Offering your hand would be perfectly acceptable. You'll find Faysal is a charming gentleman.'

'Right.' Charlie looked down at her hands and realised

she should probably have painted her nails. She looked at her simple T-shirt and trousers. 'I should probably change into something a bit dressier.'

'Not at all. You'll be fine, Charlie. Relax.' Rafe closed his laptop and slipped it into an overhead locker. 'It's time to strap ourselves back into the seat belts for landing.'

The flight attendant collected their coffee trays, and, once they were belted, she disappeared as the plane began its descent.

In her seat beside Rafe, Charlie couldn't resist asking more questions. 'So, this Faysal—how many wives does he have?'

This brought another chuckle. 'None at all so far. He's still enjoying the life of a bachelor.'

'Right. So he's a playboy?'

'Of course,' Rafe said with a knowing smile.

And I suppose you were a playboy, too, before your father died.

This sudden realisation bothered Charlie more than it should have. Why should she care about Rafe's sex life? It was none of her business—although it did make her wonder again about why Olivia had run away from him.

'And for your information, Faysal's father only has *four* wives,' Rafe said.

'Oh?' she replied airily. 'Only four?'

Rafe shrugged. 'It's a sign of the times. His grandfather had forty.'

Good grief.

After only a very short time in Dubai, Charlie realised how truly ignorant she was about this part of the world. Of course, she'd expected to see regal and haughty, dark-bearded men in flowing white robes, and she knew these men were extraordinarily wealthy and heavily into horse-racing and speed-cars and living the high life. But she hadn't been prepared for the over-the-top opulence.

On the short journey from the airport to Sheikh Faysal Daood Taariq's home, she saw a car painted in gold—and yes, Rafe assured her, it was *real* gold—and another studded with diamonds. And good grief, there was even, in one bright red sports car, a leopard!

A proper live, wild creature. Massive, with a glorious coat of spots and a silver lead around its neck. The leopard was sitting in a front passenger seat beside a handsome young man in white robes and dark sunglasses.

Gobsmacked, Charlie turned to Rafe. 'That wasn't really a leopard, was it?'

He grinned. 'It was indeed.'

'But it couldn't be. How can they?'

Rafe shrugged. 'Welcome to Dubai. Extravagance abounds here and dreadfully expensive exotic pets are all the rage.'

'But surely—' Charlie wanted to protest about the dangers. About animal rights, but she stopped herself just in time.

'Listen, Charlie.' They were in the back seat of a huge limousine and Rafe leaned a little closer, speaking quietly. 'Try not to be too surprised by anything you see here.' He waved his hand to the view beyond the car's window, as they passed a grand palace at the end of an avenue lined on both sides with fountains and palm trees.

'I can't help being amazed,' she said somewhat meekly. But she knew she had to try harder. 'I guess Olivia's used to all this,' she said. 'Her jaw wouldn't be dropping every five minutes.'

Rafe nodded. 'Exactly.'

In that moment, Charlie realised something else.

'You've brought me here to your friend's house as a test, haven't you? It's a kind of trial run for me?'

Rafe's only answer was a smile, but Charlie knew she was right. Visiting his good friend, Faysal, was a kind of fast-track apprenticeship for her in her new role as Rafe's fiancée. If she made any gross mistakes here, the errors would remain 'in house' so to speak.

But she wasn't going to make mistakes. She could do this. In Sheikh Faysal's home, she would ensure that she had perfect posture and perfect manners. She would remember to stand straight, sit with her knees together, and never cross her legs, always be polite and eat neatly, and—

And it would be exhausting to be a full-time princess.

But Charlie was determined to pass any test Rafe St Romain presented. Of course, she could hold her tongue and play the role she'd been assigned. After all, he was paying her *very* handsomely.

Now, with her thoughts sorted, she realised that their car was turning. Huge iron gates were rolling open to allow them entry to a gravelled drive and a tall, white, three-storeyed house decorated with arches.

The car stopped at a heavily embossed front door, which opened immediately to reveal a dark-haired, olive-skinned man almost as handsome as Rafe.

'Rafe and Olivia!' he cried, throwing wide his arms. 'How lovely to see you both again. Welcome!'

Breakfast at Faysal's was wonderful, as always, and to Rafe's relief Charlie behaved admirably.

They dined on the terrace beside the swimming pool, where they were served Arabic coffee made from coffee beans ground with cardamom and saffron, as well as spicy chick peas and *balabet*, a dish of sweetened vermicelli mixed with eggs and spices. There were also delicious pancakes flavoured with cardamom and coloured with saffron and served with date syrup.

Charlie was on her best behaviour, and Rafe knew she was trying hard not to be too overly impressed by everything she saw and tasted. But he could also tell that she was enjoying the meal immensely, possibly even more than she'd enjoyed last evening's meal on the plane.

Just the same, she managed not to gush over the food, and she only jumped once when Faysal called her Olivia.

She couldn't quite hide her fascination with her surroundings, though. Her bright blue eyes widened with obvious delight at the fountains and the terraced gardens and the arcade decorated with exquisite blue and gold tiled mosaics. And Rafe thought she was just a little too impressed by Faysal, who was, as always, handsome and ultra-charming.

Nevertheless, the meeting went rather well, and Rafe was feeling relaxed when Charlie retired to the powder room.

As soon as she'd left, however, Faysal, who had dressed today in European trousers and a white polo shirt instead of his customary white robes, looked across the table to Rafe with a narrowed and sceptical dark gaze.

'So,' he said, his lips tilting with amusement. 'Who the hell is that girl, Rafe?'

Inwardly groaning, Rafe feigned ignorance. 'You know who she is. She's my fiancée, Olivia. What game are you playing?'

'That's the very same question I want to ask you. You're trying to pull a swift one over me, old boy.' Faysal nodded to the corridor where Charlie had disappeared. 'That girl is Olivia's double, I'll grant you that, but, unless she's had a complete personality transplant, she is not the girl I met in Saint-Tropez and again at your engagement ball.'

Rafe sighed heavily as he remembered the extravagant ball he'd hosted. At the time he'd needed to make a big stir about his engagement and to show Chancellor Pontier how serious he was. He hoped there hadn't been too many guests as astute as Faysal. 'Is it really that obvious?'

Faysal's smile was sympathetic as he nodded. 'I'll admit I observe women with a deeper interest than most.'

This was true, but still Rafe was afraid he had a problem.

'Her name's Charlie,' he said. 'Or rather, Charlotte. She's Olivia's twin sister. I tracked her down in Australia.'

'Australia? So that was the accent.'

Rafe grimaced. 'Is that what gave her away? Her accent?'

'Not really.' Faysal eyed Rafe with a level and serious gaze.

'What, then?' Rafe demanded impatiently.

'Her sincerity.'

Hell.

Rafe knew exactly what Faysal meant. There was a genuineness about Charlie that had been totally absent in her sister. He gave a helpless shrug. 'I can't do much about that.'

'No,' Faysal observed quietly. Then he frowned. 'So what happened to Olivia? She hasn't been abducted, has she?'

'No, I wouldn't be sitting here passing the time of day with you if that was the case.' Rafe shrugged. 'She ran away.'

Faysal looked only mildly surprised. 'She panicked, in other words.'

'Yes, I think she must have.'

His friend gave a slow, thoughtful nod. 'Getting engaged to that girl wasn't your smartest move, my friend.'

'I know.' Rafe sighed again. 'As you know, it was all about convenience. It was such a shock when my father died. So unexpected.'

'The pressures of being an only child,' Faysal mused. 'If your mother had still been alive…'

Faysal didn't finish the sentence, but Rafe knew exactly what he was implying. His mother had died three years ago, but if she'd still been alive she would have seen through Olivia Belaire in a heartbeat. And in no time at all, his mother would have produced a list of a dozen or more highly suitable young women for him to choose from.

These girls would have been from good schools and families. They would probably have all had university degrees and perfect deportment and grooming and impeccable manners and be interested in good works. The list of his mother's requirements for a princess were numerous. She had never approved of the girls Rafe had dated.

His criteria for selecting a female companion had been quite different from his mother's. But those carefree days were over.

'If you can see through Charlie,' he said, somewhat dispiritedly, 'I've got a problem on my hands, haven't I?'

His friend shook his head and smiled. 'No, not a problem, Rafe. If you play your cards correctly, I'd say your Charlie could be quite an asset.'

No, Rafe thought, *Faysal's reading this wrong.* His friend might have approved of Charlie's prettiness and sincerity, but he hadn't seen her horror at the thought of actually having to marry him.

'She's a temporary stopgap,' he said firmly. 'That's all.'

CHAPTER FIVE

'So, ARE YOU going to give me a performance appraisal?'

Charlie and Rafe were back in the plane and taking off for Europe when she posed this question.

She'd tried her hardest to be cool and sophisticated in Faysal's home and she needed to know if her efforts had been satisfactory. After all, there wasn't much time to lift her act before they arrived in Montaigne.

She was watching Rafe intently, waiting for his answer, and she didn't miss his frown, although he very quickly hid it behind a smooth smile.

'You were perfect,' he said.

'Are you sure?' She'd tried really hard to lose her accent, but she suspected that he wasn't being totally honest. 'I need to hear the truth, Rafe. I don't want to let you down.'

Which was a noble way of saying that she didn't want to face the embarrassment of being caught out.

'You were fine,' he said with a hint of impatience.

Charlie wasn't sure that 'fine' was good enough, but she didn't want to pester him and become annoying. She consoled herself that Rafe would have told her if she'd made a major blunder.

'So there's nothing you need to warn me about before I arrive in your country?' she tried one more time.

Rafe smiled. 'No, just be yourself, Charlie. It would be different if you really were my fiancée, but for now, I think you'll do well just as you are.'

'Right.' Charlie wished the mention of Rafe's 'real' fiancée didn't bother her so much.

'Just try to look as if you're enjoying yourself,' he said.

She couldn't help smiling. 'That shouldn't be too hard.'

It was true. Everything about this trip so far had been wonderfully exciting. If Charlie hadn't been so worried about poor little Isla, she would have looked on this as the adventure of a lifetime.

As soon as they reached their cruising height, Rafe opened his laptop again. Apparently, he was studying everything he could about mining, so that he could out-wit the Leroy Mining Company who wanted to wreck his Alps.

For most of the flight Charlie watched movies. Her head still buzzed with a host of questions—questions about Rafe, about his family and his country, and what he expected of her—but he was clearly preoccupied. And, as he'd made it quite clear, she didn't have the responsibility of a 'real' job.

That belonged to Olivia.

Her sister.

Charlie felt a deep pang at the thought of the girl who was her mirror image. *Her sister*. They shared the same mother. Had shared the same *womb*. The same DNA.

How could her father have kept this secret from her? Learning about it now, Charlie felt hurt. Deeply hurt, as if she'd been denied something precious. The other half of herself.

She wondered how on earth the decision had been

made. Obviously her parents had decided to split and take a child each. But how had they made that choice?

Tossed a coin? Drawn straws?

Charlie wouldn't dwell on the fact that her mother had rejected her and chosen Olivia. It could warp her mind if she let that sink in too deeply. The important thing to remember was that she loved her father very much. She'd had a wonderful childhood and they'd shared many adventures, and they had a great relationship. She couldn't imagine her life without her sweet, dreamy dad.

But she also couldn't deny that her feelings about Olivia were incredibly complicated. On one level she longed to meet her sister and get to know her, but on another level she was stupidly jealous that Olivia was going to marry this deadly handsome Prince.

When Rafe found her.

They arrived in Grenoble mid-afternoon, descending through thick clouds into a world of whiteness. Snow blanketed every rooftop and field and Charlie was so excited she could hardly drag herself from the window when the flight attendant delivered her coat and scarf.

'Do you have boots?' Rafe asked, eyeing Charlie's flimsy shoes. 'You might need them.'

'They're packed away in my suitcase.'

'Hmm.' He came closer and fingered the fabric of her coat.

Charlie could tell by his frown that the coat was inadequate.

'This should be OK to get you from here to my car,' he said. 'But you'll have to get something thicker and warmer for Montaigne.'

'Yes, I dare say.' The new coat would probably need to be a good deal more glamorous, too, Charlie thought, as she noted the elegant cut of Rafe's thick overcoat. In other words, she would have to spend a big chunk of her meagre savings on a coat that she'd only need for a couple of weeks. But she couldn't bring herself to ask Rafe for more money.

Despite Rafe's warning, Charlie wasn't prepared for the blast of frigid air that hit her as she stepped out of the plane. The cold seemed to bite straight through her coat and penetrate to her very bones.

'Are you OK?' Rafe asked, slipping an arm around her shoulders. 'Charlie, you're shivering. Here, take my coat.'

'No, it's all right. We're almost there.'

Welcome warmth enveloped them as they left the tarmac and the airport's doors slid open for them. But now there was something else to worry about.

'Are there likely to be paparazzi here?' she asked.

Rafe slanted her a smile. 'There shouldn't be. I've tried to keep my movements undercover.'

Just the same, Charlie turned up the collar on her coat and tried to look relaxed when heads turned their way. She kept a fixed little smile in place as she walked with Rafe to the chauffeur waiting with a sleek black, unmarked car. All was well. So far.

Grenoble lay at the very foot of the Alps, so it wasn't long before the car was climbing the mountainous slopes. Snowflakes drifted all around them, and Charlie watched through the car windows in delight.

'It doesn't snow in Sydney,' she told Rafe. 'I've seen snow in the Blue Mountains and on the tops of the peaks in Nepal, but we were there in summer. I've never seen it like this. With snow simply *everywhere*.'

It was only then that she caught Rafe's warning frown

and his quick glance to the chauffeur sitting just in front of him.

Oh, help.

Charlie flinched. What an idiot she was. Of course, this chauffeur would talk to the rest of Rafe's staff about the strange change in their master's fiancée. Damn. She'd only just arrived and already she'd made a huge blunder.

Her face was burning as she pressed her lips tightly together. She was such a fool. Turning away sharply, she held her eyes wide open to try to hold back any hint of tears.

Until now, she hadn't doubted that she could do this, but with this first silly gaffe the enormity of her task almost overwhelmed her. There would be so many chances to make mistakes—with servants, with government officials, with Rafe's friends, shopkeepers…

Rafe reached for her hand and she jumped, but his touch was gentle.

'Don't worry,' he murmured, giving her hand an encouraging squeeze.

'But—' Charlie nodded meaningfully towards the back of the chauffeur's head.

'It's OK,' Rafe said quietly, still holding her hand. 'I'll speak to him.' After a bit, he added, 'You'll probably prefer not to have a personal maid.'

Heavens no. Charlie supposed Olivia might have had a maid, but she was bound to make way too many slip-ups under that level of vigilant attention. 'I don't think a maid will be necessary,' she said carefully.

Rafe nodded.

Deeply grateful, Charlie managed a weak smile. 'I'll get the hang of this,' she promised.

'Of course you will.'

His hand was warm on hers.

Already, she was beginning to like Rafe. Too much.

The early twilight was growing darker by the minute. Below them, the lights of Grenoble twinkled prettily, and as the road wound ever upwards, night pressed in. They passed clusters of steep-roofed chalets that glowed with welcoming warmth, but for most of the journey the Alps loomed dark and slightly ominous, the car's headlights catching huge rocky outcrops topped with snow.

Charlie wondered how long it would take to reach Montaigne, but she refrained from asking Rafe and once again exposing her ignorance. It wasn't easy for a natural chatterbox to remain silent, but discretion was her new watchword.

From time to time, Rafe talked to her about matters that he needed to attend to over the next few days. Meetings, luncheons, more meetings, dinners.

'You'll be busy,' Charlie said, and she wondered what she would do while Rafe was buzzing around attending to his princely duties.

'You'll probably need to attend some of these functions,' he said. 'Especially the dinners, but I'll try to keep your duties light. You'll have plenty of time for shopping.'

Shopping. *Oh, dear.*

It was about an hour and a half later that they reached Montaigne perched high in an Alpine valley. The capital city was incredibly pretty, bathed in the clear moonlight, with lights shining from a thousand windows. The valley looked like a bowl of sparkling, golden flakes.

'Home,' said Rafe simply.

'It's very beautiful,' Charlie told him.

He nodded and smiled. 'You must be so tired. It's been a long journey.'

They were pulling up at the front steps of a fairy-tale castle. Charlie forgot her tiredness. She was far too excited.

'*Bonsoir,* Your Highness. *Bonsoir, mademoiselle.*'

A dignified fellow in a top hat and a braided great-coat opened the car door for them. Another man collected their luggage.

Rafe ushered Charlie up a short flight of snow-spotted steps and through the huge open front doors. A woman aged around fifty and dressed in a neat navy-blue skirt and jacket greeted them with a smile.

'Good evening, Chloe.' Rafe addressed her quickly in French, as she greeted them and took their coats. 'Made-moiselle Olivia is very tired, so we'll retire early this evening, but we'd like some coffee and perhaps a little soup?'

'Yes, I'll have it sent up straight away, Your Highness.'

'That would be very good, thank you.'

Charlie managed with difficulty to refrain from star-ing about her like an awestruck Aussie tourist, but Rafe's castle was amazingly beautiful. There were white marble floors and enormous flower arrangements, huge gold-framed mirrors, chandeliers, and a grand marble stair-case carpeted in deep royal blue.

Despite her nervousness, she planned to drink in every moment that she spent here, and one day she would tell her grandchildren about it. But she wasn't sure she could ever get used to hearing Rafe addressed as 'Your High-ness'. Thank heavens she was only *mademoiselle*.

'I'll show you to your room,' Rafe told her.

To her surprise, they didn't proceed up the staircase. A lift had been fitted into the castle.

'My grandfather had this lift installed for my grandmother,' Rafe told her. 'Grandmère had a problem with her knees as she got older.'

'It must make life a lot easier for everyone else, too,' said Charlie.

'Yes. Here we are on the second floor. Your room is on the right.'

Charlie's room was, in fact, an entire suite, with a huge bedroom, bathroom and sitting room. And although the castle seemed to be heated, there was even a fireplace, where flames burned a bright welcome, and off the bedroom a small study, complete with a desk, a telephone and an assortment of stationery ready for her use.

The whole area was carpeted in a pretty rose pink with cream and silver accessories, and there were at least three bowls of pink roses. Charlie's suitcase had already been placed at the foot of the bed and it looked rather shabby and out of place.

'This is rather old-fashioned compared with your flat in Sydney,' Rafe said.

'But it's gorgeous,' protested Charlie, who couldn't believe he would even *try* to make a comparison. 'Oh, and look at the view!' She hurried over to the high, arched window set deep in the stone wall with a sill wide enough for sitting and dreaming.

Below, the lights of Montaigne glowed warm and bright in the snowy setting.

'I can't believe this.' She was grinning as she turned back to Rafe. 'It's so incredibly picture perfect.'

'There's a remote control here beside the bed.' Rafe picked it up and demonstrated. 'It makes the glass opaque for when you want to sleep.'

'How amazing.' Charlie watched in awe as the glass grew dark and then, at another flick of the switch, became clear again. 'It's magic. Like being in a fairy tale. Aren't you lucky to actually live here?'

His smile was careful. 'Even fairy tales have their dark and dangerous moments.'

'Well, yes, I guess.' Charlie wasn't sure if he was joking or serious. 'I suppose there are always wicked witches and wolves and evil spells.' And in Rafe's case, a wicked Chancellor and evil miners who wanted to wreck his country. 'But at least fairy tales give you a happy ending.'

'Unless you're the wolf,' suggested Rafe.

Charlie frowned at him. 'You're very pessimistic all of a sudden.'

'I am. You're right. I apologise.' But Rafe still looked sad as he stood there watching her.

Charlie wondered if he was thinking about his father who had died so recently. Or perhaps he was thinking about Olivia, wishing his real fiancée were here in his castle, preparing for their marriage. Instead he was left with an improvised substitute who would soon leave again.

Or were there other things worrying him? He'd mentioned the mining threat, but he probably had a great many other issues to deal with. Affairs of state.

She was pondering this when he smiled suddenly. 'I must say I'm not surprised that you believe in happy endings, Charlie.'

She thought instantly of Isla. 'It's terribly important to think positively. Why not believe? It's better than giving up.'

He dismissed this with a shrug. 'But it's a bit like asking me if I believe in fairies. Happy endings are all very well in theory, but I find that real life is mostly about compromise.'

Compromise?

Charlie stared at him in dismay. She'd never liked the idea of compromise. It seemed like such a cop-out. She never wanted to give up on important hopes and dreams and to settle for second best.

She wanted to protest, to set Rafe straight, but there was something very earnest in his expression that silenced her.

She thought about his current situation. He'd been forced to arrange a hasty, convenient marriage to save his country, instead of waiting till he found the woman he loved. That was certainly a huge compromise for both Rafe and for Olivia.

When Rafe looked ahead to the future, he could probably foresee many times when he would be required to set aside his own needs and desires and to put duty to his country first.

It was a chastening thought. Charlie supposed she'd been pretty foolish to come sailing in here, all starry-eyed, and immediately suggest that living in a castle was an automatic ticket to a fairy-tale life. She was about to apologise when there was a knock at the door.

A young man had arrived with their supper.

'Thanks, Guillaume,' Rafe said as the fellow set a tray on the low table in front of the fire. To Charlie, he said, 'I thought we'd be more comfortable eating in here tonight.' When Guillaume had left, he added, 'You don't mind if I join you?'

'No, of course not.' After all, it was what the servants would expect of an engaged couple.

They sat on sofas facing each other. The coffee smelled wonderful, as did the chicken soup, and the setting was incredibly cosy. Charlie looked at the flickering flames, the bowls of steaming soup and the crusty bread rolls.

The scene was almost homely, hardly like being in

a royal castle at all, and for Charlie there was an extra sprinkle of enchantment, no doubt provided by the hunky man who, having shed his overcoat, looked relaxed again now in his jeans and dark green sweater.

Rafe's comments about compromise were sobering though, and no doubt they were the check she needed. Royals might not be dogged by the money worries that had plagued her for most of her life, but their money came with serious responsibilities.

Was that why Olivia ran away?

When they finished their soup, Rafe called for a nightcap, which was promptly delivered, and as he and Charlie sipped the rich, smooth cognac he watched the play of firelight on Charlie's curly hair, on her soft cheeks and lips. It was only with great difficulty that he managed to restrain himself from joining her on her sofa.

But man, he was tempted. There was a sweetness about Charlie that—

No, he wasn't going to make comparisons with her sister. He couldn't waste time or energy berating himself for the error of judgement that had landed him with Olivia Belaire. Regret served no useful purpose.

'Tomorrow, when you're ready, my secretary, Mathilde, will bring you a list of your engagements,' he said, steering his thoughts strictly towards business. 'Including your shopping and hair appointments.'

Charlie looked worried. 'But I won't have *appointments* for *shopping*, will I?'

'Yes. The stores find it helpful to plan ahead. They can make sure that the right staff is available to give you the very best assistance.'

'I see.' Charlie still looked worried. 'Will your secretary also give me a list of the sorts of clothes I need?'

'No, Monique at Belle Robe will look after that. If you show Monique your list of engagements, she'll be able to advise you on dresses, shoes, handbags or whatever.'

'I—I see.'

Was it his imagination, or had Charlie grown pale?

Why? Surely all women loved shopping? Her sister had enthusiastically embraced the shopping expeditions he'd paid for. Unfortunately, Olivia had also taken all those clothes with her when she left. They would have fitted Charlie perfectly.

'You'll have to try to enjoy the experience,' he said.

'Yes, of course. I'll try to behave like Olivia. I suppose she loved shopping.'

'Yes, she had quite a talent for it.'

Charlie lifted a thumbnail to her mouth as if she wanted to chew it. Then she must have realised her mistake and quickly dropped her hand to her lap with her fist tightly curled. 'So I need to be enthusiastic,' she said. 'I can do that.'

'And don't worry about the expense.'

To his dismay, Charlie looked more worried than ever. 'What's the matter, Charlie?'

She flashed him a quick, rather brave little smile. 'No problem, really. It's just that I'm so used to living on a budget and it's hard to throw off the habits of a lifetime.'

Rafe couldn't remember ever dating a girl who was cautious with money. This was a novel experience. 'These clothes won't have price tags,' he reassured her. 'So you needn't know the cost. And remember they're just costumes. They're your uniform, if you like, an important part of the job.'

'Of course.'

'And you don't have to worry about jewellery either,'

he said next. 'There's a huge collection here in the castle vault. All my mother's and grandmother's things.'

'How—how lovely.'

'I imagine that sapphires and diamonds will suit you best.'

Charlie fingered one of her simple, pearl stud earrings, and Rafe suppressed yet another urge to join her on the couch, to trace the sweet pink curve of her earlobe, preferably with his lips. Then he would kiss her smooth neck—

He sat up straighter, cleared his throat. 'And you'll have a driver to take you everywhere.'

'Thank you.'

'Are you sure you wouldn't like a maid as well? A female companion?'

Charlie shook her head. 'If I had another girl hanging out with me, I'd be sure to chatter and give myself away.'

He smiled, knowing that this was true. Charlie was so honest and open, but he wished she weren't still looking so worried. He felt much better when she was smiling. He'd been growing rather used to her smiles.

He hoped his next suggestion wouldn't make her even more worried. 'I was hoping you might be able to visit a children's hospital,' he said carefully. 'It would be very helpful for your image.'

The change in Charlie was instantaneous. Her shoulders visibly relaxed and she uncrossed her legs and, yes, she actually smiled. 'Sure,' she said. 'I'd love that. I love kids. That's a great idea.'

The sudden reversal was puzzling until Rafe remembered that his men had reported Charlie visiting a hospital in Sydney just before she'd made her final decision to accompany him to Montaigne.

What was her interest in hospitals? He hadn't asked his men to follow up on this, but now he recalled the upsetting phone call from her father and wondered if that was the connection. He would have liked to question Charlie about it. But if she'd wanted to tell him, she would have done so by now, and there were limits to how far he could reasonably expect to pry into her private affairs.

After all, their relationship was strictly business.

Charlie yawned then, widely and noisily, and Rafe was instantly on his feet. 'It's time I left you. You need to sleep.'

'I *am* pretty stuffed,' she admitted with a wan smile.

They both stood. Beside them, the fire glowed and danced.

'Goodnight, Charlie.'

'Goodnight, Rafe.'

Her eyes were incredibly blue, their expression curious, and he supposed she was wondering if he planned to kiss her.

He certainly wanted to kiss her. Wanted to rather desperately. He wanted to taste the sweetness of her soft lips. Wanted to kiss her slowly and comprehensively, right there, on the sofa, by the warmth of the fire. Wanted to feel the softness of her skin, feel the eagerness of her response. Rafe imagined that Charlie's uninhibited response would be rather splendid.

'I'll see you in the morning,' she said, eyeing him cautiously.

Rafe came to his senses. 'Yes.' He spoke brusquely, annoyed by his lapse. 'I usually have breakfast at seven-thirty, but you will be tired from the jet lag, so sleep as long as you wish. There's a phone by your bed, so just call for a maid when you wake. Have coffee, breakfast, whatever you want, brought here to your room. Take your time.'

'Thank you.'

Stepping forward, he kissed her politely on both cheeks. *'Bonne nuit,'* he said softly, and then turned and left her without looking back.

Don't do it, Rafe told himself as he walked away. *Don't mess with this girl. You know you'll only end up hurting her.*

Problem was, the habits Rafe had developed during his years of freedom were strong. He'd grown used to having almost any girl he fancied, usually without any strings attached.

Now he was surrounded by restrictions and almost every breath he took had a string attached. The press was watching him. Chancellor Pontier was watching him. For all he knew, the whole country was watching him. His enemies were waiting for him to stuff up, while his people were waiting for him to step up to the mark.

At times the weight of expectation and responsibility pressed so heavily Rafe could barely breathe. Even Charlie, despite her willingness to help him, was just another responsibility.

For her sake, he had to remember that.

Charlie checked her phone before she went to bed, but there was no message from her father. She pressed the remote to darken the window and climbed into bed. The sheets were smooth and silky, they smelled of lavender and were trimmed with exquisite lace and embroidery. The pillow was soft but firm.

Nevertheless, she lay awake for ages, worrying about Isla. Did no news mean good news? Or was her father too busy to bother with texting? Were he and Skye and Isla already in the air on their way to Boston?

How was Isla?

She remembered the lecture she'd given Rafe about positive thinking. She should follow her own advice. She had to believe that all would be well. Isla's tiny heart would survive the long plane flight and the highly skilled doctors in Boston would make her well. The money Rafe had so generously handed over would be put to good use and this whole crazy venture would be worthwhile.

The money...

This was another thing for Charlie to worry about. How on earth could she afford the clothes she needed to carry off the role of Prince Rafael's fiancée? Why on earth hadn't she foreseen this problem?

Anxiously she tossed and turned, playing with the notion of coming clean, of telling Rafe about Isla and explaining what she'd done with his money. But there were problems with this revelation.

First, there was a chance that Rafe might not believe her and they could end up having a row about it. It was an unlikely outcome, Charlie admitted. Rafe appeared to be quite generous and reasonable.

But Charlie certainly didn't want to take advantage of his good nature. The thing was, she'd struck a deal with him and now she had to keep up her end of the bargain. To ask for more money on top of his ample payment would feel totally shabby.

Besides, if she tried to tell Rafe about her baby sister's condition and the impending surgery, she would almost certainly offload all her fears and then blubber all over him.

This was the last thing Prince Rafael of Montaigne needed. He hadn't brought her here to listen to her problems.

He had enough problems of his own.

Once she'd thought things through to this point, Charlie felt calmer. Lying in the darkness, she watched the flickering firelight and she thought about the lovely evening she and Rafe had spent together. She remembered the moment before he'd left when he stood there in the firelight, looking at her. So tall and dark and sexy, with an expression in his eyes that had set her heart thumping.

So intense he'd looked. For a giddy moment, she'd thought he was going to kiss her. Properly. Passionately. Her heart had carried on like a crazy thing, thrashing about like a landed fish.

Such a ridiculous reaction. Perhaps she could blame the jet lag. Tomorrow she'd feel much more like her old self.

CHAPTER SIX

WHEN CHARLIE WOKE the next morning, she took a moment to get her bearings. She couldn't remember another time she'd ever woken to such sumptuous surroundings.

She reached for the remote and pressed the button, and—hey, presto! Bright sunlight streamed into her room.

She wondered how late she'd slept and snatched up her phone to check the time. It was nine o'clock, and there were four new messages on her phone.

Three messages were from her father. One told her that he and Skye and Isla were leaving for Boston. Another gave her their flight's departure and arrival times. A third message asked where she was.

Charlie didn't answer this specifically.

Have a safe flight, she wrote. Sending my love to you and to Skye and Isla. All's well here. C xxx.

She'd crossed so many time zones, she didn't even try to calculate where they might be by now. It was just good to know Isla was on her way and, at this point, all was well. Charlie sent up a prayer.

Keep Isla safe. Hang in there, sweetheart.

The last text message was from Rafe.

Good morning. I hope you've slept well. My secretary, Mathilde, would like to meet with you at eleven. Is this suitable?

Quickly she typed back that this would be fine.

Great, wrote Rafe. Any problems, give me a call.

Charlie wondered where he was. Then her tummy rumbled. She needed breakfast. Rather nervously, she lifted the phone beside the bed.

Immediately a woman's voice at the other end said, '*Bonjour*, Mademoiselle Olivia.'

'Oh,' said Charlie. '*Bonjour.*' In her best French she asked, 'Could I please have some coffee in my room?'

'Certainly, *mademoiselle*. Would you also like breakfast? An omelette perhaps?'

'An omelette would be lovely. *Merci.*'

'It will be with you very soon, Mademoiselle Olivia.'

'Thank you.'

This done, Charlie heaved a huge sigh of relief. Her first hurdle might have been a rather low bar in the scheme of things, but at least she'd cleared it without mishap.

A much higher hurdle came later, after the secretary Mathilde had given Charlie her engagement itinerary. She was expected to start clothes shopping this very day.

Not only did Charlie need a warmer overcoat, a new outfit was required for dinner this evening, another to wear for a daytime engagement the next day and a special gown for a gala event to be held in the castle in two evenings' time.

Charlie almost whimpered when she saw the list. She knew Rafe never dreamed that she would be paying for these clothes out of her own money, but she felt she had no other option. The problem was, her bank account wouldn't stretch to *four* expensive items of clothing, all fit for a princess. She would be lucky if she could afford one of these outfits, which meant she had no alternative but to get a cash advance on her credit card.

Ouch.

Shivering inside her inadequate coat, Charlie stepped out of the castle to find that fresh snow had fallen during the night. Now, in the early afternoon, it was clear and sunny, but the air was freezing. A chauffeur was waiting for her at the foot of the steps.

He was understandably surprised when Charlie asked him to take her to a bank before delivering her to Belle Robe, but he discreetly refrained from making any comment. Fortunately, the bank teller didn't seem to recognise her as the Prince's intended bride. Her cards were accepted without a hitch and she was able to withdraw a sickening amount of money.

Belle Robe was around the next corner.

Gulp.

Charlie had seen expensive clothing boutiques in Sydney, so she was used to store windows decorated with elegant mannequins dressed in glamorous gowns, but she'd never been inside one of these places before. Now she tried hard not to be overawed by the top-hatted doorman, the wide expanses of cream carpet, the gilt-framed floor-to-ceiling mirrors.

Madame Monique, who'd been assigned to attend to Charlie's needs, was pencil thin with cut-glass cheekbones and she was dressed in a severely straight black dress of fine wool. She also wore glasses with trendy black and white frames and her iron-grey hair was pulled tightly back into a low ponytail.

Another woman might have looked plain in such restrained attire but Monique managed to look incredibly elegant. No doubt her bright scarlet lipstick and nail polish helped.

Charlie supposed she should have painted her nails, too. She wondered if Olivia had always worn nail polish. It was another detail she should have checked with Rafe.

Monique was very organised and had a page set aside for Charlie in a thick gold-edged notebook. 'Welcome back again, Mademoiselle Olivia,' she said with a careful smile.

'Thank you,' said Charlie. 'How are you, Monique?'

Surprise flashed briefly in the woman's eyes, as if she hadn't expected this question. 'I'm very well, thank you, *mademoiselle*.' Her smile brightened. 'And now, His Highness has ordered quite a few more items for you, I believe.'

'Yes, I'm afraid so.'

Monique looked a little puzzled at this and Charlie winced. *Afraid so?* Had she really said that? What an idiot she was. She would have to behave far more confidently if she wanted to convince the people of Montaigne that she was Olivia Belaire. She was supposed to *adore* shopping.

She laughed quickly to try to cover her gaffe. 'So,' she said, brightly. 'I'm sure you have some wonderful suggestions.'

'Of course,' said Monique. 'I have a very good idea what suits you now, so I've made a few selections to get us started.'

'Lovely,' Charlie enthused. 'I can't wait to try them on.'

They started with the coats and it was so hard to choose between a beautiful long red coat with a leather belt and another in black and white houndstooth. Eventually, with a little prompting from Monique, Charlie settled on the red.

For this evening's dinner, she chose a timelessly styled blue dress made from exquisitely fine wool. It was rather figure-hugging and designed to catch the eye, but Charlie supposed it was the sort of thing Rafe wanted her to wear. She tried not to blush when she saw her reflection in the mirror, but, heavens, she'd had no idea she could look so glamorous.

'Do you know what the daytime event for tomorrow will be?' asked Madame Monique, watching Charlie closely.

Charlie was relieved that she could answer this. 'I believe I'll be visiting the children's hospital.'

The woman's eyebrows rose, but she made no comment as she showed Charlie a rather demure dress in grey with a box neckline and a wide band around the waist.

'Hmm,' said Charlie. 'That's lovely, but do you have anything that's a bit more—fun?'

'Fun, Mademoiselle Olivia?' Madame Monique was clearly surprised.

Charlie wondered if she'd used the wrong French word. 'Something more appealing to the children, something a little more—relaxed?'

'Oh, I see, of course.' Monique went back to her racks, frowning.

Charlie followed her. The clothes were extremely elegant, but there were rather a lot of beiges and greys and blacks. She was wondering if she would be better off just wearing a pair of jeans and one of her own sweaters when something caught her eye.

'What about this?' she said, lifting out a hanger to inspect the dress more closely. It was a feminine shift dress with elbow-length sleeves and a delicate all-over print of little red sail boats with white sails on a navy-blue background. 'This would be perfect. Do you have it in my size?'

Now Monique looked worried. 'But, *mademoiselle*, don't you remember? You already have this dress. You bought it two weeks ago.'

'Oh.' Charlie wished she could sink through the floor. 'Yes, of course,' she said shakily. 'How silly of me. I—I took it home to Saint-Tropez, you see, when I—when I visited my mother—and I—'

It was awful to lie so blatantly and just saying the word 'mother' felt terribly wrong. She couldn't quite finish the sentence, but if Monique was baffled, and Charlie was sure that she had to be, she discreetly covered the reaction.

'What about this?' Monique lifted out a white dress with black polka dots and a short black jacket. 'I think this would suit you beautifully. And it certainly looks… *détendu*.'

This outfit did indeed suit Charlie very well and it had the right playful vibe she'd been hoping for. It was added to the stash, along with an *oh-my-God* evening gown of pale sea-green satin that was the most elegant and glamorous thing Charlie had ever clapped eyes on, let alone worn.

She felt a little faint as she wondered what the price tag might be.

'And now for your shoes,' said Monique.

The fainting sensation grew stronger for Charlie. *Oh, dear.* She had to sit down.

Monique fussed. 'Mademoiselle Olivia, are you all right? What can I get you? A glass of water perhaps? Coffee?'

'Perhaps some water,' said Charlie. 'Thank you.'

Monique tut-tutted when she returned with the water. 'Perhaps you are not well, *mademoiselle*.'

'No, I'm fine,' Charlie insisted, after taking several reviving sips. 'It's probably—' She was about to use jet lag as an excuse when she remembered that her sister, Olivia, hadn't been flying halfway across the world in a jet. 'I'm just a bit tired,' she said instead. 'And I was wondering—before we start on the shoes, would you mind telling me how much I have spent so far?'

This time, Madame Monique didn't try to cover her surprise. Her eyebrows shot high above her black and white spectacle frames. 'But you know there's no need to concern yourself, my dear. This goes on the St Romain account, does it not?'

Charlie had no idea what arrangement Rafe had made with Olivia. All she knew was that he'd paid her, Charlie, an extremely generous sum and she wouldn't dream of asking him for anything more.

'I'm paying for today's purchases,' she said, but as the words left her mouth she saw Monique's expression of jaw-dropping shock and knew that she'd made yet another mistake.

The dinner that evening was an official affair with some of Montaigne's most important businessmen and their wives. Charlie wore the blue wool dress and a new pair of skin-toned high heels that she hoped would go with almost everything, although Madame Monique had persuaded her that she needed black boots to go with her overcoat.

'You look beautiful,' Prince Rafael told her when he saw her.

'Thanks.' It was the first time that day that Charlie had seen him and, to her dismay, just watching him walk into the drawing room in a dark suit and tie caused a jolt to her senses. To make matters worse, he reached for her hand.

Ridiculous tingles shot over her skin.

'Did your shopping expedition go well?'

'Yes, thanks. Monique—was very helpful.' Although Charlie was miserably aware that tongues would be wagging at Belle Robe.

'Something very strange has happened to Olivia Belaire, the Prince's fiancée. I think she must be unwell. She looked very pale.'

'Can you believe she wanted to pay for the clothes with cash? And then she didn't have enough.'

At some stage this evening she would have to confess to Rafe that she'd needed to use his money as well, but she was sure she should leave it until after the dinner.

Rafe must have noticed her distress. He gave her hand an encouraging squeeze. 'I think you need jewellery to set that dress off. Sapphires perhaps?'

Charlie gulped, touched a hand to her bare throat. Before she could answer, Rafe was summoning Jacques, his right-hand man—or perhaps his valet, Charlie wasn't sure—telling him to bring the single-strand Ceylon sapphires.

'Don't look so worried,' Rafe told her as the man hurried away. His smile was a little puzzled. 'I've never met a woman who didn't like shopping or jewellery.'

Charlie shrugged. 'If you transplant an ordinary Aussie girl into a fairy-tale European kingdom, you've got to expect a few surprises.'

Rafe's eyes gleamed as he smiled. This time he lifted her hand to his lips. 'Touché,' he murmured.

To Charlie's dismay, he left a scorch mark where his lips touched her hand.

* * *

The sapphires were promptly delivered and they were perfect to complement the simple lines of her sky-blue dress—a single strand of deep blue oval stones surrounded by delicate clusters of tiny white diamonds and set in white gold.

'Allow me,' Rafe said, lifting the necklace and securing it around Charlie's neck.

The skin around his eyes crinkled this time when he smiled. 'Perfect,' he said softly. 'Oh, and there are matching earrings. You might like to wear them as well. Take a look in the mirror.'

Charlie was a little stunned by her reflection. Who was this elegant creature?

But her cheeks were flushed pink and her fingers fumbled as she tried to fit the earrings to her lobes. Crikey, she had to calm down or she'd drop a royal sapphire and have the Prince of Montaigne down on his knees, searching for it in the thick carpet.

At last the earrings were secure.

'You look like a princess,' Rafe told her.

Yes, it was amazing what expensive clothes and jewellery could do for a girl. Charlie drew a deep breath. Tonight she would have to pretend that she was a princess-to-be. Princess Charlie or, rather, Charlotte.

What a laugh.

Any urge to laugh soon died when Rafe took her hand again. She was super-aware of his warm, *naked* palm pressed against hers, of his long fingers interlaced with hers, as he led her down the formal staircase to greet their guests.

She kept her smile carefully in place and concentrated hard on remembering everyone's names as she was introduced, but the task would have been a jolly sight easier if her pretend fiancé hadn't kept touching her. For Rafe, it meant nothing to place a hand at her elbow, on her shoulder, at the small of her back. For Charlie, it was intensely, breath-robbingly distracting.

The castle's dining room was a long rectangular space decorated with rich red wallpaper as a background for impressive paintings and gold-framed mirrors. An enormous picture window with a spectacular view of the valley took up most of the far wall. The table was exquisitely set with candles and flowers, gleaming silver and shining glassware, and everything was arranged so perfectly that Charlie could imagine a ruler had been used to align the place settings.

Throughout the delicious four-course meal, Rafe conversed diplomatically with his important guests, but his eyes constantly sought Charlie out. Many times he sent her a smouldering smile across the table.

She knew his smiles weren't genuinely flirtatious. He was playing the role of an affectionate fiancé for the sake of their guests. So, of course, she tried to remain cool and collected, to pay studious attention to the conversations all around her. Actually, she had no choice but to pay *very* careful attention, because everyone spoke rather rapidly in French and she could only just keep up with them. And she tried hard to not let Rafe's sexy smiles affect her too deeply.

Unfortunately, her body had a mind of its own, firing off heat flashes whenever her gaze met Rafe's across the table. It didn't help that she was terribly worried about the conversation she must have with him as soon as his guests had departed.

* * *

It was late when everyone finally left. Much to Charlie's amazement, the men had withdrawn to linger over coffee and cognac—she thought that kind of antiquated custom had gone out with the ark.

'This is when the men settle their important business,' one of the wives told her as their coffee was served. 'They're all so worried about this Leroy Mining Company.'

'While we just want to gossip,' said another woman, an attractive brunette.

Seeing their expectant smiles, Charlie was suddenly nervous again. Were these businessmen's wives expecting her to supply them with gossip? What would Olivia have done in her shoes? She hadn't a clue.

She didn't even know if these women had known Olivia.

'I'm all ears,' Charlie said, managing an extra-bright smile, despite the roiling tension in her stomach.

For a moment the women looked baffled. Clearly, this wasn't the response they'd expected. They were hoping for news from her, but just when things were about to get very awkward one of the women laughed, as if Charlie had actually cracked a wonderful joke, and then the others joined in.

After that, knowing it was her duty as hostess to lead the conversation, Charlie asked them if they were coming to the ball on the night after next and it seemed that all of them were. From then on, she was fielding questions about which band would be playing on the night of the ball and whether Princess Maria or Countess von Belden had been invited.

'I'm sorry,' Charlie said. 'I've been visiting my mother In Saint-Tropez and I've left all those arrangements to Rafael.'

* * *

Somehow, she got through the interrogation without too many sticky moments. She wondered if Rafe had ensured that the guests were first-timers who hadn't met her sister. Even so, the night was an ordeal. She was battling jet lag and she was almost dropping with exhaustion. This 'princess' gig was so much harder than it looked from the outside.

She was sure Rafe must be tired, too, but after the guests left he still came to her room, as he'd warned her he must, for his expected 'nightly visit'.

'Thank heavens that's over,' he said, taking off his coat and carelessly draping it on the end of a sofa, then flopping into the deep cushions and loosening his tie and the buttons at his throat.

Charlie hadn't meant to stare as he performed this small act, but everything about the man was so utterly eye-catching. She found herself mesmerised by the jutting of his jaw as he loosened his collar, by the sudden exposure of his tanned throat, and even the way he sat with his elbows hooked over the back of the sofa, his long legs sprawled casually.

Everything about this Prince was super-attractive and manly.

Rafe caught her watching him. She looked away quickly, cheeks flaming, and then tried to make herself comfortable as she sat on the opposite sofa. But it was hard to feel comfortable with a huge weight on her mind.

There was only one thing for it, really—she had to get her worries off her chest quickly, before Rafe launched into another cosy fireside chat.

Charlie sat forward with her back straight, her hands tightly clasped in her lap. 'Rafe, I have a confession to make.'

Unfortunately, he merely looked amused, which wasn't at all helpful. 'I thought something must be troubling you.'

'Did it show tonight? I'm sorry. Do you think your guests noticed?'

'No, Charlie, relax.' He gave a smiling, somewhat indulgent shake of his head. 'It's just that I've learned to read the signs. There's a certain way you hold your mouth when you're distracted or worried, but as far as anyone else is concerned you were perfect tonight. You look very lovely, by the way.'

'Yes, you told me.' She refused to take his flattery seriously. 'It's the dress, of course.'

This brought another slow, knowing smile tilting the corners of his sexy mouth. 'Of course. We'll blame the dress. Now, what's your problem?'

Charlie's problem was the same problem that had dogged her all her life. 'Money.'

'Money?' Rafe looked understandably puzzled. 'So what's the problem exactly? You have too little or too much money?'

She couldn't imagine ever being worried about having too much money. 'Too little, of course. I'm sorry, I—'

A crease furrowed between Rafe's dark brows. 'Dare I ask about the two hundred and fifty thousand dollars I gave you? I know it's not really any of my business, but you haven't spent that already, have you?'

'Well, yes—I have—actually.' Charlie almost added an apology as she made this confession, but stopped herself just in time. She would only make matters worse if she behaved as if she were guilty. 'I'm only telling you this, because I went shopping today, and I tried to buy the clothes out of my own savings. But I didn't have quite enough, not for the shoes and boots, as well as the coat and the dresses.'

'But *you* weren't expected to pay for the clothes out of your own purse. Surely Monique explained?'

'I think she may have tried to. She said something about a St Romain account, but I wanted to pay for them, Rafe. You've already given me so much money.'

'Which you've managed to spend in forty-eight hours. That's no mean feat, Charlie.'

She had no answer for this. At least Rafe didn't ask her what she'd spent the money on. She still felt too tense about Isla to try to talk about that situation.

No doubt he assumed she'd bought a yacht or an apartment, or even that she'd used his money to pay off old debts.

A deafening silence followed her admission. In the midst of the awkwardness, she heard a *ping* from her phone, which she'd left on her bedside table.

'Do you mind if I get that?' she asked.

'By all means.' Rafe gave a stiff nod of his head and he spoke with excessive, almost chilling politeness.

Charlie knew she'd disappointed him and she might have felt guilty if she hadn't been so very anxious about her family. They must be in Boston by now. Her stomach was churning as she dashed to the phone.

CHAPTER SEVEN

RAFE KNEW IT was foolish to feel disappointed in Charlie simply because she'd dispensed with his money so easily. She was perfectly entitled to do what she liked with the cheque he'd given her.

She was fulfilling her obligations—she'd accompanied him to Montaigne and was acting as a stand-in for her sister, and that was all he'd asked of her. How she spent the money was none of his business.

Besides, he was using Charlie to his own ends, so he was in no position to make moral judgements about the girl.

To Rafe's annoyance, these rationalisations didn't help. He *was* disappointed. Unreasonably, illogically, stupidly disappointed.

Unfortunately, in the same short couple of days that it had taken Charlie to spend his payment, he'd allowed her—an unknown girl from the bottom of the planet—to steal under his defences.

Thinking back over the past forty-eight hours, Rafe couldn't believe that he'd allowed Charlie to cast a spell over him. But, surely, that must be what had happened. Somehow, despite the lectures he'd given himself, he'd allowed himself to become intrigued by the possibility that he'd discovered a rare creature—a lovely, sexy girl with genuine *heart*, who wasn't a grasping opportunist.

Foolishly, he'd decided that Charlie was different from her sister Olivia and from the other frustratingly shrewd and calculating young women in his social circles.

Rafe had been beguiled by Charlie's air of apparent naivety, and, even though he'd known that she wouldn't remain in his life beyond a few short weeks, he'd wanted to thoroughly enjoy the novelty of her company while he could.

She'd been a refreshing experience.

Or so he'd thought.

He consoled himself that he wasn't the only one who'd been hoodwinked. Even his good friend, Sheikh Faysal, had been taken by Charlie and had made remarks about her sincerity.

What had Faysal said? *'If you play your cards correctly, I'd say your Charlie could be quite an asset.'*

Ha! They'd both been conned.

Charlie was nervous as she picked up the phone. As she'd hoped, it was a message from her father.

Arrived safely. Dr Yu has assessed Isla and it's all systems go. Surgery scheduled for nine a.m. tomorrow EDT. Thank you, darling!! Love you loads, Dad & Skye xx

It was such a relief to hear from him. Almost immediately, Charlie could feel her shoulders relax and her breathing ease. Isla was in the best possible place, under the care of the brilliant doctors in Boston.

But her relief brought a welling of tears and she had to close her eyes to stop them from spilling. She drew in a deep breath, and then another.

She wasn't ready to share this news with Rafe. It was too private, too desperately scary to talk about. And it wasn't over yet. Poor little Isla still faced surgery and that was probably the most dangerous time of all.

Opening her eyes again, she caught a glimpse of Rafe's cautious, frowning expression. She supposed he'd been watching her, but as she returned to the sofa he paid studious attention to his own phone, which he slipped back into his pocket as she sat down.

For a tense moment, neither of them spoke. And then they both spoke together.

'That was a message from my father,' Charlie said.

'I was just checking the weather forecast,' said Rafe.

They stopped, eyed each other awkwardly.

'All's well with my family,' offered Charlie.

'There's more snow predicted,' said Rafe.

Charlie managed a tiny smile. 'At least I have a warm coat now.'

'Yes.'

She swallowed, wondering what on earth they could talk about when the mood was so strained. Rafe's smiles had vanished. There was no chance of regaining the warmth of last evening's conversation.

She touched the sapphires, lying cool and solid against her throat. 'Do these need to be returned to a vault, or something?'

Rafe nodded. 'I'll see to it.'

He sat, watching her with a hard-to-read, brooding gaze as she removed the necklace and the earrings and placed them back in their velvet-covered box. This time, he made no attempt to help her. Without the jewellery, she felt strangely naked.

'So, tomorrow you go to the children's hospital,' Rafe said.

Charlie nodded. 'Yes.'

'I hope that's not too much of an imposition.'

'No, I think I'll enjoy it.' She would feel closer to her family. The connection was important.

Another awkward silence fell and Rafe stared at her thoughtfully. 'I don't have any pressing appointments in the morning. I'll accompany you.'

This was a surprise—and not a pleasant one either. Under normal circumstances, Charlie wouldn't have minded. She enjoyed Rafe's company very much, probably *too* much. But now she was sure he was only going to the hospital to keep an eye on her, which meant he didn't trust her, and that possibility disturbed her.

'I'll look forward to your company,' she said quietly, knowing she had little choice.

Rafe nodded, then stood. 'The breakfast room is on the ground floor, in the south wing. I'll see you there at eight tomorrow?'

'Yes—sir.' Charlie couldn't help adding the cheeky 'sir'. Rafe was being so stodgy and formal.

He didn't smile, but one dark eyebrow lifted and a flicker of something that might have been amusement showed briefly in his eyes. He left quickly, though, with a curt *'bonne nuit'*. No kisses on the cheek tonight.

Visiting a children's hospital with a prince in tow was a very different experience from any previous hospital visit that Charlie had made.

After a polite and rather formal exchange at breakfast, she and Rafe left the castle in a sleek black, chauffeur-driven car that sported the blue and gold flags of Montaigne fluttering from its bonnet. And as they passed through the snowy streets, people turned to stare, to point and to wave excitedly. Finally, when the car pulled up outside the hospital, there was a group of reporters hovering on the footpath.

From the moment the chauffeur opened the door for Charlie, cameras were flashing and popping and she felt so flustered she almost stumbled and landed in the newly snow-ploughed gutter. The possibility of such an ignominious christening for her long red coat and knee high boots ensured that she navigated the footpath super carefully. Rafe's hand at her elbow helped.

A team of doctors, nurses and administrators from the hospital greeted them on the front steps. Charlie remembered to smile while Rafe introduced her as his fiancée, Olivia Belaire, and she did her level best to remember names as she shook everyone's hand.

Then the hospital team, plus Rafe and Charlie and the reporters, all processed inside.

Charlie leaned in to speak in a whisper to Rafe. 'Surely, all these flashing cameras will frighten the sick children?'

'They won't all be allowed into the wards,' Rafe assured her.

Indeed, as Charlie's and Rafe's coats were taken and they continued to the wards, only one television cameraman and one newspaper journalist were allowed to continue, along with the entourage of hospital staff. Charlie decided to ignore the other adults as best she could. The children were her focus and they were delightful.

Over the next hour or so, she and Rafe met such a touching array of children. Some were very sick and confined to bed, while others were more mobile and were busy with various craft activities. They talked to a little boy in a wheelchair who was playing a game on a tablet and another boy presented Rafe with a colourful portrait of himself and Olivia, both wearing golden crowns.

A little girl wearing a white crocheted cap to cover her bald head performed a beautiful curtsy for them.

'Oh, how clever you are!' Charlie told her, clapping madly. Prince Rafael, however, went one better. Responding with a deep bow, he took the little girl's hand and gallantly kissed her fingers.

The smile on the child's face was almost as huge as the lump in Charlie's throat and she knew this was a moment she would remember forever.

Of course, the cameras were flashing and whirring throughout these exchanges, but by now Charlie, glad of her jaunty polka-dot dress, had learned to ignore them. They moved on to a room that looked like a kindergarten where children were sitting at tables and busy with crêpe paper and scissors and wire.

'So what are you doing?' Charlie asked, kneeling down to the children's level.

'We're making roses,' she was told by a little girl with a bandage over one eye. 'And we made one for you!'

'Oh!'

Charlie's gratitude and praise for the pink and purple concoction were heartfelt and, although she felt quite emotional at times, she managed to keep her smile in place. Until they reached the sick babies.

Suddenly, her stomach was churning. At least there were no babies awaiting heart surgery in this ward, but she was given a warm, blanketed bundle to hold, and from the moment the little one was placed in her arms she was battling tears.

Of course, she was thinking of Isla, and of course, the cameramen zoomed in close, capturing every emotion. She didn't dare to catch Rafe's eye.

* * *

They were driving back to the castle, after morning tea with a selection of hospital staff, before Rafe commented on the experience. 'That seemed to go well,' he said, although he didn't look particularly happy.

'It was amazing,' Charlie declared firmly. 'The children were so excited to see you, Rafe. That little girl with the curtsy was gorgeous. I hope she gets better. Her doctor said he was optimistic.'

'That's good,' Rafe said warmly. 'Everyone loved you—especially the children, but you were a hit with the staff as well.'

Charlie couldn't help feeling chuffed. 'I guess I was channelling my inner princess.'

Rafe's response was an incomprehensible smile, and he looked more worried than pleased.

What was wrong? Charlie wondered with a sigh. She felt a spurt of impatience. She'd done her level best this morning. He'd said she'd done well. What more did he want?

'Why do you look so worried, Rafe? I thought you just told me that the visit went well. I thought you were happy.'

'Of course the visit went well. You were perfect.' He gave a slow shake of his head. 'That's the problem.'

This made no sense at all. 'Excuse me?'

'You've set rather a high standard for Olivia to follow.'

'Oh.' Charlie hadn't considered this possibility. 'Are you suggesting that visiting a children's hospital might not be her cup of tea?'

'Exactly,' Rafe said grimly.

Charlie had no answer for this. She'd done what she'd been asked to do. She could do no more. 'Do you think there'll be a photo in the newspaper tomorrow?'

Rafe nodded. 'Almost certainly.'

'I wonder if Olivia will see it. Gosh, imagine how shocked she'll be.'

This brought another frown from Rafe. 'At least, she might make contact then.'

'And that's a good thing, surely?'

But his expression was still serious and thoughtful as he looked away out through the car's window. A woman and a little girl out on the street saw him and waved excitedly, but he seemed too preoccupied to notice. He didn't wave back.

Charlie, feeling sorry for them, waved instead.

The car returned to the castle and Charlie expected that Rafe would leave her now. She had no other commitments for the day, but he would almost certainly be busy. She wasn't looking forward to the next few hours of anxiously pacing the floor, trying to fill in time until she heard news from her father.

In the castle's enormous, white-marbled entrance, she hesitated, expecting Rafe to dismiss her.

Instead, he stood, tall and wide shouldered, in his large, heavy wool overcoat, with his black leather gloves clasped in one hand, watching Charlie with unexpected vigilance, almost as if she were a puzzling, troublesome child.

She was getting rather tired of trying to understand what this Prince really wanted of her. She was about to demand what his problem was when he spoke.

'Charlie, can I ask a personal question?' His manner was perfectly polite, but there was an intensity in his grey gaze that made her suddenly nervous.

In an attempt to cover this, she shrugged, rather like a teenager put on the spot by an inquisitive parent. 'I guess. What do you want to know?'

'Would you be prepared to explain why I've seen you on the verge of tears on at least three separate occasions now?'

Her cheeks flamed hotly. 'Three times?'

'Yes,' said Rafe. 'You've been upset twice on the phone when you were speaking to your father and then today at the hospital with that tiny baby in your arms.'

'You're—you're very observant.'

'Look, I don't want to pry, Charlie,' Rafe said more gently. 'I'm fully aware that I dragged you away from your life in Sydney without really asking if it was convenient, but if something is causing you distress, perhaps I should know.'

She would burst into tears if she tried to talk about Isla, especially now with the scheduled surgery only hours away. 'I'm just a bit tense,' she hedged.

Rafe's grey eyes narrowed. 'And this tension relates to your father?'

'Sort of…yes.' It was the best she could manage. She crossed her arms tightly over her chest and hoped this was the end of Rafe's interrogation.

'Is there any way I can help?'

This was so unexpected.

Charlie had never had a drop-dead handsome man offer to help her. For a moment she was tempted to pretend that Rafe really was her fiancé, to tell him everything that was bothering her as she threw herself into his arms and sobbed on his strong, capable shoulder.

Just in time, she dragged her thoughts back to reality. 'It's kind of you to offer to help, Rafe. But, actually, I haven't talked to you about—my concerns—because I knew you might want to help. And you can't really, and if you did try, then there'd probably be all kinds of publicity and—'

'I can avoid publicity when I need to,' Rafe cut in. 'My press secretary is very good at managing these things.'

Charlie supposed this was true. There would be many times when a royal needed to avoid the press, and other times when he would welcome the attention. She supposed Rafe had been well aware that his presence at the hospital today would be a draw-card for journalists. Perhaps, Charlie realised now, he'd been using the hospital visit as some kind of bait to lure Olivia out of hiding.

This thought drew Charlie up sharply. But she didn't want to think too deeply about Rafe's relationship with Olivia. She especially didn't like to contemplate the regrettable reality that Rafe planned to go ahead with his marriage to her sister, even though he didn't love her and she clearly didn't love him.

On the other hand, when Charlie considered what she'd been prepared to do to save Isla, she supposed Rafe might go to any length to save his country. It was all rather depressing, really.

And Rafe was still waiting for her answer.

She pulled her phone from her pocket to check the time. It was only midday, and by her calculations Isla's surgery was scheduled for three pm Montaigne time. She still had to wait hours and hours before she knew the outcome.

'I appreciate your concern,' she told him. 'But now is not a good time to talk about it.'

'When will be a good time?' Rafe persisted.

'By the end of the day.' She had no idea how she would fill in the rest of the day. 'I just wish this day would go faster,' she said, thinking aloud.

'So, why don't you allow me to divert you for an hour or so with lunch in one of our finest restaurants?'

Charlie was momentarily dumbstruck. 'Aren't you too busy?'

'Not today. I've kept my schedule clear.' A smile shimmered in his eyes as he waited for her answer.

'Will there be lots of people staring at us?'

'Not at this place. Most of Cosme's clientèle are famous in their own right. Come on, Charlie. I'll drive you there myself. Let me show you a little more of my country and one of my favourite places.'

The smile he gave her now would have done Prince Charming proud, and Charlie had to admit that the thought of a pleasant lunch in a lovely restaurant was way more appealing than pacing alone in her room and uselessly worrying.

Really, when the man invited her so nicely, she'd be churlish to refuse, wouldn't she?

Rafe drove to Cosme's in a flashy silver sports car, with the hood up against the biting cold. As far as Charlie could tell, most of the city's roads seemed to be narrow and winding, which must have made life difficult for the guys with the snowploughs. Many streets were ancient and cobbled and crowded in by tall buildings made from centuries-old stone. She was sure she would have been nervous if she'd been behind the wheel, but Rafe drove his car skilfully and with obvious enjoyment.

She wondered how often he got to taste this kind of freedom, although she supposed he wasn't ever completely free. His minders were still following at a discreet distance.

The restaurant, simply called Cosme's, was in an old building that might have once been a castle. Two pine trees stood like sentries in huge pots on either side of a bright red door, making a bright splash of welcome colour.

Inside, Charlie and Rafe, with their coats and scarves taken care of, were led up a winding stone staircase to a spacious dining area made completely of stone and warmed by a blazing, crackling fire, a proper open fire with logs. The other diners scarcely paid them any attention as they were shown to their table set in an alcove.

It was all wonderfully simple, but perfect—a starched white tablecloth, gleaming, heavy silver, a small candle in a pottery holder and another spectacular view.

Charlie was rapt as she looked out through their alcove's arched window to the pale winter sky and a steep, snow-covered mountainside. 'This is absolutely gorgeous, Rafe. Thank you for bringing me here.'

He grinned. 'The pleasure's all mine. But wait till you try the food.'

The menu was large and of course everything was in French.

'You know the menu well,' Charlie said. 'I think I'd like you to choose. What do you suggest I should try?'

'Well, you can't beat the traditional French favourites,' Rafe suggested. 'Cosme has perfected them. I'm sure you'd enjoy his *soupe à l'oignon*.'

'Oh, yes.' A proper French onion soup on a cold winter's day sounded perfect.

'But perhaps, first, you would like to try an entrée? How about something local, like goat's cheese baked with Alpine honey?'

Charlie grinned. 'Yes, please. It sounds amazing.'

And, of course, it was totally delicious. For Charlie, who was used to cramming in a hasty sandwich at her desk in the gallery, this leisurely, gourmet lunch was the ultimate luxury.

As she tasted her first sip of a divine vintage Chablis, she couldn't help asking, 'Has Olivia been here?'

Amusement flickered in Rafe's eyes and at the corners of his mouth. 'Actually, no, she hasn't.'

She knew it was small-minded of her to be pleased about this. Surely it was shameful to have feelings of sibling rivalry for a sister you'd never even met.

Charlie's soup arrived, along with a veal dish for Rafe. The soup was wonderfully rich and savoury with a to-die-for golden, cheesy bread crust. It was so good she couldn't talk at first, apart from raving, but after a bit she encouraged Rafe to tell her more about Montaigne.

She was keen to learn more about its history and its traditions, about the mining threat and his plans for his country's future. So he told her succinctly and entertainingly about the country's history and the jewellery-making craftspeople and the famous Alpine skiers. As he talked she could feel how genuinely he loved this small principality and its people.

Charlie decided there was something very attractive about a man whose vision extended beyond his own personal ambitions. Not that she should dwell on Prince Rafael of Montaigne's attractions.

She was halfway through the soup, when she asked, in a burst of curiosity, 'What's it like to be you, Rafe? To be a prince? Does it do your head in sometimes?'

He frowned. 'My head in?'

'Does it ever feel unreal?'

He seemed to find this rather amusing. 'Mostly, it feels all too real.'

'But you must have met a lot of famous people. I guess you must have an awesome Christmas card list.'

This time Rafe laughed out loud, a burst of genuine mirth. 'Yes, I suppose it is an awesome list,' he said eventually.

'Will you add me?' Charlie couldn't resist asking. 'After all this is over?'

Any amusement in his face died. 'Yes,' he said quietly. 'If you'd like a Christmas card, I'd be happy to add you to my list, Charlie.'

The thought of being back in Australia and finding Prince Rafael's card in the mail wasn't as cheering as it should have been.

Charlie promptly changed the subject. 'Do you ever wish you could just be plain old Rafe St Romain?'

He wasn't smiling now. 'Many, many times. But hardly anyone can have exactly what they want, can they?'

'I—I guess not.'

'That's why life's a compromise.'

'Yeah,' said Charlie softly. But today she really needed a fairy tale for Isla. 'I suppose your parents drummed that into you?'

He gave this a little thought before he answered. 'It was my granny, actually. She was a crusty old thing, prone to giving lectures. Her favourite lesson was about the need to put duty before personal happiness. I must admit, I ignored her advice for as long as I could.'

'How long was that? Until your father died?'

His eyes widened. 'You're very perceptive, aren't you?'

Charlie dropped her gaze. 'Sorry, I have a bad habit of asking nosy questions.'

But Rafe shook this aside. 'You're quite right,' he said. 'I spent far too long living the high life. It's my deepest regret that my father died not knowing if I'd give up the nonsense and step up to the mark as his heir.'

His jaw was stiff as he said this, his mouth tight, as if he was only just holding himself together. An unexpected welling of emotion prompted Charlie to reach out, to give his hand a comforting squeeze.

Rafe responded with a sad little smile that brought tears to her eyes.

'Anyway,' he said quickly. 'I don't think Granny was ever very happy herself, and she was forever warning me that I couldn't expect to be as carefree and contented as my parents were.'

'Well, at least you must be reassured to know that your parents were happy.'

'Yes.' This time Rafe's smile wasn't quite as sad. 'My mother was from Russia. She was the daughter of a count. Her name was Tanya and she was very beautiful. My father worshipped her.'

'Wow.'

Charlie thought how sad it was that Rafe, by contrast, was arranging to marry for convenience, to save his country, tying himself into a contract with a girl he didn't seem to particularly admire.

If her sister ever came out of hiding.

To Charlie this seemed like a compromise of the very worst kind.

'By the way,' he said suddenly, changing their mood with a sudden warm smile, 'you should finish this meal with one of Cosme's chocolate eclairs. That's a happy ending you can always rely on.'

'Oh,' Charlie moaned. 'I don't think I have room.'

'We can ask for a tiny bite-size one. I promise, they're worth it.'

Charlie checked her phone again as they were getting back into the car. Rafe had noticed her checking it twice, very quickly, during the meal.

'When do you expect to hear something?' he asked.

She looked at him, her blue eyes wide, almost fearful.

'You're obviously waiting for a phone call,' he said.

She nodded sadly. 'But it won't come for ages yet. It's only just starting.'

Rafe had turned on the ignition and was about to drive off, but now he waited. Charlie had been relaxed and animated during lunch, but now she was tense and pale. 'What has just started, Charlie?'

She opened her mouth, as if she was going to tell him, and then, annoyingly, shut it again.

Rafe sat very still, but with poorly contained patience. 'What?' he asked again, but she didn't reply.

He watched her trembling chin, knew she was struggling not to cry, and couldn't believe how the sight of her distress bothered him as much as it frustrated him. He almost demanded there and then that she tell him about it.

He certainly would have done so, if they weren't in a car on a narrow street with curious pedestrians on either side. Instead, with grim resignation, he put his foot down on the accelerator and the car roared off.

When Rafe pulled up at the castle steps a valet was waiting to open Charlie's door and to park the car. Charlie wondered if ancient dungeons had been turned into underground car parks and she might have asked Rafe about this, but the question died when he linked his arm with hers and kept a firm hold on her as they went up the steps and inside the huge front doors.

'We'll have coffee in Olivia's room,' he told the waiting Chloe.

Charlie had expected to be alone now. She wanted to focus on Isla, to send positive thoughts while she waited for news. Just in time, she remembered not to show that she minded Rafe's company. No matter how tense she was, she couldn't let him down in front of the watchful eyes of his staff. She was supposed to be his loving fiancée, after all.

She waited until they were in the lift. 'You don't need to come to my room, Rafe.'

His eyes were cool grey stones. 'But I choose to.'

He said this with such compellingly regal authority Charlie knew it was pointless to argue. She supposed she should be grateful for his company. Try as she might to send positive thoughts, she would probably end up sitting alone, unhelpfully imagining all kinds of gruesomeness as a surgeon's scalpel sliced through poor Isla's tiny chest.

Upstairs once again, she and Rafe sat opposite each other on the sofas. It was a scene that was beginning to feel very familiar, with the fire flickering, the huge window offering them its snowy view of the city and a coffee pot and their mugs sitting on the low table between them.

'Shall I pour?' Charlie asked.

Rafe nodded gravely. 'Thank you.'

The coffee was hot and strong. Charlie took two sips then set her mug down.

'How long do you have to wait for this news?' Rafe asked.

'I don't know. I guess it depends—' It was ridiculous to avoid telling him now. 'I have no idea how long it takes to operate on a not quite two weeks old baby's heart.'

She watched the shock flare in his eyes.

'This is your little half-sister?' he said, eventually.

Charlie swallowed. 'You knew?'

'I knew you had a baby sister, your stepmother's child. You visited her in Sydney before you left.'

She supposed his 'men' had told him this. 'Her name's Isla,' she said. 'She was born with a congenital heart defect.'

'Oh, Charlie.'

She held up a hand to stop him. 'Don't be nice to me, or I'll cry.'

Rafe stared at her, his expression gravely thoughtful. 'Where is this surgery taking place?'

'In America. In Boston. The surgeon is supposed to be brilliant. The best.'

'I'm sure you can rely on that brilliance,' Rafe said, and this time his voice was surprisingly gentle.

Charlie nodded. Already, after getting this sad truth out in the open, she was breathing a little more easily.

Rafe was looking at his phone. 'I guess the Internet should be able to tell us how long these sorts of operations might take.'

'I guess.' Charlie hugged her coffee mug to her chest as she watched him scroll through various sites.

'Hmm…looks like it could take anything from two and a half hours to over four hours.'

'Oh, God.'

Poor Isla.

Rafe looked up from his phone, his gaze direct, challenging. 'This is what you wanted the money for, isn't it?'

The tears she'd warned him about welled in her eyes. Fighting them, Charlie pressed her lips together. She nodded, swallowed deeply before she could speak. 'Do you mind?'

'Mind? No, of course I don't mind. How could I mind about my money being spent on something so—so decent and honourable?' His mouth twisted in a lopsided, sad smile.

'Oh, Charlie,' he said again and his voice was as gentle as she'd feared it would be.

Oh, Charlie.

With just those two words, Rafe unravelled the last shreds of her resolve.

The tension of the past few days gave way. She could feel her face crumpling, her mouth losing its shape. Then suddenly Rafe was on the sofa beside her and he was drawing her into his arms, bringing her head onto his shoulder.

For a brief moment, Charlie savoured the luxury of his muscled strength, the reassuring firmness of his considerable chest through the soft wool of his sweater, but then the building force of her pent-up emotions broke through and she wept.

CHAPTER EIGHT

RAFE KNEW THIS was wrong. A weeping Charlie in his arms was not, in any way, shape or form, a part of his plans. But he was still trying to digest her news and its implications.

Surely he shouldn't be so deeply moved by the fact that Charlie had used his money for such a worthy cause?

It had been much easier to assume that she'd wasted it.

Now, disarmed by the truth, Rafe knew he had to get a grip, had to throw a rope around the crazy roller coaster of emotions that had slugged him from the moment Charlie hurled herself into his embrace.

These emotions were all wrong. So wrong. He'd struck a business deal with this girl, and a short term one at that. She was a conveniently purchased stopgap. Nothing more. He wasn't supposed to feel aching tenderness, or a desperate need to help her, to take away her worries.

The problem was—this girl had already become so much more than a lookalike body double that he could parade before Montaigne like a puppet. Charlie Morisset was brave and unselfish and warm-hearted and, when these qualities were combined with the natural physical attributes she shared with her beautiful sister, she became quite dangerous. An irresistible package.

But somehow Rafe had to resist her appeal. He'd made

his commitment. He'd chosen Olivia as his fiancée. They'd signed a contract, and even though she'd disappeared he was almost certain she was playing some kind of game with him and would turn up when it suited her.

Meanwhile, Charlie was being predictably sensible. Already, she was pulling out of his arms and gallantly drying her eyes, and making an admirable effort to regain her composure.

She gave him a wan smile and they drank their cooling coffee. Outside, the afternoon was turning to early twilight.

Rafe stood and went to the window, looking out. 'It's not snowing. Perhaps we should go for a walk. All the lights are coming on, so it should be quite pleasant, and you still have a long time to wait.'

He was sure a long walk in fresh air and a chill wind were what they both needed. Anything was safer than staying here on the sofa with Charlie. The temptations were huge, overwhelming, but only a jerk would take advantage of her when she was so distraught.

'Won't you be mobbed if you try to walk out on the streets?' Charlie asked.

'It's not too bad at this time of the year. With an overcoat and a woolly cap and scarves, I can more or less stay incognito.' He smiled at her. She should have looked pathetic, so wan and puffy-eyed from crying, but she brought out the most alarming protectiveness in him. He held out his hand to haul her to her feet. 'Come on.'

Charlie had the good sense to recognise that Rafe's suggestion of a walk was the right thing to do under the circumstances. Sitting here, feeling sick and scared, was not going to help anyone in Boston. She could change into jeans and a sweater, and she'd bought a warm hat,

as well as a scarf and gloves, so she would be well protected against the cold.

Besides, it was incredibly considerate of Rafe to put
up with her weeping and to devote this entire day to her.
The least she could do was accept his kind suggestion.

Outside, the sky and the air were navy blue, on the
very edge of night. Lamplight glowed golden, as did the
lights from shops and houses, from the headlights of cars.
Pulling their hats low and winding their scarves tighter,
they set off together, with Charlie's arm linked in the
crook of Rafe's elbow.

Ahead stretched the long main street that led from
the castle. On either side were pastel-coloured buildings
from different eras, mostly now converted into shops,
hotels and restaurants.

'This section of the city is called Old Town,' Rafe told
her. 'New Town starts on the far hillside, beyond that tall
clock tower.'

He seemed to enjoy playing tour guide, pointing out
the significance of the clock tower and the statue of his
great-great-grandfather in full military regalia, complete
with medals. When they rounded the next corner and
came across a small cobblestoned plaza with a charming statue of a young boy with a flock of goats, Rafe told
her the story of the goatherd who was Montaigne's national hero.

'His name was Guido Durant,' Rafe said. 'He acted
as a kind of unpaid sentry up in the high Alps. When
the Austral-Hungarians were making their way through
a narrow pass in winter, planning to invade our country, Guido dug at rocks and stones and managed to get a
snow slide going. It turned into a full-blown avalanche
and blocked their way. Then he ran through the night all
the way to the castle to warn my great-great-grandfather.'

'So he's Montaigne's version of William Tell?' Charlie suggested.

Rafe shot her a surprised smile. 'You know about William Tell?'

'Of course. My father used to love telling me that story. He used to play the opera, too, turning the music up really loud. It's very dramatic.'

'Yes, it is,' Rafe agreed. 'It was one of my father's favourite operas, actually.'

'My father's, too.' Charlie laughed. 'Crikey, Rafe, we do have something in common after all.'

'So we do,' he said quietly and his grey eyes gleamed as their gazes connected, making Charlie feel flushed and breathless. For a crazy moment, she thought he was going to do something reckless like haul her into his arms and her skin flashed with heat, as if she'd been scorched by a fireball.

Then the moment was over.

They walked on and the smell of cooking reached them from the many cafés, but they weren't very hungry after their substantial lunch.

Montaigne's capital city was packed with charm. Charlie loved the cobblestoned alleys, the arched doorways with fringes of snow, the shop windows with beautifully crafted wares, including jewellery that Rafe told her was locally made from gemstones found right here in the Alps. She especially loved the glimpses into cosy cafés where laughing people gathered.

'Can you ever go into places like that?' she asked him, as they passed a group at a bar who were guffawing loudly, obviously sharing a huge joke.

He shrugged. 'I have a few favourite cafés where I like to meet with friends.'

'Thank heavens for that.'

'Are you worried about me, Charlie? You think I'm not happy?'

'Well, no, of course not,' she said, which wasn't true. She wasn't sure that anyone who believed life was a compromise could really be happy.

His smile was complicated as he tucked her arm more snugly in his.

They went on, past a tenth-century cathedral, which, according to Rafe, had beautiful frescoes in its cloisters, past a museum of culture and local history, a monastery where a choir was practising, sending beautiful music spilling into the night.

Once again, Charlie imagined herself at some point in the distant future, when she was middle-aged and married to some respectable, ordinary Aussie man, telling others, perhaps her children, about this magical mountain kingdom that she'd once visited with a handsome prince.

She didn't suppose anyone would believe her.

Rafe's phone rang twice during their walk, but the calls seemed to be business matters that he was able to deal with quite quickly. Just once, Charlie checked her phone. There wasn't any news about Isla. She had known there wouldn't be, but she'd had to check anyway.

Always, throughout the walk, her fear about her baby sister sat like a heavy rock in her chest.

They were almost back at the castle, passing a market stall that sold arts and crafts and local honey, when Charlie heard the ping of a text message.

Her heart took off like an arrow fired from a bow. She came to a dead stop in a pool of yellow lamplight, felt sick, burning, and was almost too scared to look at her phone.

Rafe stood watching her, his eyes brimming with gentle sympathy. He smiled, a small encouragement.

Terrified, Charlie drew the phone out from the depths of her overcoat pocket. She was so scared she could hardly focus on the words.

Isla out of surgery and Dr Yu is happy. She'll be in Intensive Care for about four days, but so far all good. Love, Dad xxx

'Oh!' She wanted to laugh and cry at once.

Unable to speak, she held up her phone for Rafe to read the message, but she was shaking so badly, he had to clasp her hand tightly to steady it before he had any chance of reading it.

'She made it!' His cry was as joyous as Charlie's and he looked so relieved for her that she couldn't help herself. Launching towards him, she threw her arms around his neck, and hugged him hard, and then, impulsively, she kissed him. On the mouth.

No doubt it was an unwise move for an Australian commoner to kiss a European crown prince in such a public place. Fortunately the Crown Prince didn't seem to mind. In fact he gathered the commoner into his arms, almost crushing her as he held her tightly against him, and he returned her kiss with breath-robbing, fiery passion.

It seemed fitting to go into a café to celebrate the good news. Rafe took Charlie's hand and showed her a place tucked away in a back street that seemed to be carved out of stone like a cave. As they went inside, another welcoming fire burned in a grate, rows of bottles and glasses reflected back the cheerful light, and although there were one or two excited glances and elbow nudges from curious customers, they didn't hassle the newcomers as they perched on tall wooden stools at the bar.

Charlie's head was spinning.

Calm down, girl, it was just a kiss.

But it wasn't just *any* old kiss. She knew she'd never been kissed with such intensity, such excitement, had never experienced such a soul-searing thrill.

But he's a prince, a jet-setter, a playboy. He's had masses of practice. A kiss like that means nothing to him.

Could she be sure? It had felt very genuine.

Yes, that's the problem.

She had to stop thinking about it. Had to concentrate on Isla.

None of this would have happened if Isla had been well.

Rafe ordered *vin chaud*, which proved to be a delicious mulled wine laced with cinnamon, cloves and juniper berries.

'Here's to Isla,' he said, clinking his glass against Charlie's.

'Yes. To Isla.' Charlie lifted her glass. 'Hang in there for another four days, kiddo.' She took a sip. 'Wow, this is amazing.'

'It's a favourite drink with the skiers,' Rafe told her.

'I can certainly understand why.' Charlie drank a little more. 'I've never been skiing.'

He pretended to be shocked. 'That's something we'll have to remedy.'

The thought of skiing with Rafe was thrilling, but Charlie doubted they would have time. Apart from the hospital visit this morning, today had been unusually free of engagements. The private time alone with Rafe had been an unexpected bonus, but she knew he had commitments that were bound to keep him very busy. And tomorrow evening, there was to be the grand ball.

Charlie had never been to a ball and the very thought of it made her nervous. She would have to wear that beautiful, and incredibly expensive, pale green gown, and her schedule tomorrow included appointments with a hairdresser and a beautician.

It was best not to think about that tonight while they lingered over their *vin chaud*.

Eventually, they continued on their way, stopping to buy hot roasted chestnuts from a stall on a street corner and eating them from a paper cone. When they reached the castle, Rafe ordered a light supper to be brought to Mademoiselle Olivia's room.

In the lift, Charlie gave herself a stern lecture.

Forget about that kiss. You started it, remember?

Yes, and Rafe was just being kind.

Kind? Really?

That's probably how a playboy expresses kindness.

It won't happen again.

Delicious mini-pizzas arrived, topped with caramelised onions, black olives and Gruyère cheese. And there were cherries for dessert along with a pot of the most divine hot chocolate.

As they enjoyed their supper, Rafe filled Charlie in about the important dignitaries who would attend the ball tomorrow evening.

'You won't be expected to know everyone,' he assured her. 'But I'll ask Mathilde to give you a list with photos, so you can at least learn some of the names.'

'That would be helpful, thank you.' Charlie remembered something else that was bothering her. 'What about the dancing?'

'Ah, yes.' Rafe frowned. 'I should have thought about that earlier. Can you waltz?'

'No, not really. I mean—we learnt a little ballroom dancing at school and I've watched people waltzing on TV. I know it's basically one-two-three, one-two-three, but—' Charlie grimaced awkwardly. 'I don't suppose there'll be any disco dancing?'

Rafe smiled. 'There'll be some, I should imagine. But you'll be expected to know how to waltz.'

'Could Olivia waltz?'

'Yes. She's quite a good dancer, I must admit.'

Damn. 'Any chance we could have a bit of practice before tomorrow night?'

'Of course,' Rafe said without hesitation.

It was silly to feel so self-conscious, almost blushing at the thought of dancing in his arms, their bodies lightly brushing.

'You don't want to start worrying about that now, though,' he said. 'I'll see you tomorrow evening, say an hour early, before the ball, and we can have a little practice. Your room's carpeted, so it won't be the same as dancing on a proper dance floor, but at least we can run through the basics. I'm sure you'll pick it up very quickly.'

'OK. Thank you.'

The charming meal was a lovely end to a perfect day. All too quickly, it seemed to Charlie, it was time for Rafe to leave. He rose from the sofa, taking both her hands in his and drawing her to her feet.

Her heart began a silly kind of drumming.

Stop it.

'Thanks for giving up so much time to be with me today,' she said. 'It's been—' She was about to tell him it had been wonderful, a stand-out, red-letter day that she would never forget. But perhaps over-the-top enthusiasm wasn't wise at this point. It was time to remind herself that this was only a role that she was being paid to fulfil.

Instead of gushing, she said carefully, 'I appreciated your company. It was—very nice.'

'Very nice?' Rafe repeated in a tone that implied she had somehow insulted him.

'Well…yes.'

Leave it at that, Charlie. Too bad if he's disappointed. It's important to keep your head.

Perhaps Rafe understood. He responded with a courteous nod. 'I enjoyed the day, too. You're great company, Charlie, and I was very pleased to share the good news about your little sister.'

It felt strained to be so formal after the closeness they'd shared today, but Charlie told herself that this new, careful politeness was desirable. This was how matters must be between herself and the Prince. Even though Rafe was still holding her hands, it was time to retreat from being overly familiar.

It was time to remember the reality of their situation. She was only a temporary fill-in until Olivia was found—or until Olivia returned of her own accord.

Charlie was pleased to have her thoughts sorted on this matter, but then Rafe spoiled everything by clasping her hands more tightly and holding them against his chest.

Big mistake. She could feel his heart beating beneath her palm.

In response, her own heart was hammering. She tried to ignore it.

'You're a very special girl,' he said with a wry smile. 'Note I said *special*, not just very *nice*.'

'Special is open to interpretation,' Charlie said more curtly than she meant to.

'So it is.' Rafe lifted her hands to his lips. 'Perhaps

you'd prefer nice?' Keeping his grey gaze locked with hers, he kissed her hand, and his lips traced a seductive path over her knuckles.

Of course, Charlie's skin burned and tingled wherever his lips touched, and she knew what would come next. At any moment, Rafe would take her into his arms again and he would kiss her. Already, she could imagine the exquisite devastation of his lips meeting hers.

She had never wanted a kiss more, but she had to remember why this shouldn't happen.

'D-don't play with me, Rafe.'

He frowned as he stared at her, trying to read her.

Time seemed to stand still.

And poor Charlie was already regretting her plea, as the wicked vamp inside her longed for Rafe to go on kissing her hands, kissing her mouth, kissing any part of her that took his fancy.

But he was letting her hands go. 'Forgive me, Charlie. I did not intend to take liberties.'

It was ridiculous to feel so disappointed. Charlie knew she should be relieved that her message had got through to the playboy Prince.

'I'll see you at breakfast in the morning,' he said politely. 'Sleep well.'

With another formal bow, he backed out of the room, but the blazing signal in his eyes was anything but formal, and there was no way Charlie could miss its message. She only had to say the word and Rafe would drop the formalities. In a heartbeat, she would be in his arms, in his bed, discovering what it was like to make love to a prince. All night long.

Somehow, she stood super still until the door closed behind him.

Oh, help. Now she would have the devil's own job getting to sleep.

CHAPTER NINE

NEXT MORNING, WHEN Charlie went down to the breakfast room, she half expected to find that Rafe had left already, but he was still at the table, polishing off a croissant stuffed with smoked salmon and scrambled eggs. After a restless night, she felt a little uncertain about his mood, but he greeted her with a smile.

'*Bonjour*, Olivia.'

'*Bonjour*,' she responded carefully, knowing there were servants within hearing range.

Rafe immediately shot a pointed glance towards the newspaper on the table beside him.

The headline jumped out at Charlie.

OLIVIA LOOKS FORWARD TO MOTHERHOOD!

She gasped, caught Rafe's eye. He gave a helpless shrug.

The headline was accompanied by a photo of Charlie standing in the hospital's nursery in her new black and white polka-dot dress, holding the snugly wrapped baby and gazing at it wistfully, while Rafe watched with a smile that might easily be interpreted as fond.

The accompanying story began: *Olivia Belaire's motherly instincts were on clear display yesterday when she and Prince Rafael visited Montaigne's Royal Children's Hospital...*

Charlie skipped the rest of the story to check out another smaller headline.

ROYAL-IN-WAITING BRINGS CURTSIES AND SMILES.

The photograph beneath this caption showed Charlie and Rafe in the children's ward, standing close together, grinning with delight and applauding as the little girl in the crocheted cap performed her curtsy.

Charlie wondered what Olivia would make of these stories, if she saw them.

'Are you happy with this?' she asked Rafe, holding up the paper.

'My press officer's happy, so that's the main thing.' Over his coffee cup, he smiled at her again. 'You did well. I told you that yesterday. Everyone loved you.'

Charlie supposed she should be pleased, but she didn't really know how to feel about this. It was all too weird, and now that she wasn't quite so stressed about Isla she found herself wondering about her other sister. Olivia.

What was the real reason for Olivia's decision to take off? Would these photos of her double bring her out of hiding? If so, when would she show up? How would that scene play out?

Charlie couldn't help wondering if Rafe had thought this charade through properly, considering all possible consequences.

Then again, Charlie knew that for herself there was only one possible outcome. As soon as Olivia returned, Charlie's role at Montaigne would be over, which meant she could be gone from here within a matter of days.

Hours?

In no time she would find herself back in Sydney, back in her little flat that she'd decorated so carefully. She would be reunited with Dolly, her cat, and she'd see all her friends again and resume her role at the gallery. Once again she would be living in hope that she might sell her father's paintings for an enormous sum.

Taking her seat at the breakfast table, Charlie wished she felt happier about the prospect of going home. It didn't make sense to feel miserable about going back to her own world and her old life, the life that had been perfectly satisfactory until she'd been so suddenly plucked from it.

Her low mood was annoying. Puzzling, too. She knew she couldn't have fallen in love with Rafe in such a short space of time. And anyway, even if she had, foolishly, lost her head, it couldn't be an emotion of the lasting kind.

She was simply dazzled…starstruck. This man and his castle and his beautiful principality were all part of a fairy tale, after all. This world wasn't real—not for an everyday average Aussie girl.

'Is everything all right?' Rafe asked her in French.

Charlie blinked and it took her a moment to compute his simple question. 'Of course,' she said at last. 'I was just wondering when a certain person might be found.'

'Oh, yes, I know.' He frowned. 'It's very frustrating.'

Charlie suspected that Rafe might have said more, but a young man with carefully slicked-back hair, dressed in a pristine white shirt and black trousers, appeared to pour her coffee and to politely offer her warmed platters of food awaiting her selection. She copied Rafe and took a croissant with scrambled eggs and a little smoked salmon.

'I'm going to be busy for most of today,' Rafe told her as the young man hovered to pour his second cup of coffee and to make sure Charlie had everything she needed.

'But I've arranged for Mathilde to give you that VIP guest list with the photos.'

'Thank you.'

'And I won't forget our arrangement to meet prior to the ball. I think seven o'clock should give us enough time.'

'Yes, I'll make sure I'm ready.' Charlie was rather looking forward to their dancing lesson.

Rafe nodded. 'There's nothing else you need today?' And then almost immediately, he answered his own question. 'Of course, you'll need jewellery for tonight.'

'Well, yes, I suppose I shall.'

'What colour is your gown?'

Charlie thought about the beautiful gown hanging in her wardrobe. She remembered the slinky sensation of the fully lined satin and the way it had clung and rippled about her body as she moved. Now that the ball was drawing close, she was a bit self-conscious about wearing it in public.

'It's a sort of pale green.' she said. 'Not an apple green, a pale—I don't know, a smoky green, perhaps?' The colour was hard enough to describe in English, but trying to do so in French was almost impossible. Charlie knew she was making a hash of it. 'I think Monique may have called it sea foam, or something like that.'

'Sea-foam green?' Rafe's grey eyes widened. He didn't look impressed.

Charlie lifted her hands in a helpless gesture. 'Don't worry, Rafe, it works. That colour shouldn't suit me with my blue eyes, but it seems to.'

'I'm sure it's very beautiful, Char—Olivia.' It was the first time Rafe had ever slipped up with her name. Was it a sign that he was nervous about her performance tonight? This would be her first real test in front of all the most important people in Montaigne. She was beginning to wish that she'd chosen a nice safe white or blue dress.

But then, to her surprise, Rafe said, 'I can't wait to see you wearing it.' And he sent her a smile so smouldering it should have been illegal. Charlie was too busy catching her breath to reply.

'I imagine,' he said next, 'that pearls and diamonds might be best suited to your sea foam.'

'Yes,' Charlie agreed, very deliberately calming down, despite the exciting prospect of wearing royal pearls and diamonds. 'I think they'd be perfect.'

'Good. I'll arrange to have them sent to your room before seven.'

'Thank you.'

It was yet another day of new experiences. Charlie had been to hair salons before, of course, and had once indulged in a spray tan at a beauty salon in Sydney. But she'd never been to a suite of salons as grand and luxurious as the place Rafe's chauffeur delivered her to for today's appointments.

She'd certainly never been so pampered. By the end of the day she'd been given a warm oil body massage and a winter hydrating facial, as well as a manicure, pedicure and eyebrow wax—and of course, there had been a beautiful healthy lunch that included a ghastly looking green smoothie that was surprisingly delicious.

Charlie's hair had been given a special conditioning treatment, too, and her scalp had been massaged, her curls trimmed.

'Oh, my God, Olivia! Your hair has grown so much since your last cut!'

Charlie merely nodded at this. 'It grows fast,' she agreed, crossing her fingers under her cape.

After a short but intense discussion among the hairdressers about the Prince's expectations for the ball, Charlie's hair was styled into a glamorous updo. And then her make-up was applied. She'd been rather nervous about this. She was worried that the make-up would be too heavy, that it would involve false eyelashes and she'd end up looking like a drag queen. She wanted to be able to recognise herself when she saw her reflection.

There was no problem with recognition, however. In fact, the results were amazing. The girl in the mirror was the same old Charlie, but her skin now had a special glow, a feat she had never managed before without making her nose shiny. Her eyes seemed to have acquired an extra sparkle and glamour. Her hair was glossy, her curls artistically tamed. The result was faultless.

Charlie was a little overawed by this newly refined and sophisticated version of herself. She *almost* felt like a princess. She quickly stomped on that thought before it took root.

By seven o'clock the names and faces on the supplied list had all been memorised—Charlie had tested herself several times—and she was dressed and ready. The seafoam dress still looked good, she was relieved to see.

It was sleeveless with a scooped neckline and an elegant, low cowl back, but it was the slinky way the dress flowed, responding to every subtle movement of her body, that made it so special.

She had never gone out of her way to draw attention to herself, but she knew this was the sort of dress that would let everyone, male and female, know she was in the room. The addition of Rafe's heirloom pearls and diamonds—delivered by his valet, Jacques—completed her transformation. She had expected a necklace and earrings, but there was a tiara as well, which Jacques kindly helped her to secure.

When the valet left she was rather stunned when she saw herself in the mirror. The dress was a dream, the make-up dewy-perfect. The elegant up-sweep of her hair and the gleaming pearls and sparkling diamonds of the tiara had combined to create the perfect image of a princess.

Charlie Morisset was in for a *big* night.

For Rafe's sake, she only hoped she could get through it without making too many blunders.

Rafe was due at any moment and, rather than waiting for him to knock, Charlie opened her door, ready for his arrival. As she did so she heard strange noises—blasts and ripples of music floating up the staircase from the grand ballroom on the lower floor. Trumpets, clarinets, saxophones and flutes. The band was warming up.

Excitement and anticipation pinged inside her and she drew a quick, steadying breath. Not that it did her any good, for a moment later Rafe stepped out from a doorway across the hall and she completely forgot how to breathe.

He was dressed in a formal black military uniform with gold braid on his shoulders, a colourful row of medals and a diagonal red and gold sash across his broad chest. His dark hair, as black as a raven's wing, gleamed in the light of overhead chandeliers and he looked so handsome and so splendidly royal that Charlie's knees began to tremble.

Drop-dead gorgeous had just been redefined.

It didn't help that Rafe had come to a complete standstill when he saw her, or that his smile was replaced by a look of total surprise.

The trembling in Charlie's knees spread to the rest of her body and she might have stumbled if she hadn't kept a death grip on the door handle. She wished that Rafe would say something—*anything*—but he simply stood there, staring at her with a bewildered smile.

After an ice age or two, she managed to speak. 'Are you coming in?'

Rafe nodded and she stepped back to allow him to enter her room. 'That's an amazing uniform,' she said, hoping to ease the obvious tension. 'You look very—regal.'

'And you look, *literally*, breathtaking, Charlie.' He turned to her and gave a shaky smile as he let his burning gaze ride over her from head to toe and back again. 'You're going to steal the show tonight.'

She managed to smile. 'You had your doubts about the sea foam.'

Rafe shook his head. 'I knew you would choose well.'

'I'm glad it's OK, then.'

'OK? *C'est superbe. Magnifique!*'

As Charlie closed the door Rafe stepped towards her, reaching for her hands. His grey eyes were shining so brightly they'd turned to silver. A knot in his throat moved as he swallowed. 'My dear Charlie,' he whispered, taking her hands in his and drawing her nearer. 'I think I've made the most terrible mistake in bringing you here.'

Charlie's throat was suddenly so painfully tight she could barely squeeze out a response.

'Why is that?' she managed at last.

Rafe's mouth twisted, as if he was trying for a smile, but couldn't quite manage it. 'I don't know how I'll ever be able to let you go.'

Oh, Rafe.

She wanted to weep, to melt in his arms, to acknowledge the unmistakable emotions that eddied between them, to give in to the sizzling chemistry. But a warning voice in her head reminded her that she had to be sensible.

In less than an hour they were expected to host a royal ball that would be attended by all the local VIPs, including Rafe's enemies. Being seen at such an occasion was the very reason she'd been brought to Montaigne. Decorum was required. Dignity, not passion.

She shook her head at him. 'Don't pay me compliments, sir. Not now. You'll make me cry, and that will spoil my make-up, and I'm sure it cost you a small fortune.'

A rueful chuckle broke from him. 'I've never met a girl so worried about money. But, OK, no more compliments.'

'Good.' Although Charlie feared that a dancing lesson with Rafe would be even more dangerous than his compliments.

'I'll have to kiss you instead,' Rafe said next. 'Perhaps there is no make-up here?'

Before she quite realised what was happening Rafe touched his fingers to her bare shoulder and, before she could gather her wits to stop him, he pressed his warm, sexy lips to the same patch of skin.

Charlie gasped as his lips brushed her in the gentlest of caresses. Her skin tingled and flamed. The blood in her veins rushed and zapped.

'Or perhaps here?' Rafe murmured as he pressed another kiss to Charlie's neck and caused a starburst of heat, just above the pearls and diamonds.

'What about here?' he whispered, and Charlie had no choice but to cling to him, grabbing at the stiff cloth of his jacket, closing her eyes, as he kissed the sensitive skin just beneath her ear. And then gently nibbled at her earlobe.

She tried to tell herself that he was just being a playboy, and she might have believed this, if she hadn't already seen that shimmer of a deeper emotion in his eyes.

And now she was only too painfully aware of the truth about her own feelings. She was in love with this man. Totally. Utterly. Deeply.

It didn't make sense, she knew it was wrong, but she couldn't help it. From the moment she'd left Australia, this Prince had charmed every cell in her body. Right now, she was powerless.

'You do crazy things to me, Charlie.' Rafe's arms tightened around her and his voice was hoarse and breathless as he whispered close to her ear. 'You make me want to forget everything, throw off my responsibilities. You make me want to believe in your fairy tales.'

Oh, Rafe. Charlie's throat ached with welling tears. *What have we done?*

And now, his grey eyes were fierce, burning with an intensity that was almost scary, as he ever so gently touched the backs of his fingers to her cheek. 'I've never really believed in love till now. But my problem was that I'd never met the right girl. And now I have. Now I want to believe.'

Emotion and longing rioted through Charlie. She thought she might burst.

Rafe's sad smile was breaking her heart. 'Is it safe to kiss your lips?' he whispered.

She knew she should step back, tell him no. If he kissed her mouth, heaven knew what else might happen.

But it was so hard to be sensible. To her dismay, she heard herself say, 'I have a new lipstick for touch ups.'

Idiot.

It was all the invitation the Prince needed. Slipping his arms around Charlie's waist, he gathered her closer, and now she could smell the expensive cloth of his jacket, the light cologne on his skin.

His lips found hers and her heart seemed to burst into flames. She tipped her head to access the dizzying pleasure, and worried, fleetingly, that her tiara might slip, but this worry and all others were shoved aside as Rafe's lips worked their magic. His kiss was all-seeking and possessive, commanding every shred of her attention.

Happiness and hunger in equal parts rose through Charlie like a bubbling geyser. She no longer cared that she'd fallen under this Prince's spell. She would happily hand him her heart on a platter.

With unforgivable ease, he had won her completely and, as his kiss deepened deliciously, a soft moan of deepest pleasure escaped her.

But the moan was cut short as the door burst open.

A woman's voice yelled, 'What the hell's going on?'

CHAPTER TEN

OLIVIA.

The woman bursting through the door couldn't be anyone else. An exact replica of Charlie, she was dressed in a magnificent white fur coat and elegant, knee-high white boots. She looked stunning. Stunning and very angry.

Ignoring Rafe, the newcomer directed her glaring gaze straight to Charlie. 'What the hell are you doing here?'

'Olivia.' Rafe had gone pale, but he managed to sound calm. 'What impeccable timing you have.'

Slamming the door behind her, Olivia flounced past them into the room and flung her expensive copper-toned handbag onto the nearest sofa. 'Don't talk to me about timing, Rafe. I deserve an explanation. What's going on? What's *she* doing here?'

Hearing herself called 'she', Charlie felt weirdly dislocated from this scene, as if a real-life version of herself had taken centre stage, and she was an invisible spectre watching on.

'I'll explain in due course,' Rafe told her coolly. 'Just as soon as you've apologised for your disappearance. You knew full well that you'd cause me enormous problems by taking off like that, without warning or explanation. You knew my country was left in grave danger.'

Olivia pouted. 'I always planned to come back.'

Rafe looked unimpressed. 'It would have been helpful if you'd informed me of your plans.'

This brought a shrugging eye roll from his fiancée. Olivia reminded Charlie of a petulant teenager.

Rafe was standing with his shoulders braced, his eyes wary but determined. 'Where have you been, Olivia?'

'In Monaco.' She gave another offhand shrug, as if her answer was obvious. 'I needed to—see someone.'

Charlie could sense the fury mounting in Rafe as he glared at her sister.

Olivia pouted back at him. 'You haven't explained what she's doing here.'

'Isn't it obvious? You know very well that I needed a fiancée. A *visible*, *available* fiancée.' Rafe turned to Charlie and his grey eyes now betrayed a mix of sadness and resignation. With a courteous nod to her, he said, 'Charlie, allow me to introduce you to your sister, Olivia Belaire. Olivia, this is Charlotte Morisset, from Australia.'

If Charlie had dreamed of being greeted by Olivia with a sisterly hug, she was promptly disappointed. Olivia didn't so much as offer a handshake, let alone a kiss on the cheek. Instead she lowered herself onto the arm of the nearest sofa, letting her fur coat fall open to reveal a tight, tiny, copper silk dress.

Then she crossed her legs, which looked rather long and sexy in the knee-high white boots. 'Yes,' she said airily. 'I know who she is. I rang my mother and got the whole story from her.'

'So you never knew about me either?' Charlie couldn't help asking. 'Not till today?'

'No.' As she said this, Olivia finally lost some of her belligerence. 'It was a terrible shock to see those photos of you at the hospital.'

Charlie could well believe this. She remembered her own shock and disbelief back in Sydney when Rafe had first shown her the photo of the girl on the beach in Saint-Tropez. It was astonishing to think that she and this girl had shared their mother's womb, had been babies together until their parents' divorce.

She wondered what had caused the bust up. Had the birth of twins been the final blow for an already shaky relationship between a woman who loved the high life and a dreamy, impoverished artist? She saw her puzzlement reflected in Olivia's blue eyes. No doubt her sister was asking herself similar questions.

'How on earth did you find her?' Olivia asked Rafe.

'My men were searching high and low for you, Olivia, but you were very good at keeping under the radar. And then we were sure we'd found you in Sydney.'

'But that's ridiculous. Why on earth would I go to Australia?' Olivia said this as if Australia were still a penal colony.

'We have beaches, too,' Charlie couldn't help snapping. 'Beaches and snowfields and casinos. Sydney's not Mars, you know?'

Rafe sighed, shifted his cuff to check the gold watch on his wrist. 'Anyway, we don't have much time to thrash this out now. There's a grand ball due to start in less than thirty minutes.'

'Yes, so I gathered from all the fuss downstairs. Obviously, that's why you two are all dressed up.' Olivia's eyes narrowed as she studied Charlie in her finery. Then she smiled archly and gave another shrug. 'Well, I'm back now.'

'For how long?' asked Rafe.

'For as long as you need me, Rafey. I've sorted everything out with my boyfriend.'

This brought a further stiffening of Rafe's shoulders, a deeper frown. 'You never mentioned a boyfriend.'

Olivia gave yet another nonchalant shrug. 'I know. Andre and I had a fight just before I met you. Well, a bit of a tiff. I'd gone home to Saint-Tropez in a huff.'

Rafe glared at her now and Charlie could imagine what he was thinking—that Olivia had agreed to the fiancée role in a fit of spite to get back at her boyfriend. How awful.

'But surely this fellow's not prepared to let you marry me?' Rafe said.

Olivia's jaw jutted stubbornly. 'He is, actually. He's prepared for me to complete the terms of our contract.'

So there was a contract. It was all signed and sealed. Charlie felt ice water pool in her stomach. For her, then, this was it. Her exit line. She was no longer needed.

As if to confirm this, Olivia shot another glance Charlie's way. 'It was good of you to fill in for me, Charlotte.'

'It was *indeed* very good of Charlie,' Rafe cut in coldly. 'She dropped everything to help me out.'

'Yes, but I'm sure you paid her very well.'

This brought another glare from Rafe as Olivia sat there in her fur coat and boots, with one crossed leg swinging, while she smiled at him shrewdly. He looked as if he would have liked to shake her, but instead he clasped his hands behind his back and stood with the stiff, unhappy dignity of a prince who had been schooled by his granny to put duty before personal desires.

Rafe should have known this would happen. It was no doubt typical of Olivia to turn up at the very worst possible moment, but he couldn't believe he'd made such a serious error of judgement and recklessly chosen her in a moment of panic. He was a fool, the very worst version of a thoughtless idiot.

And now, what about Charlie? What the hell had he been thinking when he'd started kissing her? Damn it, he hadn't merely kissed her, he'd been seducing the poor girl, when he'd known all too well that he had absolutely no right to toy with her emotions.

There was no point in trying to excuse himself now, by trying to pretend that Charlie was simply irresistible. Sure, he'd found himself daydreaming about her constantly and, yes, he was desperate to make love to her. Even though they'd only shared a kiss or two, he'd sensed an exciting wildness in Charlie that had only fired his own desire to greater heights. Their few, sweet kisses had been just enough to tease him, to give birth to a deep and painful longing, the whisper of a promise, a burning question without any answers.

It had been such a delightful surprise to discover that a girl who looked so much like Olivia could be so very different beneath the surface. Beyond the beauty, there'd been so much to *love* about Charlie—her openness, her sudden surprise questions, her selfless concern for her baby half-sister. But all these differences should have warned him to protect Charlie, not to expose her.

Olivia might have been out of sight, but, although Rafe had only known her for a painfully brief time, he'd been almost certain that she would turn up again, when she was good and ready. And he'd also been fully aware that he'd signed a contract with her, a contract which he now had no choice but to honour.

The terms of their contract were clear. Rafe was paying Olivia a sum of money that was enormous, even by his standards, to take on the role of his wife. At a future date, when Pontier and the Leroy Mining Company threats were satisfactorily resolved, Olivia would then be free to divorce him. No doubt, she would go back to this boyfriend, who would enjoy sharing her profits. By then, Rafe should supposedly have found a more suitable bride.

These plans had all been so clear and watertight.

Before he'd walked into a certain art gallery in Sydney.

And now… Rafe couldn't bear to see the hurt and shock and disappointment in Charlie's eyes. He knew full well that he'd caused her this pain. He'd played with her feelings unforgivably.

He'd gambled recklessly with his own feelings as well. In a moment of weakness he'd allowed himself to imagine—or to hope, at any rate—that life wasn't the compromise he'd always believed it to be, and that Charlie's happy endings were indeed possible.

Fool.

Now there was no way to resurrect this situation without making things worse for Charlie.

'So.' Olivia was smiling smugly as she finally rose from her perch on the arm of the sofa. 'It's obvious from the little scene I've so recently interrupted that you two have grown quite pally.' The smile she sent Rafe and then Charlie was condescending in the extreme.

Charlie had no choice but to ignore the piercing pain in her heart. She tried to hide her distress with a defiant tilt of her chin. But she didn't dare to catch Rafe's eye.

'But like it or not, it's time for me to relieve you of your duties, Charlotte,' Olivia said next. 'I'm sure you'll agree that *I* should attend tonight's ball with Prince Rafael.'

No-o-o! Just in time, Charlie jammed her lips tightly together to hold back her cry of protest.

It didn't really help that Rafe looked angry, as if this new possibility hadn't occurred to him.

'That's not very practical,' he told Olivia. 'As you can see, Charlie's all ready to—'

But Olivia, having thrown Charlie a quick look that was probably meant to be pitying, stopped him with a raised hand. 'If I'm to be your wife, Rafe, I'm the one who needs to meet all these important people tonight.'

Rafe's eyes narrowed. 'In theory, that's true. But the ball's about to begin,' he said. 'And Charlie has gone to a great deal of trouble.'

'I'm sure she has, and, yes, she looks beautiful,' Olivia admitted grudgingly. 'And I suppose I should apologise if my arrival has been a trifle inconvenient, but *I* want to go to the ball. I believe I should go. It doesn't make sense for her to carry on as my double now that I'm here.'

Olivia didn't quite stamp her foot, but she might as well have. The insistence in her voice was equally compelling.

Rafe, however, could match her stubbornness. 'Olivia, be reasonable. It's too late.'

'Oh, for heaven's sake, Rafe, don't tell me you're taking her side.'

'It's not a matter of taking sides.'

Charlie couldn't stand this debate. 'It's not too late,' she shouted.

The other two turned and stared at her, both obviously surprised that she'd spoken up.

'It's not too late,' Charlie said again, hoping desperately that her voice wasn't shaking. 'It won't take me long to get changed.' She knew there was no other choice, really.

Olivia was right. Rafe had made a legal and binding commitment, and, as his future wife, Olivia should be at the ball tonight, mixing with Montaigne's VIPs.

Charlie knew that Rafe was aware of this. He'd only protested because he felt sorry for her.

And that was rubbish.

There was no point in feeling sorry for her. She'd completed her commitment and now she was free. Free to leave Montaigne. Why prolong the torture by attending a silly ball and dancing with a ridiculously handsome prince, spending an entire night at his side, pretending to be his chosen bride?

All those touches and smiles from the Prince would be sure to completely break her already shattered heart. She'd been stupid to allow herself to get so hung up on him. Now, there really was no valid reason for her to stay another moment in these clothes, living the lie.

'I can be undressed in a jiffy,' she told them. 'At least we know Olivia and I are the same size.'

Rafe looked grim.

Olivia looked satisfied and ever so slightly triumphant.

Charlie lifted her head even higher. 'If you'll excuse me—'

With that, she retired to her adjoining bedroom, walking very deliberately with her shoulders back and her head bravely high, closing the door quietly but firmly behind her.

'Would you like a hand?' Olivia called after her.

'No, thanks!'

Don't cry, Charlie warned herself as she sank back against the closed door. *Don't you dare waste a moment on crying. You'll only look ridiculous with make-up streaking down your cheeks and you'll slow down this whole horrible, inevitable process.*

Best to get it over with.

Drawing a deep, shuddering breath, she stepped away

from the door and turned her back on the full-length mirror with its taunting reflection. Methodically, she began to undress.

First she unpinned the tiara and set it on the quilted bedspread. The pearl and diamond earrings and necklace came off next and Charlie placed them carefully back in their box, which she set on the bed beside the tiara. She kicked off her silver shoes, set them neatly on the floor at the end of the bed.

With the removal of each item, she could feel herself stepping further and further away from Rafe. She tried not to think about the exciting ballroom downstairs, the musicians on their special dais, the white-coated waiters with their silver trays of drinks, the enormous flower arrangements, the brilliant chandeliers, the enormous ballroom floor polished to a high sheen. Not to mention the long staircase where she and Rafe had planned to descend, her arm linked with his, as they went to receive his official guests.

Unlike Cinderella, she wouldn't have to leave before midnight—she wouldn't make it to the ball at all.

She knew she was foolish to feel so disappointed. She'd only ever been a stopgap, a fill-in. It was time to get out of the dress.

The zipper for the ball gown was discreetly hidden within a side seam beneath her left arm. Charlie carefully slid the zipper down, then gently, somewhat awkwardly, eased out of the gown.

The silk-lined satin whispered and rustled about her as she dragged it over her head, taking care not to smudge the shiny fabric with her make-up. She really could have done with help for this manoeuvre, but eventually she got the dress off without a lipstick smear, or a split seam.

She arranged the gown on a hanger on the wardrobe

door. The pale sea-foam satin shimmered, making her think, rather foolishly, of mermaids. Hadn't there been a poem she'd learned long ago about a forsaken merman?

One last look at the white-wall'd town...

For heaven's sake! Her mind was spinning crazily, throwing up nonsense. *Stop it!*

She let out the breath she'd been holding, collected the white towelling bathrobe from a chair where she'd left it, pulled it on and tied the sash at her waist. She took the carefully chosen lipstick from her evening bag and set it on the bed, where Olivia could find it, beside the jewellery.

There. It was done. She was no longer a princess, not even a pretend one. She was Charlie Morisset once more.

Unfortunately, this thought brought no sweet rush of relief.

Resolutely, she returned to the bedroom door and opened it.

Rafe and Olivia were still there, more or less where she'd left them. They were standing rather stiffly and neither of them looked happy and Charlie wondered what they'd been saying to each other.

'Over to you, Olivia,' she said quietly.

'Thank you, Charlotte.'

'Would you like me to help you?'

'I—' Olivia hesitated. 'I'm not sure. I'll call out if I need you.'

'OK.'

As the door closed on her sister, Charlie rounded on Rafe, needing to speak her piece before he could try to apologise, as she was sure he would.

'It's OK,' she told him quickly. 'I'm fine about this,

Rafe. Honestly. If I'd gone to the ball, I probably would have made a hash of things, getting people's names wrong, making mistakes with my French, standing on your toes when we were trying to waltz.'

His sad smile was almost her undoing. 'You've been very gallant, Charlie, but I do owe you an apology.'

Why? For kissing me?

She would break down if he tried to apologise for that.

'Save it for later,' she said as toughly as she could. 'I'll be fine here in my room, if someone could send me a little supper.'

'Of course.'

'I'm assuming I can keep this room for tonight?'

'Most definitely. I wouldn't dream of asking you to leave. There are other rooms that Olivia can use. And I'll arrange for a special meal to be sent up for you.'

'Your staff will be gobsmacked to realise there are two of us.'

'Perhaps, but they're trained to be very discreet. Just the same, I'll have a word with them to smooth the waters.'

Charlie nodded. 'Thank you.' She looked down at her bare feet beneath the white bathrobe. After the pedicure, her toes were looking especially neat and smooth with pretty, silvery green nail polish. She supposed it had been a whimsical choice to wear nail polish to match the seafoam dress when her toes wouldn't even be seen. Anyone would think she'd been planning to wear glass slippers.

Hastily, she lifted her gaze from her feet, only to realise that Rafe was staring at them, too. Feeling self-conscious, she rubbed one bare foot against the other as she tried to banish stupid thoughts about what might have happened tonight, after the ball, if she and Rafe had opted to pick up where their kiss had left off.

Before she could stop her reckless thoughts, they rushed away, and she was picturing the two of them in bed—her bed, his bed—it didn't matter whose bed—and it wasn't just her feet that were bare.

Stop it!

'Have you had news about Isla this afternoon?' Rafe asked.

Desperately grateful for the change of subject, Charlie smiled. 'I was able to speak to my dad,' she told him. 'Isla's still doing well. Dad said the doctors were very happy with her progress and he sounded so relieved. It was lovely to hear the happiness in his voice.'

Rafe nodded. 'That's very good news.'

'It is.'

She was wondering what they might talk about next, when a voice called from inside.

'Charlotte, can you give me a hand with this tiara?'

'Coming,' Charlie called back, and she hurried to her sister's assistance, without another glance in Rafe's direction.

She'd thought she was prepared for the sight of Olivia in the ball gown, in *her* ball gown, but the reality was even more startling than anything she'd imagined.

Olivia was stop-and-stare gorgeous. The softly shimmering gown clung to her body in all the right places, the deep cowl back was divine, and the pale fabric rippled sensuously as she moved.

'Wow!' Charlie said. 'I hope you like the gown.'

Olivia grinned. 'It's adorable, isn't it?'

'Yeah,' Charlie said flatly.

'A good choice. Is it from Belle Robe?'

Charlie nodded.

'Monique's brilliant.' Olivia grinned. 'I'm looking forward to another shopping spree. But right now I need a couple of pins to anchor the ends of this tiara.'

'Yes, I can do that.' Charlie obliged, marvelling as she did so at the incredible similarity between her hair and her sister's. It was amazing now, up close, to see that Olivia's tresses were the exact same colour of wheat, had the same amount of curl, were the same texture. She was suddenly overwhelmed by the enormity of their connection.

They'd come from the same egg. For nine months they'd nestled together in the same womb. She wondered who had been born first. Had her father been present for their birth?

Olivia, however, was busily applying another layer of Charlie's lipstick. 'Well,' she said. 'I think I'm ready.'

'You look lovely,' Charlie told her. 'Like a proper princess.'

'That's the general idea.' Olivia picked up the beaded silver evening bag, popped the lipstick inside.

Charlie blinked, desperate to hide any hint of tears as her lookalike headed for the door.

Just before she reached it, Charlie had to ask, 'Why did you do it, Olivia? When you already had a boyfriend, why did you agree to marry Rafe?'

Her sister smiled archly. 'For the same reason as you, my dear Charlotte. For the money, of course.'

CHAPTER ELEVEN

CHARLIE DIDN'T WATCH Olivia and the Prince as they left for the ball. Excusing herself quickly, she retired to her room. Tears threatened, but she gave herself a mental shake. She'd known from the start of this mad adventure with Rafe that it would all end with her sister's return, so it made absolutely no sense to feel sorry for herself.

But she wasn't going to beat herself up either. Sure, she'd been reckless. Any way you looked at it, agreeing to pretend to be a foreign prince's fiancée was pretty damn crazy. Many would call it foolish in the extreme.

But Charlie consoled herself that at least her original motives hadn't been merely mercenary, and Isla was out of the woods, so that was a huge positive. Her mistake had been getting sidetracked by all the trimmings—a handsome and charming prince and his beautiful castle and his gorgeously romantic Alpine principality.

And at least she'd learned one or two things from this wildly unreal experience. She no longer believed any of that nonsense about fairy tales and happy endings. Sadly, Rafe's depressingly realistic theory was correct. Life *was* a compromise.

For Charlie Morisset, it was time to remember who she really was. An everyday, average girl from Down Under. And a poor one at that.

Right, come on, girl. Get a grip on reality. Deep breath.

* * *

When the first strains of waltz music drifted up from the ballroom, she turned on the television. She'd hardly watched any TV since she'd arrived in Montaigne, but tonight she curled up on the sofa in front of the fire and scrolled through channels till she found a romantic movie, so old it was in black and white. It was also in French, without subtitles, but Charlie could just keep up.

She refused to think about the laughter and the music and glamour downstairs and she refused to give a moment's thought to Olivia dancing in Rafe's arms. The film was very good, and she managed to remain deeply engrossed until a knock at the door signalled the arrival of her dinner.

'Please, come in,' she called.

Guillaume appeared, bearing a heavily laden tray and looking deeply distressed. 'His Highness ordered a special dinner for you, *mademoiselle*.'

Charlie smiled bravely. 'How kind of him.'

Guillaume set the tray on the coffee table, then gave a deep bow. He looked as if he might have been going to say something of great importance, but after standing with his mouth open for a rather long and awkward moment, he swallowed, making his Adam's apple jerk nervously, then said simply, *'Bon appetit, mademoiselle.'*

'Merci, Guillaume.' For his sake, Charlie replied with as much dignity as she could muster, while seated in her bathrobe, and she waited until he'd gone before she examined her meal.

As the door closed behind him, she lifted the lid on a small casserole dish and was greeted by the tantalising aroma of beef in red wine with herbs and mushrooms. On checking out the other covered dishes, she found *foie gras* and toast fingers, and wedges of several different cheeses. Yet another little dish housed crème caramel.

Oh, and there was a selection of Belgian chocolates! And as if these luxuries weren't enough, there was a bottle of Shiraz *and* an ice bucket with champagne, plus the appropriate glasses.

I could get well and truly plastered.

It was a tempting thought. Charlie could have used a little cheering up, although the last thing she wanted was to leave the castle with a hangover. Even so, it was very thoughtful of Rafe to make sure she had such a wonderful selection.

And it didn't help at that moment, to remember the Prince's many kindnesses.

Rafe wasn't just the hunkiest guy she'd ever met. He really was, despite his princely status and his many regal responsibilities, the most thoughtful man she'd ever known. She was used to her dad's vagaries, and none of her boyfriends had been especially considerate or caring. Rafe, however, had gone out of his way to make sure she'd thoroughly enjoyed her short stay in his country.

And then, of course, there were his kisses…

Would she ever forget the way he'd kissed her tonight, taking such exquisite care not to mess her make-up? All those delicious sexy kisses to her neck, to her throat and ears…

Until their caution gave way to passion.

Oh, such blissful passion!

No wonder she needed to cry.

It was hours later when Charlie's phone rang. She had fallen asleep on the sofa at some unearthly hour, having found a second movie to watch while drinking yet another big glass of the deliciously hearty red wine. It took her a moment to find her phone among the scattered dishes on the coffee table. Her fingers finally closed around it just as it was due to ring out.

'Hello,' she said sleepily.

'Charlie, I'm sorry if I've woken you. It's Dad.'

A chill skittered through her. Suddenly terrified for Isla, Charlie sat up quickly, heart thumping. 'Yes, Dad? How's Isla?'

'Isla's OK,' her father said quickly. 'Actually, she's better than OK. She's coming out of ICU tomorrow.'

'Oh, that's wonderful.'

'Yes, it is. I'm not ringing with bad news, Charlie. It's good news, rather amazing news, actually. It's about my paintings.'

'Really?' Charlie was waking up fast. 'Don't tell me you've sold one?'

'Not just one painting, Charlie. I've sold five!'

'Oh, wow! How?' She was wide awake now. 'Tell me all about it.'

And, of course, her dad was more than happy to recount his amazing story. 'I happened to meet this fellow here in Boston called Charles Peabody. He works here at the hospital, some kind of world-famous surgeon, actually, absolutely loaded. Anyway, Dr Yu introduced us, just out of politeness, but it turns out Peabody's wife was born in Sydney, so he has a bit of a soft spot for the place. *And* he's apparently something of an art collector.'

'That was very handy.'

'Wasn't it? It's as if my stars were all aligned. Anyway, we were yarning and I happened to mention my paintings.'

'As you do.'

Her father laughed. 'Of course. Anyway, Peabody was really interested. Afterwards, he got in touch with his

New York dealer, who was able to show him my paintings online. And he fell in love with the painting of the alley. You know the one—you've always liked it, too— *View from Cook's Alley*?'

'Yes, of course,' said Charlie. 'That's always been my favourite.'

It was a remarkable painting, she'd always believed. It showed a view down a steep, narrow alley that had grimy, old buildings on either side that served as a frame for a sparkling view of Sydney Harbour. The slice of the bright blue sky and sunlit water with pretty sailing boats and the curve of the Harbour Bridge made a startling contrast to the narrow dark alley with dank gutters, a stray cat and newspapers wrapped around the bottom of a lamp post.

'That's so fantastic, Dad. I always knew someone would realise you're a genius. I'm so happy for you. I hope this Peabody fellow is paying you top dollar?'

'Top dollar? You wouldn't believe the sum the dealer managed to sell it for. I still can't bring myself to say it out loud, in case it breaks a spell or something.'

Charlie chuckled. No wonder she was superstitious. She got it from her dad.

'But the amazing thing is,' her father went on, 'the dealer's already sold four more paintings to American collectors—in New York, in Seattle, San Francisco and New Orleans. After all these years, it seems I've become an overnight international success.'

Charlie's laugh was a little shaky. She was feeling teary again. 'That's so fantastic. Totally deserved, of course.'

'Thanks, darling.' Her dad's voice sounded a bit choked now. 'And I mean that. I owe you heartfelt thanks, Charlie. I'm pretty sure I would have fallen by the wayside without you there to prop me up more than once.'

Charlie had to swallow the lump in her throat before she could speak. 'And these sales might never have happened if it wasn't for Isla,' she said.

'Correction. They wouldn't have happened if it wasn't for you, Charlie. I don't know how you found that money, or who the kind benefactor was, but we're so, so grateful.'

Now she gripped the phone harder, fighting more tears.

'You know what this means, don't you, love?' her father said next.

'Your money worries are over.' At last. Finally. 'Dad, you so totally deserve this.'

'But it also means I can pay you back for Isla's operation, and you can pay whoever you borrowed the money from.'

'Yeah.' Charlie knew it made no sense to be sobered by this prospect. The timing was perfect. Now she wasn't only free to leave Montaigne, she would also be able to hand the money back to Rafe, even though he didn't expect it, and her ties with him would be severed. Neatly. Cleanly. Permanently.

If only she could find a way to feel happy about that.

As dawn broke over the castle, Rafael St Romain paced the carpeted floor in his private suite. He was bone weary, but he was also bursting with impatience. Except for the night of his father's death, this night of the Grand Ball had turned out to be the most unexpectedly significant and pivotal night of his life. As a result, he hadn't slept a wink.

It had all begun quite early in the evening. The business of greeting the long line of guests was just coming to an end, when the head of police, Chief Dameron, stepped up to Rafe, leaning close to his ear.

'We've got him,' he whispered excitedly.

Rafe immediately knew who the man was referring to. It had to be Montaigne's Chancellor, Claude Pontier.

The news was exhilarating, but Rafe hid his surprise behind a frown. 'You've made an arrest?'

'Better than an arrest, Your Highness. Would it be possible to have a private audience?'

The last of the guests had been presented, so Rafe excused himself, murmuring his apologies to Olivia, before retiring with his police chief to a small salon. There he was given details of the good news. The police had intercepted several important phone calls from Claude Pontier and now they had irrefutable evidence of his corrupt dealings with the Leroy miners who threatened Montaigne with so much damage.

Chief Dameron handed Rafe a document. 'And here is Pontier's signed resignation.'

This time Rafe's jaw dropped. 'He's resigned as Chancellor? Already?'

'Yes, Your Highness.' Chief Dameron allowed himself a small smile. 'Given the man's options, resignation seemed to be his wisest choice.'

Rafe was elated, of course, but he didn't like to think too deeply about the techniques his police might have used to persuade the Chancellor to roll over so quickly. Dameron was a gracious and gentlemanly old fellow, but Rafe could almost imagine him threatening Pontier with some ancient punishment for treason, possibly involving menacing machinery and dark, unpleasant dungeons.

'Well,' he said, shaking off these thoughts as the good news sank in. 'We'll need to appoint a new Chancellor.' Which also meant he had the chance to appoint a citizen who was unquestionably sympathetic to his country's best interests.

The police chief nodded. 'If you'll pardon my forwardness, Your Highness, might I make a suggestion?'

'By all means.'

'I'd like to highly recommend the Chief Justice, Marie Valcourt, as someone very suitable to be the next Chancellor.'

'Ah, yes.' Rafe smiled. Marie Valcourt was indeed an excellent choice. Apart from her inestimable legal skills, she was fiercely loyal to Montaigne. Her family's history in this region went back almost as far as his own. Besides, he rather liked the idea of a woman as Chancellor. His father would possibly roll in his grave, but it was time his country moved with the times.

'I'm sure we can trust Marie to act with Montaigne's best interests at heart,' he said.

'I'm certain of it.' Chief Dameron's smile broadened. 'If this were medieval times, Justice Valcourt would be donning blue-grey armour and standing at the city gates, sword in hand.'

Rafe laughed. 'She's a wonderful champion of our cause, that's for sure. A first-class suggestion, Chief.'

After that, it was almost bizarre how quickly everything had turned around. By midnight, while the Grand Ball continued with music and waltzing and an endless flow of champagne, Rafe had consulted in private chambers with his minsters and, with their consent, he'd spoken at some length to Justice Marie Valcourt. Within a matter of hours, he had appointed her as Montaigne's new Chancellor.

It had been well after midnight when the final guests eventually left. Of course, Olivia had known that something was in the wind, but fortunately she'd been happy enough to spend the evening dancing with just about every available male.

Olivia had done this with very little complaint, for which Rafe was excessively grateful, and afterwards, as he explained the new situation to her, he couldn't blame her for being instantly wary.

'So what does this mean for me, Rafe?'

'Chancellor Valcourt agrees that the constitutional requirements regarding my marriage are totally out of date and unnecessary,' Rafe told her. 'There's to be a special meeting of Cabinet tomorrow to repeal the old law. I'm assured it will be passed, without contest, which means—'

'I'm no longer needed here,' Olivia supplied.

He nodded. 'If that's what you wish, yes, you are free.'

'I can tear up our contract?'

'Yes, you can.'

'But I can keep the money?'

He suppressed a weary smile. 'Of course.'

Olivia brightened instantly. 'That—that's very kind, Rafe.'

'No, it's you who has been kind,' he assured her. 'I'm very grateful to you for stepping up to the plate. My country would have been in deep trouble without your help.'

'And Charlotte's help, too,' Olivia said with unexpected generosity. Then her eyes narrowed as she shot Rafe a cagey glance. 'I suppose my sister will go home now as well?'

'I suppose—'

Rafe paused in his pacing and stood at the window, looking out over the familiar view of snowy rooftops, which were only just visible in the pre-dawn light. It was almost eight. A reasonable hour, surely? He didn't think he could wait much longer before he went to Charlie's room.

Of course, he wanted to ask her to stay.

All night, during the ball, throughout the political ma-
noeuvres and the diplomatic tensions, Rafe had been battling with thoughts of Charlie and their interrupted kiss.
He couldn't get the honeyed taste of her kisses out of
his mind. He kept remembering the exquisite pleasure
of holding her in his arms, her breasts pressed against
his chest, her stomach crushing against his hard arousal.

He kept hearing the soft needy sighs she'd made as she
wound her arms more tightly around him, driving him insane with the knowledge that she was as ready as he was.

Now that he'd had hours to pace impatiently, his memories of her were at fever point. Rafe desperately needed
more of Charlie. He needed her spontaneity and respon-
siveness. He'd been waiting all night.

He was dizzy with wanting. He wanted her. Now.

At eight-fifteen Rafe left his room, his pulses drumming
crazily as he crossed the carpeted hallway to Charlie's
door. He knocked quietly, and held his breath as he waited
for her response.

There was no sound from within.

Perhaps she was still asleep? He waited a little longer,
listening intently for the smallest sounds, but Charlie's
suite was fully carpeted, so her footsteps would almost
certainly be silent.

After what felt like an age, but was probably no more
than thirty seconds, Rafe knocked again, more loudly
this time.

There was still no response. He remembered the two
bottles of wine he'd sent to her room last night. Perhaps
she'd been a little too indulgent and was sleeping it off?

He called, 'Charlie? Charlie, are you awake? It's Rafe.'

When there was still no response from within he began
to worry. Swift on the heels of his worry came action.

Pushing the door open, Rafe marched into the sitting room, where Charlie had dined last night. It was all very tidy now. No sign of her meal. Even the cushions on the sofas were plumped and in place.

The door to Charlie's bedroom was closed, however. Rafe crossed to it and knocked again. 'Charlie?'

Again, there was no answer and he felt a fresh stirring of alarm.

'Charlie!' he cried more loudly, pushing open the door as he did so.

The bed was empty.

In fact it was neatly made up. And there was no sign of her belongings. Thoroughly alarmed, Rafe flung the wardrobe doors open. The long red coat, the blue dinner dress and the black and white polka-dot outfit from Belle Robe were still hanging there—but not the ball gown, which was now in Olivia's possession. All Charlie's other clothes and her suitcase were gone.

He knocked on the door to the en-suite bathroom, then opened it. Again, it was empty and cleared of Charlie's things.

Dismayed, Rafe went back to the bedroom. And that was when he saw the small folded sheet of white paper on the snowy pillow. With a cry, he snatched it up.

He hardly dared to read its contents. By now, he had no doubt that the news wouldn't be good.

His fears were quickly confirmed.

Dear Rafe,
  Goodbye and thanks so much for everything. Your country is beautiful and you've been a wonderful host. It's been an amazing experience.
  My bank will be in touch to repay you the money in full. I wish you and Olivia every happiness.

Oh, and I've borrowed your chauffeur.
Apologies for the inconvenience,
Charlie xx

If Rafe had thought he'd cared about Charlie before this, now the true weight of his feelings crashed down on him. The thought of losing her was as painful as cutting his own heart out with a penknife.

He couldn't possibly let her go without making sure she understood how he felt.

He wasted no time on a second reading of her note. Grabbing his phone, he speed-dialled his chauffeur.

'Tobias, where are you?'

'Good morning, Your Highness. I have just driven Mademoiselle Morisset to Grenoble.'

'You're there already?'

'Yes, Your Highness.'

Rafe cursed. It was rather telling that Tobias had referred to Charlie by her correct name—*Morisset*. 'I gave you no such instructions,' he barked.

'Forgive me, Your Highness, but you told me to make myself available to the *mademoiselle* at all times.'

This was damn true, Rafe remembered now, through gritted teeth. And perhaps he shouldn't be surprised that Charlie had won over his staff. 'So you're already at the airport?'

'I am, sir.'

'And Mademoiselle Morisset has already booked her flights.'

'I believe so, Your Highness.' After a small silence. 'Yes, she has.'

Damn.

As Rafe disconnected he was already racing through the castle. He had no choice but to drive his own car down the mountain as quickly as possible. No matter what risks were involved, he couldn't let Charlie simply fly away.

It was freezing when Charlie stepped out of the car at Grenoble airport. She almost wished she'd brought her lovely new overcoat with her, but she was determined to leave behind everything that meant she was in any way indebted to the Prince.

Now, she knew that Tobias had been speaking to Rafe on the phone. In other words, Rafe knew where she was, so on the off chance that he might, for some crazy reason, try to follow her, she shouldn't linger over farewells.

She needed to get away, to get safely home to Sydney and to put this whole heartbreaking experience behind her.

'Thank you, Tobias,' she said as he set her suitcase on the footpath. 'I really appreciate everything you've done for me, especially your skilful driving down those steep snowy roads.'

'Thank you, *mademoiselle*. It's been my pleasure.'

'I hope Prince Rafael won't be too angry with you for bringing me here this morning,' she said.

Tobias shrugged. 'Don't give it another thought. Would you like me to help you with your suitcase?'

'No, thank you. It has wheels. It's as easy as pie.' She pinned on a smile as she held out her hand. 'Goodbye, then, Tobias.'

'*Adieu, mademoiselle.* I wish you a safe journey.' To Charlie's surprise, a look of genuine warmth shone in the chauffeur's eyes as he smiled. 'I and the rest of the castle staff will miss you, *mademoiselle*.'

Miss me? This was so unexpected, Charlie felt a painful lump in her throat. Her vision grew blurry. Why, oh, why was she so susceptible to people saying nice things about her?

She managed a shaky, crooked smile. 'I'll miss you, too. I've had a wonderful stay in your country.'

Then quickly, before she made a total fool of herself, she grabbed the handle of her suitcase, yanked it into its extended position, gave a hasty wave, and hurried away, dragging the wobbling suitcase behind her as she went through the airport's huge sliding glass doors.

Rafe drove as quickly as he dared down the steep, winding mountain road. Of course, there were princely responsibilities that he should have been attending to this morning, but right now finding Charlie before she boarded a plane was far more important than anything else.

He couldn't bear to think that Charlie might slip away before they had a proper conversation. Charlie knew nothing about the way his entire situation had changed overnight. He had to tell her that he was free from the pressure to marry her sister. More importantly, he had to tell her the truth that lay in his heart.

Unfortunately, it was going to be a damned difficult conversation to get right. Rafe needed Charlie to understand the true strength and depth of his feelings for her.

Some might say this was an unreasonable expectation, given that Rafe hadn't really understood these feelings himself until this morning. It was only when he'd read Charlie's note and realised that he was going to lose her that he'd faced a moment of terrifying truth. Everything had been suddenly, frighteningly clear.

Charlie Morisset was desperately important to his future happiness.

Rafe had known many women—all glamorous, beautiful or charming in their own way—but he'd never known a woman like Charlie. Charlie was not only beautiful and sexy, but she was honest and genuine and caring and funny and kind.

In just a few short days, she had become so much more than a girlfriend Rafe wanted to bed. She'd become a rare and real friend. She'd answered a deep need in himself that he hadn't even realised existed. Until now.

Unhappily, he knew it would be asking a great deal to expect Charlie to believe in the truth of his rapid transformation. It would be especially difficult when time was so pressing. Charlie had every right to tell him to take a flying leap.

Rafe cursed aloud, but it wasn't the particularly sharp bend in the roadway that bothered him. It was the harrowing possibility that he might let Charlie go.

And yet…if he was honest, he had to admit that he had used the girl to his own ends, with very little regard for her finer feelings. Now he wanted to make amends, but there was only the briefest window of opportunity to set things right.

As the Prince of Montaigne spun the steering wheel back and forth, negotiating yet another set of hairpin bends at the fastest possible speed, he tried to practise what he must say to his no-nonsense, straight-shooting Australian.

If only it could be as easy as it was in the movies when a guy chasing a girl could win her with a simple *I love you*.

CHAPTER TWELVE

CHARLIE FELT CALMER once she'd emerged from the long queue in Customs and was safely in the departure lounge. In less than an hour now she would be on a flight home to Sydney via Paris, this time without a diversion to Dubai and a handsome sheikh's residence.

She bought herself a cappuccino, a croissant and a paperback novel. She chose a murder mystery, rather than a romance. It would probably be years before she could bear to read another romance. She now knew better than to believe in happy ever after.

Settling at a table in the corner of the café, she took a sip of her coffee and opened the paperback with a great sense of purpose.

Focus, girl, focus.

The story was set in the American Midwest, thousands of kilometres from anywhere Charlie had ever been. It was midsummer, apparently, and the hero cop had a doozy of a hangover. There was a body lying in the middle of a cornfield. Flies were buzzing around it.

Charlie sighed and closed the book. She wasn't normally squeamish, but this morning she wasn't in the mood for blood and gore. Problem was, she wasn't in the mood for any form of entertainment, really.

Her mind, her whole body, felt numb. She broke off a

corner of her croissant. She hadn't had any breakfast and she should have been hungry, but even the sweet pastry filled with strawberry jam seemed tasteless.

It was as if her senses had been dulled. She had left Montaigne and sent herself into self-imposed exile, and nothing would ever be the same again.

No Rafe.

Forget him.

But how could she forget him? How could she forget the whole prince-Alpine-castle fairy tale? The gorgeous lunch at Cosme's. The walk with Rafe through the snowy streets, holding hands. The look in his eyes when he saw her in the ball gown. His kiss.

Oh, help, that kiss.

How was a girl supposed to get over something as life-changing as that?

Heading to the opposite hemisphere is supposed to help. Aren't distance and time supposed to cure all wounds?

Yes, once she was back in Sydney, surrounded by everything that was familiar and dear, she'd feel so much better. All she wanted was for this flight to be over.

She needed to be home.

Rafe's car skidded to a halt in the airport car park. As he leapt from the driver's seat an attendant glared at him. Rafe pressed several large notes into the man's beefy hand. 'Be a good fellow and park this for me.'

'But—'

'This is an emergency.'

Without waiting to see the attendant's reaction, Rafe took off on foot, racing into the airport terminal, heedless of the surprised stares of staff and travellers. He was a man on a mission, a desperate mission as far as he was concerned. He *had* to see Charlie. He couldn't let her go back to Australia without speaking to her, without making sure she understood that everything about his situation had changed.

Mathilde had tracked down Charlie's flight and had texted him the details. Now, in the middle of the busy airport, he scanned the list of flights that were preparing for departure.

Already, Charlie's flight was boarding. A chill swept through him. He still had to wrangle with Security and Customs, had to persuade them to let him get through to her.

But he would do this. He was the Prince of Montaigne. With luck, someone at the Customs gates would recognise him, but if that didn't happen he would wave his royal passport in their faces and make them understand.

He would do whatever was necessary to stop that plane.

Flying home was going to be a very different matter from the flight in Rafe's luxurious chartered jet. Charlie was crammed into economy class beside a little Japanese man who seemed to go to sleep as soon as he sat down and a very large American businessman who only just managed to get his seat belt done up.

Wedged between them, Charlie tried to look on the bright side. She could watch back-to-back movies if necessary and, if she didn't sleep, at least she would be home inside twenty-four hours and then she could sleep for a week.

She had hoped to keep Rafe out of her thoughts, but she found herself wondering if he was awake yet. No doubt he'd slept in quite late after the Grand Ball, but he might be up by now.

Had he seen her note? Would he be upset that she'd left without saying a proper goodbye? Or would he simply move Olivia back into her room and get on with his life?

This possibility was so depressing, Charlie picked up her novel and tried again to read, forcing herself to concentrate on the words on the page and to ignore the questions in her head, the heavy weight in her chest.

'Miss Morisset?'

Charlie had actually made it to page three—after having read the second page several times—when she heard her name. She looked up to see a pretty, auburn-haired flight attendant fixing her with a wide-eyed, fearful stare, almost as if she suspected Charlie of being a terrorist or something equally horrifying.

Charlie tried not to panic. 'Yes?' she said.

'Could you please come with me?' the attendant asked.

A shaft of white-hot panic shot through Charlie. What could possibly have gone wrong now? Was there a mistake with her ticket? She'd never bought a plane ticket using her phone before. But surely a problem would have been picked up at the airport desk. Not now, at the last moment.

Despite her profuse apologies, the large American wasn't happy about getting out of his seat to make room to let Charlie past. She tried to ignore all the curious stares of the other passengers, but her cheeks were flaming as she followed the flight attendant back down the long narrow aisle, through business class and first class, where people were already sipping champagne, to the very front of the plane.

'What's the matter?' she asked, when the attendant finally stopped at the plane's front door. 'Is there a problem with my ticket?'

'There's someone here who needs to speak to you,' the girl said, nodding towards the air bridge. Her eyes were bigger than ever, and a couple of other attendants were also staring at Charlie.

Crikey, anyone would think she was a celebrity or something. Or had something terrible happened? Was it a message from her father? Were the police trying to contact her?

Stiff with fear, Charlie forced her feet to move forward, through the doorway. Then she saw the tall, dark-haired, masculine figure in a long charcoal overcoat and her knees almost caved.

It didn't make sense. What was he doing here? Was she dreaming?

'Charlie!' A huge smile lit up Rafe's handsome face as he stepped forward, reaching for her hands.

'Wh-what are you d-doing here?'

'I had to see you. I couldn't let you go.'

'Why? Is something wrong?'

'No, not at all. Everything's fine, in fact. Very fine indeed. That's why I had to see you, to let you know.'

And suddenly, standing in the air bridge, holding her hands tightly in his, Rafe told her a crazy story about his Chancellor and some Chief Justice and an overnight change in Montaigne's laws. He said that he and Olivia weren't going to marry after all, and now he wanted Charlie to know how he really felt about her.

Her head was spinning.

'I haven't slept all night for thinking of you,' Rafe said.

Charlie hadn't slept for thinking about him, but she wasn't about to admit that now when her mind was made up. She'd put too much hard thinking into reaching this point.

Now she didn't know whether to laugh or to cry. This

was like something out of a dream—or a nightmare; she wasn't sure which.

'I want you to stay.' Rafe's gaze was intense. 'I need you to come back with me, Charlie, so I can explain everything to you properly. I want us to have another chance. A proper chance.'

Another chance.

Charlie's whole body swayed dizzily. It was just as well Rafe was holding her hands or she might have fallen.

He stepped closer, and she smelled the faintest trace of his cologne as he leaned in to speak softly in her ear. 'I know this is the wrong place and the wrong time, but I've fallen in love with you, Charlie.'

In love. In love. In love.

The words circled in her head, but they felt unreal, like part of a magic spell.

Rafe clasped her hands more tightly. 'Please come back to Montaigne with me.'

Oh-h-h.

She couldn't believe this was happening now.

It was everything she wanted. It was too much to take in. Her poor heart was soaring and swooping like a bird caught in a whirlwind. She longed to lean into Rafe, to be wrapped in his strong arms, to just let him sweep her away.

But she had to be sensible. She had to remember how she'd sat in her room in the early hours of this morning, alone in Rafe's castle, thinking carefully and rationally about everything that had happened between them. She had reminded herself then how very, very easy it was to be blinded by this handsome Prince, by his charm, by his wealth and power.

She knew she had to be super careful now, or she could make a very serious mistake.

* * *

Rafe saw the fear in Charlie's pale face and his heart sank. Had he done this to her? Surely he hadn't made her feel so scared? It was the last thing he wanted. 'Charlie, I only want to talk to you, to try to explain.'

She was shaking her head. 'I'm sorry, Rafe. It's too much. Too much pressure.'

'But I wouldn't try to force you into anything.'

'You already have,' she said.

'No, Charlie, I—'

He was silenced by the stubborn light in her eyes. It reminded him of the tough little terrier he'd met in the Sydney art gallery. Right now Charlie looked both tough *and* scared.

'You're trying to get me off this plane, Rafe. What's that if it's not bullying?' Charlie's lovely mouth twisted as if she was trying very hard not to cry.

Again, she shook her head. 'Believe me, I've thought this through properly. We come from totally different worlds. We connected for a couple of days and it was fun. But you were right all along. Happy endings are for dreamers. Real life is all about compromise and common sense.'

Despair ripped through Rafe. He couldn't bear to lose her, to let things end this way.

'Thanks for everything, but I'm going home,' Charlie told him quietly, and then, before he could find the all-important words that might stop her, she turned. Her shoulders were ramrod-straight as she walked back into the plane.

The flight attendants quickly turned from their whispering huddle when Charlie appeared, but not before she heard snatches of their conversation.

'Rafael...'

'Prince of Montaigne...'

'Playboy...'

She didn't bother to speak to them. With her head high, her eyes stinging but dry, she made the hideously long journey back down the aisle to her seat.

Her large neighbour wasn't happy about having to get out again to let her past. She thanked him and, as soon as she was buckled in her seat, she found the eye mask for sleeping and slipped it on.

Eventually, the huge plane rolled forward on the tarmac, gathering speed, and she told herself over and over that she'd done the right thing, the only sensible thing. She could only hope that if she kept saying this until she reached Sydney, she might at last believe it.

CHAPTER THIRTEEN

Six weeks later

AFTER YET ANOTHER unsuccessful job interview, Charlie climbed the stairs to her flat, lugging grocery bags with food for her cat, as well as the ingredients for her own dinner.

She was now at the end of her second full week of job hunting and she'd lost count of the number of interviews she'd endured. If she'd known it would be this difficult to get another job, she might not have accepted the gallery's redundancy so readily. Not that she'd had much option.

From the moment her father had been heralded as the art world's latest sensation, the directors of the gallery where Charlie had worked for five years had promptly decided to employ experts with 'proper' qualifications. Charlie hadn't been to university, so her intimate knowledge of the work of local artists hadn't counted.

The dismissal had upset her for a day or two. Her father had protested and wanted to fight for her to stay, but she'd begged him not to cause a fuss. In her heart of hearts, she'd already accepted that it was time to move on. After all, the gallery was a constant reminder of a certain tall, commanding figure who'd come striding through the doors to turn her world upside-down.

Now it was late on a Friday. Charlie reached the landing at the top of the steps and set down her shopping while she fished in her jeans pocket for her keys. It was a warm afternoon at the end of summer. Edna from next door had left her door open to catch a breeze and the smell of her baking wafted down the hallway.

The tempting aroma of freshly baked chocolate cake was accompanied by the sound of voices—Edna's voice and a masculine baritone. Judging by the happy chatter, the two of them were having a jolly old time. Disturbingly, the man's voice reminded Charlie of Rafe's.

So annoying to have yet another reminder of the man she was trying so hard to forget. Pushing the key roughly into the lock, Charlie shoved at the door, holding it open with her knee, while she gathered up the shopping bags.

Meow!

Her darling cat, Dolly, pattered down the hall, eager to greet her. 'Hello, beautiful girl, you're going to love me when you see what I've bought for your dinner.'

Dolly answered with another meow and rubbed her silky black and white body against Charlie's shins. Then she began to sniff at the shopping bags.

Charlie was closing the door when Edna's voice called from the next flat, 'Yoo-hoo! Is that you, Charlie?'

'Yes, Edna, just home.' Charlie tried to inject a little enthusiasm into her response, but she knew from experience that Edna liked to drag her in for a cuppa and to meet her friends. She wasn't in a sociable mood this evening.

If she was honest, she hadn't been in a sociable mood for weeks. A broken heart could do that to a girl, and losing her job hadn't helped. Charlie's dad and her neighbour had both commented on her low moods, but so far they'd been tolerant, sensing that something 'deep' was the cause. However, she knew their tolerance would turn to annoyance before too long.

'Ah,' said Edna's voice.

Charlie turned to see her neighbour beaming from her doorway.

'I told him you should be home soon,' said Edna.

Told *him*?

Charlie's heart began a fretful kind of pounding. 'Told who?' she asked shakily.

Edna's beaming grin broadened. 'Your lovely friend.'

'My—'

Rafe appeared in the hallway behind Edna, and Charlie froze. He was dressed in casual blue jeans and a white T-shirt. His black hair was a little longer and shaggier than she remembered, and his jaw was shadowed by the hint of a beard. He seemed a little leaner and more strained, and yet Charlie thought he'd never looked more gorgeous.

Why was he here?

She had relived the details of their farewell a thousand times, torturing herself with questions about what might have happened if she'd gone with Rafe instead of walking away.

Regrets? Yes, she'd had more than a few, but for the sake of her sanity she'd chosen to believe that she'd done the right thing, the only sensible thing.

Now, amazingly, after six long weeks, here Rafe was. Truly. In the flesh. Charlie was so blindsided she couldn't speak, couldn't think how to react. Could only stand there stupefied.

'Hello, Charlie,' he said.

She might have nodded. She couldn't be sure.

'Rafe told me you weren't expecting him,' Edna explained self-importantly, almost hugging herself with excitement. 'Isn't this a lovely surprise for you?'

'I—guess,' Charlie muttered faintly.

Her neighbour turned to Rafe. 'Well, I really enjoyed meeting you again, Rafe, and thank you so much for our lovely chat.'

'Thank you for the tea and chocolate cake,' he responded with his customary courtesy.

'I'll leave you two to have a really nice catch-up now.' Edna winked rather obviously at him.

Crikey, thought Charlie. *The poor woman would probably have a heart attack if she knew she was winking so brazenly at a European prince.*

With a final smiling wave, Edna closed her door.

Charlie swallowed as she looked at Rafe. Her impulse was to rush into her flat and slam the door in his face, but that would be childish, not to mention rude. And it would leave her with too many unanswered questions.

Her second thought was to hold Rafe at bay, here on the landing, while she demanded that he explain exactly why he had come all this way. She was still thinking this through when Rafe spoke.

'How's your baby sister?' he asked.

It was the last thing Charlie had expected him to say and, in an instant, she could feel her resistance crumbling.

'Isla's doing really well,' she said. 'She's home again and she's getting fatter. She even gave her first smile last week.'

'That's wonderful.'

'Yes, it is.' He looked so gorgeous and, with so much emotion shimmering in his eyes, Charlie wanted to hurl herself into his arms. 'I guess you'd better come inside,' she said instead.

'Thank you, Charlie. I'd like that.'

In the hallway, she bent to pick up her shopping.

'Here, let me.' Rafe bent down too and their hands bumped together as they both tried to grab the bags at the same moment.

Lightning flashes engulfed Charlie. She stepped away, her hands clenched to her sides as she thanked him weakly. 'Can you bring the bags through to the kitchen?'

She couldn't believe she was conversing about ordinary everyday things like her shopping bags with Rafe St Romain. Shouldn't she be *demanding* to know exactly why he was here? Why he'd crossed hemispheres to be here?

But those questions felt too huge. Charlie had spent six long weeks trying to get over this man. Unfortunately, she now knew for sure that her efforts had been in vain. The mere sight of him stirred up every last vestige of the old longing and pain.

Oh, help!

Dolly rubbed at her ankles again, meowing more insistently. 'She can smell her dinner,' Charlie said, glad of the distraction. 'I'd better feed her, or she'll drive us mad.'

'By all means.'

She nodded to a red kitchen stool. 'Pull up a pew. Or if you'd prefer, you can sit in the lounge. I won't be long.'

'Here in the kitchen is fine, thanks.'

'Would you like another cup of tea?'

Rafe smiled, rubbed a hand over his flat stomach. 'No, thanks, I'm swimming in tea.'

'Wine?'

He shook his head, and smiled again. 'Take care of your cat.'

Charlie felt as if she'd woken in the middle of a weird dream as she unwrapped the fish she'd bought for Dolly and set it on a chopping board to dice. 'When did you arrive in Sydney, Rafe?'

'A couple of hours ago.'

'You must be feeling jet-lagged.'

'It's not too bad.'

She transferred the fish to Dolly's stainless-steel feeding bowl, set it on the floor, where Dolly greeted it with ecstatic, purring delight.

Rafe laughed. 'That's one happy cat.'

'It's a special treat. Fresh fish is like *foie gras* and champagne for her.' Charlie washed her hands at the sink, dried them on a hand towel hanging on a hook, then turned back to Rafe without quite meeting his gaze. Under normal circumstances she would start cooking her own meal now.

These were anything but normal circumstances.

'I was hoping that you might be free,' Rafe said. 'So I could take you out to dinner tonight.'

'Oh, I—um—' Charlie's head spun dizzily as she imagined dining somewhere glamorous with this man. He would be sure to choose a restaurant with sensational gourmet food, first-class wines, candlelight and ambience by the truckload. She saw herself falling under his spell. Again.

Be careful, girl.

'Actually, I—I was about to cook my dinner,' she told him. 'Why don't you join me here?' She couldn't quite believe she'd said that, but she could hardly send him packing, and surely it was far safer to eat in her kitchen than to go to a restaurant? At least she would be able to keep busy here. She could distract herself with any number of small kitchen tasks.

'There's enough for two,' she said. 'That's if you don't mind a Thai prawn stir-fry?'

Rafe's grey eyes gleamed with an intensity that made her heart stumble. 'Thank you, Charlie. I'd like that very much.'

She swallowed. Now she felt stupidly nervous about cooking a meal in front of this Prince, even though she'd made the dish so many times she could practically do it in her sleep.

'What can I do to help?' Rafe asked.

She blinked at him. 'Do you know how to cook? Have you ever been in a kitchen?'

He smiled. 'Not since I was a small boy, but I used to love sneaking downstairs to help the cooks to peel apples, or to cut out gingerbread men.'

It was an endearing thought, and, despite her qualms, Charlie set two chopping boards and two knives on the counter. 'You can help with chopping the veggies, then. I'll do the onions—I'd hate to see a grown man cry. You can do the carrots. Or would you prefer—?'

'Carrots are fine.'

It was surreal. Six weeks ago, they had parted at the door of an international jet amidst a huge amount of embarrassment and tension and now there were still huge questions hanging in the air. But Rafe seemed perfectly happy to help with preparing their dinner as if they were an old couple who'd lived harmoniously together for ages.

Charlie showed him how to cut carrots on the diagonal for stir-frying, rather than in strips or rounds.

'Stir-frying needs to be very quick and this way there's more of the carrot's surface area coming in contact with the heat.'

He nodded. 'That makes sense.'

As they chopped capsicum, shallots and fresh ginger Charlie asked about Tobias and Mathilde, Guillaume and Chloe. Rafe told her they were all well.

He looked up from his task, sending her a glance that hinted at amusement. 'They all asked to be remembered to you.'

'Oh.' This was a surprise. Her face flamed as she nipped the ends off snow peas, and she refrained from asking any more questions as she set jasmine rice cooking on a back burner.

Charlie found the fish sauce she needed and combined it with soy sauce, sesame oil and honey in a small bowl. Luckily the prawns were already peeled, so she could avoid that messy task.

As she set the wok on the gas flame she wondered what Rafe was *really* thinking. She felt tense as a bowstring. Questions kept popping into her head, but they were so very personal and important that to ask them felt as reckless as running through a field of unexploded landmines.

She forced herself to concentrate on her task, working calmly and methodically, cooking the prawns in the hot oil with garlic and chilli.

'When do the vegetables go in?' Rafe asked as he came to stand beside her.

'Soon. They only take a few minutes.'

'It smells sensational.'

Her skin was flaming—not from the cooking heat, but from his proximity. 'Would you—ah—mind setting the table? The plates and bowls are in the cupboard up there.' She pointed. 'And the cutlery's in that drawer.'

Rafe set the table with black place mats and white china and Charlie's red-handled cutlery, while Charlie transferred the stir-fry and the rice into two black and white ceramic bowls.

'Wine!' she announced. She suddenly, most definitely, needed wine. 'There's a nice cold white chilling in the fridge. I'll get the glasses.'

But she'd run out of delaying tactics. In a matter of moments, everything was ready. Rafe was sitting opposite her at her dining table, and he was smiling—looking unaccountably happy, actually—and drop-dead sexy in his casual jeans and T-shirt. And Charlie knew her efforts to keep herself busy and diverted had been no help whatsoever.

Even without the glamour of a fancy restaurant and mood lighting, even here in her ordinary little flat with a simple home-cooked meal, Prince Rafael of Montaigne was as attractive and charming as ever. And she was still totally, hopelessly under his spell.

Worse, she knew they could no longer avoid the important conversations they'd been dancing around, although Rafe seemed in no hurry to broach them.

'This is delicious,' he said. 'The flavours are fantastic.'

'I'm glad you like it.' The meal wasn't exactly flash.

'I love it, Charlie. This is exactly what I hoped for.'

'Prawn stir-fry?'

He chuckled. 'To see you in your natural environment.'

'You make me sound like some kind of rare animal.'

'Sorry.' He gave a dismayed shake of his head. 'Am I making a hash of this?'

Was he? Charlie thought he was being rather lovely, just as he'd been in Montaigne, although she was still uncertain and confused about the purpose of his surprise visit.

'You were right,' Rafe said suddenly, after he'd helped himself to another spoonful of veggies. 'I should never have tried to drag you off that plane. I was an egotistical bully. I realised that, as soon as you turned and walked away from me. I couldn't believe I'd been so crass.'

He looked so repentant, the final wedge of resistance in Charlie's heart melted.

'I shouldn't have run away,' she admitted. 'I should have at least stayed at the castle until I'd thanked you for your wonderful hospitality. I should have said goodbye properly.'

Rafe shrugged. 'I couldn't really blame you for rushing off. You'd been through the wringer. I'd dragged you across the world and you had the stress of trying to pretend to be someone else. Not to mention all the worry about your little sister.'

'And I also had a certain playboy prince kissing me senseless when he wasn't supposed to.'

The smoulder in Rafe's eyes sent Charlie's skin flaming again. 'I'm not going to apologise for kissing you.'

The air seemed to crackle with the chemistry sparking between them. Charlie dropped her gaze. 'It was pretty awkward to have Olivia turning up just at that moment—'

'It was,' Rafe agreed. 'Her timing was uncanny.'

He set down his fork. To Charlie's surprise, he smiled and leaned back in his chair, looking totally relaxed.

'So how is Montaigne's political situation now?' she asked, having deliberately avoided searching the Internet for news of his country. It had seemed sensible to try to put the whole experience behind her, but now, with Rafe here in her flat, dining at her table, she needed to get her facts straight before her brain went into total meltdown. 'Is everything settled?'

Rafe nodded. 'Our new Chancellor is brilliant. Leroy Mining have pulled in their horns. Everything's back to the way it should be as far as I'm concerned.'

'That must be a relief. And where's Olivia these days?'

'On her honeymoon, I imagine.'

Charlie's eyes widened. 'She's married already? To her fellow in Monaco?'

'Yes. His name's Frederick Hugo.' Rafe took a lazy

sip of his wine. 'And she has also spilled her story to the press.'

'About you—and—'

'And about you,' Rafe supplied smoothly. 'Olivia's big reveal. It was a double-page spread in a really popular glossy. Everything out in the open about how she only became engaged to me to help Montaigne, and the real love of her life was Frederick.'

'Gosh.'

Rafe didn't look the slightest bit put out. 'No doubt the magazine paid her a fortune. That's fine.' He smiled. 'She's saved me from having to explain how there came to be two of you.'

Charlie swallowed. 'So that's in the magazines, too? About Olivia and me being identical twins?'

'Yes, including photos of you at the hospital. Olivia declared she was ever so grateful that her sister stepped in when she had her little crisis.'

'So now your whole country knows who I really am?'

'Well, those who read gossip magazines, at any rate. But it means,' Rafe added carefully, 'that if you ever wanted to come back to Montaigne, we wouldn't have to worry about awkward explanations.'

'I—I see.'

'Of course,' he added, 'I'm being plagued with questions about you, especially about why I let you go.'

Charlie found this hard to believe. 'Who would ask about me?'

Rafe smiled again. 'Absolutely everyone. My staff. My good friend Faysal. Monique at Belle Robe. The people at the hospital. Just about anyone who's met you, Charlie.'

She had no idea what to say to this. She was astonished that these people even remembered her, let alone cared about her. Totally flustered, she stood abruptly and wondered if it was too soon to start clearing the table.

Rafe stood too and he moved towards her, reached for her hand before she could try to pick up a plate.

'Charlie,' he said softly.

'What?' She could barely hear her nervous response above the thumping of her heart.

'You were right to be cautious. We do hardly know each other.' His hand closed around hers. 'But I meant what I said at the airport. I want us to have a second chance.'

A second chance...

Charlie was as enchanted by Rafe's touch, by the pressure of his fingers wrapped around hers, as she was by his words. But there were things she needed to sort out. This man was supposed to be finding himself a wife to help him to rule Montaigne. He had access to the wealthiest and most beautiful women in Europe and he now had time to court one of these women properly. So what was he doing in a suburban flat in Sydney?

'What sort of second chance are we talking about, Rafe? Last time you wanted me to pretend to be your fiancée.'

'I know, I know.' He gave a soft groan. 'Looking back it was crazy, but it was the best crazy thing I've ever done.'

Now he reached for her other hand and held them both together, cradled against his chest.

Charlie could feel the heat of him through his thin white T-shirt, feel the thud of his heartbeats. She blinked back tears and tried to breathe. *Don't cry. Not now.*

'Charlie, I've missed you so much I thought I was going out of my mind.'

She couldn't speak. All the air had been sucked out of her lungs.

'But I owe it to you to do better,' Rafe said. 'I want us to go about dating the way any other couple might. No pressure, no huge expectations. Just the two of us getting to know each other, seeing how things work out.'

'Where—where might this happen?'

'Here. In Sydney.'

'You mean, you'd stay here in Sydney?'

'For a while, a couple of weeks at least. I'd love to explore this place with you. Bondi Beach, the harbour, maybe the Blue Mountains.'

It was Charlie's idea of bliss and she could no longer think of reasonable objections. 'Well, I don't happen to have a job any more, so I'm actually free.'

'That's handy.' Laughter shone in Rafe's eyes.

Charlie tried to smile back at him, but she couldn't see him now for tears.

It didn't matter. Rafe's arms were around her. Strong and reassuring and safe. She closed her eyes, let her head rest against his chest. It felt like coming home.

He didn't kiss her immediately. For long lovely moments he just held her close as if she was the most precious thing in the world. And when his lips finally found hers, his kiss was lazy and lingering, and the magic was there from the first contact.

Charlie felt the heat and the power of him flowing through her, touching flashpoints, igniting the yearning that had never really gone away.

Rafe in jeans and a T-shirt, here in Australia, was every bit as sexy and dangerous as he'd been in his castle in full princely regalia. Desire curled through Charlie like smoke. Like smoke and flames and she wanted to press close to him, to wriggle against him, to tear off her clothes.

Between increasingly frantic kisses, she asked, 'Have you booked into a hotel?'

'Yes. Somewhere near the harbour.'

'But you said you wanted to see me in my natural environment.'

Rafe smiled. 'That's true, I do.'

'Then you should cancel your booking,' she suggested recklessly. 'Stay here.'

She heard the sharp rasp of his breath. 'That would be perfect.'

Then in a burst of unbelievable confidence, she said, 'But, of course, you'd need to check my bedroom first. Make sure the mattress is up to scratch.'

Now he laughed. 'Have I ever told you I love the way you think, Charlie girl?'

In one easy motion he swept her high, holding her with an arm beneath her knees and another around her shoulders. 'Which way is the bedroom?'

Charlie pointed.

Of course, she knew she should be nervous about directing a royal prince to her boudoir. She had no idea what happened when a girl let a fairy tale and real life collide. But she was too entranced to analyse the problem, too impressed by Rafe's strength, by the easy way he carried her as if she were a featherweight.

'It's like a glamorous cave in here,' he said as he set her down on the snowy white bed in her black-walled bedroom with just a single lamp glowing in the corner.

'I got carried away with the black and white theme.'

'It's great. I love it.' He sat on the bed beside her, and her body hummed with anticipation as he leaned over her, supporting himself with a hand on the mattress on either side of her.

Please, she whispered silently. She'd never felt so ready, so wanting.

Bending closer, he kissed her throat, her chin, her brow and, in that moment, as her eyes drifted closed, he pressed gentle kisses to her eyelids, and Charlie forgot the whole prince thing. This was Rafe and that was all that mattered. Rafe, the hunkiest *and* the nicest guy she'd ever met, who'd come all this way to get to know her.

'I've missed you so much I thought I was going out of my mind,' he'd said.

He kissed her mouth, teasing her lips apart with his tongue, and any last efforts to think dissolved as sensation claimed her, washing over her in heated, hungry waves. She wound her arms around his neck, and her hips bucked, needing him closer still.

It should have been gentle and lingering, this first time, but they'd been waiting too long. Need built fast and furiously, breaking through any final barriers of politeness. Everything went a little wild and slightly desperate as they helped each other out of their clothes and then scrambled to be close again. Skin to skin.

At the centre of the wildness there was happiness, too. For Charlie, a fierce, bubbling, over-the-top joy. She and the man who'd stolen her heart were together at last, and everything was OK. It was perfect.

It was ten days later when Charlie got the phone call. For Rafe they had been ten glorious days, spent exclusively with Charlie, exploring Sydney, dining out, cooking at home, talking, talking, making love. A kind of honeymoon without the wedding. A perfection they both knew couldn't last.

On this particular day they had been to the Blue Mountains, hiking, checking out the gift shops and dining in a hotel with an amazing view of craggy cliffs and a deep, tree-studded valley. Rafe was driving his hire car back into Charlie's garage when her phone rang. She had to fish the phone out of her bag.

'I've no idea who this can be,' she said as she checked the caller ID. She climbed out of the car to answer the call.

Rafe collected their sweaters from the back seat, locked the car, and indicated to Charlie that he would go ahead to open the flat.

Still intent on the phone conversation, she nodded.

He was in the kitchen, giving Dolly a welcome scratch behind her ears, when Charlie came in. Charlie's eyes were wide, as if she'd had a shock, but there was also a tightness in her expressive face that suggested she might not want to share her news.

'That was unexpected,' she said, setting her phone on the kitchen counter.

'Is everything OK?' Rafe asked cautiously.

'Well, I guess. I've been offered a job.'

An unwelcome chill spread over his skin. Charlie had already told him about her father's sudden rise to fame and the changes at the art gallery where she used to work. But they hadn't talked about her future plans. They'd been busy making the most of their time together, and Rafe had promised Charlie there would be no pressure or expectation, so he'd been careful to hold any discussion about the future at bay. Charlie hadn't mentioned any job prospects.

'It's weird,' she said now. 'I've applied for all kinds of positions and been knocked back and now I'm offered a job I never even applied for.'

Rafe's throat tightened. 'What kind of offer?'

'To run another art gallery at the Gold Coast. In

Queensland.' Her eyes widened and it was clear she was impressed. 'There's a big tourist market up there,' she said. 'A huge turnover.'

'A big responsibility, then.' Rafe spoke quietly, despite the chilling lump of dread that had settled in his gut.

Now he regretted his reticence to talk about their future. He hadn't wanted to rush Charlie, to overwhelm her with the truth about his deep feelings for her. But the past days had only served to prove to him how important she was to him.

In every way, Charlie was the most desirable woman he'd ever known, but his feelings went way beyond their incredible chemistry. With her own special brand of wisdom, Charlie brought the perfect balance to his world.

As he juggled the privileges of royalty with its responsibilities, he needed this sunny, open-hearted and genuine girl in his life. By his side.

Hell. Had he left it too late?

Charlie stood very still with her arms folded tightly over her chest, trying hard not to mind that Rafe had taken her news so calmly, as if he wasn't in any way a part of her future.

A big responsibility, then.

Was that all he could say?

After ten of the best days of her life? After ten ecstatically beautiful days filled with fun and laughter and their deepening friendship, not to mention sublimely satisfying sex?

Foolishly, she'd spent these ten days falling more deeply and helplessly in love with the man, despite the fact that there'd been no talk at all about where any of this was leading.

Now Charlie hugged herself tighter and tried not to

panic. But Rafe was taking her news so calmly. Too calmly. Had she been a total fool? Had she totally misunderstood where their relationship was heading?

Was the new job opportunity a turning point? Was Rafe about to gently let her go?

It was really nice knowing you, Charlie, but I'm royalty after all, and I'm afraid you're not quite up to scratch.

'I didn't realise you were still job-hunting,' Rafe said.

Charlie shrugged miserably and kept her gaze on the black and white floor tiles. 'I wasn't really hunting for this job.'

'If I'd known you were looking for work, I might have spoken earlier,' he said. 'I'd like to offer you a job.'

She stiffened. A job offer from Rafe was like a slap in the face. What did he have in mind? To employ her as some kind of secretary-cum-mistress?

How dared he?

'No, thanks,' she snapped, jamming her lips tightly together to bite back the sob that threatened.

'Because being my wife is a kind of job, I'm afraid.'

At first, Charlie thought she'd misheard him.

'As you know,' Rafe went on with uncharacteristic earnestness, 'there are certain expectations and responsibilities. But I think—no, I don't just think, I *know* you'd be brilliant at that particular job, Charlie. So I was hoping you'd do me the honour—'

He stopped talking and looked at her with a smile that was both shy and hopeful.

Charlie stopped hugging herself. Instead she gripped the counter before her knees gave way. 'I'm sorry,' she said shakily. 'I think I might have missed something. What exactly are you asking me?'

And that was when it happened. Tall, impossibly handsome Rafael St Romain, Prince of Montaigne, got down on one knee on her kitchen floor and placed a hand over his heart.

'I love you, Charlie. I suspect I've been in love with you from the day I first met you, but now I know it for certain and it's a relief to be able to tell you at last.'

Oh.

'I'm desperate to spend the rest of my life with you.'

'Oh-h-h-h.'

'And I'm shamelessly begging you to marry me.'

'Oh, Rafe.' Charlie dashed at tears with one hand while she held her other hand out to him. 'I've been the same.' Her voice was very wobbly as she linked her fingers with his. 'I didn't know it was possible to love someone so deeply. I had no idea till I met you.'

The intensity in his face was heart-stopping. 'So you'll marry me?'

Charlie was grinning now, with tears streaming down her face. 'Only if you get up off that floor and kiss me.'

Leaping to his feet, Rafe was more than happy to oblige. 'I promise I'll make you happy,' he said as he gathered Charlie close.

'And if marrying you is a job, my first job will be to keep you happy, too,' she told him.

A pleading meow sounded at their feet. Charlie felt a silken pressure against her ankles and looked down to a swishing black and white tail. 'Oh, dear. If we get married, what will happen to Dolly?'

Rafe smiled. 'No worries, as you Aussies say. She'll fit in just fine in the castle.'

And then he kissed her and, despite the thousand wonderful kisses they'd shared, this was the very best kiss of all.

EPILOGUE

THE BELLS RANG LOUDLY, pealing from churches all over Montaigne, echoing from the mountainsides and rolling down the valleys. Loudest of all were the bells from the cathedral where Prince Rafael and his bride, Princess Charlotte, were to be married.

The joyful sounds surrounded Charlie and her dad as they drove through the streets, lined with crowds of cheering well-wishers who were waving flags or home-made signs.

We love you, Charlie!
Bonne chance!
Félicitations!

Charlie couldn't help being overwhelmed by all the excitement and goodwill. She felt quite nervous by the time she and her father arrived at the cathedral and the bells were replaced by thundering organ music, lifting to the magnificent soaring ceilings.

Is this real? Is this really happening to me?

As she stood in the enormous cathedral doorway, Charlie trembled as she saw the splendour of it all—the stained-glass windows, the candles, the bishop in his robes, the pews filled with grand-looking strangers. She was almost too scared to look properly at Rafe, who stood at the far end of the very long aisle, incredibly splendid in a red jacket with gold braid and black trousers. She was so overcome she feared she might weep.

In that moment, however, her eye was caught by a bobbing flash of deep purple right at the front of the congregation. Someone had turned to grin and to wave excitedly. Charlie realised it was Edna.

Her neighbour had been over the moon to be invited to the royal wedding and today she looked magnificent in a purple lace suit, with a lavender fascinator, complete with feathers, perched rather precariously on her head.

The sight of her old neighbour's familiar beaming grin was enough to calm Charlie.

She looked again at Rafe. And he smiled.

His smile was for her. Only for her. She could feel his love reaching her down the full length of the red-carpeted aisle, and she knew that, despite the over-the-top pomp and ceremony, Rafe was just a normal guy who needed her. He had told her this over and over during the past few days.

They loved each other. They might be a royal couple, but they were also good mates. Everything was OK.

With a happy, calming, deep breath, Charlie turned her attention to Arielle, her flower girl, who had just arrived in the car that followed close behind.

Arielle was one of the first people Charlie had visited on her return to Montaigne. The little girl's hair had grown back since the day they'd first met in the hospital, when she'd worn a crocheted cap and had won Rafe and Charlie's hearts with her curtsy. On Charlie's second visit, she had met Arielle's parents as well. Since then her friendship with the family and with many other patients had deepened.

Today the excited little girl looked beautiful with her

mop of short dark curls adorned by a circlet of roses that matched her floor-length dress of palest pink. Olivia looked beautiful too in a gown in the same shade. She'd been thrilled and touched when Charlie had invited her to be her matron of honour.

And Suze, Charlie's best friend since kindergarten, was also a bridesmaid, looking perfectly lovely, but slightly overawed by the fact that her groomsman partner was a handsome sheikh.

Now, with everyone assembled, Charlie sent them all a final smile and then linked arms with her dad. Michael Morisset had taken a while to get used to the idea of his daughter marrying a prince. At first he'd thought Charlie was pulling his leg. It was too preposterous to believe.

Fortunately, once he'd got to know Rafe, he'd calmed down. Eventually, he'd declared his prospective son-in-law to be a regular 'good bloke'.

'I was worried Rafe wouldn't understand how lucky he was,' Charlie's father had confided. 'But he seems to truly appreciate how wonderful you are, my duckling, so I'm happy to give you my blessing.'

Now her dad smiled at her. His eyes were a tad too shiny, but he still looked happy. 'I'm so proud of you, kiddo,' he said fondly, a beat before the organist struck the opening chords of the processional hymn.

The congregation rose, the music swelled and flowed, and Charlie kept her smile just for Rafe as she made her way down the long, long aisle. Throughout the procession, her Prince didn't take his eyes from her and his message was clear and shining.

This day wasn't just a happy ending, it was the very happiest of new beginnings.

* * * * *

THE MILLIONAIRE'S ROYAL RESCUE

JENNIFER FAYE

For Mona and Louie.
Thanks for the smiles and the reminder
that there's more to life than work.
I hope your dreams come true.

PROLOGUE

ANOTHER DISASTROUS DATE.

Lady Annabelle DiSalvo's back teeth ground together as memories from the night before came rushing over her. It was tough enough finding a decent guy who liked her for herself and not for her position as the daughter of the Duke of Halencia, but then to expect him to put up with her over-zealous security team was another thing altogether.

And so when her date had tried to slip away with her for a stroll beneath the stars, her bodyguard had stopped them. Heat rushed to Annabelle's face as she recalled how the evening had ended in a heated confrontation between her, him and her unbending bodyguard. It had been awful. Needless to say, there'd be no second date.

The backs of Annabelle's eyes stung with tears of frustration. She couldn't stand to live like this any longer. Her friends were all starting to get married, but she was single with no hope of that changing as long as her every move was monitored. She just wanted a normal life—like her life had been before her mother's murder.

If only her mother were here, she could talk some sense into Annabelle's overprotective father. She missed her mother so much. And the fact that her father rarely spoke of her mother only made the hole in Annabelle's heart ache more.

She clutched her mother's journal close to her chest. Maybe she shouldn't have been snooping through her mother's things, but her father had left her no other choice. How else would she ever really get to know her mother?

Annabelle slipped the journal into her oversized purse and rushed down the sweeping staircase of her father's vast estate in Halencia. At the bottom of the steps her ever-vigilant bodyguard, Berto, waited for her. There was actually a whole team of them, all taking turns to protect Annabelle.

Ever since her mother had died during a mugging, Annabelle had been watched, night and day. And since her mother's murderer had never been caught, Annabelle had understood her father's concerns at the time. But now, eleven years later, the protective detail assigned to her felt claustrophobic and unnecessary.

She'd thought by moving to Mirraccino, her mother's home country, that things would change, but with the king of Mirraccino being her uncle, she was still under armed guard. But Annabelle had a plan to change all of that. And she was just about to put that plan in motion.

"Berto, I'm ready to go."

The man with short, dark hair and muscles that were obvious even with his suit jacket on, got to his feet. He was the quiet sort and could intimidate people with just a look. Annabelle was the exception.

She'd known him since she was a teenager. He was a gentle giant unless provoked. She thought of him as an overprotective big brother. They moved to the door. Annabelle was anxious to get back to Mirraccino for a pivotal business meeting—

"Not so fast," the rumble of her father's voice put a pause in her steps. The Duke of Halencia strode into the spacious foyer. His black dress shoes sounded as they struck the marble floor. "I didn't know you were leaving so soon." He arched a brow. "Any reason for your quick departure?"

"Something came up." Her unwavering gaze met her father's.

He tugged on the sleeves of his suit, adjusting them. "What's that supposed to mean?"

"It means I have responsibilities in Mirraccino. Not that you would understand." Her voice rose with emotion as memories of last night's date flashed in her mind.

"Annabelle, I don't understand where this hostility is coming from. It's not like you."

"Maybe it's because I'm twenty-four years old and you will not let me live a normal life."

"Of course I do—"

"Then why do you refuse to remove my bodyguards? They're ruining my chances of ever being happy. Momma's been gone a long time. There is no threat. All of that died with her."

"You don't know that." Her father's dark bushy brows drew together and his face aged almost instantly.

Her patience was quickly reaching the breaking point. "You're right, I don't. But that's nothing new. I've been asking you repeatedly over the years to tell me—to tell both myself and Luca why you're worried about us—but you refuse."

Her father sighed. "I've told you, the police said it was a mugging gone wrong."

"Why would a mugger come after us?"

"He wouldn't."

"But?" He couldn't just stop there.

"But something never felt right."

At last some pieces of the puzzle were falling into place. "Because her jewelry and wallet were taken, the police wrote it off as a mugging, but you know something different, don't you?"

Her father's lips pressed together as his dark brows gathered. "I don't know any more than the police."

"But you suspect something. Don't you?" When he didn't respond, she refused to give up. This was too important. "Poppa, you owe me an explanation."

He sighed. "I found it strange that your mother phoned me from the palace to say something was not as it seemed, but she wouldn't go into details on the phone. And two days later, she…she's killed in a mugging."

"What wasn't as it seemed?"

"That's it. I don't know. It might have been nothing. That's what the police said when I told them. All of the evidence said it was a mugging."

"But you never believed it?"

He shook his head. "When the king didn't know what your mother had been referring to, I hired a private investigator. He combed through your mother's items and talked with the palace staff. He didn't come up with anything that would have gotten her killed."

"Maybe the police were right."

Her father shook his head. "I don't believe it."

"Even though you don't have any evidence?"

"It's a feeling." His face seemed to age right before her. "And I'm not taking any chances with you and your brother. You two are all I have left."

"I know you're worried but you can't continue to have us followed around and spied upon like we're criminals. It's so bad Luca never comes home anymore. And—" She thought of admitting that was why she still lived in Mirraccino, but the pain reflected in her father's eyes stopped her.

"And what? You just want to go about as though nothing happened? There's a murderer still on the loose."

Annabelle had placated him most of her life because she felt sorry for him as he continued to grieve for her mother. However, living in Mirraccino for these past couple of years had given her a different perspective. If she didn't stand up for herself, she would never gain her freedom. She would never be able to experience a lot of her dreams. She would forever live under her father's thumb and that was not truly living.

Many people were put off by her security detail. She ended up refraining from doing things just because it was easier than following security protocol and having people send her strange looks, not to mention the whispered comments. Most guys she might have a chance with quietly backed off after meeting Berto. The ones that persisted, she'd learned the hard way, were trouble, one way or the other. And so her dating life was sporadic at best.

"I'm not backing down, Poppa. I'm twenty-four now. I deserve to have my own life—"

"You have a life."

"No, I don't. My every move is analyzed before I do it. And then it is reported back to you. That is not a life."

Her father sighed. "I'm sorry you feel that way, but I'm just doing what I must to protect you and your brother. I don't hear him complaining."

"That's because Luca doesn't care what you or anyone says. He does exactly what he wants."

Her father ran a hand over his clean-shaven jaw. "I know. I know."

"Is that what you want me to do?"

"No!" Her father's raised voice reverberated off the walls.

"Then maybe you need to back off. I'm not wild like Luca, but if that's what you want—"

"Don't you dare. I have enough problems with your brother, but that's going to come to an end. If he wants to inherit my title, he has to earn it."

She couldn't help her brother, not that Luca would want or accept her help, but they were getting sidetracked. "My brother can fight his own battles. This is about you and me. I need you to back off or…"

Her father's gaze narrowed. "Or what?"

She didn't have an answer to that question. Or did she? There was something that had come to mind more than once when she'd felt smothered.

"Or else you'll leave me no choice. I'll leave Halencia and Mirraccino." She saw the surprise reflected in her father's eyes. She hated to do this to him, but perhaps that's what it would take to get her father to understand that she meant business.

He didn't say anything for a moment. And when he did speak, his voice was low and rumbled with agitation. "Your threats won't work."

"Poppa, this isn't a threat. It's a promise. And it's not something that I take lightly."

Her father stared at her as though gauging her sincerity. "Why don't you and your brother understand that I just want to protect you?"

"I know you are worried about our safety after…after what happened to Momma, but that was a long time ago. It was just a mugging—there's no threat to us. You can relax. We'll be safe."

He shook his head. "You don't know that. I can't remove your security detail. I… I have to be sure that you're mature enough—competent enough—to take care of yourself."

The knowledge that her father thought so little of her stabbed at her. But she refused to give in to the pain. This was her chance to forge ahead. "I will prove to you that I'm fully capable of taking care of myself and making good decisions."

Business was something her father understood and respected. She told her father how she'd taken over the South Shore Project. With the crown prince now occupied with his new family and assuming more and more of the king's duties, he didn't have time to personally oversee the project. And Annabelle had happily stepped up. And she almost had the entire piazza occupied. There was just one more pivotal vacancy that needed to be filled. And not just by anyone, but a business that would draw the twentysomething crowd— the people with plenty of disposable cash that would keep the South Shore thriving long into the future.

"And you think you can do this all on your own?" There was a note of doubt in her father's voice.

Her back teeth ground together. Her father was so old-fashioned. If it were up to him, she'd be married off to some successful businessman who could help sustain her father's citrus business.

Annabelle lifted her chin as her gaze met his. "Yes, I

can do this. I'll show you. And once I do, you'll remove the bodyguards."

Their gazes met and neither wanted to turn away. A battle of wills ensued. Obviously her father hadn't realized that he'd raised a daughter who was as stubborn as him.

All the while, she wondered if there was any truth to her father's suspicions about her mother's death. Or was he just grasping for something more meaningful than her mother had died over some measly money and jewelry?

CHAPTER ONE

THIS DAY WAS the beginning of a new chapter…

Lady Annabelle DiSalvo smiled as she walked down the crowded sidewalk of Bellacitta, the capital of Mirraccino. Though the day hadn't started off the way she'd hoped, she had high hopes for the afternoon.

With a few minutes to spare before her big meeting, she planned to swing by Princess Zoe's suite of offices. They had become good friends since Zoe and the crown prince had reconciled their marriage. Annabelle admired the way Zoe insisted on being a modern-day princess and continued with her interior design business—although her hours had to be drastically reduced to accommodate her royal duties as well as being a wife and mother. If Zoe could make it all work, so could Annabelle. She just had to gain her freedom from her father's overzealous security.

It wasn't until then that Annabelle recalled the email Zoe had sent her. Zoe had left town with her husband on an extended diplomatic trip. And with the other prince in America, visiting with his wife's family, the palace was bound to be very quiet.

Someone slammed into her shoulder. Annabelle struggled not to fall over. As she waved her arms about, the strap of her purse was yanked from her shoulder. Once her balance was restored, her hand clenched the strap.

No way was this guy going to get away with her purse—with her mother's final words in a journal lying at the bottom of the bag. For the first time ever, Annabelle regretted forcing Berto to walk at least ten paces behind her. This was all going down too fast for him to help.

Knowing the fate of the journal was at stake, she held on with all of her might. But the short lanky kid with a black ball cap was moving fast. His momentum practically yanked her arm out of its socket.

Pain zinged down her arm. The intense discomfort had her fingers instinctively loosening their grip. And then they were gone—the purse, the journal and the thief.

"Hey! Stop!" Annabelle gripped her sore shoulder.

"Are you okay?" Berto asked.

"No. I'm not. Please get my purse! Quick!"

The man hesitated. She knew his instructions were to stay with her no matter what, but this was different. That thief had her last connection to her mother. Not wasting another moment while the culprit got away, Annabelle took off with Berto close on her heels.

"Lady Annabelle, stop!" Berto called out.

No way! She couldn't. She wasn't about to let another piece of her past be stolen from her. The hole in her heart caused by her mother's death was still there. It had scar tissue built up around it, but on those occasions when a mother's presence was noticeably lacking, the pain could be felt with each beat of her heart.

Annabelle's feet pounded the sidewalk harder and faster. "Stop him! Thief!"

Adrenaline flooded her veins as she threaded her way through the crowd of confused pedestrians. Some had been knocked aside by the thief. Others had stopped to take in the unfolding scene.

It soon became apparent that she wasn't going to catch him. And yet she kept moving, catching glimpses of the kid's black ball cap in the crowd. She wouldn't stop until all hope was gone.

"Stop him! Thief!" she yelled at the top of her lungs.

Frustration and anger powered her onward. Berto remained at her side. She understood that his priority was her, but for once, she wished he would break the rules. He had no idea what she was about to lose.

Annabelle's only hope was that a Good Samaritan would step forward and help. *Please, oh, please, let me catch him.*

"Stop! Thief!"

* * *

So this was Mirraccino.

Grayson Landers adjusted his dark sunglasses. He strolled down the sidewalk of Bellacitta, admiring how the historical architecture with its distinctive ornate appearance was butted up against more modern buildings with their smooth and seamless style. And what he liked even more was that no one on this crowded sidewalk seemed to notice him much less recognize him as…what did the tabloids dub him? Oh, yes, the slippery fat cat.

Of course, they weren't entirely off the mark with that name. A frown pulled at his lips. He jerked his thoughts to a halt. He refused to get lost on that dark, miserable path into the past.

He scratched at the scruff on his face. It itched and he longed to shave it off, but he really didn't want to be recognized. He didn't want the questions to begin again. The minor irritation of a short beard and mustache was worth his anonymity. Here in sunny Mirraccino he could just be plain old Grayson Landers.

In fact, in less than a half hour, he had a meeting for a potential business deal—a chance to expand his gaming cafés that were all the rage in the United States. Now, it was time to expand into the Mediterranean region.

And Mirraccino offered some perks that had him inclined to give it a closer look. He couldn't imagine that it'd be hard to attract new employees to the sunny island. This island nation was large enough to offer them a choice between city life or a more rural existence. And there was plenty of room on the South Shore for a sizable facility.

His board would love the revenue growth from the international venture. Adding Mirraccino as the hub would give them diversification. It could be the beginning of great things.

"Stop! Thief!" screamed a female above the murmur of voices.

The next thing Grayson knew a young lanky guy bumped into him as he ran up the walk. Grayson reached out, grabbing him as he passed.

The kid yanked, trying to escape the solid hold Grayson had on his upper arm. Between his grip on him and the fact that Grayson had almost a foot on the guy and at least thirty pounds, the kid wasn't going anywhere.

"Thief! Stop him!" again came the female voice and it was growing closer.

Could this guy be the person in question? Grayson gave the teenager a quick once-over. "I'm guessing that's not yours." Grayson gestured to the purse in the kid's hand.

"Yes, it is."

"It's not exactly your color." The purse was brown with pink trim and a pink strap.

The guy continued to struggle, obviously not smart enough to realize that he wasn't going anywhere until the cops showed up. "Let me go!"

Grayson narrowed his gaze on the guy. "If you don't stand still, you won't like what I do next."

"Dude, you don't understand." The kid glanced over his shoulder. "They're after me."

"Probably because you stole," Grayson snatched the purse while the guy wasn't paying attention, "this."

The kid with a few scrawny hairs on his chin turned to him. "Hey, give that back." He glanced over his shoulder again as a crowd formed around them. "Never mind. You keep it. Just let me go."

"I'll keep it and you."

"I called the cops," someone in the crowd called out.

Inwardly, Grayson cringed. The very last thing he wanted to do now was deal with more cops. A little more than a year ago, he'd answered enough questions to last him a lifetime. He was really tempted to let the kid get away and then Grayson could quietly slip into the thickening crowd.

Before he could make up his mind whether to do the right

thing for some stranger or protect himself from yet another interrogation, the whoop-whoop of a police car blasted into the air. Then there was the slamming of a car door.

The suspect in Grayson's hold fought for his freedom with amazing force for someone so slight. The punch that landed in Grayson's gut made him grunt. Anger pumped in his veins. No matter what it cost him personally, this guy needed to learn a lesson.

The crowd parted, allowing the police officer to make his way over to them. Thankfully the officer immediately took custody of the feisty young man and restrained him.

"Move aside." A deep gruff voice shouted. "Let the lady pass."

Grayson glanced up to find the most beautiful young woman standing at the edge of the crowd. Immediately he could see that there was something special about her. Maybe it was her big brown eyes. Or perhaps it was the way her long flowing dark brown hair framed her face. Whatever it was, she was definitely a looker.

It was only then that Grayson noticed the big burly man at her side. Her boyfriend? Most likely. The stab of disappointment assailed him.

Not that he was interested in starting anything romantic. He'd learned his lesson about affairs of the heart—they made you do things you wouldn't normally do and in the end, you got your heart broken, or in his case ripped from his chest. No, he was better on his own.

He was about to turn away when he realized the young woman looked familiar. And then it came to him. She was Lady Annabelle DiSalvo—the very woman he was here to meet with.

The police officer turned to the crowd. "There's nothing here to see. Everyone, please, move on."

Lady DiSalvo didn't move. Was she that fascinated? Or could she be the victim in this case?

This was not the way he'd planned for their relationship

to start—their business relationship that was. And then her gaze moved to him. He waited, wondering if she recognized him. Nothing appeared to register in her eyes. And then she turned to talk to the man at her side.

A camera flash momentarily blinded Grayson.

Seriously? Could this day get any worse?

Where is it?

It has to be here.

Annabelle craned her neck. Her gaze frantically searched for her purse. *Oh, please, let this be the right person. Let him still have my purse.* And then she realized that during the foot chase he could have ditched it anywhere along the way. Her elation waned.

Her gaze latched on to the tall, dark and sexy man standing in the center of the scene. She'd sensed him staring at her earlier. But with those dark sunglasses, she couldn't make out his eyes. He was tall with an athletic build. Her gaze took in the heavy layer of scruff trailing down his jaw, and she couldn't help wondering what he'd look like without it. The thought intrigued her, but right now she had more pressing matters on her mind.

She was about to glance away when she noticed that he was holding her purse. Her gut said he wasn't the thief. The young man next to him giving the policeman a hard time was wearing a dark ball cap. That had to be the culprit. The kid had the right build as well as a smart mouth.

"Hey you! That's my purse!" Annabelle called out, hoping the stranger would hear her. "I need it back."

A reporter positioned himself between them. The man with her purse began backing away and turning his face away from the camera. What was up with that?

She had to get to the man with her purse. And it'd probably go better if she didn't have Berto in tow. Even though she knew he was a gentle giant, strangers found his mammoth size and quiet ways a bit off-putting.

While Berto glanced over the crowd for a new threat, she quietly slipped away. She threaded her way through the lingering crowd. There was a lot of *pardon me* and *excuse me*. But finally she made her way over to the man with her purse in his hand just as the officer was escorting the thief to the police car.

Annabelle had to crane her neck to gaze into the man's face.

"Thank you so much. I didn't think I'd ever see my purse again. You're quite a hero."

The man looked uncomfortable with her praise. "I'm glad I could help."

"Well, I really appreciate it."

"No big deal."

It was a huge deal, but she didn't want to get into any of that right now. "If you'll just give me my purse, I'll be going."

Even standing this close to the man, she couldn't make out his eyes through the large, dark sunglasses. His brows rose in surprise, but he didn't make any motion to give it back.

"Is there a problem?"

"I can't hand it over." The man's voice was deep and smooth like a fine gourmet coffee.

He couldn't be serious. She pressed her hands to her hips. "I don't think you understand. That's my purse. He," she gestured to the thief, who was struggling with the police officer, "stole it from me."

"And it's evidence. You'll have to take it up with the police."

Really? He was going to be a stickler for the law. "Listen, I don't have time for this. I have a meeting—"

"I have to give this to the police. I'm sorry." There was a finality to his tone.

What was it with this day? First, there was the scene with her father. Then she missed her flight. And if that wasn't enough, she'd nearly lost her mother's journal. And now, this man refused to return her belongings.

Maybe she just needed to take a different approach. "If it's a reward you want, I'll need my purse back in order to do that."

The man frowned. "I don't need your money."

This couldn't be happening. There had to be something she could say to change his mind before the policeman turned his attention their way. At last, she decided to do something that she'd never done before. She was about to play the royalty card. After all, desperate times called for desperate measures. And right now, she was most definitely desperate.

But then she had a thought. "If I don't file charges, it's not evidence."

"You'll have to take it up with the officer."

Seriously. Why was the man so stubborn?

"Do you know who I am?"

Before the man could respond, the policeman strode over to them. "I'll be taking that."

The mystery man readily handed over her purse. She glared at him, but she didn't have time to say anything. Her focus needed to remain on getting the journal back.

"That's my purse. I need it back," Annabelle pleaded with the officer. "All of my important things are in there."

"Sorry, miss. Afraid it's evidence now." When the young officer glanced at her, the color drained from his face. "Lady Annabelle, I didn't know it was you. I… I'm sorry."

She smiled hoping to put him at ease. "It's all right. You're just doing your duty. As for my purse, could I have it back now?"

Color rose in the officer's face. His gaze lowered to the purse in his hand. "The thing is, ma'am, regulations say I have to turn this in as evidence. My captain is always telling us to follow the regs. But seeing as it's you, I guess I could make an exception—"

"No." The word was out of her mouth before she realized what she was saying—or maybe she did realize it. She didn't want this young man getting in trouble with his captain because she had him break the rules. "You do what you need to do and I'll come by the police station to pick it up later."

The officer's eyes widened in surprise. "Much appreciated, ma'am, especially seeing as you're the victim. I'll need you to file a complaint against the suspect."

"I… I'm not filing charges."

The officer frowned at her. "That would be a mistake."

He went on to list the reasons that letting the kid get away with this crime would be a bad idea. And he had some good points. In the end, she had to agree with him.

"Okay. I'll need you and the man who caught the thief to make statements down at the station." The officer glanced around. "Where did he go?"

She glanced around for her hero, but there was no sign of him. How could he vanish so quickly?

"I didn't get a chance to catch his name much less take a statement." The officer shook his head as he noted something on the pad of paper in his hand.

Why had the man disappeared without giving his statement? Was he afraid of cops? Or was it something else? Something that had him hiding behind dark sunglasses and a shaggy beard?

Or perhaps she'd watched one too many cop shows. She'd probably never know the truth about him. But that didn't stop her from imagining that he was a bad boy, maybe a wrongly accused fugitive or a spy. Someone as mysterious as him had to have an interesting background. What could it be?

CHAPTER TWO

AT LAST SHE'D ARRIVED.

Annabelle checked the time on her cell phone. Luckily, she'd had it in her pocket or it would have been confiscated with her purse. She had two minutes to spare before her meeting with an executive of the Fo Shizzle Cafés. Her name was Mary and they'd corresponded for the past few weeks. It seemed Grayson Landers, the CEO and mastermind behind the hip cafés, was only hands-on once a site had been vetted by a trusted member of his team.

Annabelle took a seat at one of the umbrella tables off to the side of the historic piazza in the South Shore. She glanced around, but there weren't any professional young women lurking about.

Annabelle looked down at the screen of her phone. Her social media popped up. There were already numerous posts about the incident with her purse. There were photos of her, but no photos of her hero's face. Too bad.

And then a thought came to her. Perhaps a phone call to the police station would hurry along the return of her possessions. Her finger moved over the screen, beginning the search for the phone number—

"You're seriously not going to let me through?"

The disgruntled male voice drew Annabelle's attention. She glanced up as Berto blocked a man from getting any closer. She swallowed hard. It didn't matter how many times it happened, she was still uncomfortable having security scrutinize everyone that came within twenty meters of her.

Berto stood there like a big mountain of muscle with his bulky arms crossed and his legs slightly spread. Annabelle had no doubt he was ready to spring into action at the slightest provocation. He'd done it before with some overly enthusiastic admirers. Okay, so having him around wasn't all bad, but she did take self-defense classes and knew how to protect herself.

"You'll have to go around. The lady does not want to be disturbed." There was no waver in Berto's voice.

"I'd like to speak to the lady."

"That's not happening."

Annabelle couldn't see Berto's face, but she could imagine his dark frown. He didn't like anyone messing with his orders and that included keeping strangers at a distance.

Annabelle's gaze moved to the stranger. She immediately recognized him. He was the man who'd rescued her purse from that thief. What was he doing here?

He was a tall man, taller than Berto, but not quite as bulky. The man's dark hair was short and wavy, just begging for someone to run their fingers through it. And those broad shoulders were just perfect to lean against during a slow dance.

He was certainly handsome enough to be a model. She could imagine him on the cover of a glossy magazine. He didn't appear threatening. Perhaps he was interested in her. What would it hurt to speak to him?

Annabelle slipped her phone in her pocket. "Berto, is that any way to treat a hero? Let him through."

There was a twitch of a muscle in Berto's jaw, letting her know he wasn't comfortable with her decision. If it were up to him, her father or even the king, she'd never have a social life. It was getting old. And if this man was bold enough to stand up to Berto, she was intrigued.

Without another word, Berto stepped aside.

The man approached her table. He didn't smile at her. She couldn't blame him. Berto could put people on edge.

"I'm sorry about Berto. He can be overprotective. I'd like to thank you again. You're my hero—"

"Stop saying that. I'm no one's hero."

"But you stopped that thief and without you, I probably

wouldn't have gotten my purse back." Or more importantly, the journal.

"I was just in the right place at the right time. That doesn't make me anything special."

"Well, don't argue with me. It's all over social media." She withdrew her phone. She pulled up the feed with all of the posts that included photos of this man holding her purse, but his head was lowered, shielding his face.

She noticed how the muscles of his jaw tensed. He took modesty to a whole new level. What was up with that? She was definitely intrigued by this man.

"I'm guessing you didn't track me down to claim a reward."

The man in a pair of navy dress shorts and a white polo shirt lowered himself into a seat across the table from her. "You don't recognize me, do you?"

Was this man for real? "Of course I do."

He shook his head. "I meant, do you know my name?"

She was definitely missing something here, but what? "I take it you know me."

"Of course. You are Lady Annabelle DiSalvo, daughter of the Duke of Halencia and niece of the king. Also, you are in charge of the South Shore Project."

If he was hoping to impress her, he'd succeeded. Now, she had no choice but to ask. "And your name would be?"

"Grayson Landers."

Wait. What? He was the genius multimillionaire?

Surely she couldn't have heard him correctly. He removed his sunglasses and it all came together. Those striking cerulean blue eyes were unforgettable—even from an online photo. At the time, she'd thought they'd been Photoshopped. They hadn't been. His piercing eyes were just as striking in person—maybe even more so.

Somehow, someway she'd missed a voice mail or an email because the last she knew she was supposed to be meeting Mary. She swallowed hard. She should be happy about this change of events, but her stomach was aflutter with nerves. She resisted the urge to run a hand over her hair, wishing that she'd taken the time to freshen up before this meeting.

"Mr. Landers, it's so nice to meet you." She stretched her hand across the table.

His handshake was firm but brief. She had no idea if that was a bad sign or not.

"I, uh, wasn't expecting you."

"I know. You were expecting Mary, but my plans changed at the last minute, making it possible for me to attend this meeting."

"I see. I… I mean that's great." She sent him a smile, hoping to lighten the mood.

There was just something about this man that made her nervous, which was odd. Considering who her uncle and her father were, she was used to being around powerful men.

But most of the men in her life wore their power like they wore their suits. It was out there for people to see, maybe not flaunting it, but they certainly didn't waste their time trying to hide who and what they were. But this man, he looked like an American tourist, not a man who could buy a small country. And that beard and mustache hadn't been in any of the photos online.

His brows rose. "Is there something wrong with my appearance?"

Drat. She'd let her gaze linger too long. "No. No. Not at all. In fact, you look quite comfortable."

Her words did nothing to smooth the frown lines marring his handsome face. "Do I need to change for today's meeting?"

"Um, not at all." She jumped to her feet. "Shall we go?"

He didn't say anything at first. And then he returned his sunglasses to the bridge of his nose as he got to his feet. There was something disconcerting about not being able to look into his eyes when they spoke.

The sooner she got this presentation under way, the sooner it'd be over. "Would you like a tour of the South Shore?"

"Yes."

Short and to the point. She wondered if he was always so reserved. She started to walk, thinking about where she should begin. Of course, she'd given this tour a number of times before to other potential business owners, but somehow it all felt different where Mr. Landers was concerned. Everything about him felt different.

Annabelle straightened her shoulders as she turned to the small piazza where an historic fountain adorned the center. "I thought we would start the tour here. The South Shore is a historic neighborhood."

"I see that. Which makes me wonder why you think one of my cafés would fit in?"

"This area has had its better days." She'd hoped her presentation would make the answer to his question evident, but she hadn't even started yet. She laced her fingers together and turned to him. "Where buildings had once been left for nature to reduce them to rubble, there is now a growing and thriving community."

"That's nice, but you haven't answered my question."

She moved closer to the ancient fountain where four cherubs in short togas held up a basin while water spouts from the edge of the fountain shot into the basin. At night, spotlights lit up the fountain, capturing the droplets of water and making them twinkle like diamonds. Too bad she couldn't show him. It was a beautiful sight.

"If you will give me a chance, I'm getting to it."

He nodded. "Proceed."

She turned to the fountain. "This is as old as the South Shore. The famous sculptor Michele Vincenzo Valentini created it. It is said that he visited Mirraccino and fell in love with the island. Wanting to put his mark upon the land he loved, he sculpted this fountain as a gift to its people. The sad thing is that not long after the project was completed, he passed on."

"Interesting." Grayson glanced over his shoulder at Berto. "Will he be coming with us?"

"Yes." Without any explanation about Berto's presence, Annabelle moved toward one of her favorite shops lining the piazza, the bakery. She inhaled deeply. The aroma of fresh-baked rolls and cinnamon greeted her, making her mouth water. Perhaps they should go inside for a sampling. Surely something so delicious that melts in your mouth would put a smile on her companion's handsome face.

"This bakery is another place that's been around for years. In fact, this family bakery has been handed down through the generations. And let me tell you, their baked goods can't be surpassed. Would you care to go inside?"

He didn't say anything at first and she was starting to wonder if he'd even heard her. And then he said, "If that's what you'd like."

Not exactly the ringing endorsement that she'd been hoping for, but it was good enough. And the only excuse she needed to latch on to one of those cinnamon rolls. She yanked open the door and stepped inside. The sweet, mouth-watering aromas wrapped around her, making her stomach rumble with approval. It was only then she realized that due to her flight delay not only had she missed an opportunity to freshen up but she'd also missed her lunch.

After Grayson had enjoyed a cannoli and some black coffee and she'd savored chocolate-and-pistachio biscotti with her latte, they continued the tour. They took in the new senior facility that was housed in a fully refurbished and modernized historic mansion. They walked along the waterfront and visited many of the shops and businesses where Annabelle was friends with most everyone.

"This place must be very special to you," Grayson said.

At last, he was finally starting to loosen up around her. She knew fresh pastries and caffeine could win over just about everyone. "Sure. I've been working on the project for two years now. It's given me a purpose in life that I hadn't realized before."

"A purpose?"

She nodded. "I like helping people. I know from the outside it might seem like I'm doing the crown's bidding, but it's a lot more than that. I've been able to help people find new homes here in the South Shore. We created that new seniors' residence. Wasn't that seashore mural in the ballroom stunning?"

"Yes. It was quite remarkable. And it's very impressive how you've taken on this project and found a deeper meaning in it than just selling parcels of land. But I meant you personally—you seem to have a strong link to this place. When you talk about it, your face lights up."

"It does?" Was this his way of flirting with her? If so, she liked it.

"Did you spend a lot of time here as a child? The way you describe everything is way more personal than any sales pitch I've ever heard. And trust me, I've heard a lot of them."

"Well, thank you, I think." She smiled at him, still not quite sure how to take him or the things that he said. "But I didn't spend much time here as a kid. I grew up in Halencia. It's a small island not too far from here." But he was right, this place did have a very familiar vibe to it. She'd noticed it before when she was working but had brushed off the sensation. "My mother grew up here. When she talked about her homeland, it always seemed as though she regretted having to leave here. But as for me, until recently, I only came here for the occasional visit."

"Really? Hmm… I must have been mistaken."

"I think it must just be from me working so closely on this project."

"Of course. Mirraccino seems like it would be a great place for a young family. And that fountain, I can imagine kids wanting to make wishes there. And that bakery, it was fantastic…"

Grayson's voice faded into the background as Annabelle latched on to a fuzzy memory of her mother. They'd been here, in this very piazza the day before her mother was murdered. The memory was so vague that she was having a hard time focusing on it. But she did recall her mother had been upset. She definitely hadn't been her usual happy, smiling self.

"Annabelle? Are you okay?"

Grayson's voice jarred her back to reality. Heat rushed up her neck and settled in her cheeks. She was embarrassed that in the middle of this very important meeting she'd zoned out and gotten lost in her memories. "I'm sorry. What did you say?"

"I can see something is bothering you." He led her over to one of the benches surrounding the fountain and they sat down. "I know we barely know each other, but maybe that's a good thing. Sometimes I find it easier to talk to a stranger about my troubles."

What did she say? That she had some vague flashback? And why did she have it? What did it even mean?

It was best to deflect the question. "What troubles do you have?"

He glanced away. "We…um, aren't talking about me right now. You're the one who looked as though you saw a ghost."

So he did have a skeleton or two in his closet. Was it bad that she took some sort of strange comfort in knowing that he wasn't as perfect as she imagined him to be, not that she'd done any digging into his past. When she'd done her research on Fo Shizzle, she'd been more interested in his company's financial history and their projections for the future—all of which consisted of glowing reports.

"Annabelle?"

"Okay. It's not that big of a deal. I was just remembering being here with my mother."

His brows drew together. "I don't understand. Why would that upset you?"

She'd told him this much; she might as well tell him the rest. After all, it wasn't like the memory was any big deal. "It's just that the memory is from a long time ago and it's vague. I remember that day my mother wasn't acting like herself. She was quiet and short-tempered. Quite unlike her."

"Was your father with you?"

Annabelle shook her head. "I don't know where he was. I'm assuming back home in Halencia with my brother."

"You have a brother?"

She nodded. "He's six years older than me. But what I don't get is why I'd forgotten this."

"It's natural to forget things that don't seem important at the time. Do you think the memory is important now?"

"I have no idea."

"Why not just ask your mother about it?"

"I can't." Though Annabelle wished with all of her heart that she could speak with her mother.

"You don't get along with her?"

In barely more than a whisper, Annabelle said, "She died."

"Oh. Sorry. If you don't mind me asking, how old were you at the time?"

"I was thirteen. So I wasn't really paying my mother a whole lot of attention."

"I remember what it was like to be a kid. Although I spent most of my time holed up in my bedroom, messing around on my computer."

"So that's how you became so successful. You worked toward it your whole life."

He leaned back on the bench and stretched his legs out in front of him. "I never set out to be a success. I was just having fun. I guess you could say I stumbled into success."

"From what I've read, you learned to do quite a bit as far as computers are concerned."

"Coding is like a puzzle for me. I just have to find the

right connections to make the programs do what I want." He glanced at her. "It's similar to the way you have snippets of a memory of your mother. You need to find the missing parts for the snippets to fit together and give you a whole picture."

Annabelle shrugged and glanced away. "I'm sure the memory isn't important."

"Perhaps. Or maybe it is and that's why you've started to remember it."

"It's not worth dwelling on." Who was she kidding? This was probably all she'd think of tonight when she was supposed to be sleeping. Was there some hidden significance to the memory?

Just then she recalled her mother raising her voice. Her mother never shouted. Born a princess, her mother prided herself in always using her manners.

"You remembered something else."

Annabelle's gaze met his. "How do you do that?"

"What?"

"Read my mind."

"Because it's written all over your face. And just now, you went suddenly pale. I take it whatever you recalled wasn't good."

"I'm not sure."

"Maybe it would help if you remembered a little more. Perhaps it's not as bad as you're thinking."

"Or maybe it's worse." She pressed her lips together. She hadn't meant to utter those words, but the little voice in her head was warning her to tread lightly.

"Close your eyes," Grayson said in a gentle tone.

"What?"

"Trust me."

"How can I trust you when I hardly even know you?"

"You have a point. But think of it this way, we're out here in the open and your bodyguard is not more than twenty feet away. If that isn't enough security, there are people passing by and people in the nearby shops. All you have to do is call out and they'll come running."

"Okay. I get the point."

"So do it."

She crossed her arms and then closed her eyes, not sure what good this was going to do.

"Relax. This won't work otherwise."

She opened her eyes. "You sound like you know what you're doing. Are you some kind of therapist or something?"

"No. But I've been through this process before."

"You mean to retrieve fragmented memories?"

"Something like that. Now close your eyes again." When she complied, he said, "Recall that memory of your mother. Do you have it?"

Annabelle nodded. All that she could see was the frown marring her mother's flawless complexion and the worry reflected in her eyes.

"Now, was it sunny out?"

What kind of question was that? Who cared about the weather? "How would I know?"

"Relax. Let the memories come back to you. Do you recall perhaps the smell of the bakery?"

"I've heard it said that smell is one of the strongest senses—"

"Annabelle, you're supposed to be focusing."

And she was dodging the memories, but why? Was there something there that she was afraid to recall?

She took a deep breath and blew it out. She tried to focus on any detail that she could summon. Together they sat there for countless minutes as she rummaged through the cobwebs in her mind. Grayson was surprisingly patient as he prompted her from time to time with a somewhat innocuous question. These questions weren't about her mother but rather about sensory details—she recalled the scent of cinnamon and how her mother had bought her a cinnamon roll. The sun had been shining and it had taken the chill out of the air, which meant that it was morning.

"And I remember, my mother said she had to speak to someone. She told me to wait on a bench like this one and she would be right back."

"She left you alone?" There was surprise in his voice.

"No. She stayed here in the piazza, but she moved out of hearing range. There was a man that she met."

"Someone you know?"

"I'm not sure. I never saw his face. I just know their conversation was short and he left immediately after they spoke."

"What did your mother say to you?"

Annabelle opened her eyes. "I don't know anymore. I don't think she said much of anything, which was unusual for her. She was always good at making casual conversation. I guess that's something you learn when you're born into royalty—the art of talking about absolutely nothing of relevance."

"At least nothing bad happened."

"Thanks for helping me to remember."

"I wonder what it was about that day that the memory stuck in your mind."

"I'm not sure."

The truth was, it happened a day or two before her mother died. Could it mean something? Had the police been wrong? Was her mother's death more than a mugging? Or was she just letting herself get caught up in her father's suspicions?

Annabelle didn't want to get into details of the murder with Grayson. As it was, she'd exposed more of herself to this stranger than she'd ever intended. It would be best to stop things right here.

CHAPTER THREE

G<small>RAYSON HAD RESERVATIONS.</small>

The site for Fo Shizzle was not what he'd been envisioning.

Sure, what he'd seen so far of Mirraccino was beautiful. Maybe not as striking as Annabelle, but it definitely came in a close second. The South Shore was a mix of history and modernization. The view of the blue waters of the Mediterranean was stunning. But it just didn't seem like the right fit for one of his Fo Shizzle Cafés.

"So what did you think?" Annabelle's voice drew him from his thoughts.

"I think you've done a commendable job with this revitalization project. I think it's going to be a huge success." Now how did he word this so as not to hurt her feelings? After all, she'd been a wonderful hostess. And to be honest, he didn't want this to end. This was the most relaxed he'd felt in more than a year…ever since the accident and the ensuing scandal.

"But…?"

"What?" He'd let his mind wonder and hadn't heard what she'd been saying.

"You like the South Shore, however I detect there's a but coming. So out with it. What isn't working for you?"

He paused, struggling to find the right words. "I was under the impression that the site of the café would be in the heart of the city. This area is nothing like the locations of the other cafés. The way the South Shore was described in the proposal was that it was an up-and-coming area. This," he outstretched his arms at the varying shops, "is very reserved. It's an area that would be frequented by a more mature clientele."

"We are in the process of revitalizing the area—the proposal was a projection. I was certain if I could get a representative of Fo Shizzle here that they would see the potential.

I'm sure your café will be a huge draw. I've spoken with the tourism department and they can insert photos and captions prominently in their promo."

His brow arched. He had not expected this bit of news. He couldn't deny that free advertising would help, but would it be enough? "The thing is, my cafés are designed for younger people, high school, college and young adults. The cafés do not cater to a more mature audience. They can be a bit loud at times, especially during an online tournament. The decor is a bit dark with prints of our most popular avatars. Do you know much about our games?"

She shook her head. "Since you can only play on a closed circuit within one of your cafés, I've never had the opportunity. But the research looks intriguing. And I think it would be a hit here with the young crowd."

"To be a success, this area would have to be heavily frequented by young people—"

"And that's what we want." She smiled at him as though she had all of the answers. "I have research studies broken out by demographic."

He liked numbers and charts. "Could I take a look at them?"

She nodded. "Most definitely. I had a copy in my purse, but I also have them at the palace along with an investment package with detailed figures and projections. I wanted you to have a feel for the area before we dove into the numbers."

He glanced around the piazza. "I'm just not sure about this setting. Don't get me wrong—it's beautiful, but it's not quite as urban as our other locations."

"In the reviews I've read about Fo Shizzle, they say young people come from miles away just to hang out and take part in the high-stakes gaming tournaments. You've definitely latched on to a great idea. And I hear the coffee's not so bad either."

"The coffee is actually quite good." He'd made sure of that. Being a coder, he lived on a steady stream of caffeine when he was on a roll. And he was picky about the flavor. He wouldn't have anything less than the best for his cafés—just as he would only have the top-of-the-line games. The newest titles. And the best quality.

Annabelle gave him a speculative look as though figuring out his unshaven appearance and his longer-than-usual hair. It was not his standard appearance—not unless he was on a deadline for a new program rollout. When it came to business, all else came in a distant second, third or lower ranking.

When she didn't vocalize her thoughts about his appearance, he added, "I'm usually a little more cleaned up." Why was he making excuses for his appearance? It wasn't like he was going to ask her out on a date or anything. Still, he heard himself say, "It's just with the media and all, sometimes it's easier to travel incognito."

She nodded but still didn't say anything.

He hated to admit it, but he really did want to know what she was thinking. Did he really look that bad? His hand moved to his jaw. His fingers stroked his beard. It was quickly filling in. Soon it would start to get bushy. He didn't warm to the thought.

Beards were okay on some guys, but not him. It just wasn't his thing. "Is it really that bad?"

She shrugged. "It's okay."

Definitely not a ringing endorsement for his new look.

"I guess it doesn't matter much if I shave or not now that my picture is all over social media. And it's not like I'm going to be here much longer—"

"What? You mean you're leaving? Already?"

He nodded. "I have to keep scouting for a headquarters for my Mediterranean expansion."

"But this is it. The South Shore will be perfect."

Was that a glimmer of worry reflected in her eyes? Surely she couldn't be that invested in doing business with him. And if she was, he had to ask himself why. What was driving her to close this deal?

He cleared his throat. "I'm not ready to make a decision of this magnitude. I have plans to visit Rome, Milan and Athens next."

"And when will you be leaving?"

"In the morning—"

"But you can't." She pressed her lips together as though regretting the outburst.

"Why not?"

"Because you still have to file a report with the police. There's the theft and…and you're an eyewitness. They'll probably want you to testify."

She had a point. And as much as he would like to fly off into the sunset, he wouldn't shirk his duty. "You know, the only reason I walked away is because you said you weren't going to press charges so I figured there was no reason for me to stick around."

"I was truly considering it, but the policeman convinced me it wouldn't be in anyone's best interest. So it looks like you'll be hanging around Mirraccino a bit longer. And I would love to show you more of this beautiful land."

How much more was there to see? And did she really think another day of playing tourist was really going to change his mind?

"I don't know." He glanced at his wristwatch. It was getting late. "Maybe I could swing by the police station now and give them my statement."

"It's Friday. And it's late in the afternoon. I'm sure the people you'll need to speak with will be gone for the weekend or at least have one foot out the door."

"Can't I just give my statement to an officer? Surely the whole police force doesn't go home early for the weekend."

Annabelle smiled. "Funny. But I meant you'll probably have to speak with some of the clerical or legal people."

He nodded. "I suppose they might do things a bit differently from what I'm accustomed to in the States."

Annabelle nodded. "Now let's see about getting you situated."

"I have a room at the hotel in the city."

"I was thinking of something different. How about being a guest at the royal palace?"

Had he heard her correctly? She was inviting him to stay in the palace with the king? "Are you serious?"

"Of course I'm serious. The king is my uncle."

"And you live there—at the palace, that is?"

"At the moment, I do. I've been living there while working in Mirraccino for the past couple of years."

There was a lot about Lady Annabelle that intrigued him. And honestly, what would it hurt if he took a few more days before moving on?

Annabelle was the first person to interest him in a long time—just not romantically. It wasn't that he didn't find her exceedingly attractive. He did. But he refused to get sucked into another relationship. He'd been through enough. His heart was still mending.

"Oh, please say that you'll stay. I've already had a suite made up for you. And…and the King is expecting you at dinner tonight."

"The king wants to meet me?"

Her cheeks bloomed with color and her gaze didn't quite meet his as she nodded.

He suspected she was just saying anything to get him to stay. He had to admit no one had ever dangled an invitation to meet a king before him in order to help with a business deal. What made this amazing woman feel as though she had to jump to such lengths to get him to close this deal?

"Tell the truth," he said. "The king, he isn't expecting me at dinner, is he?"

Her gaze finally met his. "No, but I'm sure it won't be a problem. The suite truly is prepared and awaiting your arrival, as well as the financial projections. We can go over them together if you like."

He couldn't help but smile at the eagerness reflected on her face. "You know, I've never stayed in a palace before." When her eyes widened and her glossy lips lifted into a smile, he said, "We'll just need to pick up my luggage at the hotel and then I'd very much enjoy staying with you—erm, staying at the palace."

A visit to a royal palace, what could possibly go wrong?

Security would be heavy and the paparazzi would be non-existent. It would be a win-win.

But who would keep him from getting lost in Lady Annabelle's brown eyes?

At last, Annabelle got through on the phone to the police department.

And without playing the royal card, she was able to speak with someone in authority. They told her to stop by in the morning and they'd see about getting some of her possessions back to her. She wasn't sure what *some* consisted of, but it was a start.

"Everything okay?" Grayson asked.

She nodded. "They'd like you to stop by tomorrow and give them a statement."

He didn't say anything as he turned to stare out the window as they approached the palace gates. She chose to take his silence as a good sign, but she couldn't help but worry just a bit about the impression he'd gotten of Mirraccino. She could only hope the financial projections packet she'd put together would outweigh everything else.

Annabelle sat in the back of her sedan with Grayson as Berto ushered them past the security gates and onto the royal grounds. Annabelle had to admit that after living here for the past couple of years she'd begun to take the palace's beauty for granted.

She turned to Grayson to find him staring out the window. He seemed to be taking in the manicured lawns, the towering palm trees and the red-and-white border of flowers lining the long and winding drive.

"This place is remarkable." Grayson said, drawing her from her thoughts. "We have nothing like this where I come from."

"You're from California, right?"

He nodded, but he never took his gaze off the colorful scenery. "I couldn't even imagine what it must be like to live here."

"You get used to it." As strange as that might sound, this big place felt like home to her. "Is this your first visit to Mirraccino?"

"Yes." He still didn't look at her.

The turrets of the palace were first to come into view. They were colorful with stripes of yellow, pink, aqua and gold. Annabelle found herself looking at them through new eyes.

And then the palace in its entirety loomed. It was enormous, even compared to her family's spacious mansion back in Halencia. While her home in Halencia was all white, the palace was created in warm shades of tan and coral with some accents done in aqua. It was simple and yet stunning.

And with the afternoon sun's rays, the palace practically gleamed. When she was a little girl, she'd thought the palace was magical. She'd always wanted to be a princess, but her mother assured her that she didn't need to be a princess to be special.

Being the daughter of the Duke of Halencia, she was addressed as Lady Annabelle. It gave her recognition in high society but not much else. Her father's estate would eventually revert to her older brother, the Earl of Halencia. She used to think it was unfair, but now she appreciated having choices in life.

The car pulled to a stop outside the palace. Berto rushed to get the car door. Annabelle alighted from the car followed by Grayson.

Grayson turned to her. "Why is the South Shore so important to you that you'd go out of your way for me?"

She schooled her features, trying to hide any hint of her desperation. "The South Shore was a pet project of the crown prince. He brought me in on the project at the beginning. When his responsibilities drew him away, I promised to see that it was finished."

"So you're keeping a promise to the prince?" Grayson arched a brow.

"He's my friend as well as my cousin," she was quick to clarify.

"That's right. You did mention the king was your uncle. So this is a family favor of sorts?"

"Yes. You could put it that way." If that's what he wanted to believe, who was she to change his mind? Because in the beginning that's all it had been. Now it was her way to prove herself to her father. "But in the process, I've really come to care about the people of the South Shore and I want to see it flourish."

He smiled at her, making her stomach quiver with the sensation of butterflies. "In that case, lead the way."

She didn't normally enter through the main door, but Grayson was a special guest—pivotal to her future. It wouldn't hurt to give him the VIP treatment.

Berto swung open the enormous wooden door with the large brass handle. They stepped inside the palace and once again she consciously surveyed her surroundings from the marble floor of the grand entryway to the high ceiling with the crystal chandelier suspended in the center. As a little girl, when there was a royal ball, she'd sneak down here and dance around the table in the center of the floor. She'd pretend that she truly was a princess attending the ball. Oh, the silly things kids did.

Grayson took in the opulent room. "I couldn't even imagine what it must be like to live here."

She shrugged. "It has its protocols and a system that it's

best not to tamper with, but other than that I imagine it's like most other homes."

Grayson laughed. "I don't think so."

Just then, Alfred, the butler, came rushing into the room. "Lady Annabelle, I'm sorry. I didn't hear you arrive."

"No problem. I was just showing Mr. Landers around."

The butler gave her guest a discerning once-over. "Yes, ma'am. Is there anything I can do for you?"

"No, thanks. I was just going to show Mr. Landers to his suite of rooms so he can freshen up. Could you let the kitchen know that there will be one more for dinner?"

"Yes, ma'am. Shall I inform the king?"

Normally, she would say yes, but seeing as Grayson was a special guest who could make such a difference to her future, she said, "I'll speak to my uncle. Thank you."

Annabelle showed Grayson to the sweeping steps to the upstairs. A comfortable silence engulfed them as Grayson continued to take in his surroundings. She had to admit the palace was a lot more like a museum than a home. There were so many priceless works of art and gifts from other nations.

But more than anything, she wondered what thoughts were going through Grayson's mind. There was so much she wanted to know about him. As her uncle said often, knowledge was power. And she needed the power to push through this business deal.

She tried to tell herself that was the only reason she wanted to know more about Grayson. After all, it had nothing to do with his good looks or the way he was able to connect with her back at the piazza.

No. It was none of those things. It was purely business.

CHAPTER FOUR

Okay. So maybe this isn't so bad.

A vacation in a Mediterranean palace.

In fact, the palace is the perfect inspiration for a new game for Fo Shizzle.

Grayson sat in the formal dining room at a very large table. Did they really eat here every day? He might be rich, but he'd come from a humble beginning. He didn't stand on airs and most of the time his dinner was eaten alone in front of his desktop computer.

Meeting the king had been a great honor. Thankfully Annabelle had instructed him on the proper protocol while they were in the car. He wondered how he should have greeted her considering she was the daughter of a duke. He'd hazard a guess it wasn't to argue about what to do with her purse after the theft.

And try as he might, he couldn't help but like Annabelle. Not that he would let her sunny smiles get to him. He'd learned his lesson about love, especially about loving someone in the spotlight. And Annabelle, with her constant bodyguard, was definitely someone who was used to living in the spotlight—a place where he felt uncomfortable.

"Mr. Landers, you picked an optimal time to visit Mirraccino," the king said as their dinner dishes were cleared from the table.

How exactly did one make small talk with a king? Grayson swallowed hard. "Please call me Grayson." When the man nodded, Grayson continued. "If you don't mind me asking, why is this an optimal time?"

The king turned to Annabelle. "You didn't tell him about the heritage festival?"

"It slipped my mind." Color rushed to her cheeks. "I mean, there was so much going on this afternoon. I apologize. You are most definitely welcome to stay and partake in the festivities."

"No apology is necessary." Grayson could understand that the theft had shaken her up.

"Annabelle," the king said, "you need to slow down. I think you're becoming a workaholic."

Feeling bad for Annabelle, Grayson intervened. "I'd love to hear more about this heritage festival."

The king leaned back in his chair as the wait staff supplied them with coffee and a dessert plate of finger foods. "The heritage festival is an annual event. It's held in Portolina, which is a small village within walking distance of the palace. The villagers get together—actually people from all over the nation make the pilgrimage to Portolina for the four-day celebration."

Grayson took a sip of his coffee and then gently set it back on the fine china saucer which had tiny blue flowers around the edge. He didn't think he'd ever used such delicate dishes. With his big hands, he was afraid of touching such fragile items. He had no doubt that they were antiques. And he didn't even want to imagine their value. He might be wealthy, but there was a vast difference between his wealth and that of the king.

Grayson pulled his dessert plate closer. "I actually don't know if I'll be here that long."

The king picked up a mini pecan tart. "You really don't want to miss the event. Maybe you could extend your vacation. You would be my guest, here at the palace."

"Thank you, sir. I… I'll see if I can adjust my schedule."

"Good. You'll enjoy all of the activities." The king acted as though Grayson had said yes. The king added some sugar to his coffee and stirred. "You are here to determine if the South Shore is appropriate for your business. I hope you found it as beautiful as we do."

"I did, sir." That was certainly not one of the reasons he was hesitant to put in one of his cafés. But he really didn't want to get into the details with the king. "I'd like a chance to check into a few more locations before I commit my company. And as soon as this situation with Annabelle and the police is wrapped up—"

"Police?" The king sat up straight. A distinct frown marred his face as he turned to his niece. "Why is this the first I'm hearing of an incident with the police?"

Color flooded Annabelle's face. "It's not a big deal."

"I'll be the judge of that." The king turned back to Grayson. "What exactly happened?"

"Uncle, I'll explain." Annabelle sent Grayson a warning look. "There's no need to drag Grayson into this."

"It appears he's already a part of it. He at least knows what happened, which is more than I do." The King turned back to him and gestured for Grayson to spill the details.

Grayson swallowed hard. "It really isn't that big of a deal."

"If it involves my niece, it's a very big deal."

Grayson glanced down at the small plate filled with sweets. He suddenly lost his appetite. He launched into the details of his first meeting with Annabelle. He tried to downplay the events, realizing how much the king worried about her. And Grayson knew what happened when a high-profile person didn't heed safety protocols.

When Grayson finished reciting the events as best as he could recall them, the king gestured for the phone. He announced that he was going to speak with the police.

"Uncle, I have everything under control."

The man sent her a pointed look. "It doesn't sound like it. You don't have your purse and you don't know what's going to happen to that thief." He shook his head as he accepted the phone that had already been dialed for him. "What is this world coming to when you can't even walk down the street without being accosted?"

"Uncle, it was nothing. I don't know who is worse. You, or my father?"

"We just want you to be safe." The king pressed the phone to his ear and began talking.

Grayson found the whole dynamic between these two quite interesting. They were comfortable enough with each other even though they were in opposition. Annabelle was noticeably seething under all of the fuss, but she restrained her emotions. And her uncle looked worried. These two obviously loved each other deeply.

The king didn't say much during the phone conversation. It seemed as if he was getting a blow-by-blow explanation of the chain of events. Grayson glanced at Annabelle, who looked miserable. He was sorry that he'd opened his mouth. He had thought the king would have been informed. After all, Annabelle was his niece.

"There. That's resolved," the king said as he disconnected the call. "You and Grayson are to go to the police station tomorrow morning. They will be expecting you. Grayson needs to give his statement, as do you. As for your belongings, they should be able to give you your wallet but the rest is evidence."

"I know," Annabelle said.

The king's eyes widened. "What do you mean, you know?"

"I'd already called and made arrangements to go to the station in the morning."

For a moment her uncle didn't say a word and neither did anyone else.

Finally, the king got to his feet. "Now, if you'll excuse me. I am needed elsewhere."

Grayson didn't know whether to stand or remain seated. When Annabelle stood, he followed her lead. They didn't sit back down until the king was out of sight. Once seated again, Grayson took a sip of coffee and waited until Annabelle was ready to speak.

"I'm sorry about that," she said while staring at her coffee cup.

"It's no big deal."

"But you didn't come here to witness some family drama."

"It's okay. I understand." Grayson didn't. Not really. His parents lived in rural Ohio and were so caught up in their own lives that they never gave him a second thought. He didn't know what it was like to have your every move under a microscope. He imagined that it would be quite oppressive.

"No, you don't," Annabelle said wearily. "My life…it's complicated."

If he were smart, he'd get to his feet and head for his suite. They'd done enough sharing for one day, but he couldn't turn his back on her. She obviously needed someone to lend her an ear.

He cleared his throat while searching for some words of comfort. "Everyone's life is complicated. It's how you get through it all that matters."

She arched a fine brow. "Even yours?"

He nodded. "Even mine."

"But you're rich and you run your own company. You don't have people telling you what to do and thinking they know better. You get to call all of the shots."

Grayson laughed. "If that's what you think, then you've got it all wrong. My name may be on the company letterhead, but I have a board and shareholders to answer to. A lot of those shareholders think they have all of the answers, even though they are far removed from our target clientele and know nothing about our product and its design."

"Oh. I didn't realize." She paused as though letting this information sink in. "But you only have to deal with it as far as your business is concerned. At least, they aren't involved in your personal life."

Grayson rubbed the back of his neck. Now she was heading into exceedingly uncomfortable territory. Time for a change of subjects. "Should we go to the police station together in the morning?"

"After what happened with my uncle, I didn't think you'd want anything to do with me."

"Seriously? That was nothing. Trust me, my father ruined more dinners than I could ever count. What your uncle did was just his way of showing that he cares about you and is worried about your safety."

Her eyes widened with surprise. "You really believe that? Or are you just trying to make me feel better?"

He wasn't going to feed her a line. Other people had done that to him and he knew it wasn't helpful. "How about a little of both?"

A small smile pulled at her lips. "Thanks for being honest. I really appreciate it."

"You're welcome."

She studied him for a moment, making him a little uncomfortable.

"Do I have something on my mouth?" When she shook her head, he asked, "My nose? My chin?" She continued to shake her head but a smile had started to lift her lips. "Then what is it?"

"You look tired. Is it jet lag?"

"Actually, it is. I can't sleep on planes." He always envied those people who could snooze after takeoff and wake up at landing.

Annabelle got to her feet. "Why don't we call it an evening?"

"But the financials?"

"Can wait until tomorrow." She started for the door and he followed.

It wasn't until she paused outside his room that he realized she hadn't answered his question. "About the police station—"

"Oh, yes. We can go together. Is first thing in the morning all right?"

"It's fine with me. Just ignore the jet lag."

Then hesitantly she asked, "Will it be a problem if my bodyguard accompanies us?"

"Not a problem at all." A question came to his mind although he wasn't sure if he should ask, but seeing as they were starting to open up to each other, he decided to go with it. "Are you always under protection?"

"Yes. Ever since my mother was murdered."

"Murdered?"

Annabelle averted her gaze and nodded. It was obviously still painful for her. He couldn't even imagine the pain she'd been living with.

Grayson cleared his throat. "I'm sorry."

Her gaze finally met his. "Thank you."

"Your father, he thinks the person is going to come after you? After all of this time?"

"I don't know what he thinks. The official report says that she died during a mugging. My father doesn't believe it, but he has no proof of anything to the contrary. And it isn't just me that my father has a protective detail on. It's my brother too. But Luca doesn't let it bother him. He still keeps up with his globe-trotting, partying ways. Maybe that's his way of dealing with everything. I don't know. We've grown apart over the years."

"I take it you don't believe your father's suspicions?"

"Quite honestly, today is the first time he's shared this information with me. And I don't know what to make of it."

"So your brother doesn't know?"

She shook her head. "I wouldn't even know what to tell him."

The look in her eyes told Grayson this was all very troubling for her. It was best to change the subject. "I always wanted a brother or sister, but fate had other ideas. And now looking back on things, I guess it was for the best. They were spared."

"Your home life was that bad?" She pressed her lips together as though realizing she was being nosey. "Sorry. I shouldn't have asked."

"It's okay. I started this conversation. As for my family, we saw things differently. My father grew up working with his hands, tilling the ground and planting seeds. I was never interested in that sort of life and it infuriated him. He thought I should do the same as he'd done and follow in the family tradition of farming." Grayson shifted his weight from one foot to the other. "Let's just say those discussions became heated."

"And your mother?"

"She always sided with my father. They were always so worried about what I should be doing with my life that they never stopped and asked what I wanted to do with it."

"I'm sorry. That's tough. But somehow you overcame it all and made yourself into a success."

"Trust me. It wasn't easy. And I wouldn't want to do it again."

"Do you still speak with your parents?"

"I haven't seen them in years. When I walked out, my father told me that if I left I would never be welcome again. I guess he meant it because I've never heard from them."

"That's so sad."

"The reason I told you that is because I don't want to see the same thing happen with you and your family."

"But this is different—"

"Not that much. You are struggling for your freedom and they are struggling to keep you safe. You can't both have your own way. Someone is going to win this struggle and someone is going to lose. The key is not to destroy your relationship in the process."

"You sound so wise for someone so young."

"I don't know about that. Maybe I just wish someone had given me some advice along the way instead of me always having to learn things the hard way."

"Well, don't worry. Things are about to change." She

pressed her lips together and glanced away as though she'd just realized she'd said too much.

"Ah, you have a plan."

"It's nothing. I should be going. I've forgotten to give the king a message from my father." And with that she rushed off down the hallway.

Grayson watched her go. He couldn't help but wonder about this plan of hers and if it was going to get her into trouble. It was obvious that she wasn't ready to share the details with him. But that didn't keep him from worrying about this *plan*. His mind told him it was absolutely none of his business, but his gut told him that she might get herself into trouble trying to prove a point.

And he might have just met her, but he already realized she was stubborn. Stubborn enough not to ask for help? But what was he supposed to do about any of it?

CHAPTER FIVE

ALONE AT LAST.

The next morning, Annabelle hurried to her suite of rooms as soon as she'd returned from the police station. Grayson had stayed behind in Bellacitta to meet with a business associate. They'd agreed to meet up later to go over the financial projections for the South Shore Project.

She'd been relieved to have a little time to herself. At last, she'd recovered her mother's journal, and she had some privacy to look at it. And if she'd had any qualms about invading her mother's privacy, the police had remedied them. They had her open the journal and read just a bit to herself to verify it belonged to her. She didn't correct their assumption that it was her journal.

Alone in her room, Annabelle sat down at her desk in front of the window that overlooked the blue waters of the Mediterranean. And though usually she took solace in the majestic view, today her thoughts were elsewhere.

As the hours ticked by, she turned page after page. There were old snapshots stuffed between the pages. Some of her mother and father. Some of Annabelle and her brother. There was so much history crammed between the leather covers that it floored her.

And thankfully, there was nothing scandalous or cringeworthy within the pages. Not even anything blushworthy lurked in the passages, which was a gigantic relief to Annabelle. It was almost as if her mother had known that one day one of her children would be reading it.

Instead, the journal read more like the highlights of a royal's life. There were mentions of birthday celebrations, picnics, holidays and countless other events that Annabelle had either been too young to remember or hadn't bothered to really notice. But her mother had remembered and made note of colorful details that brought the passages to life. And it had been a nice life, not perfect, but the bad times were smoothed over and the good times highlighted. That's how she remembered her mother—always trying to fix things and make people smile.

Annabelle didn't even notice lunchtime coming or going. At some point, she moved from the desk chair to the comfort of her big canopied bed with its array of silken pillows. She couldn't remember the last time she'd curled up in bed with a book in the middle of the day. It felt so decadent. She continued devouring word after word, feeling closer to her mother than she'd felt in a very long time.

Knock. Knock.

Annabelle's gaze jerked to the door, expecting one of the household staff to enter with fresh flowers or clean linens. A frown pulled at her lips. She really didn't want to be disturbed. She still had a lot of pages to read.

Knock. Knock.

"Annabelle? Is everything okay?"

It was Grayson. And something told her he wasn't going to leave until they spoke. With a sigh, she closed the journal and set it off to the side of the bed. Hating to leave her comfy spot, she grudgingly got to her feet.

She moved to the door and then paused to run a hand over her hair. Deciding that it was good enough, she reached for the doorknob.

"Hi." She couldn't help but stare at his handsome face and piercing blue eyes. Now that he'd shaved, his looks were a perfect ten.

He frowned. "Why do you keep looking at me that way?"

"What way?" She averted her gaze. She was going to have to be more covert with her admiration in the future.

He sighed. "Never mind."

She stepped back, allowing him to enter the room. "Come in."

He stepped into her spacious suite and glanced around. She followed his gaze around the room, taking in the settee, the armchairs, a table with a bouquet of flowers and her desk. She noticed how his gaze lingered on the king-size bed.

At last, his gaze met hers. "You missed lunch?"

"Did we have plans?" She didn't recall any. In fact, Grayson had said he planned to remain in the city for most of the day.

"No, we didn't. But I wrapped up my meeting early and returned to the palace. I thought I would see you at lunch and when you didn't show up, I... I just wanted to make sure everything was all right."

"Oh, yes, everything is fine. I was reading." She gestured toward the now rumpled bed.

Grayson's gaze followed her hand gesture. "It looks like I must have startled you."

"What?"

He moved toward the bed where he knelt down and picked up the journal from the floor. But that wasn't the only thing on the floor. The precious pictures were scattered about.

"Oh, no." She rushed over.

"No worries. Nothing's ruined."

"You don't have to pick that up," Annabelle said, kneeling down next to him. "I can get it."

"I don't mind." He picked up a photograph and glanced at it. "Is this you as a child?"

She looked at the photo and a rush of memories came back to her. "Yes. That's me and my brother, Luca."

"You were a cute kid."

"Thanks. I think." Her stomach quivered as Grayson's gaze lingered longer than necessary. She swallowed hard. "I can't believe my mother kept all of those pictures stuffed in her journal."

"Ah...so that's your mother's. It explains why you're so protective of it. I thought you were going to jump across that desk at the police station when the officer said he couldn't release it to you."

Heat rushed up Annabelle's neck and settled in her cheeks

as she realized how that incident must have looked to others. But she'd been desperate to hang on to this link to her mother. And by reading the pages, she already felt as though she knew her mother so much better.

"Thanks for stepping up and reasoning with the officer," Annabelle said. "I just couldn't get him to understand my urgency."

"You're welcome."

"You know, you're not such a bad guy to have around."

His voice grew deep and gentle. "Is that your way of saying you'd like me to stay for the heritage festival?"

"Maybe." Did her voice sound as breathless to him as it did to her?

His head lifted and their gazes met. There was something different about the way he looked at her. And then it struck her with the force of an electrical surge—there was desire reflected in his gaze. He wanted her.

It was like a switch had been turned on and she was fully aware of the attraction arcing between them. Annabelle had never felt anything so vital and stirring with anyone else in her life. Maybe she'd led a more sheltered life than she'd ever imagined. Sure there had been other men, but those relationships had never had this sort of spark and soon they fizzled out.

With them kneeling down on the floor side by side, their faces were only mere inches apart. Did he have any idea what his close proximity did to her heart rate, not to mention her common sense?

His gaze dipped to her mouth and the breath hitched in her throat. Was he going to kiss her? And was it wrong that she wanted him to?

Not waiting for him to make up his mind, she leaned forward, pressing her lips to his. If this was too bold, she didn't care. She'd been cautious all of her life, while her brother had been reckless. If she wanted things to change, then *she* had to change them, by taking more chances.

His lips were smooth and warm. Yet, he was hesitant. His mouth didn't move against hers. Oh, no! Had she read everything wrong?

Her problem was her lack of experience. She hadn't gotten out enough. She didn't know how to read men. Here she'd been thinking that he desired her and the thought had probably never crossed his mind. She was such a fool.

She started to pull back when his hand reached up, cupping her cheek. Her heart jumped into her throat. Then again, maybe she had been right. As he deepened the kiss, her heart thump-thumped. He did want her. And she most definitely wanted him.

Her hands slid up over his muscled shoulders and wrapped around the back of his neck. All the while, his thumb stroked her cheek, sending the most delicious sensations to her very core, heating it up and melting it down.

She didn't know where this was headed and she didn't care. The only thing that mattered was the here and now. And the here and now was quite delicious. Quite addictive—

Footsteps echoed in the hallway. Annabelle recalled leaving the door wide open.

She yanked back. Grayson let her go. It was as though they both realized that what was happening here wasn't practical. They came from different worlds and worse yet, they were involved in a business deal. She couldn't lose her focus.

Annabelle averted her gaze as she ran a shaky hand over her now tender lips. How could she face him again after she'd initiated that kiss—that soul-stirring kiss?

She glanced down at the mess still on the floor. Focus on anything but how good that kiss had been. Annabelle began picking up the papers when there was a knock at the door. She glanced up. "Come in."

A member of her uncle's staff appeared, holding a tray of food. "Excuse me, ma'am. The king asked that this tray be brought to you since you missed lunch."

"Oh. Thank you." She forced a smile. "You can leave it on the desk."

"Yes, ma'am." The young woman deposited the heavily laden tray and then turned for the door.

The door snicked shut as Annabelle turned back to Grayson. He was picking up the last of the photos and papers. They were now sorted into two piles. One of snapshots and one of scraps of papers.

"I think I got it all," Grayson said but his gaze never quite met hers.

So he regretted what just happened between them. She couldn't blame him. She'd let the attraction she'd felt since she first met him get the better of her. Now, she had to somehow repair the damage if she had any hope of getting him to bring his state-of-the-art gaming café to Mirraccino. And it wasn't just the café Grayson would bring to the area, but it would also be the headquarters for the Mediterranean arm of his business—an employment opportunity that would help Mirraccino.

"I'm sorry." They both said in unison.

The combined apology broke the tension. They both smiled—genuine smiles. Maybe this situation wasn't beyond repair after all. A girl could hope, couldn't she?

"I shouldn't have kissed you," Annabelle confessed.

"You didn't do it alone."

"But still, I initiated it. This is all on me."

He arched a brow. "I don't think so. I could have stopped you...if I'd wanted to."

Had she heard him correctly? Or was she just hearing what she wished to? "Are...are you saying you didn't want it to stop?"

His gaze searched hers. "If we're to continue to do business together that probably shouldn't happen again."

"Agreed." She averted her gaze. "And I think you're going to be impressed with the incentives we're willing to offer you to bring your business to Mirraccino."

"I'm looking forward to seeing the package."

As Annabelle continued to gaze down at the Oriental rug covering the wood floor, she noticed a cream-colored slip of paper sticking out from the edge of the bed. It must have come from the journal. She bent over and picked it up.

"Sorry," Grayson said. "I must have missed that one."

"It was most of the way under the bed. It's no wonder you missed it."

Wanting something to distract her from the jumble of emotions over Grayson's pending departure, she unfolded the slip of paper. Inside was a message. A very strange message.

"What's the matter?" Grayson asked.

"It's this note. It seems odd. Why would my mother have a note addressed to Cosmo? I don't even know any Cosmo."

"Do you mind if I take a look?"

There certainly wasn't anything personal in the note so she handed it over. It honestly didn't mean anything to her. Why in the world had her mother kept it? And why would she have placed it with her most sacred papers?

Grayson read the note aloud:

Cosmo, tea is my Gold. I drink it first in the morning and at four in the afternoon.

for you. I hope you enjOy. Am hopiNg The Queen Is weLL. Visit heR oftEn? Nate is Well. yOu muSt see Sara. She's growN very much. Everything is As you requesTed. Don't terry. Get goin noW. WishIng you all of tHe best.

"What do you make of it?" Annabelle asked.

Grayson stood up and turned the paper over as though searching for more clues as to why her mother had kept it. "You're sure it doesn't strike any chords in your memory?"

"None at all. In fact, can I see it again?" Annabelle examined the handwriting. "That's not even my mother's handwriting."

"That's odd. You're sure?"

"Positive." She moved to the bed and retrieved her mother's journal and flipped it open to a random page. "See. Very different handwriting."

"I have to agree with you. Perhaps it wasn't in the journal. Maybe someone who stayed here before you dropped it."

"Impossible. I've been in this room for a couple of years and trust me when I say they clean the palace from top to bottom without missing a thing. No, this had to have come from the journal. But my question is why did my mother keep such a cryptic note?"

Grayson backed away. "I can't help you with that."

She folded the note and slipped it back in the journal. It was just one more mystery where her mother was concerned. Annabelle would try to figure it out, but later. Right now, she had to convince Grayson that Mirraccino was a good fit for Fo Shizzle.

"We should go over those financial projections now." She glanced at him, hoping he'd be agreeable. "Unless you have other plans."

He shook his head. "I'm all yours."

His words set her stomach aquiver with nervous energy. She knew he'd meant nothing intimate by the words, but it didn't stop her mind from wondering *what if*?

A couple of hours later, Annabelle stared across the antique mahogany table in the library at Grayson. She'd successfully answered all of his questions about the financial projections and the future of the South Shore.

He was still reading over the material. There was a lot of it. She'd worked hard to present a thorough package. But she had one other idea up her sleeve.

Grayson straightened the papers and slid them back in the folder. "You've certainly given me a lot to think about.

Between the proposed national advertising campaign and the tax reduction, I'm impressed."

"Good." But he still didn't seem thoroughly convinced and that worried her.

He picked up the folder. "I appreciate your thoroughness."

She refused to stop while she was on a roll. If she could bring this deal about, the South Shore would have an amazing facility for seniors in need of assistance. It would have decent-priced housing for young families. And this café would give young people a reason to hang out in the South Shore without causing a ruckus. And from the reviews she'd read about the cafés in other cities, it would provide a popular tourist destination.

"Why not hang out with me today?" she asked in her best cajoling voice. When his gaze narrowed in on her, she smiled.

"I have some reports to review and emails to answer."

"Can't they wait just a little bit?" She had to think fast here. "After all, it's a beautiful day in Mirraccino. And this is your first and perhaps your last trip here. And you haven't seen that much of the island."

"I've seen enough—"

"To know that it's beautiful. But I haven't yet shown you other parts of it. Mirraccino is a complex nation. It has a rich history, but it is also a thriving community with a technology base that tops the region. And there are lots of young people—young people who would like the opportunity to remain here in Mirraccino when they complete their education."

Grayson rubbed a hand over his clean-shaven jaw. "I don't know."

The way his eyes twinkled told her he was playing with her. She asked, "Are you going to make me beg?"

Surprise and interest lit up his handsome face. "I— think—"

"You'll be a gentleman and accept my invitation without making me go to such great extremes."

He smiled and shook his head. "Boy, you know how to take the fun out of things."

"I thought fun was what we just had before we were interrupted." She was blatantly flirting with him, something she rarely did, but there was something about him—something that brought out the impish side of her.

"Is that what we were doing?"

He wanted her. It was written all over his face and as much as she'd like to fall into his arms, they'd both agreed it wasn't a good idea. There was work to be done. And she wasn't about to confuse her priorities again.

Before lunch, she'd had the forethought to set up some appointments at the university with the faculty and some of the computer science students. She had a feeling if he were to see this island nation for all of its benefits, he'd change his mind about expanding his business here. At least she hoped…

And what was in it for her? Besides helping her community once their business was concluded, she wouldn't mind another of those mind-blowing kisses. Not that she was anxious for anything serious. She didn't have time for a relationship. But if he were to set up a business in Mirraccino, she might be able to make time for a little fun. As it was, all work and no play made for a dull Annabelle. That's what her brother always used to tell her. Maybe he wasn't all wrong.

Grayson quietly studied her for a moment. "Okay. You've won me over. Let's go."

Yay! This plan would work. She knew what he wanted and now she could show him that Mirraccino could provide it. "Just give me a second to freshen up."

"Do you mind if I take another look at that cryptic note?"

His question surprised her, but she didn't see how it would hurt. While Grayson read over the note, Annabelle touched up her makeup and swept her hair up into a ponytail. She knew that it was fine just the way it was, but she had an impulse to look her best. Not that she was trying to impress anyone of course…

CHAPTER SIX

"WELL?"

Grayson couldn't help but smile at Annabelle's enthusiasm. Her eyes twinkled when she was excited and she couldn't stand still. She stared at him with rapt attention.

"It'd been a long time since someone had looked at him like he was at the center of their world. He'd forgotten how good it felt for someone to care about his opinion. Was it wrong that he didn't want it to end?

"Grayson, please, say something."

"I really enjoyed today. Thank you."

Her smile broadened and puffed up her cheeks. She was adorable. And a business associate—nothing more. It was for the best. "How much?"

"How much what?"

"How much did you enjoy today?" She clasped her hands together. "Enough to seriously consider Mirraccino for your new headquarters?"

He couldn't help but laugh at her eagerness. "How could I say no to that pleading look?"

"You mean it?"

He nodded. What he didn't tell her was that he'd made up his mind after reviewing the financial package. "I sent the figures to my team to consider."

"I knew you'd like it here."

Grayson began walking along the sidewalk of the great Mirraccino Royal University with Annabelle by his side. He didn't say things that he didn't mean. And he wasn't truly impressed that often, but today he had been.

He was glad that he'd relented and decided to give Annabelle…erm… Mirraccino another try. Annabelle had arranged for a most impressive tour of the up-to-date campus. He'd talked with the professors in the computer science department. And he'd even agreed to give a spontaneous guest lecture.

To his relief, the lecture had gone well and the students had been quite receptive to his talk on his company's cloud technology and how they'd harnessed it to make their café games relevant and constantly morphing into something bigger and better.

"Really? You were honestly impressed?" Annabelle came to a stop in front of him. Hope reflected in her eyes.

"Yes, I meant it. Why do you sound so surprised?"

"I don't know. I'm not. It's just—"

"You weren't so sure about today, were you?"

She shrugged. "Not really. I wanted to believe you'd see the full potential that Mirraccino could offer you—offer your company, but yesterday you seemed to have made your mind up about everything."

He couldn't let her stop there. "And what have I decided about you?"

Annabelle glanced away. "That I'm spoiled and over-protected."

"That isn't what I think. That is what *you* think, but it shouldn't be. I think you work hard for what you want. Setting up everything today couldn't have been easy, especially when it was done at the last minute."

Her gaze met his. "I called in every favor I had here at the school. But to be honest, when I spoke to the head of the computer science department and told him who I wanted to bring for a visit, he was more than willing to help. You have quite an amazing reputation in your field."

"I don't know about that, but I appreciate your kind words."

When she gazed deep into his eyes, like she was doing now, it was so hard to remember that they were supposed to be doing business together and not picking up that kiss where they'd left off. His gaze latched on to her tempting mouth. What would she say? His gaze moved back to her eyes. Was that desire he spied glinting within them?

He didn't know how long they stood there, staring into each other's eyes. In that moment, there was nowhere else he needed to be—nowhere else he wanted to be. There was a special quality about Annabelle that sparked life back into him. She filled in all the cracks in his heart and made him want to face whatever life threw at him.

A motion out of the corner of his eye reminded him they weren't alone. Today there was a female bodyguard escorting them. She was not the friendly sort—always on guard. He recalled Annabelle calling the woman Marta.

Having a bodyguard watch over them dampened his lusty thoughts. He didn't like an audience and he preferred not to end up in one of those reports sent off to the Duke of Halencia. But that didn't mean their outing should end just yet.

"How about we go to dinner? I'd enjoy trying one of the local restaurants."

Surprise lit up Annabelle's eyes, but in a blink her enthusiasm dimmed. "Um, sure."

"What's the matter?"

"Why does anything need to be the matter?"

"Because it was written all over your face and it was in your tone."

"It's nothing. You're just imagining things." She glanced away and pulled out her phone. "I know the perfect spot. I'll just call ahead and let them know we're on our way."

He didn't believe her protests. There was something weighing on her mind, but he didn't push the subject. If she wanted to confide in him, she would have to do it of her own accord. Once she made the call, they started across the campus toward the parking lot.

After touring this university with its state-of-the-art facilities and cutting-edge technology, he realized there was a lot more to this island nation than its obvious beauty and rich history. The university was surprisingly large, drawing students from all over Europe and there were even some Americans in the mix.

There was a wealth of knowledge here. Some of the students had heard of his cafés and had pleaded with him to build one in Mirraccino. And there were other students who were anxious to work for him.

It would mean his company wouldn't have to go outside Mirraccino every time they needed to hire personnel for the technological portion of the business. And with some combined initiatives with the university, word about the café would reach the targeted demographic.

"What has you so quiet?" Annabelle asked, interrupting his thoughts.

"I was just going over the events of the day."

"I'm glad you enjoyed your visit. You know, I graduated from this university with a business degree. I never knew what I'd do with it, but the South Shore Project has been good for me. I like getting up in the morning and having a purpose. Too bad the project is winding down."

"Then why don't you find another job?"

She shrugged. "It's hard to have a normal job when you have someone shadowing your every move."

"Maybe your circumstances will change and you'll be able to do as you please."

Annabelle lowered her voice. "That's my plan."

Again the warning bells went off in his mind. He couldn't resist asking, "What plan?"

She glanced over her shoulder as though making certain her bodyguard wasn't within earshot. "I plan to show my father that I'm fully capable of caring for myself and that he no longer has to watch over me. And when you sign on with the South Shore, he'll have to acknowledge that fact."

"And if your father doesn't agree? Then what?"

"Then I'm leaving. I've always wanted to travel. Maybe I'll go to London, Paris," she paused and stared at him, "or perhaps I'll go to California."

He didn't believe she'd actually do it. "Could you really walk away from your father and uncle?"

"Why not?" she said with bravado. "It'll make their lives easier. After all, you left your family. Why shouldn't I?"

"My circumstances were different." There was no comparison between their situations. He had to make her understand. "Your father and uncle love you very much. That's why they worry so much. I never had anyone worry about me."

"I'm sorry. I… I shouldn't have said anything."

He couldn't leave off there. He had to stop her from making a big mistake. "When I left, my parents didn't try to stop me. When I rejected their way of life, I became dead to them. But if you leave here, your father and uncle will never stop looking for you."

"So they can stick their security detail on me—"

"No, because they love you and your absence would make them sad. Please tell me you understand what a gift you have here."

"I… I do." She twisted her purse strap around her fingers. "But somewhere along the way that love started to smother me. My father doesn't accept that my mother has been dead for eleven years and if there were any lingering dangers, something would have happened by now."

He sure hoped she was right. Still, there was an uneasy feeling in his gut. But then again he probably wasn't the best judge of danger. His thoughts strayed back to his last girlfriend. A harmless day of fun had turned deadly. And he'd missed all of the signs. So maybe he was just being overly sensitive now.

They rounded the corner of the administration office when a group of reporters rushed them. Grayson's whole body tensed. He'd known this moment would come sooner or later. He'd been hoping for later.

Annabelle's bodyguard rushed in front of them, waving off the paparazzi.

Members of the press started yelling out questions. "Lady Annabelle, is it true? Do you have a new love interest?"

"Does the king approve?"

"How long have you two been involved?"

The questions kept coming one after the other in rapid succession. Thanks to social media, they couldn't even visit the university without the whole world knowing.

He glanced over at Annabelle and was surprised to find her keeping it all together. But then again as a member of the royal family, she was probably used to these occurrences. Now he better understood her father's reluctance to lift the security detail.

Campus security quickly responded. Grayson guessed that the bodyguard had alerted them. With help, they made it to their car. Marta drove as he sat with Annabelle in the backseat. But when they took off out of the parking lot, they were followed.

As their speed increased so did Grayson's anxiety. His fingers bit into the door handle. His body tensed as memories washed over him. Usually he only visited this nightmare when it was late and he was alone. But now it was happening right before his wide-open eyes.

His past and present collided. He recalled the moments leading up to the hideous chain of events. It was like a horror movie playing in his mind and he was helpless to stop it.

"Grayson, are you okay?" Annabelle asked.

He nodded, not trusting his voice at that moment.

"No, you're not." She pressed a hand to his cheek. "You feel okay, but you're pale as a ghost."

"I'm fine," he ground out.

Just then there was a bang. He jumped, nearly hitting his head on the roof. In the next instant, he was leaning over to Annabelle and pulling her as close as possible with seat belt restraints still on.

"Grayson, let me up." She pushed on his chest.

He hesitated. Not hearing any further gunfire, he moved, allowing Annabelle to sit fully upright.

"What was that?" she asked, uneasiness filling her voice.

Grayson didn't dare say what he thought it was. He didn't

want to scare her any more than necessary. Sadly, he knew what a gunshot sounded like from inside a vehicle.

"A vehicle backfired," Marta said from the driver's seat.

Annabelle's hand slipped in his and squeezed.

A backfire? That knowledge should make him feel better and put him at ease, but it didn't. There were still paparazzi in cars and motorcycles swarming all around them. Their chaotic and unwanted caravan was flying down the highway now.

"Marta, take us back to the palace," Annabelle ordered.

The bodyguard never took her gaze off the road. "Understood. I'll let the palace know we're coming in hot."

Annabelle leaned her head against Grayson's shoulder. "I'm so sorry. Don't worry. We'll be at the palace soon."

"I'm fine." Why did he keep saying that? He was anything but fine. It was just that he wasn't ready to open up about his past. He didn't want to see the disappointment in Annabelle's eyes when she knew that he wasn't such a great guy after all.

"No, you're not. If it's the paparazzi, I'm sorry. I guess I didn't think about them getting wind of us being at the university. But I'm sure some of the students got excited and were posting pictures and messages about the visit on their social media accounts."

They remained hand in hand the rest of the way back to the palace where there was a heavy contingent of armed guards. There was no way any reporter was going to get past the gates.

As the gates swung closed behind them and their speed drastically reduced, Grayson could at last take a full breath. He felt foolish for letting the incident affect him so greatly. It'd been a while since he'd had a panic attack. There'd been a period after the accident when he'd stopped leaving his Malibu beach house for this very reason.

It'd been more than a year since the accident. He'd thought that he would have been past it by now. But the idea of the same thing happening to Annabelle shook him to the core.

When the vehicle pulled to a stop in front of the palace, he immediately jumped out. He'd made an utter fool of himself. How could he not tell the difference between a gunshot and a car backfiring? What was the matter with him?

He needed some fresh air and a chance to pull himself together before he faced Annabelle's inevitable questions. He couldn't blame her for wondering what was going on with him, but he didn't know what to tell her. He'd never discussed that very painful episode with anyone but a counselor. And he wasn't going to start now.

He took off in the direction of the beach. He knew from talking to Annabelle that it was private. He would be safe from prying eyes there.

"Grayson, wait," Annabelle called out.

He kept moving.

"Let him go," Marta said.

"But he…" Annabelle's voice faded into the breeze.

The more he walked, the calmer he got. And his jumbled thoughts smoothed out. Needing a diversion, he pondered the strange note that Annabelle had found among her mother's things. There was something about the message that continued to nag at him.

He pulled his phone from his pocket. On it was an image of the note. He'd taken the photo because his gut was telling him there was something about it that wasn't quite right. But what was it?

He read the note once, then twice and a third time. Was it the misspelled words that bothered him? Or perhaps the mix of lowercase and uppercase letters? Or was it the fact the message just didn't say much of anything?

Who in the world would write such a cryptic note?

And why would Annabelle's mother place it in her journal?

There was more going on here than they knew. But what was it?

CHAPTER SEVEN

THIS WAS HER FAULT.

Annabelle felt horrible about the paparazzi's appearance at the university and the ensuing chase. Though Grayson was a multimillionaire and famous, he didn't appear used to the hounding press.

She hadn't thought of that aspect when she'd made arrangements to take him there. She'd been so anxious to show him how well his business would fit in here that she hadn't taken time to plan a rear exit from the campus to avoid the press.

If it hadn't been for Grayson's adverse reaction, she might have turned the situation around and given a public statement about the pending contract with the Fo Shizzle Café chain. But on second thought, she would have been rushing things. There was no verbal or paper contract…yet.

And after today, there might not be one. Unless she could turn things around. First, she needed to get the press off their trail. And then she needed to smooth things over with Grayson.

She called the palace's press secretary and set up a brief statement to be given just outside the palace gates where the paparazzi were lying in wait. She knew from past experience that they wouldn't go away until they got a story—whether it be the truth or a bit of fiction that they conjured up.

And next, she called the kitchen and requested a candlelit dinner to be served on the patio overlooking the sea. She didn't know if Grayson would be in any mood to join her, but she wanted to make the effort since their prior dinner plans had been ruined.

With all of the arrangements made, she put on a pair of dark jeans, a white blouse and a navy blazer. She piled her hair atop her head. She wore a modest amount of makeup and chose gold hoop earrings and a necklace to match. Simple and presentable.

Her stomach churned with nerves. She never liked talking with the press. Some would say that she should be used to it, being part of a royal family. But she was the same as everyone else and longed for a private life.

Knowing she had to do this if she wanted the press to lay off, she made her way down the grand staircase. In her mind, she went over and over what she would say to the reporters. It was her intention to give a statement and not accept questions because quite honestly, she wouldn't know how to answer any questions about her relationship with Grayson. It was very complicated to say the least.

This time not only was her bodyguard present, but a bunch of palace security met her in the grand foyer of the palace. And then she spied her uncle talking with the palace guards. She inwardly groaned.

Knowing there was no way to avoid the king, she walked directly toward him. "Hello, Uncle."

"Don't hello me. What's going on?" His voice grew husky with concern. "I heard there was a high-speed pursuit with the paparazzi today. You know that's dangerous. You should have used the protocols that we have in place if you are going to do something high profile."

"But it wasn't high profile. It was a visit to the university."

"The university?"

Annabelle explained what had led her and Grayson to the school. And she admitted to the fact that she hadn't anticipated the students making a big deal of the visit via social media. It was her slipup and no one else's.

The king nodded in understanding. "You have to be careful. Your life is not like other peoples'. You must take precautions."

"You know, sometimes when you say that you sound just like my father."

"Well, that's because your father is right."

"Right or wrong, I have to go talk to the press."

"You could let the press secretary handle it. That's what we pay her to do."

Annabelle shook her head. "I started all of this and if there is to be any peace for the remainder of Grayson's stay, I must fix it."

Her uncle sighed. "You always were a stubborn girl. So much like your mother. Do what you must, but a full security team will accompany you."

She knew better than to argue with the king. There was only so much he was willing to concede and she knew she'd hit that limit. She was fine with the escort as long as they hung back.

She gave her uncle a hug. "I'm sorry I worried you. That was never my intention."

"I know. Though some may think otherwise, it's not always an easy life. There are limitations to what we can or should do."

"I understand. I will be more cautious."

And with her uncle's blessing she set off down the drive to address the media. Though her insides shivered with nervous energy, she kept moving. She would fix this and then she would speak with Grayson.

The household knew to alert her when he returned from his walk. So far she hadn't heard a word. Surely he'd be back soon.

CHAPTER EIGHT

IT WAS A CIPHER.

Grayson picked up his pace as he retraced his footsteps back to the palace. The calming sound of the water and the gentle breeze had soothed his agitation as he'd hoped it would.

And now he had to find Annabelle. He had to tell her what he'd uncovered. Something told him that she'd be just as intrigued as he was.

As the last lingering rays of the sun danced over the sea, Grayson took the steps trailing up the side of the cliff two at a time. He knew she'd also want an explanation for his peculiar reaction in the car.

And as much as part of him wanted to avoid her and those uncomfortable questions, there was another part of him that was excited to tell her what he'd figured out. And yet, the conclusions he'd arrived at only prompted more questions. Hopefully Annabelle would have the necessary answers. He just had to find her.

When he reached the patio area overlooking the beach, he stopped. There before him was a beautiful dinner table set with fine linens and china. It was lit with candles, giving it a warm and romantic atmosphere.

He inwardly groaned, realizing that he'd stumbled into someone's special plans. Someone was going to have a nice evening—a very nice evening. He couldn't even remember the last time he'd wined and dined someone.

Thankfully no one appeared to be about. He made a bee-line for the door, hoping to get away without being noticed.

"Mr. Landers," the gravelly male voice called out.

He stopped in his tracks, feeling as though he were back in elementary school. The principal had more than once caught him pulling pranks on his classmates. Sometimes he'd done it just to make them smile, but more times than not it was because he was bored senseless. No one had recognized that he had excelled far beyond his class. Not his teachers and not his parents. As long as he maintained good grades, no adult paid him much attention.

Grayson turned to find out what he'd done this time. "Yes."

The butler stood there. His face was void of emotion. Grayson couldn't help but wonder how many years it'd taken the man to perfect that serious look. Grayson didn't think he could mask his emotions all day, every day. It definitely took skills that he didn't possess.

"Lady Annabelle requested that you wait here for her. She will be here momentarily."

"You mean the table, it's for us?"

The man nodded and then withdrew back behind the palace walls.

Grayson wasn't sure what to make of this scene. He moved to the wall at the edge of the patio. He stared off at the peaceful water while a gentle breeze rushed over his skin. This whole thing felt like a dream, but it wasn't.

He turned back to the table. It was most definitely real. What exactly did Annabelle have in mind for this evening? It was obvious he hadn't scared her off with that meltdown in the car. But how was that possible? Was she used to people freaking out when the paparazzi were in hot pursuit?

"Grayson, there you are," Annabelle crossed the patio to where he stood next to the wall. "Listen, I'm so sorry about earlier. But no worries, I took care of it."

"You took care of it?" He sent her a puzzled look.

"The press. I gave them a statement. I'm sorry that I had to out us."

Out them? His gaze moved from her to the candlelit table with the rosebud and the stemware. What exactly did she want to happen this evening?

He cleared his throat. "You told them about us?" His voice dropped an octave. "What exactly did you tell them?"

Her eyes widened. "Not that."

He breathed a little easier. Sure, the kiss wasn't anything scandalous. Far from it. But he didn't need any more sparks fanning the flames with the media. He had enough rumors following him about and not only did they conjure up horrific memories for him, but they also put his board on edge as it reflected poorly on the leadership of the company.

"Then I don't understand," Grayson said. "Why did you talk to them?"

"So they would leave us alone. I told them we are in negotiations over the South Shore property."

"Oh." That was so much better than anything that had crossed his mind.

"I know that it was presumptive, so I made it clear that no deal has been reached and that we are still in the negotiating stage."

He nodded. "I understand. Did they go away?"

"Actually, they did. They seemed disappointed that it was all about business. Can you believe that? This is a huge deal for Mirraccino. I thought they'd be excited and asking for an exclusive, but nothing."

Grayson's mouth drew upward at the corners. "I think they were hoping for some romance and the promise of a royal wedding."

She shook her head. "That's not happening. Besides, my cousin just got married a couple of years ago. They don't need another wedding already. I have other things on my mind right now."

"You mean dealing with your father?"

She nodded. "But I don't want to talk about that now. I'm hungry."

He thought of what he'd discovered about the note, but he decided it could wait for a bit. Some food did sound good. He glanced over at the candlelit table and wondered if Annabelle was hungry for food…or was she hoping for more kisses?

* * *

Dinner was amazing.

Annabelle hated to see the evening end. This was the most enjoyment she'd had in a long time. Grayson had opened up more about his childhood in Ohio. She wasn't surprised to find out that his IQ was genius level and that he'd grown bored of school. Her heart had gone out to him when she learned that his parents had done nothing to nurture his special gift.

With the dinner dishes cleared, every bit of crème brûlée devoured and the hour growing late, they headed inside. She noticed Grayson had grown quiet. Perhaps he was just tired. They had had a long day. Or perhaps he was still rattled by the paparazzi and the chase back to the palace.

Annabelle had made a point of avoiding the topic during dinner, not wanting to ruin the meal. But perhaps it would be best to clear the air.

"Grayson, about earlier at the university, I'm sorry. I hadn't considered that the press would show up. I know I should have, but I was distracted."

"It's not your fault. I shouldn't have let it bother me."

It did a whole lot more than bother him. "Do you want to talk about it?"

Grayson's gaze didn't quite meet hers. He shook his head.

"I understand." She didn't. Not really. "Have you decided what you'll do about tomorrow?"

This time he did look directly at her with puzzlement reflected in his eyes. "What about tomorrow?"

"You're supposed to leave. But I was hoping after the visit to the university that I'd convince you to stay and give the South Shore and Mirraccino more consideration. Of course, I hadn't counted on the press messing up everything."

He reached out to her, but his hand stopped midway. He lowered his hand back to his side. "They didn't ruin anything. It was no big deal."

She didn't believe him, but she wasn't going to push the

matter. "Does this mean you'll accept my uncle's invitation to stay for the heritage festival?"

A small smile pulled at his lips. "How could I turn down an invitation from a king?"

"He will be pleased." She started to turn for the door to her suite, wishing he were staying for her instead. "You should get some rest."

"Annabelle, wait. I'm staying for more than just that."

She turned back to him, hesitant to get her hopes up. "What reason would that be?"

"Do you have to ask?"

"I do."

"I'm staying because of you."

Though she tried to subdue her response, it was impossible. Her heart fluttered in her chest and a smile pulled at her lips. "You're staying for me?"

He nodded. "I think you did a terrific job today swaying my decision on the viability of establishing my Mediterranean headquarters here. The projections and incentives were impressive and well thought out. And the programs at the university were current and cutting-edge."

"Thank you for the compliment. I hope it all works out." And that he spends a lot more time in Mirraccino. "It's getting late. We should call it a night." Before she did something she might regret—like kiss him again.

"Oh, okay. It's just I had something I wanted to talk to you about."

"Do you mind if it waits? I need to be up early tomorrow. I have a couple of things I need to do for my uncle first thing."

"Um, sure. I'll see you in the morning." For a moment, he didn't move. It seemed as if he was considering whether he should kiss her or just walk away.

Was it wrong that she willed him to kiss her again? Her gaze sought out his lips, his very tempting lips. She'd never been kissed quite like she had by him. It had rocked her world right off its axis. What would one more kiss hurt?

Her heart pounded harder, faster. Her gaze focused on his. Was it her imagination or were their bodies being drawn toward each other? If she were just to sway forward a little, their lips would meet and ecstasy would ensue.

Grayson backed away. "I'll see you in the morning."

Maybe she shouldn't have rushed him off. Maybe she should have said that she'd talk to him as long as he wanted. But he was already walking away. She sighed. Tomorrow was another day. Hopefully it would go smoother than this one.

"Good night."

She turned to her suite. Something told her that sleep was going to be elusive that night.

CHAPTER NINE

HAD HE BEEN imagining things last night?

Grayson assured himself it had been a bunch of wishful thinking on his part. It was the best explanation he could come up with for that tension just before he'd walked away from Annabelle. After all, she was royalty and he was just a techno geek from Ohio. Definitely worlds apart.

Grayson ate his breakfast alone. So far there'd been no sightings of the king or Annabelle. Before coming to breakfast, Grayson had checked her room, but she hadn't been there. She must have urgent things to do. Grayson couldn't even imagine what it must be like having your uncle be the king. The responsibilities must be enormous.

But he had to gain Annabelle's attention long enough to ask her some questions about the cryptic note. And no one he'd spoken to seemed to know where she might be. After breakfast, he checked the gardens and the beach. No sign of her.

He was about to head back upstairs to check her room again when he passed through the grand entryway. It was then that he noticed a folded newspaper sitting on a table. If he couldn't find Annabelle, perhaps he'd do a little reading about Mirraccino. The more he learned about this Mediterranean paradise, the easier time he'd have selling the idea to his board of directors.

He glanced around for one of the many staff to ask them if he could borrow the paper, but no one was about. He picked up the paper and unfolded it. The breath caught in his throat when he saw a picture of himself.

His gaze frantically scanned the picture. It was of him and Annabelle. They were staring at each other. The photo made it look like they were about to kiss. But that wasn't possible. The only kiss they'd shared had been in the privacy of Annabelle's room. And this photo, it was taken outside, and from the looks of it at the university.

His gaze scanned up to the headline—Hero To The Rescue!

He was not a hero. Why did people keep saying that? He inwardly groaned, his hands clenching and crinkling the newspaper. If he were a hero Abbi wouldn't be dead.

Blood pulsated in his temples. Why couldn't the paparazzi find someone else to torment? He'd had enough of it back in California after the car accident.

Grayson's attention returned to the brief article. It was pretty much what he'd expected. Innuendos and assumptions. But what he didn't expect was a quote from Annabelle.

"We are together."

She'd said that? To the media? Why would she tell them such a thing? It wasn't true. He'd made sure to keep his distance since their one and only kiss—no matter how tempting he found her. What was she up to?

"Grayson, there you are." Annabelle's voice called out behind him. "I've been looking everywhere for you."

He choked down his outrage at the headline. He could only be thankful that the Mirraccino media hadn't dug into his past, but something told him they would soon. "Apparently you didn't look hard enough." He closed the paper along the fold. "I've been right here."

"I'm sorry things took so long this morning. There was more to do than I anticipated."

He nodded. His mind was still on the newspaper article. "Really? It seemed like you took care of everything last night."

She sent him a strange look as though she didn't know what he was talking about. "I, ah, had some last-minute details to take care of for the heritage festival."

His gaze lowered to the photo of them. It had to have been digitally altered because there was no way he'd looked at Annabelle like…like that—like they were lovers.

"Grayson, what's the matter?"

He wondered if she'd seen the photo yet. "Why do you think something is the matter?"

"Because you've barely said a word to me. And you keep scowling. Now what's the matter? Have I done something to upset you?"

"You might say that." He held out the newspaper. "When were you going to tell me about this?"

She retrieved the newspaper from his hand. Her mouth gaped open. He wanted to believe that this was as much a surprise to her as it was to him, but he couldn't let go of the fact that there was a quote from her.

"Aren't you going to say anything?" His voice came out more agitated than he'd intended.

"You think I did this?" Her free hand smacked off the paper.

"It has you quoted in the article."

"I'm surprised you took time to read it." She tossed the paper back on the table. "For the record, I didn't imply that you and I are lovers. They did that all on their own. I don't know why you're making such a big deal about this. Surely someone of your position must be used to the media by now."

That was the problem. He was all too used to them. He knew how much their words could cut and he thought at last the rumors had died down. But there hadn't been a word about the accident in the paper. Maybe he was being over-sensitive.

He shouldn't have been so quick to think the worst of her. Is that what he'd let happen to him? Had his bad experience jaded him?

"I thought you and I were friends, but obviously I was wrong." Annabelle's voice drew him from his thoughts. "I won't make that mistake again." She turned to walk away.

He couldn't let her walk away. Not like this.

Grayson cleared his throat. "Annabelle, wait."

She hesitated but didn't turn around. Her shoulders were

rigid. And if he could see her eyes, he'd bet they were glowing with anger.

"I'm sorry," he said. Those words didn't often cross his lips. But he truly owed her an apology. He couldn't take out what had happened to him in the past on her. "I shouldn't have accused you of anything. I know the media can turn the most innocent of comments around."

She turned to face him. Her expression was stony cold. "I appreciate the apology."

He couldn't tell if she truly meant that or not. He'd really messed things up. He raked his fingers through his hair.

"I've got things to do." Annabelle walked away.

He picked up the paper again and held it before him. He studied the photo of them. Is that really how she looked at him? There was a vulnerability in her gaze as her body leaned toward him. This knowledge started a strange sensation swirling in his chest.

Then his gaze moved to the image of himself. He looked like he was ready to sweep her into his arms and have his way with her. Was that really what he'd felt in that moment? He recalled the desire to taste her sweet kisses once more, but he'd thought he'd covered it up. Obviously, he'd failed. Miserably.

Footsteps sounded in the hallway. He glanced up hoping to find Annabelle returning so that they could smooth things over—so they could resume the easy friendship that they'd developed. But it wasn't her. It was Mr. Drago, one of the king's men.

"Can I help you, sir?" The man was always so formal.

"Uh, no." Grayson returned the paper to the table. "I was just going to look for Annabelle."

"I believe I saw her go out to the patio."

"Thank you." Grayson walked away.

Part of him told him to leave things alone. It was best that they didn't reconnect. After all, it wasn't like he was ready for anything serious. He didn't know if he ever would be. He'd already failed so miserably.

And since that deadly car accident, he'd cut himself off from everything outside his board of directors, and his assistant. He'd forgotten how much he'd enjoyed laughing with someone and just sharing a casual conversation.

Annabelle had given that back to him and he wasn't ready to give it up. He wasn't ready to give her up. Not yet.

What was he supposed to do now? He just couldn't leave things like this. And then he thought of the cryptic note. He hadn't had a chance to tell her his suspicion about it. Maybe that could get them back on friendly terms.

He picked up his pace.

Insulting.
  Insufferable.
  Annoying.

Annabelle muttered under her breath as she strode down the hallway with no actual destination in mind. She just needed some space—make that a lot of space—between her and Grayson before she said something she might regret. How dare he accuse her?

Like she would do anything to help the media. What did he take her for? A fool? Or was he just another man who thought she wasn't savvy enough to take care of herself and watch what she said to the press?

Her back teeth ground together as she choked back her exasperation. What was it with the men in her life? She found herself headed for the patio. It was her place of solace, well, actually the beach was. The sea called to her. She stared out at the peaceful waters as the sunshine danced over the gentle swells.

She longed to go for a walk and let the water gently wash over her feet. It was so therapeutic. The more she thought about it, the more tempted she became. After all, she didn't have anything else that needed her attention. Why not go for a walk on the beach?

Without any more debate, she set off down the steps. The warm breeze rushed through her hair, brushing it back over her shoulders. Later, she might go for a dip. It'd been a long time since she'd gone swimming, too long in fact.

She slipped off her shoes and walked to the water's edge. She enjoyed the feel of the sun-warmed sand on her feet and then the coolness of the water as it washed over them.

"Annabelle!" The all-too-familiar voice called out to her. Grayson.

She groaned inwardly. She wasn't ready to deal with him. Not yet.

She started walking like she hadn't heard him. Maybe he'd get the hint and leave her in peace, but something told her that man hadn't gotten to the position of head of his own multinational company by letting people brush him off.

"Annabelle, wait up!"

He definitely wasn't going to relent. She stopped and turned, pausing for him to catch up. What did he want now?

He jogged up to her. "Mind if I walk with you?"

"Suit yourself."

They walked for a few minutes in silence. Surprisingly it was a comfortable silence. Maybe she'd overreacted too. It just hurt when Grayson thought she'd betrayed his trust. When had he come to mean so much to her?

"I wanted to talk to you about that note you found in your mother's journal. There's just something about it that's not quite right."

That's what he wanted to talk about? A little smile pulled at her lips. "What doesn't seem right to you?"

"It's not any one specific thing. It's more like a bunch of small things. You said the handwriting wasn't your mother's, right?"

Annabelle nodded. "My mother was a perfectionist when

it came to penmanship. She would never abide by that mix of upper and lowercases in every word."

"Do you know of your mother keeping secrets? Or sneaking around?"

"My mother? Never." And then the memory of that day at the South Shore came back to her. "Then again, there was that strange man that she was arguing with."

"Maybe your mother was holding the note for someone else. Do you think that's possible?"

Annabelle shrugged. "At this point, I guess most anything is possible."

"Then I'm about to tell you something and I don't want you to freak out."

"Now you're worrying me."

"I just told you to stay calm."

"You can't tell someone not to freak out and expect them to remain calm." She stopped walking. She drew in a deep breath of sea air and blew it out. "Okay. Now tell me."

His gaze met hers. "I think the note is some sort of cipher."

"A cipher?"

"Yeah, a code. A secret message."

"I know what a cipher is. I just don't know what my mother would be doing with such a thing. Surely you must be wrong."

"I don't think I am. Back in college, my buddy and I would write them just to see if we could outsmart each other with some unbreakable code."

"Seriously? That's what you did for fun?"

Grayson shrugged. "Sure. Why not? The party scene just wasn't for me."

"You'd rather exercise your brain."

"Something like that."

"How good were you?"

"Let's just say the government got wind of what we were up to and wanted to recruit us out of college."

"I take it you didn't accept their offer."

"I didn't. But my buddy did. He works for one of those three-letter agencies."

Wow. She'd never met someone so intelligent that they sat around writing coded messages for fun. Who did that? A genius of course. And Grayson was the cutest nerd she'd ever met.

"So what did this message say?" Annabelle asked, more curious than before, if that were possible.

"I didn't start working on it. I mean, I wanted to, but I wanted to check with you first."

"Yes, decode it. I need to know what it says."

Grayson's brows drew together. "Are you sure? I mean, it could be anything. Something innocent. Or it could be something about your mother that you never wanted to know."

"You mean like she was having an affair?"

He didn't say anything, just nodded.

Annabelle didn't believe it. "I realize there's a lot about my mother I don't know, but there is one thing I do know and that is my parents truly loved each other. She wouldn't have cheated on my father. Whatever is in that note, it's something else. And it just might be what got her killed."

"Have you recalled meeting anyone by the name of Cosmo?"

"I've thought about it a lot and I have nothing."

"You mentioned that you have a brother. Could you check with him?"

She pulled out her cell phone and pulled up her brother's number. Thanks to palace security, they made sure that cell service was available down on the beach.

"What are you doing?" Grayson asked.

"Calling my brother like you asked." The phone was already ringing. She held up a finger for Grayson to give her a minute.

Her brother's familiar voice came over the phone. "Hey sis, now isn't a good time to talk."

"Is that any way to greet your only sibling?"

He sighed. "Sorry. It's just that I'm late to meet Elena."

"Is there something going on with you two?"

"Why do you always insist that something must be going on with me and Elena? Can't we just be friends?"

"When Elena is gorgeous, not to mention an international runway model, no, you can't just be friends. Her days as a tomboy are long gone. Don't tell me you haven't noticed because then I'll have to take you to the eye doctor."

"Sis, enough. We're friends. Nothing more. Besides, you know I don't do serious relationships."

"And that's what Elena wants?"

"I don't know."

"Are you in Paris?"

"Perhaps. Now, why did you call?"

She went on to ask him about the name on the note but made sure not to mention the cryptic message. Her gut told her to hold her cards close to her chest until she knew more.

Her brother didn't recall meeting or hearing of anyone with that name. But it spiked his curiosity and she quickly diverted his attention. He might have his issues with their father, but that didn't mean he wouldn't inform their father of her activities if he thought it was for the best. He was yet another protective male in her life. She was surrounded by them.

As soon as she disconnected the phone, Grayson asked, "So what did he say?"

"He's never heard the name. So does that help or hinder us?"

"It doesn't help us. But it shouldn't hurt us if it truly is a code."

"Oh, good. At last, my family will have some answers."

"Don't go getting your hopes up." Grayson looked very serious in that moment. "I've been known to be wrong. I haven't started working with it."

Annabelle stopped walking. "Well, what are you waiting for? The note is back the other way."

"You mean you want to work on it now?"

"Maybe my father was right. Maybe there is more to my mother's death than a mugging. Either way, I need to know. I owe my mother that much."

CHAPTER TEN

EVENING HAD SNUCK UP on them.

It was nothing new for Grayson. There were many days that came and went without much notice by him as he pounded away on his keyboard. He couldn't help it. He loved what he did for a living. In fact, he thrived on developing software. Watching a program he'd written from scratch come to life was a total rush.

Running a corporation, well, that was something that didn't exactly excite him. There was a lot more paperwork and decisions that had nothing to do with his computer programs or the functioning of the cafés. And administrative issues seemed to crop up when he was right in the middle of a big breakthrough.

But squirreled away in the palace in this enormous library with just about every edition of the classics on the shelf, he found himself distracted. And it wasn't the moonlight gleaming through the tall windows. Nor was it the priceless artwork on the walls or the artifacts on display. No, it was the beautiful woman sitting next to him.

Annabelle yawned and stretched.

"Getting tired?"

She shook her head. "No. I'm fine."

He didn't believe her. It was getting late and they should call it a night.

"Okay, so it isn't all of the capitalized letters," Annabelle said. "And it's not any of the other combinations we've tried. What else could it be?"

"Let me think." He shoved his fingers through his hair. He'd run the note through a program he had on his computer and searched for different variables. Nothing came up...at least nothing that made the least bit of sense.

She sighed and leaned back in her chair. "Are you sure there's something here?"

"You sound skeptical."

"I am."

"If you want, we can forget I ever said anything."

She didn't respond for a moment, as though she were weighing her options. "It won't hurt to work on it some more."

"There's a message here. I know it. Those random capital letters must mean something."

"I guess I should let you know that I already signed us up for some of the games at the heritage festival tomorrow—"

"You did what?" Grayson frowned at her. "You probably should have checked with me first. I'm not that sports oriented unless it's on a digital screen."

"Good."

That certainly wasn't the response he was expecting. "Why good?"

"Because then you can't show me up at the games."

He shook his head. "You're something else."

"I hope that's good." She smothered another yawn.

"Let's just say you keep me guessing."

Her eyes lit up. "Good. I never want to be accused of being boring. Now what should we try next?"

"We're obviously spinning our wheels right now. Maybe if we take a break for the night something will come to one of us by morning."

With Annabelle in agreement, they turned off the lights in the library and closed the door behind them. The palace was quiet at this hour. But then again, Grayson had noticed that for the most part the palace was quite tranquil. He didn't know if that was due to the large size and the noise not carrying throughout or if it was a request of the king. It was a lot like living inside a library and every time Grayson went to speak, he felt as though he should whisper.

They stopped outside Annabelle's suite. Grayson really didn't want the night to end. All afternoon and evening, he'd envisioned running his fingers through her long, silky hair. And showering kisses over her lips, cheeks and down her neck.

"What are you thinking about?" Annabelle sent him a smile as though she could read his mind.

He cleared his throat. "I was just thinking some more about the note."

She nodded, but her eyes said she didn't believe him. "Well, you better get some rest. We're going to be very busy tomorrow."

"I'd be better off here, working on deciphering the note."

"And I think you need to get out and experience a bit of Mirraccino. After all, the contract isn't signed yet. I still need to give you a good impression of our nation."

His gaze strayed to her lips before returning to her eyes. "I have a very good impression already."

"Why Grayson, if I didn't know better I'd think you were flirting with me." She sent him a teasing smile. "I must be more tired than I thought. Good night." And with that she went into her room and closed the door.

He stood there for a moment taking stock of what just happened. He'd been soundly turned down. That had never happened to him. In fact, he was normally the one who turned away women.

Annabelle was most certainly different. And it had nothing to do with her noble birthright. It was something deep within her that set her apart from the other women who'd crossed his life.

"I can't believe you talked me into this."

The next morning, Grayson stood in the middle of the road. He hunched over at the starting line of the chariot race. His hands wrapped around the handles of the wooden cart. Why exactly had he agreed to this? And then he recalled Annabelle's sunny smile and the twinkle of merriment in her eyes. That had done in all of his common sense.

And now he was the horse and she was the driver. Go figure. What part of not being athletic didn't Annabelle get? And worst of all, the king was in attendance. Grayson could feel the man's inquisitive gaze following him.

"What did you say?" Annabelle asked. "I can't hear you from back here."

Before he could answer a horn was blown.

"Hold on!" Grayson yelled and then he lifted the front of the wooden chariot and set off.

Annabelle of course got to stand in the rustic chariot. He could hear her back there shouting encouragements. It wasn't helping. Why did people find getting all hot and sweaty so exhilarating? He jogged each morning, but that was for the health benefits, not because he enjoyed it. His favorite part of running was when it was over. He was more than fine with a tall cold drink and his laptop.

Lucky for him Annabelle didn't weigh much. He kept his gaze on the finish line. He'd told Annabelle not to get her hopes up for winning. He was definitely not a sprinter, but now that the race was under way, his competitive streak prodded him onward.

He looked to his right. They'd passed that team, leaving only one other team in this heat. He quickly glanced to the left to find two guys. They were slightly ahead.

"Go, Grayson!" Annabelle cheered. In his mind's eye he could see her smiling. "We can do this!"

She was right, he could catch them. Adrenaline flooded his veins.

He just had to push harder. This wasn't so bad. In fact, he kind of liked it.

"Grayson, straighten up."

He glanced forward and realized that he'd listed to the left. Oops. But it wasn't such an egregious error that it couldn't be fixed. He just had to stay focused. The further they went, the heavier his load became. His leg muscles burned, but he refused to slow down. Annabelle was counting on him.

His breathing came in huffs. He really needed to take his

running more seriously in the future. Who knew when the next chariot race would pop up? He'd laugh, but he was too tired.

He was running out of energy. Still, he kept putting one foot in front of the other. The finish line was just a little farther. Keep going. Just a little farther.

He.

Could.

Do.

It.

When his chest struck the ticker tape, a cheer started deep in his chest and rose up through his throat. He lowered the cart. He drew in quick, deep breaths.

The next thing he knew, Annabelle ran up to him. With a great big smile, she flung her arms around him. "We did it! We did it!"

He wasn't so sure how much of a "we" effort it was, considering all she'd had to do was hold on, but he wasn't about to deflate her good mood. He wrapped his arms around her, pulling her close and enjoying the way her soft curves molded to his body.

But then she pulled away—much too soon. She was still smiling as she leaned up on her tiptoes and swayed toward him. She was going to kiss him. That would make this torture he'd gone through totally worth it.

And then something happened that he hadn't expected; her lips landed on his cheek. His cheek? Really? He deserved so much more than that.

Totally deflated, he struggled to keep the smile on his face as the official made his way over to congratulate them and let them know that they would be racing later that afternoon in the final heat.

Yay! Grayson couldn't wait. Not. But when he looked back at Annabelle, who was still grinning ear to ear, his mood lifted. How could he complain when it obviously made her so happy? Besides, it meant that he didn't have to go running later this evening or tomorrow morning. He could deal with that.

When they set off to get drinks, Annabelle glanced his way. "See, that wasn't so bad, was it?"

"If you say so." He refused to tell her that she was right. If he did, he worried about what she'd come up with next for them to do.

"And I bet you thought all of these old games would be boring. Sometimes you don't need technology to have a good time. Doing things the old-fashioned way can be fun too."

There was something in what she said that struck a chord in his mind. While Annabelle got them some cold water to drink, he thought about what she'd said about not needing technology and doing things the old-fashioned way.

"Here you go." She held the water out to him.

He readily accepted it. He could feel the icy-cold liquid make its way down his parched throat. It tasted so good that he ended up chugging most of it.

"You know, you're right," he said.

"Of course I am." Then she paused and sent him a puzzled look. "About what exactly?"

"Not needing technology. Sometimes old school works."

"I'm not following you."

He lowered his voice, not wanting to be overheard. "The note. I was trying more modern ways of cracking it but I need to try a more old-school method."

"Oh." Her eyes lit up. "That's great." Then the smile slipped from her face.

"What's the matter now?"

"You won the race."

Leave it to Annabelle to confuse him once again. "I thought that was a good thing."

"It was until you figured out what to do with the note. Now we have to stay for the final heat and the note is back at the palace."

"Stop fretting. It isn't going anywhere." He glanced

around. "Why don't you show me around the village before lunch?"

She hesitantly agreed and set off. He found it interesting that the streets within the village were blocked off to cars and trucks. The cobblestone paths were for two-legged and four-legged passersby only.

Annabelle pointed out historic buildings with their stone-and-mortar walls. Each building was unique, from their materials to the layout, and even the doors were all different shapes. There were no cookie-cutter replicas anywhere.

Walking through Portolina, Grayson felt as though he'd stepped back in time—at least a couple of centuries. He enjoyed visiting, but he definitely wouldn't want to stay. He had a soft spot for all things technological starting with his computer and microwave.

The villagers were super friendly. Many of them made a point of greeting Annabelle. They didn't treat him as an outsider but rather drew him into the conversation. He'd never visited such a friendly place.

The cobblestone path wound its way through the village, past the tailor, baker and schoolhouse. Whatever you needed, it was within walking distance. It was such a simple way of life. The exact opposite of his high-tech, state-of-the-art existence.

But not all of Mirraccino was locked in the past. This island nation had the best of both worlds. It tempted him to consider purchasing a vacation home here.

He glanced over at Annabelle. She was all the incentive he needed to spend more time here.

He halted his thoughts, startled that he was beginning to feel something for Annabelle. But that couldn't be. He wouldn't allow himself to get emotionally invested.

If he were smart, he'd catch the next plane to Rome. But he'd already obligated himself to decipher the note and there was the pending proposal for the café. He was stuck.

He'd just have to proceed carefully and not risk his scarred heart.

CHAPTER ELEVEN

SHE HAD TO HURRY.

That evening, Annabelle rushed out of the kitchen. She paused in front of an ornate mirror in the hallway to run a hand over her hair. She considered going back to her room to touch up her makeup, but she didn't want to waste any more time. She was already ten minutes late to meet Grayson.

The day had rushed past her in a heartbeat. In between the chariot races, the tour of the village and the quaint shops, they'd sampled many of the local culinary treats. Truth be told, she'd had a fantastic day. She'd had more fun with Grayson than she'd had in a long time. She hadn't realized until then how much she'd let her work take over her life. And that had to stop.

She promised herself that once she finished the South Shore Project she would start living her life and having some fun. If she'd learned anything from her mother, it was that life was too short not to enjoy it. And she enjoyed it a lot more with Grayson in it. He'd been such a good sport that day with the chariot races. And she had a surprise for him tomorrow at the festival.

But now it was time to puzzle over that note again. It wasn't like she could make anything of it. She honestly didn't think there was anything to it. However, she didn't mind spending more time with Grayson while he worked on it.

Annabelle rushed into the library to find Grayson already there. "Sorry I'm late. Things took longer than I'd planned."

He glanced up from where he was sitting on the couch. "No problem. I haven't been here that long. I had a lot of emails to answer and a couple of phone calls to return."

"Sounds like you were busy. I hope there aren't any problems with your business."

"No. Nothing serious. Just the usual things that need answering or approval. If it isn't one thing, then it's something else. I also did some thinking about that note. Do you think Cosmo is some sort of nickname that your mother had?" Grayson asked. "Maybe something from her childhood?"

"Not that I know of. Does this mean you think the note was written to her?"

"It's just a thought."

She stood behind him as he sat on the couch. She leaned over his shoulder, getting a better look at the note. "But if this note was written to her, I'm confused. So she gave someone tea who must have known her when she was a child? It just doesn't make any sense."

"Which is why I think it's a cipher."

She picked up the note and stared at it, wishing something would pop out at her. "In the beginning I thought the chance of this note being some sort of cipher was a bit far-fetched."

"And now?"

"I'm still skeptical but the mix of random upper and lowercase letters is odd. And then there's the strange wording. I mean, do people really say that tea is their gold. Isn't that a bit of overkill?"

"What do you think?"

She moved around the couch and sat down. "Maybe Cosmo is some sort of code name."

Grayson smiled. "Have you been watching a lot of 007 movies?"

She shrugged, not really in a jovial mood. Maybe it was just exhaustion settling in. Or maybe it was her rising frustration. "I just want to know the truth. I want to know if there's more to my mother's death than anyone has acknowledged. Maybe unraveling what exactly happened to her and who killed her will help my father. I don't think he's ever really recovered from the event. He's always worried about me and my brother."

"And you think that if you can figure out what happened then your family can have a normal life?"

"Maybe not normal precisely. I'm not even sure what that

is anymore, but something less stressful than what we have now. My father is always worried, checking in every evening. And my brother, well, he says that he's fine, but he's never home. He's always on a new adventure. Last I heard he was in Paris, visiting an old friend of ours. It seems like my family is never in the same place at the same time."

Grayson reached out and took her hand in his. "I'm sorry. I hope you're able to change things. I know what it is to live without any family around. It can get pretty lonely, especially around the holidays."

"Why don't you try talking to your family?"

He shook his head. "That chapter of my life is over."

"A lot of time has passed since you've spoken to them—tempers have cooled, expectations have adjusted and regrets have set in." She didn't want him to pass up a chance to reconnect with his parents. If she could have one more day with her mother it would mean the world to her. "When was the last time you spoke with them?"

He cleared his throat. "When I got a scholarship to college. I was sixteen."

"Sixteen. Wow. How did you make it on your own?"

"I worked. Hard. I took every job I could find. I ate a lot of ramen noodles and cans of tuna."

"Surely they miss you."

He shook his head. "They made their feelings bluntly obvious."

"A lot of time has passed. Maybe you could try again."

"Annabelle." There was a definite warning tone to his voice.

She understood this was a sensitive subject for him, just as her mother's murder was sensitive for her. If she could pay him back for all of his assistance by helping to find a bridge back to his family, she had to try.

"I'm sure they regret the way things ended."

"Stop." Grayson's body grew visibly stiff. "Now, do you want to go over this note or not?"

Perhaps she shouldn't have pushed the subject of his family so much. "I only meant to help."

"I know." He turned his attention back to the note and then began typing on his computer.

She glanced at the monitor. "Your idea of this being old-school coding, what did you mean?"

"I think this note could simply be a case of letter replacement or taking every other letter or so."

"What can I do to help?"

He explained his plan to unravel the note. It sounded simple enough. She just wondered if it'd work.

Annabelle made a stack of photocopies, even though Grayson offered to write a computer program to sort out the correct letters. She said they could do it just as quickly by hand. And she wanted to be able to contribute. So with copies of the note and highlighters, they started going through the note, highlighting every capital letter without success. Then they tried every other letter, every third letter and so on.

"This isn't working," Annabelle said in exasperation.

"I agree." Grayson studied the note for a bit. "Maybe we're jumping ahead."

"What do you mean?"

He continued staring at the copy of the note. "Perhaps the note is telling us something."

Knock. Knock.

Who could that be? Annabelle sent Grayson a worried look. No one in the palace knew what they were up to and that's the way she wanted it to remain. She quickly turned all of the pages over.

"Come in."

The door opened and Mr. Drago stepped into the room. Annabelle had known him all of her life. He was a quiet man, who never gave any outward signs of what he was thinking. Annabelle had always felt like they were strangers.

"Excuse me, ma'am. The king would like to know if you are done in his office."

"Yes, I am." Did her voice really sound off? Or was she just being a bit paranoid. "Please thank my uncle for me."

"Yes, ma'am. Is there anything I can do for you?"

"Thank you, but I think Grayson and I are good."

"Very well." He looked at her like he wanted to say something else, but then he quietly backed out of the room, closing the door behind him.

Once he was gone, she breathed easier and unclenched her hands. "Do you think he suspects something? Or worse, do you think my uncle is suspicious?"

"Why? Because he asked if you needed anything?"

She nodded. Her mind raced with potential scenarios, none of them good.

"The only reason anyone would be suspicious is because you look like you're ready to jump out of your skin. Relax," Grayson said. "I'm serious. You look like you just stole the crown jewels."

"Not me." She sat down on the couch next to him. "I'd crack under the stress."

"I don't know about that. You seem to be doing fine with our secret investigation."

"But that's different. If this note proves to have something to do with my mother's death, what we're doing is about uncovering the truth about my past—a chance for my family to heal. I'm not out to hurt anyone. Unless you consider the killer being exposed and punished."

"And for any of that to happen, we need to decode this note." Grayson paused and gave her a serious look. "Are you going to be okay if this turns out to have absolutely nothing to do with your mother's death?"

"I honestly have no expectations. Okay, that's not exactly true. I'm starting to believe you. But whether the coded message has something to do with my mother's death is questionable. And we won't know unless we get back to work."

"It's getting late. Maybe we should pick this up in the morning."

"About that...we can't." This time she avoided his gaze.

"And why would that be?"

"Because we have plans."

"Oh, no. Not another chariot race. I refuse. I ache in places that I don't think are supposed to hurt. You'll have to find yourself another horse."

Annabelle failed to suppress a laugh. "I promise it's nothing like that."

"Good. Then what plans would these be?"

"I promise no physical effort will be required, but I'm going to make you wait until tomorrow to find out the details."

"Oh, no. I don't think so." His determined gaze met and held hers. "You have to tell me or else."

She couldn't stop smiling. "Or else what?"

He reached out and started tickling her. His long fingers were gentle, but they seemed to gravitate to all of her ticklish spots. Laughter peeled from her lips as she slid down on the couch. She tried shoving him away, but he was too strong for her.

And then suddenly she realized that he was practically on top of her. He smelled spicy and manly. And her hands were still gripping his shoulders that were rock hard with muscles.

Their gazes met and her heart leapt into her throat. Did he have any idea what he did to her body? Or how much she wanted to pick up kissing him where they'd left off before?

He stopped tickling her, as though he were reading her thoughts. Was it that obvious on her face how much she desired him? And in that moment, she wanted him touching her again, not tickling her, but caressing her. And she wanted his mouth pressed to hers.

Not about to let the moment slip away, she reached up and pulled his head down to hers. She claimed his lips with all the heat and passion that she'd kept locked up inside her. His lips moved over hers with a gentleness that surprised her. His approach was much smoother than her inexperienced clumsiness.

She slowed to his gentle, enticing pace. She found the slow kiss allowed her to enjoy the way he evoked the most delicious sensations within her. She could kiss him all night long. A moan swelled in the back of her throat and grew in intensity.

The note and its meaning slipped to the back of her mind. All that mattered right now was the man hovering over her. She'd never felt like this for a man before…ever. He was sweeter than the finest chocolate cake. And he was more addictive than her caramel coffee lattes.

She had no idea how much time had passed, nor did she care, when a cell phone buzzed. Annabelle knew nothing could be as important as this moment. And apparently Grayson agreed as he continued to kiss her. But the phone kept on buzzing.

Grayson pulled back. The phone stopped ringing. Too little, too late.

He ran a hand over his mouth as though realizing the gravity of what had just happened between them. It wasn't just a passing fancy. There was something serious growing here. Annabelle wasn't anxious to examine it too closely. Everything would be better if they just kept it light and simple.

The phone began to buzz again. Grayson frowned. "I better get this."

Annabelle sat up and straightened her clothes. "Go ahead."

It was funny how things went from very heated to suddenly awkward in a matter of seconds. What in the world had come over her? She remembered their sweet moment of abandon. It had been so good. And so not what they should have been doing together. After all, she still had a deal to sign with Grayson. The last thing she needed to do was complicate matters even more than they were already.

Still… She sighed, recalling the way his lips felt against

hers. Heat swirled in her chest and rushed up her neck. She resisted the urge to fan herself.

Annabelle lifted a sheet of paper with a copy of the note. This was what she should be concentrating on, not Grayson and his tantalizing lips.

"Sorry about that," Grayson said, turning back to her. "It was business."

"Um, no problem." She pretended to be concentrating on the note, but she was having a severe problem focusing. "I was just thinking some more about this note."

"Oh, no, you don't." He swiped the paper out of her hand and set it on the coffee table.

"Hey, what did you do that for?"

"Because we weren't finished yet."

Again, heat flooded her cheeks. "Grayson, I don't think—"

"Hey, you owe me an answer and I'm not letting you get out of it."

An answer? He wasn't talking about picking up where they'd left off with the kiss? Oops. She averted her gaze, not wanting him to read her thoughts.

"Well?" he prompted.

She glanced at him, surprised to find merriment twinkling in his eyes. So, he didn't regret what just happened between them, but had she read too much into it? That must be it. She needed to lighten up.

Her thoughts were cut off when Grayson's fingers began tickling her sides again. Why did she have to be so ticklish? How embarrassing.

Laughter filled the air and her thoughts scattered. What was it about this man that made her forget her responsibilities and just want to have fun with him?

Having problems catching her breath between the laughter, she finally gasped, "Okay."

He paused and arched a brow. "Okay, what?"

"Okay, you win." She drew in one deep breath after the

other, so relieved that the tickling had subsided. "I'll tell you."

"So out with it. What devious plan do you have in store for me?"

"Eating cake."

His brows drew together. "What?"

"You're a judge for the baking contest tomorrow."

It took a moment for her words to sink in and then a smile lifted his very tempting lips. "I can do that. I like cake."

"There's more than cake. There will be cookies, bread and some other stuff."

He rubbed his flat abdomen. "Sounds good to me."

"I'm glad you approve. So it's a date?"

The startled look on Grayson's face alerted Annabelle to her slip of the tongue. She inwardly groaned. If only it were possible to go back in time, she would. In a heartbeat.

CHAPTER TWELVE

A DATE?

Was she serious?

Grayson's heart was lodged in his throat. Sure they'd had some fun this evening, well, pretty much all day. He hadn't even minded playing the part of her horse for the races. But this was going further than he'd intended.

Granted, he probably shouldn't have given in to his urge to tickle her—to hear her laugh, but hindsight was always twenty-twenty. And then he'd made things worse by kissing her. Or was it that she'd kissed him? It was all a bit jumbled in his mind.

He got up and backed away from Annabelle. Some distance would help them both think clearly. He hoped.

Because there was no way he was dating her—or anyone. He'd sworn off relationships after Abbi had died in that car crash. He couldn't make himself that vulnerable again. He couldn't go through the pain of losing yet another person who he loved.

"I… I'm sorry if you got the wrong idea," he stammered. His heart was pounding so hard now that it was echoing in his ears.

"I didn't." She glanced away and started straightening up the papers. "It was just a slip of the tongue. Honest."

He wanted to believe her, but he recalled the intensity of their kiss. And it sure wasn't just him who had been into it. She'd been a driving force that had kicked up the flames of desire.

Perhaps it was time to straighten a few things out between them. He certainly didn't want her to get the wrong idea and end up getting hurt.

"Annabelle, we need to talk."

"About the note?"

He shook his head. The hopeful look on her face fell and

he knew that he was on dangerous ground. One wrong word or look and things would go downhill quickly.

"Listen, Annabelle, I think I gave you the wrong impression." Boy, this was harder than he'd thought it would be. And with her staring right at him, he struggled to find the right words. "I didn't mean to imply with that kiss that there could be anything between us. I… I just got caught up in the moment."

Her gaze narrowed in on him and he prepared himself for her wrath. He was certain that someone as beautiful, fun and engaging as her was not used to being rejected—not that he was rejecting her. He was just letting her know that he wasn't emotionally available. And he didn't know if he ever would be.

Annabelle got to her feet. "I didn't think that this," she waved her hand at the couch, "was a prelude to marriage. I may be a bit sheltered thanks to my father and my uncle, but even I am not naive. Or perhaps that's what you're worried about, my father and uncle forcing you to marry me." Her eyes grew dark and the room grew distinctly chilly. "Trust me. That would not happen. I wouldn't allow it. And I'm sorry you think so little of me."

"That isn't what I meant."

She turned her back to him and began gathering all of the papers. Oh, boy, had he made a mess of things. Where had the smiling and laughing Annabelle gone? And how did he get her back?

He jammed his fingers through his hair. "Annabelle, that isn't what I meant. It's just that, well, I'm not ready for anything serious. And I didn't want you to get the wrong impression. I like you, but that's all it can ever be."

With all of her papers and pens gathered, she straightened. Her guarded gaze met his. "Thank you for sorting it out. I'll make sure that nothing like that ever happens again. And now, I'm going to bed. Alone."

When she started toward the door, he called out, "But what about the note?"

She paused and for a moment he wasn't sure she was going to say anything, but then she turned back to him. "That's not your problem. I appreciate what you've done. But I won't be needing your assistance going forward."

"Annabelle, I'm sorry. I didn't mean to hurt your feelings."

She turned and marched out the door.

Great! Could he have made more of a mess of things?

Frustration balled up in his gut. He felt like throwing something. He'd never felt this sort of overwhelming sense of failure. He'd meant to protect Annabelle and instead he'd done the exact opposite.

Energy built up in his body and he needed to expunge it. But when he glanced around, he knew this was not the place to take out his emotions. This palace was more exotic than any museum he'd ever visited. He might be rich, but he'd be willing to guess that most of the pieces in this room were priceless. He needed to get out of here.

He headed for the door. There was no way he'd be able to go to sleep anytime soon. He was wide awake and he had a decision to make: cut his losses and leave Mirraccino as soon as possible or stay and try to make this up to Annabelle.

Deciding to burn off some of his pent-up energy, he headed for the beach. The sand was highlighted by moonlight, but he barely noticed the beauty of the evening. His thoughts were solely on Annabelle.

He started walking aimlessly. He had to work all of the frustration out of his system so that he could think clearly. He didn't know how far he'd walked when he finally stopped.

He'd known the truth before he'd even set off on this stroll—he wasn't going anywhere. At least not yet. He had too much to wrap up here, from testifying over the purse snatching to judging at the festival. But he knew those were just excuses. He wanted to stay and make things right with Annabelle. At this point, he had to wonder if that was even possible.

By the time Grayson returned to his suite, his body was exhausted. After a cool shower, he stretched out on the king-size bed. He closed his eyes, but all he saw was Annabelle's face with that hurt expression that sliced right through him. He tossed and turned, but he couldn't find any solace or drift off to sleep.

He turned on the bedside light and reached for his phone. Annabelle may have taken all of the paper copies of the note with her, but she'd forgotten that he still had a photo of it on his phone. He pulled it up and stared at it for a moment.

For being a genius, he sure hadn't displayed much intelligence when it came to revealing the secrets of this note. What was up with that? He was usually very good at this type of thing. And then the answer came to him. He hadn't wanted to solve the mystery of the note. He liked having an excuse to spend time with Annabelle.

But now that he'd gone and ruined all of that, there was no reason for him not to finish it. Perhaps it could be some sort of peace offering. After all, he wanted Annabelle to find the truth about her mother. He just hoped it would bring her the answers she craved.

He stared at the message. He believed the key to solving it was more obvious than he'd first surmised.

He read it again. *Tea is my Gold.*

Could that mean *T* equaled *G*?

Grayson retrieved his computer and set to work setting up a spreadsheet to imitate a cipher wheel. In the end, he determined that the capital letters and misspellings were red herrings.

He set the cipher wheel with *T* equals *G*. The other sentence in the message referenced the first and forth. After trial and error, he decided that it was referring to the first letter in the first and fourth words.

In the end, he ended up with: *SUNDIAL. FIVE. TWO.*

Grayson went over the message again and again. It always came back to the same thing. He stared at the message. That had to be right.

What were the chances that he'd got it wrong and the words were so clear?

None. This was it.

He was holding the answer that Annabelle had been seeking. But where was this sundial? And what would they find when they got there?

He wanted to go wake her up, but he didn't dare. She'd been so upset with him earlier that perhaps some sleep would improve her mood.

In the meantime, he searched on the internet for a sundial in Mirraccino, but he couldn't find any. That was odd. Was it possible this mysterious sundial was on another island? Or in a different country?

He yawned. At last, he was winding down. He glanced at the time on his laptop. It was well past two in the morning. If he didn't get some sleep, he'd turn into a big grumpy pumpkin come sunup.

Talk about overreacting.

Annabelle made her way to the village for today's baked goods competition. She'd delivered her entry early that morning and returned to the palace to finish some work on another of the South Shore revitalization projects.

The truth was that she hadn't slept much the night before. Once she'd calmed down and gotten over the sting of Grayson's rejection, she'd realized that she could have taken his words better. A lot better.

Did she really have to storm out of the room? Heat rushed to her face. He was honest with her and that's what she'd wanted. She just hadn't expected him to turn away her kisses. Was she that bad at it?

The thought dug at her. Or was there something wrong

with him? After all, what did she really know about him? That he lived in California. That he was rich. And that he was estranged from his family. In the grand scheme of things, that wasn't a whole lot of information. Perhaps she'd been saved from an even bigger hurt. She clung to that last thought, hoping it would ease the pain in her chest.

She approached the tent where her triple chocolate cake was to be judged. It was then she realized that she'd forgotten to notify the festival officials that Grayson wouldn't be judging. She was certain after the scene last night that he wouldn't waste any time leaving Mirraccino.

And the fate of the South Shore? Her stomach clenched. She hated the thought of letting down her cousin, the king and the students at the university. Everyone was very enthusiastic about the trendy café.

She would reach out to Grayson after the judging and see if he would still consider taking part in the South Shore. If need be, she'd extricate herself from the project. That would make it simpler for everyone and hopefully give him less reason to take his business elsewhere.

Annabelle stepped into the white-tented area and stopped. Her gaze searched for one of the officials. At last she spotted Mr. Caruso.

She made her way over to him. He'd just finished speaking with someone and turned to her. "Good morning, Lady Annabelle. The festival is going along splendidly. I was so happy to learn that you're taking part in it this year. As a representative of the royal family, it really helps relations with the citizens."

"And I was very happy to take part. I had a lot of fun." Her thoughts momentarily strayed to Grayson. It wouldn't have been nearly as fun without him.

"I hope you'll be taking part in the community dinner as well as the masquerade ball."

"I'll definitely be here for the dinner. I wouldn't miss it."

Without Grayson around, it didn't sound nearly as inviting, but she would not let the people down. "As for the ball, I don't think I'll be able to attend."

"That's a real shame, but we're really pleased to have you here for the rest of it."

She forced a smile that she just didn't feel at the moment. This was the moment when she needed to admit that Grayson would no longer be around and there was no one to blame for that but herself. She'd driven him away.

She laced her fingers together to keep from fidgeting. "There is something I need to tell you. I'm sorry that it's last-minute, but Mr. La—"

"Is right here."

The sound of Grayson's voice made her heart skip a beat. She spun around to find him standing a few feet away. The expression on his face was blank. To say she was surprised by his appearance was an understatement. She thought for sure that he'd already be jetting off for Italy.

Regardless of why he'd stayed, she was happy to see him. Very happy.

But just as quickly, she realized that his presence probably had more to do with the South Shore Project and less to do with whatever was going on between them. That thought dampened her enthusiasm a bit.

Annabelle swallowed hard. "Grayson, what are you doing here?"

His brows drew together. "Did you forget? I'm one of the judges for today's contests."

"Oh. Of course."

Mr. Caruso spoke up. "And we're very happy to have you. Trust me, judging today is definitely a treat." The older man turned back to Annabelle. "What did you start to tell me?"

"Oh, it's nothing. Nothing at all."

She walked away, letting Grayson and Mr. Caruso talk about what was expected of him during today's baking competition. She couldn't deny that she was happy to see him. But what did this mean? Did he regret rejecting her?

And if he did, could she trust him not to hurt her again?

CHAPTER THIRTEEN

"ANNABELLE! ANNABELLE, WAIT UP!"

Grayson had excused himself, telling Mr. Caruso that he'd forgotten to relay a message to Annabelle and that he'd be right back. It wasn't exactly the truth, but it wasn't exactly a lie. He did have something that he had to tell Annabelle, but he hadn't forgotten. He just didn't want to make a scene in front of the man. There was enough gossip going around about them already.

Was she walking unusually fast? Or was he just imagining it? He picked up his pace. He wasn't going to let this awkwardness between them drag on.

"Annabelle." Foot by foot, he was gaining ground on her. When at last he was just behind her, he said, "You can keep going, but just so you know, I'll keep following you."

With an audible sigh, she stopped and turned to him. "Grayson, what are you doing here? I thought we said everything last night."

"Annabelle, I want to apologize."

She shook her head. "Don't. You were honest."

"But there was more I should have said." When her eyes lit up just a little, he knew he had her attention. "I overreacted last night and didn't handle things well. I... I don't know what I was thinking."

"It's for the best." There was a resigned tone to her voice.

"Really?" Surely he hadn't heard her correctly. "You're fine with ending things?"

"Yes. After all, it's not like there was anything serious between us." Her voice was hollow and lacked any emotion. "You made perfect sense."

He made sense? He wasn't sure how to take that.

Her gaze didn't quite meet his. "And don't feel obligated to judge the baking competition. I can make your excuses."

"You aren't getting rid of me that easily." He smiled at her, but she didn't smile back. "I'm looking forward to this."

"I just don't want you to do it out of obligation."

"I'm not—"

"And I hope this won't affect the South Shore deal."

"Business is business. I'm expecting to hear from the board today or tomorrow."

"Good. Now I have to go." She turned and walked away with her head held high and her shoulders rigid.

He blew out a frustrated breath. He'd really messed things up. He stood there watching her retreating form. She'd said all of the right things and yet he didn't believe a word of it.

He might not be in a place for a relationship, but that didn't mean he was okay with hurting Annabelle. He felt awful for his outburst the prior evening. There had to be a way to make it up to her. He wanted to make her smile again. But how?

He thought about the problem for a moment. And then he latched on to the heritage festival. Annabelle had been so excited about it. He thought about the baking contest today. It'd be great if she won, but he didn't know what she'd baked and he wasn't one for cheating. If she won, it had to be on her own merits. That was the only way it would mean anything.

No, there had to be something else. He pondered it some more as he walked over to the tent to get his judging paperwork. He was almost there when the idea hit him. A little payback for Annabelle signing him up for all of these activities. He would now sign her up for an event.

Second place.

Annabelle shook hands with so many people congratulating her on her accomplishment. She knew that it was foolish and petty, but she'd been hoping to take first place. She wanted to show Grayson what he was passing up by brushing her off.

She gave herself a mental jerk. Since when did she worry

so much over what a man thought about her? There had been no one else in her life who had ever affected her so greatly. It was best that he would be leaving soon. She needed to think clearly because she still had a note to decipher. She wasn't giving up…even if Grayson would no longer be helping her.

Having spent a few hours at the festival, and with the baking competition over, it was time she left. She didn't want to have to force a smile on her face any longer. She needed some alone time.

With Berto following close behind, Annabelle was almost to the palace when Grayson came rushing up from behind. His sudden appearance startled her. "Grayson, whatever it is, it'll have to wait."

"Hey, is that how it's going to be from now on?"

She kept walking. "I don't know what you're talking about."

"Yes, you do. You've said all of the right things, but you don't mean any of them."

She stopped and glared at him. "Grayson, what do you want from me? You said there shouldn't be anything between us. I said I was fine with that. And now you're upset because I'm trying to maintain some distance between us. You can't have it both ways."

He frowned as he considered her words. "Would it help if I admitted that I'm confused—that you confuse me?"

"No. It wouldn't." She started walking again. The palace was in sight. Just a little farther.

He reached out, touching her arm. "Annabelle, don't run away."

That stopped her in her tracks. She did not run from anything or anyone. She straightened her shoulders and lifted her chin. She turned to him. "What do you want from me?"

"Nothing."

That was not the response she was expecting. "Then why are you here?"

"It's what I can do for you. I figured out the cipher."

"You did? It really is a cipher?" The longer it'd taken them to crack the code, the more her doubts had mounted.

He smiled and nodded. "I figured it out last night."

"You did?"

"I couldn't sleep, so I worked on it."

He hadn't been able to sleep last night. The thought skidded through her mind, but she didn't have time to dwell on it. She had to know about the note. "And what did it say?"

"That's the thing. It didn't mean anything to me. I hope it makes sense to you."

"How will I know if you don't tell me?"

"It said, 'Sundial. Five. Two.'"

"That's it?" It sure wasn't much to go on. "Do you think it ties in with my mother's death?"

"The more important question is, do you believe it ties in?"

She gave it some thought. How many people possessed a coded message? And perhaps it would explain her father's inability to let go of the past. But what was her mother doing with a coded message? What was she involved in?

"Annabelle, what are you thinking?"

The concern in Grayson's voice drew her from her thoughts. "I honestly have no idea what to make of this. I've got more questions than answers."

"Then if you're willing, I think we should follow the clue. It will hopefully give you some peace of mind."

"I... I don't know. What if it's something bad? I'm not sure my family can take any more bad news."

"If you want, I can investigate on my own. And if I think it's something you should know, I'll tell you."

Her gaze met his. "You'd really do that for me?"

He nodded. "You are stronger than you give yourself credit for. And you deserve the truth."

He was right. She could do this. She slipped her hand into his. "We'll do this together."

"Good." He squeezed her hand. "Do you know where we can find a sundial?"

She stopped to think. A sundial? Really?

"Annabelle, please tell me you know of one."

Her mind raced. And then it latched on to a memory. "There's one in the garden."

"What garden? Do you mean the palace gardens?"

She nodded. "It's overgrown with ivy now. When I was a kid, my cousins, my brother and some others would play in the gardens. It's a great place for hide-and-seek. Anyway, we stumbled over the sundial."

"Do you remember where it is?"

The gardens were immense. It would take a long time to search them without some direction. But she was certain that with a little time, she could lead them to the sundial.

"Come on." She started off toward the palace at a clip.

It was only when they reached the palace gates that she realized she was holding his hand. She assured herself that it was just a natural instinct and the action had no deeper meaning. After all, he'd made his feelings for her known. Rather, that should be, he had made his *lack of* feelings for her known.

She quickly let go and pretended as though their connection had no effect over her. *Just stay focused on the note and the sundial.*

Annabelle led them straight to the gardens and suddenly it all looked the same. Sure, each geometrically-shaped garden had a different flower. But then she recalled the ivy. That's what she had to search for. They walked all through the gardens. Each path was explored. No turn was left unexplored.

"I don't understand it," Annabelle said. "I know there was ivy here at one point."

"Don't worry about the ivy. Try to remember if the ivy was near a wall. Or was it out in the open? Was there a statue nearby? I noticed there are quite a few scattered throughout the garden."

She closed her eyes and tried to pull the memory into focus. It had been a lot of years ago and she'd never suspected that she would need to know where to find the sundial.

"Maybe we should ask someone," Grayson said.

Her eyes opened. "No way. We're so close. And I don't need my uncle or father finding out what I'm up to."

"But you're a grown woman. What can they do to stop you?"

She smiled at his naivety. "You obviously have forgotten that my uncle is the king. If he says jump, people ask how high? And my father, he's a duke. He's the one who stuck my security detail on me. There's a lot they can do to make my life miserable. I'd prefer to avoid as much of it as I can."

"Okay. Point taken. But what are we going to do if you can't remember where it is? Or worse, what are we going to do if it has been removed?"

"I highly doubt that it's been removed. If you haven't noticed, my uncle doesn't like change."

"It sounds like you two have a lot in common."

She stopped walking and turned to him. "What's that supposed to mean?"

"It means that you stay here and let them influence your life instead of getting out on your own."

"I left Halencia and my father's home to come here. I can't help that he sent his security with me."

"But you didn't go very far, did you? I mean how much different is your uncle's home from your father's? They both keep a close eye on you."

She didn't like what Grayson was implying. "That's not fair." And worse, his accusation had a ring of truth. "What do you want me to do? Abandon my family like you did?" There was a flinch of pain in his eyes. She hadn't meant to hurt him. "I'm sorry. I shouldn't have said that."

"No. You're right. I did leave my family. Maybe they didn't deserve the way I cut them out of my life. Maybe I should have tried harder."

"And maybe you're right. Maybe I took the easy way out by coming here." Which went back to her thought of visiting the United States. "And once this mystery is unraveled

and the South Shore Project is resolved, I just might surprise
you and go on my own adventure."

"What sort of adventure are we talking about?"

And then it came to her. "That's it."

"What's it?"

"An adventure. It reminded me that we were role-play-
ing. The sundial was on the helm of our ship." She started
walking.

"And…"

"And it was next to a wall that overlooked the sea." She
smiled at him. "Thanks."

"Sure." He looked a bit confused. "Glad I could, uh, help."

They made their way to the far end of the garden where
there was a stone wall. They walked along it until they found
the sundial.

"It's here!" Annabelle was radiating with happiness.

They both rushed over to the historic sundial. It was made
of some sort of metal that was tarnished and weathered. It
was propped up on a rock. And just as Annabelle recalled,
it overlooked the sea.

"What else did the note say?" Annabelle asked.

"Five. Two."

"What do you think that means?"

"If I have to guess, I'd say five down and two across."

They both looked at the sundial. There was nothing there
but the big solid rock and the sundial. Annabelle tried moving the dial, but it was not meant to move.

"Try the rock wall," Grayson suggested, already scan-
ning the area for any sign of disturbance.

Together they worked for the next hour trying each and
every stone, but none of them would give way.

Annabelle kicked at the wall. "This is pointless."

"Hey, don't give up so easily."

"Why not? It's obvious that none of these rocks are going
to move. There's nothing here."

He had to agree. He didn't think this was the spot. But

the note had been so specific. If they could just find the right sundial.

"What makes you think the sundial is here in Mirraccino?" Grayson asked. He couldn't shake the thought that Annabelle and her mother had lived in Halencia and she had found the note in Halencia, yet they were looking here in Mirraccino.

"It's a gut feeling, plus the fact that my mother was murdered here in Mirraccino. It's going to be here." She turned back to the rock wall. "What am I missing?"

"Is it possible there's another sundial around here?"

Just then the butler, Alfred, came up the walk. "Oh, there you are, ma'am." He sent her a puzzled look as she stood in the dirt next to the wall. And then in polished style, he acted as though nothing were amiss. "The king would like to know if you and Mr. Landers will be joining him for dinner."

Annabelle glanced at Grayson. She didn't know where their relationship stood and she had absolutely no idea if Grayson would even be here come dinnertime. And more than anything, she didn't want to stop for dinner. She wanted to keep hunting for the other sundial.

"I had plans to take Lady Annabelle to dinner," Grayson said to her utter surprise. "But if that's a problem, we could go another time."

"No, sir. Not a problem. I will let the king and staff know that you have other plans." The man turned to walk away.

"Alfred, do you have a moment?" Annabelle made her way back to the sidewalk with Grayson right behind her.

The butler turned to her. "Yes, ma'am."

"Grayson and I were just talking about the sundial. Do you know how old it is?"

"No, ma'am, I don't. It could very well be as old as the palace."

"See," Annabelle turned to Grayson, hoping he'd play along. "I told you it was really old."

Grayson's eyes momentarily widened before they went

back to normal. "Yes, you did. I just love all of these historical artifacts. Sundials happen to be a favorite of mine."

"Alfred, do you know of any other sundials on the island?"

The butler paused for a moment as though surprised by the question. She hoped he would give them the clue they needed to find the next piece of this puzzle that her mother had left behind for her.

"Actually, ma'am, there is one other. It's in the old park in the city."

"That's wonderful." Annabelle couldn't help but smile. The butler watched her carefully and then just to cover her tracks, she said, "I'll have to show it to Grayson before he leaves the island."

"Anything else, ma'am?"

"No. Thank you."

The butler nodded and then turned and strode off.

"Do you think he suspects anything?" Annabelle asked. Her gaze trailed after one of her uncle's most trusted employees.

"Does it matter? You didn't know about the other sundial, right?" When she shook her head, Grayson added, "Without you asking him about it, we might never have found it."

"You're right." She just couldn't shake this feeling that she'd made a mistake. "Let's go into the city."

"You know, I wasn't lying when I said I wanted to take you to dinner this evening."

"Oh, but I thought you said you didn't want to get involved."

"It's dinner. I want to make it up to you…you know, for the way I acted last night."

"So what does this mean? Have you changed your mind?"

"How about, I want to be your friend?"

Friends? That wasn't so bad. There were even friends with benefits, but that was for another time. Right now, she wanted to find that sundial.

CHAPTER FOURTEEN

FIVE DOWN. TWO ACROSS.

"This is it! This is it!" Annabelle struggled not to shout it to the world. Instead, her excitement came out in excited whispers.

She worked to loosen the stone just as her phone rang for about the tenth time. And again, she ignored it. After dinner in the city at a small Italian restaurant, she'd grabbed Grayson's hand and snuck out the back while Berto waited for them by the front door.

With the darkness of evening having settled over the city, they'd been able to move quickly down the sidewalk. It was only a five minute walk to the oldest park in Bellacitta.

The hard part was searching in the dark for a sundial. Thank goodness cell phones also made good flashlights. And Grayson found the sundial on the north side of the park near a rock wall.

Once again, her phone rang. And just like before, she ignored it.

"Aren't you ever going to answer that?" Grayson asked.

"Not until I'm ready."

"Annabelle, this isn't safe. You shouldn't have ditched your security detail."

The truth of the matter was that she felt bad about slipping away without a word, but knowing Berto's allegiance was to his employer—her father—what else was she to do?

She and Berto were friendly, but he'd never let that get in the way of doing his job. And he was very good at what he did. She'd make sure to protect him from her father's wrath and somehow make this up to him.

"You do know that they're able to trace the cell phone signal?" He glanced around as though expecting an army of royal guards to arrive.

"I know I told you that my father keeps a close eye on me

and my activities, but relax a little. I don't think even he'd go to that extent. At least, not yet." She smiled at Grayson, hoping to put him at ease.

He didn't return the friendly gesture. "This isn't safe. What if your father is right and there's a real threat on your life? And your bodyguard, I'm sure he won't be happy about you giving him the slip."

"He never is. And besides, I have you to protect me."

"Wait. You've done this before?"

"Ditch Berto to go treasure hunting? No. Ditch him so I could have some semblance of a normal life? Yes. But not very often—only for really important things." She'd gone through a bit of a rebellious stage as a teenager, but unlike her brother, she'd realized there was more to life than partying. She'd wanted an education and a career. So she'd settled down to study and bring up her grades.

"I don't like this." Grayson glanced into the shadows. "We're going back."

She pressed her hands to her hips. What was it with the men in her life bossing her around? She'd been hoping Grayson would be different. "I'm not leaving here until I do what I intended."

His hard gaze met hers. For a moment, there was a mental tug of war, but she refused to give in. She had a plan and she was going to see it through to the end. She owed her mother that much.

"Okay." Grayson conceded with a frown. "But we have to hurry up."

That was good enough for her. She turned and counted out the rocks, but when she went to remove the stone, it wouldn't budge. The tips of her fingers clenched as tight as possible and she pulled, but it wouldn't move.

"Come help me. This rock is stuck."

Grayson glanced around. "You know if we're not careful, we'll be going before that judge for our own crimes."

"What crime? All I'm doing is moving a stone. And I promise to put it right back."

Grayson sighed but he moved next to her and wiggled the stone out of its spot in the wall. "See. Nothing to it."

She glared at him. "That's because I loosened it for you."

"Uh-huh. Sure."

Any other time, she'd have continued the disagreement, but not today. The important thing was solving this clue. They looked at the stone, but they didn't see anything suspicious about it. It looked like your basic stone. So what now?

Annabelle wasn't about to give up. She moved to the wall and in the dark, she ran her hand around the hole in the wall until her fingers felt something smooth in a groove. The more she ran her fingers over it, the more she realized that it was plastic. She pulled it out.

"It's here!"

"Shh… Do you want us to get caught?"

"Sorry." Annabelle glanced around but there was no one in this part of the park.

Grayson replaced the stone in the wall and joined her on the sidewalk. "Let's go."

"Don't you want to see what it says?"

"It's too dark here. Let's go back to the palace and read it there."

There was no way Annabelle was waiting any longer. Just then her phone buzzed again. She figured she'd better get it before her uncle called out every police officer on the island to search for her. She withdrew her phone. She didn't get a word out before Berto started shouting at her. She could hear the worry in his voice. She apologized profusely and promised it wouldn't happen again.

"So how much trouble are you in?" Grayson asked as she disconnected the call.

"I'm not." When she met the disbelief reflected in Grayson's eyes, she said, "Okay. Maybe just a little."

"And I'm sure your father will hear about it. What will you tell him?"

She grinned at him. "The truth."

"The truth? I didn't think you wanted your father to know about the note."

"Who said I was going to mention that? I was going to tell them that I wanted some alone time with you."

"Oh. Good idea. That will make him happy," Grayson said sarcastically.

And then without any warning, Grayson leaned down and pressed his lips to hers. At first, Annabelle didn't respond. Where had that come from? She'd thought he didn't want this. Perhaps all day he'd been trying to tell her that he'd changed his mind.

Annabelle had no idea what was up with him but she wasn't going to complain. She enjoyed feeling his lips move over hers. And soon she was kissing him back. Her heart thump-thumped in her chest.

Perhaps he truly did regret what had happened the other night. Maybe it was a lot to compute for both of them. And the evening had been beautiful…in a way. A walk in the royal gardens. Dinner in one of the local restaurants. And now a walk through the park beneath the stars.

Okay, so maybe that hadn't been exactly how the day had unfolded, but who said she couldn't use some creative license and remember the fun parts. And with Grayson's lips pressed to hers, this was the best part of all.

When he pulled back, she looked up at him. "What was that for?"

"So you don't have to lie to anyone. When they ask why you slipped away, you'll have a very good reason." His voice was warm and deep.

She wasn't quite sure what to say. In that moment, she wasn't sure she trusted herself to speak. Her heart was still beating wildly in her chest.

"What?" He studied her for a moment. "You don't have anything to say?"

She swallowed hard. "Yes. Let's look at this note."

Under a light along the sidewalk, they stopped. Annabelle carefully removed the note from the plastic, afraid the paper would disintegrate in her hands, but luckily it didn't.

When she had it unfolded, she asked, "Can you tell what it says?"

Grayson studied the paper. "There's something there, but in this light I can't make it out. We'll have to look at it when we get back to the palace."

And so they set off for home. Annabelle didn't know which had her stomach aquiver—the new message or the very unexpected, very stirring kiss.

This was impossible.

The next morning, Grayson sighed and leaned back on the couch in the palace's library. They both studied the note.

The paper was old and weathered. And worse yet, some of the ink had faded. But Annabelle refused to give up. And he couldn't blame her. If he were in her shoes, he wouldn't give up either.

"What are we going to do?" Annabelle asked, sitting down beside him.

"Find a solution." He opened his laptop and started typing keywords into the search engine about recovering writing from a faded document. Surprisingly, results were immediately available. "At last an answer."

He turned the computer so Annabelle could read the instructions. It certainly seemed easy enough. But would it work for them?

"Let's do it," Annabelle said.

"Are you sure?" he asked.

"Of course. Why not?"

"Because those are some serious chemicals. They could ruin the paper beyond repair."

"And what good is that note the way it is? We can only make out bits and pieces of the message. Certainly not enough to figure out what it says. I say let's do it."

"Okay then. Can you get the chemicals they mention in the article?"

"I think everything should be here at the palace. The trick is knowing who to ask or where to look."

He nodded in understanding. "You find what we need and I'll meet you out on the balcony."

"The balcony?"

"You surely don't want to use those chemicals in here. Do you?"

"You're right." She started for the door.

"Annabelle," when she paused and turned to him, Grayson asked, "you did read the part where the blog post said to let the paper dry for a few hours before trying to read it?"

She frowned but nodded. "This is going to be the longest few hours of my life."

"Hey, no worries. I'll keep you distracted. After all there's the heritage dinner in the village and we have to be at the courthouse soon—"

Knock. Knock.

Annabelle opened the door. The butler stood there holding a big package.

"Ma'am, this was just delivered for you."

"For me? But I'm not expecting anything."

"I assure you, ma'am that it has your name on it. But if you don't want it, I'll take it away."

"Oh, no, I'll take it." She lowered her voice. "I always do enjoy a good surprise."

Grayson couldn't help but wonder why there was only one box. He'd expected at least two boxes. Something was amiss, but he'd straighten it out later.

She moved to the table and set down the big box. The outside cardboard shipping package had already been opened. Grayson guessed that was typical protocol for the palace.

He couldn't blame them. In this day and age, one couldn't take chances when they lived in the public eye.

Annabelle lifted out a big white box with a large red ribbon. She glanced at him again. "You know what this is, don't you?"

"I'm just watching."

He enjoyed the childlike excitement written all over her face. Who'd have thought a member of royalty, who could have pretty much anything she wished for, would get so excited over a present. Or maybe the excitement was due to her utter surprise and wonderment. Whatever it was, he wanted to put that look on her face again.

She slid the ribbon from the box. She didn't waste any time and she wasn't exactly gentle. She was certainly anxious to see what was inside. Grayson stood back and smiled.

Annabelle lifted the lid and looked inside. At first, she didn't say anything. His heart stopped. That couldn't possibly be a good sign. The breath caught in his lungs as he waited.

Annabelle lifted the black sequined tulle gown from the box. He'd read the description of each gown on the internet until he found the one he thought would look best on Annabelle. He just hoped he'd guessed correctly about the size. After all, he'd never bought a gown before. But what was the good of being rich, if you didn't splurge once in a while?

She turned to him. Her mouth gaped open, but her eyes said it all.

At last, Grayson could breathe. "You like it?"

She nodded vigorously and smiled. "It's amazing. But I don't understand."

"You will. There should be more in the box."

She turned around and lifted out a Venetian mask with an intricate detail and feathers. "But I… I'm not going to the masquerade ball."

"You are now. It's called payback."

Her puzzled gaze met his. "Payback?"

"Yes, you signed me up for the chariot races and the judging. By the way, I really enjoyed the last part." When a smile lifted her lips, he knew he could get her to agree to go the masquerade ball…with very little persuasion. "And I thought it was time I signed you up for something."

Just then his phone buzzed. He wanted to ignore it, but he couldn't. He was expecting a decision from the board. As he checked the caller ID, he realized it was them.

He moved to the other end of the room to take the call. If it was bad news, he didn't want Annabelle to overhear. He'd need a moment to find the right words. But he sincerely didn't believe that it'd come to that.

A few minutes later, he returned to Annabelle. She sent him a curious look but she didn't pry.

"Aren't you curious?" he asked.

"I figured if you wanted me to know that you'd tell me."

"What would you say if I told you the board unanimously approved the South Shore Project?"

Her eyes widened. "Really?"

"Really."

She cheered and then rushed to him with her arms wide open. She hugged him tight. Her soft curves pressed against him and at that moment, he only had one thought on his mind—kissing her.

He pulled back just far enough to stake a claim on Annabelle's glossy lips. He just couldn't help himself. No other kiss had ever been so sweet. He just couldn't get enough of her.

He lowered his head—

Knock. Knock.

Grayson uttered a curse under his breath as he released Annabelle.

Her fine brows drew together. "Do I even want to know what else you're up to?"

"Me?" he said innocently. "Why are you blaming me for someone knocking on the door? Do you want me to get it?"

"No, I've got it."

She swung the door open and the butler was standing there with another large box. Annabelle immediately took it. A grin played upon her very kissable lips.

"Thank you." She started to close the door.

"Ma'am."

She turned back to Alfred. "Yes."

"The box is for Mr. Landers."

"Oh." Pink tinged her cheeks. "I'll give it to him. Thanks." When the door closed, Annabelle sent him another puzzled look. "What's this?"

He approached her and took the box from her. "This is what I'll be wearing to the ball."

"You're going?" The surprise in her voice rang out, making him smile.

"Of course. I wouldn't make you go alone." When her mouth opened in protest, he held up a finger silencing her. "And before you complain, just remember that you owe me. And be grateful that there'll be no chariots involved and that you won't have to pretend to be a horse." As she broke out in laughter, he'd never heard anything so wonderful. "By my way of thinking, you definitely win."

She subdued her amusement. "When you put it that way, I have to agree with you."

"Good. I'll take that as your acceptance. We'd better get ready to leave for the courthouse."

"I almost forgot." She checked the clock. "We don't have long. I just need to change."

"I think I will too. I'll meet you back down here."

Her gaze moved to the note. "What about this?"

"We don't have time to do anything with it now. Do you have someplace safe to keep it?"

She nodded. "My room will be safe enough." She lowered her voice even though they were the only two in the library and the doors were shut. "As a little girl, I found a loose piece of molding with space behind it. It will be the perfect place."

"Sounds good."

He knew that he shouldn't be so eager to spend time with her. After all he'd gone through after Abbi's death, he'd sworn off letting anyone get that close to him again. But if he could just maintain this friendship with Annabelle, they'd be all right.

CHAPTER FIFTEEN

WHO'D HAVE GUESSED that he could be so charming?

Annabelle's feet barely touched the floor as she made her way back to her room with her ball gown in her arms. She wondered if it'd fit. She wasn't worried. There was a woman on staff at the palace who could work magic with a needle.

She couldn't believe Grayson had bought her a ball gown. No one had ever done anything so thoughtful for her—ever. Annabelle spread the gown out over the bed. It was simply stunning, with a crystal-studded bodice. The man certainly had good taste. A smile pulled at her lips.

If he didn't want to get involved with her, he was certainly sending out the wrong signals, from the kiss in the park to this gown. Maybe he was changing his mind. And she didn't see how that would be so bad.

There was a knock at her door. She rushed over, thinking that it was Grayson. She wondered what he'd forgotten to tell her. She opened it to find a new member of the household staff standing there holding a silver tray.

The young woman smiled. "Ma'am, your mail."

Annabelle accepted it and closed the door. She was about to set the mail aside when she noticed that the top envelope didn't have a postage stamp.

She stared at it a little longer. It had her name typed out but no address. And the longer she stared at it, the more convinced she was that someone had actually used a typewriter. She was intrigued. She didn't know of anyone these days who used a typewriter.

She placed the other two envelopes on the desk before picking up a letter opener and running it smoothly along the fold in the envelope. She withdrew a plain piece of paper. When she unfolded it, she found a typed note:

This is your only warning.
Leave the past alone.
Nothing good will come of you unearthing ghosts.
You don't want to end up like your mother.

Annabelle gasped. She'd been threatened. Adrenaline pumped through her veins. The implications of this note were staggering.

She backed up to the edge of the bed and then sat down. This verified her father's suspicions. He'd been right all along. Suddenly, guilt assailed Annabelle for thinking all these years that her father was paranoid.

Her mother's killer was alive and here in Mirraccino. And this cipher was somehow tied in to it all.

She had to tell Grayson. She rushed out of her room and down the hallway to Grayson's door. Please let him be here. She knocked, rapidly and continuously.

"Okay, okay. I'm coming."

Grayson swung the door open. He was wearing a pair of black jeans and his shirt was unbuttoned. The words caught in the back of Annabelle's throat. He looked good—really good.

"Annabelle, what's the matter?" Grayson's voice shook her out of her stupor.

"I, ah…" She suddenly realized that telling him about the note probably wasn't a good idea. She moved the envelope behind her back.

The more she got to know about Grayson, the more she realized that he was cautious like her father and uncle. He'd probably want to tell the king about the note and she didn't intend to let that happen until she discovered the truth about her mother's death.

"Annabelle?"

"Sorry." Her mind rapidly searched for an answer that wouldn't raise his suspicions. She glanced up and down the hallway, making sure they were alone. Then she lowered her voice. "I just wanted to let you know that I stashed the note." Then she made a point of checking her bracelet watch. "Shouldn't we be going?"

He frowned at her. "I didn't think you'd be anxious to get to the courthouse early."

She shrugged. "It never hurts to make a good impression."

"Annabelle, there's something else. Tell me."

She frowned at him. How could he read her thoughts so easily? The truth was that she really did want to share the contents of the note with him. She'd trusted him this far, surely she could trust him with this too.

"There is one other thing." She glanced around again to make sure they were still alone. She really didn't want anyone to overhear them and report back to the king.

"Would you like to come inside?"

He didn't have to ask her twice. She stepped inside and closed the door behind her. "I received something very strange in today's mail."

"The mail? What is it?"

She held out the envelope. "Here. Maybe it'd be better if you read it yourself."

His brows drew together as he accepted the envelope. He glanced at the front which only had her name, Lady Annabelle. He withdrew the note and started to read.

He didn't say anything as his gaze rose to meet hers. And then he read it again. The continued silence was eating at her. Why didn't he say something?

At last, not able to contain herself, she said, "Well, what do you think? This is a good sign, isn't it?"

"Good? How do you get that?" His voice rumbled with emotion. "This is far from good."

Why wasn't he seeing this as a good sign? Maybe if she explained her reasoning. "Don't you see? If we weren't getting close, whoever this is wouldn't be scared that we're going to reveal the truth."

"And I think you're taking this too lightly. Annabelle,

this is a threat to your safety. You have to tell your uncle and the police."

She shook her head. "No way. This is proof that my mother's murder was something more than a mugging."

"Which is another reason to bring in the authorities."

"No." She would not bend on her decision. "They won't take it seriously—"

"They will. They'll make sure you're safe."

"But they won't reopen my mother's case."

"You don't know that for sure."

Her unwavering gaze met his. "We have no proof of foul play. Until we do, this stays between us."

Grayson blew out a deep breath as he raked his fingers through his hair. "You think we'll find the proof we need by following the clues?"

She nodded. "I promise, as soon as we have proof of my mother's murder we'll go to the police."

"Can I trust you?"

She swiped her finger over her heart, making an *X*. "Cross my heart and hope to die."

"Okay. I don't think you have to go that far. But if I agree to go along with this, you have to do something for me."

"Name it."

"You have to promise not to go out of my sight. Someone has to keep you safe—someone who knows there's a legitimate threat lurking out there."

The implications of his words struck her. "When you say not out of your sight, are we talking about sleeping and showering together?"

He frowned at her. "Any other time I'd welcome your flirting, but not now. This is serious. You get that, don't you?"

She did, but she refused to let that note scare her off. "I was just trying not to let the threat get to me, but you just went and ruined that."

"You can't pretend your safety isn't at risk." He pressed

his hand to his trim waist. "You should back off this search and let me handle it."

"That's not going to happen." She leveled him a long, hard stare, making sure he knew she meant business. "I'll take the threat seriously, but we're in this together."

"And when I tell you to do something to keep you safe, you'll do it without arguing?"

"Now you're pushing your luck." When he looked as though he was about to launch into another argument, she said, "Stop worrying. I won't do anything dangerous. Besides, you'll be right there to protect me. Now, we should get going."

There was no way Grayson was cutting her out of this hunt. They were close to solving her mother's murder. Really close.

"What's wrong?"

Annabelle's voice cut through Grayson's thoughts. They had just finished at the courthouse and had returned to the palace. She'd maneuvered her car into a parking spot off to the side of the palace with the other estate vehicles.

Grayson cleared his throat. "I didn't think you knew how to drive."

It wasn't what he was thinking about, but it gave him time to think of how to word the next thing he had to tell her.

She sent him a puzzled look. "Why would you think that? Doesn't everyone know how to drive?"

He shrugged. "It's just that since I've known you, one of your bodyguards has driven you everywhere."

She shrugged. "I guess it all depends on my mood. But as you noticed, they were right behind us."

"I only noticed because you said something."

"Someday that's all going to change. As soon as we figure this mystery out."

This was his cue to speak up. "I've been thinking."

"I know. You've been quiet ever since the judge gave the kid probation."

That wasn't what had him quiet, but the judge's sentence did give him pause. "Did you think that was a fair sentence?"

She shrugged. "After hearing the kid's side of it, I can see where desperation might have led him to do something stupid."

The teenager had been trying to help his mother financially. She'd just lost her job and he was scared of how she would make ends meet. It would be a tough position for anyone.

Grayson rubbed his clean-shaven jaw. "I'm just worried the kid might not have learned his lesson. And if he were to be put in a tough spot again, he might make the same poor choices."

"Let's hope not. But doesn't he deserve a chance to prove himself?"

Grayson glanced away. "I suppose."

Annabelle's gaze bored into him. "There's something else that's bothering you and I know what it is."

"You do?"

She whispered. "It's the note, isn't it?"

Needing some air, he got out of the car and she joined him. She kept looking at him, waiting for an answer. He had to find just the right words so she'd give credence to what he was about to say.

He held his hand out to her. "Let's go for a walk."

"But we need to take care of the note and then get ready for the festival dinner—"

"This is important. Come on." He gave a gentle pull on her arm.

For a moment, he thought that she was going to resist, but then she started moving and he fell in step with her. She was headed for the royal gardens, the exact place he had in mind. The gardens were enormous and would allow them plenty of privacy.

With the golden sun of the afternoon shining, it lit up all of the flowers from reds and yellows to purples and pinks. Plenty of greens were interspersed to offset everything. He never considered himself a flower kind of guy, but there was something truly beautiful about this place.

When they came upon a bench along one of the walkways, he stopped. "Let's sit down. We need to talk."

"I'd rather be treating the note so that we can read it."

"That can wait. This can't."

She wasn't listening to him about the threat and he had to find a way to reach her. He needed her to be cautious. But he understood her hesitation to tell her father or uncle. After all, she'd been living with security dogging her steps for years now unless she was on the palace grounds. He couldn't imagine what they might do to protect her if they found out about the note. Before he made the decision of whether to tell anyone about the threat, he had to know that Annabelle was taking it seriously.

"Okay. I'm listening." Annabelle's gaze met his.

"That's the problem. I don't think you're hearing what I'm trying to tell you. This note, it's serious."

"It's proof that we're close to the truth about my mother's murder."

"It's much more than that and you know it." He really didn't want to scare her with the stark possibilities, but what else did he have to knock sense into her?

Annabelle sighed. "I know you're worried. But I can't stop—"

"I know. I know." He understood how important this endeavor was to her.

Annabelle's determination reminded him of Abbi's. That was not a good thing. Warning bells were going off in his head. Maybe if he'd been more insistent with Abbi then they wouldn't have been in that horrible car accident that stole her life far too soon.

He took Annabelle's hand and guided it to his face. He

ran her hand down over the faint scar trailing down his jaw. "Do you feel that?"

"It's a scar?"

He nodded. "I'm going to tell you something that I've never told anyone. I mean, it was written up in the papers, but they invariably got the facts wrong. Way wrong."

Annabelle sat quietly as though waiting until he was ready to go on. The horrific and painful memories washed over him. He'd locked them in the back of his mind for so long that it was almost a relief to get them out there—almost.

He cleared his throat, hoping his voice wouldn't betray him. "When my company went public and I ended up with more money than I knew what to do with, I gained instant fame. I could have easily become a partying fool with a girl on each arm, but that just wasn't me."

"Let me guess—you preferred to spend your time working on your computer."

"Something like that. I guess when you grow up with your nose in a book or gaming on your computer, it's tough to change. One night, after a particularly successful deal was signed, a couple of friends talked me into going out to celebrate. Of course, I'm the lone guy at the table while those two were off chatting up some beautiful girls. And that's when Abbi stepped into my life. Literally. I was on my way out when she stepped in front of me."

"And it was love at first sight."

Grayson shrugged, not comfortable talking about his feelings for Abbi with Annabelle. "She was leaving too. I offered to grab some coffee with her and she agreed. There was an all-night coffee shop a couple of blocks away. I had the feeling that I should know her, but I didn't. And she was actually okay with that. She told me she was an actress. She'd just had her first box office hit. But she wasn't like the others who'd passed through my life. She didn't want anything from me. She was down-to-earth and actually interested in my games."

It'd been a long time since he was able to think about

Abbi without seeing the horrific scene of the accident with the blood and her broken body. Those images were the ones that had kept him up many nights. But these memories, he found comfort in them. He remembered Abbi smiling and laughing.

"We became fast friends."

"Uh-huh." The look in Annabelle's eyes said she didn't believe that they were just friends. And there was something else. Was it jealousy?

"Trust me. In the beginning, neither of us were looking for anything serious. We both just needed a friend—someone who treated us like normal people. And so when she wasn't filming or doing promo spots, she came and crashed at my place. We gamed a lot."

Annabelle frowned.

"What's the matter?" Grayson asked.

"I just never had anyone like that in my life. Sure, there's my brother, but other than that my father succeeded in isolating me."

"What about female friends? Didn't you have some close ones?"

She nodded. "I did. But then we grew up and went our separate ways. In fact, my brother is visiting one of our old friends right now. She's a model on the Paris runways. Who'd have guessed, given that she started off as a tomboy contrary to her mother's best intentions? She and my brother were best friends as kids. They'd fish together and go boating. You name it and they probably did it."

"But not you?"

"I guess I was too much of a girly girl. I was not into getting dirty or touching creepy, crawly things." Her face scrunched at the mere thought and he couldn't help but smile.

So once again, she'd been left out. Grayson's heart went out to her. He knew what it was to be alone and never know if the people who were in your life were there because they liked you or because they liked what you could do for them.

He couldn't blame her for doing everything she could to solve her mother's murder and to regain her freedom.

When Annabelle spoke again, her voice was soft. "Did you and this Abbi get romantic?"

"Eventually. At the same time, she got nominated for a prestigious award for outstanding supporting actress. Her fame grew exponentially overnight. In the process, she gained what she called a superfan. I called him a stalker from the get-go, but she didn't want to believe it."

Annabelle remained quiet.

"Eventually, she told her agent and the studio where she was working on a new film. They hired her a bodyguard until they could do something about the stalker. And everything quieted down. No notes. No roses. No photos. Everyone assumed the guy had given up and moved on." Grayson felt like such a fool for letting himself believe that someone that obsessed would just give up. If only he had done something different.

Grayson leaned forward resting his elbows on his knees. He stared straight ahead, but all he could see were flashbacks of the past. A nightmare that would never fully leave him.

"We felt suffocated and needed some time alone without any security watching Abbi's every move. So we snuck off to the beach—alone." The breath caught in the back of his throat as he recalled how things had gone from fun to downright deadly. "It...it was like something out of a real-life horror movie." The pain and regret stabbed at him. He lowered his head into his hands. "I keep asking myself, what was I thinking?"

Annabelle didn't say anything. Instead, she placed her hand on his back, letting him know she was there for him. The funny thing was that he was supposed to be here for her—to help her see reason. And yet here she was being supportive to him.

When he found his voice again, he said, "At first, I couldn't even believe what was happening. At a red light on the way to the beach, gunshots rang out from the car beside us. The windows shattered."

Annabelle let out a horrified gasp. "Were you hit?"

He shook his head. "I punched the gas and luckily didn't hit anyone as we cleared the intersection. It turned into a high-speed chase, but I just couldn't shake the guy. And then…"

The scenes unfolded before his eyes. To this day, he still kept thinking "what if?" scenarios. If only he'd made a different decision, Abbi might still be here.

He swallowed hard. "I came upon an intersection with heavy cross traffic. I stopped…the stalker didn't. He…he plowed into the back of my car. It sent us airborne. I can't remember anything other than Abbi's scream. The rest is a blank. The first responders said that I was thrown free, but Abbi, she, uh, was pinned under the wreckage."

"I'm so sorry." While her one arm was still draped over his back, her other hand gripped his arm. "You don't have to go into this—"

"Yes, I do. You have to understand."

"Understand what?"

He had to keep going. He had to make Annabelle understand that risky decisions had major consequences. "Abbi died on the way to the hospital. And it was my fault."

"No, it wasn't." Annabelle's voice was soft and gentle like a balm on his scarred heart.

Grayson turned to face her. "I wish I could believe that. I really do. But it was my idea to go to the beach. It…it was my idea for us to spend some time alone. I just never thought that guy was still sticking around. I failed her."

Annabelle pulled him close and held him. He knew he didn't deserve her sympathy when he was sitting here while Abbi was gone. Life wasn't fair. That's one thing his father had taught him that had been right.

When he gathered himself, he pulled back. "The media, they got ahold of the story, and they told lie upon lie about me and about Abbi. It got so bad that I didn't leave my house for a long time. I worked remotely. That's when I started working on my plan to take the cafés global."

"I'm very sorry that all of that happened to you, but why did you tell me?"

"Because I need you to take that note seriously. Abbi and I didn't take her threat seriously enough and look what happened."

Her gaze met his. "You are that worried about me?"

"Yes. I couldn't stand for anything to happen to you."

"It won't."

"Promise me that you'll be careful."

"I promise."

And then he claimed her lips, needing to feel her closeness. Her touch was rejuvenating and eased away the painful memories. He'd never forget what happened, but he knew now that he had to keep going forward because his life's journey wasn't complete. Maybe he was meant to be here and keep Annabelle safe.

But as her lips moved beneath his, something very profound struck him. Here he was warning her about unknown dangers and yet, he was the one in imminent danger—of losing his heart, if he wasn't careful.

CHAPTER SIXTEEN

"THIS IS A MOMENT we've been waiting for." The king's deep voice rang out loud and clear.

Annabelle quietly sat at the heritage dinner that evening. Back at the palace the note had been brushed with chemicals that hopefully would illuminate the print on it. And while she waited, she'd been treated to the most amazing home-cooked food.

She wasn't alone in her enjoyment. Everyone had oohed and aahed over the entrees before devouring them. And the sinfully delightful desserts had just been served, but before people could dive in, the king wanted to make a special toast.

Grayson sat next to her at the long wooden table. They were having dinner in the village streets of Portolina. It was a community affair and this was the only spot big enough for such a large turnout. Annabelle smiled as she gazed around at so many familiar faces.

Her eyes paused on the man next to her—Grayson. He'd surprised her today when he'd opened up to her with what must have been one of the most tragic moments of his life. And the fact that he'd done it because he was worried about her was not lost on her. This man who said that he wasn't interested in a relationship was now throwing out very confusing signals.

And the fact that he'd been willing to keep her secret for just a little while longer made him even more attractive. He was not like the other men in her life. He was not domineering and insistent on having his way. He was willing to listen and consider both sides of the argument. That was a huge change for her. And it was most definitely a big plus in her book.

Not to mention she was getting used to having him next to her—really used to it. She didn't know what she was going to do when he left Mirraccino. Because no matter what was growing between them, she realized that he intended to leave and return to his life in California.

"And that's why I'd like you to help me welcome Mr. Grayson Landers," the king's voice interrupted Annabelle's thoughts.

Applause filled the air as Grayson got to his feet. He smiled and winked at Annabelle before he made his way toward the king. Hands were shaken. The contract for the South Shore Project was signed. And Grayson offered a brief thank-you.

Annabelle hadn't realized how much this moment would mean to her. She thought that it would be monumental because at last she could show her father that she could take care of herself. But she realized that this moment meant so much more because Grayson now had a permanent tie to Mirraccino. He would be housing his Mediterranean operations right here in addition to starting one of his famous cafés. Maybe it wasn't such a far-fetched idea to think that they might have the beginning of something real.

"Annabelle."

She turned to find her father standing behind her. "Poppa, what are you doing here?"

"Is that the way you greet your father?"

"Sorry." She moved forward to give him a kiss on the cheek followed by a hug. "I didn't know you were coming."

"We need to talk." His voice was serious, as was the expression on his face.

She started to lead him away from the crowd. "Is something wrong?"

"Yes, it is."

Fear stabbed at her heart. It had to be serious for him to come all of this way on the spur of the moment. And then a worst-case scenario came to mind. "Is it Luca? Has something happened to him?"

"No."

She let out a pent-up breath. She could deal with anything else. Curiosity was gnawing at her. "What is it?"

"We'll talk about it back at the palace."

Annabelle walked silently next to her father. He was never this quiet unless he was really agitated. She had a sinking feeling that she knew the reason for his impromptu visit. And this evening was most definitely not going to end on a good note.

Annabelle stopped walking. "Let's have it out here."

Her father sighed as he turned to her. "Don't be ridiculous. We're not going to talk out here in public."

"There's no one within earshot. And I don't need the palace staff overhearing this and gossiping." She wasn't about to say that there was someone out there who thought they had a vested interest in anything having to do with her mother's murder. Right now, she wasn't sure who she could trust and who she couldn't.

"Fine." Her father crossed his arms and frowned at her just as he had done when she was a little girl and had gotten into the cookies right before dinner. If only this problem were so easy to remedy. "I know what you did. I know you stole some of your mother's belongings."

"Stole? Really?" The harsh word pierced her heart, but she refused to give in to the tears that burned the backs of her eyes. "She was my mother—"

"And her journal is none of your business."

"I disagree. I was robbed of really getting to know her. And you…you shut down any time I ask about her. How else am I supposed to get to know her?"

Her father's eyes widened with surprise. "Why can't you just leave the past alone?"

"How am I supposed to do that when you can't let go of it?"

Her father's gaze narrowed in on her. "There's more going on here, isn't there?"

"No." She realized that she'd said it too quickly. She'd never been capable of subterfuge and her brother never let her forget it.

"Whatever you're up to, daughter, I want it stopped. Now!" Her father so rarely raised his voice that when he did, he meant business.

"Is there a problem here?" Grayson's voice came from behind her.

She'd been so caught up in her heated conversation with her father that she hadn't even heard Grayson's footsteps on the gravel of the roadway. But she should have known that he wouldn't be far behind. He'd said he'd be keeping a close eye on her.

Her father didn't make any motion to acknowledge Grayson. Instead he continued to stare at her, bullying her into doing as he commanded. And as much as she loved him, she just couldn't abide by his wishes anymore. Their family was falling apart under the strain of what had happened to their mother. She could no longer bear the mystery, the silence, the not knowing. Someone had to do something and it looked like it was going to be her.

"Poppa, I'd like you to meet Mr. Grayson Landers. He has just bought the last property in the South Shore piazza."

The two men shook hands. All the while her father eyed up Grayson. She wasn't sure what was going through her father's mind, but she'd hazard a guess that it wasn't good.

Now was her chance to make her move. "Poppa, now that I've concluded the South Shore Project on my own, surely you must recognize that was quite an accomplishment."

Her father's bushy eyebrows rose. "Yes, you're right. You did a very good job. I'm sorry I didn't say something sooner. As you know, I had other matters on my mind."

"I understand." So far, so good. "Now you have to accept that I can take care of myself. I'd like the security removed."

"No." There was a finality in his voice.

She'd heard that tone before and knew that arguing was pointless. When her father made up his mind, he didn't change it—even when he was wrong. "One of these days you'll have to let go of me."

Her father turned to Grayson. "I see the way you look at my daughter and the way she looks at you. Make sure you take care of her."

Without hesitation, Grayson said, "I will, sir. I promise."

And then her father turned toward the palace, leaving them in the shadows as the sun set. Annabelle let out a sigh.

Grayson cleared his throat. "So that was your father?"

"The duke himself. I take it he wasn't what you were expecting."

"I guess I was just hoping that he would be warmer and friendlier than you'd portrayed."

"He used to be…when my mother was alive. Her death changed us all."

"I'm sorry." And then Grayson drew her into his strong arms. She should probably resist, but right now the thought of being wrapped in his embrace was far too tempting.

The best thing she could do was give her father time to disappear to the study for his evening bourbon and then she would head inside. She was anxious to see if they could read the note yet.

Nothing was ever easy.

Grayson sighed. The initial treatment with the note hadn't worked. Some more research on the internet had them searching for yet another chemical. But it was harder to locate and required a trip into the city. Annabelle had insisted on driving. She'd said it calmed her down when she was worked up. And so with her security in the vehicle behind them, they made yet another jaunt into the city.

This trip had been short and to the point. There had been no time for a walk around the South Shore or a stroll through the picturesque university campus. There hadn't even been a few minutes for some ice cream on this warm day. No, today they both wanted to solve this latest clue.

Like the duke, Grayson was worried about Annabelle's safety. If he could solve this mystery on his own, he would.

But he didn't know the island well enough in order to make sense of the clues—for that he needed Annabelle.

This application just had to work. Annabelle and her family deserved some answers. It wouldn't bring back Annabelle's mother, but it might give them all a little peace.

"Well, come on," she said before she alighted from the car.

Grayson opened the car door and with the necessary supplies in hand, he called out, "Hey, wait for me."

She did and then they headed inside. Annabelle agreed to retrieve the note from her hiding spot and meet him in his room. He had a feeling that the weathered paper wouldn't hold up much longer so they had to get it right this time.

When the lock on his door snicked shut, he noticed how Annabelle fidgeted with the hem of her top. Was she nervous about being alone with him? Was she secretly hoping more would happen than revealing the contents of the note?

Maybe a little diversion would help them both relax. His gaze moved to Annabelle's full, glossy lips. He took a step closer to her. What would it hurt to indulge their desires?

"Don't even think about it." And then a little softer, she said, "We don't have time."

Not exactly a rejection—more like a delay of the game. He smiled. He could work with that.

His gaze met hers. "There's always time."

She crossed her arms and arched a brow, letting him know that she meant business.

He sighed, thinking of the delicious moment they'd missed out on. But then he recalled the ball that evening and his mood buoyed. Soft music, Annabelle in his arms and the twinkling stars overhead. Oh, yeah. This was going to be a great night.

"You're right." He moved to the desk near the window. "Let's get to work."

While Annabelle peered over his shoulder, he applied the solution. All the while, he willed it to work.

At first, there was nothing and then there were the faintest letters. Together they worked, making out the wording of the note. Thankfully the person had used the same key, making decoding it quite simple.

"We did it!" Annabelle beamed.

"Yes, but what does 'Placard. Two. Three.' mean?"

The smile slipped from her face. "I have no idea."

He studied the note making sure he hadn't made a mistake. "What do you think we'll find this time?"

When Annabelle didn't respond, Grayson glanced up at her. Lines had formed between her brows and her lips were drawn down into a frown. Oh, no. There was a problem.

"Annabelle?" She didn't respond as though lost in her thoughts. He cleared his throat and said a little louder, "Annabelle, did you remember something? Do you know what this note is referencing?"

This time her gaze met his and she shook her head. "I haven't a clue."

"But something's bothering you."

She glanced away. "It's just the not knowing. It's starting to get to me."

Was that it? Or was she having second thoughts about unearthing the past? He needed to give her an out. "If you've changed your mind, we can put the note away and forget that we found it—"

"No. I can't. My mother deserves better than that."

But it wasn't her mother he was worried about right now. "You have time to think about it. We can do whatever you want." He consulted his wristwatch. "And now it's time to get ready for the ball."

"I'm not going." She stated it as though it were nonnegotiable.

She might be stubborn, but he was even more so. "You have to." When her gaze met his, he said, "You're my date. And I've never been to a masquerade ball. Look," he walked over to the bed and picked up his black mask, "I'm all set to be your mystery man."

That elicited a slight smile from her, but she was quiet. Too quiet.

"And you can be my seductive lady of intrigue," he said, trying to get her to loosen up so she could enjoy the evening.

"Intrigue, huh?"

He nodded, anxious to see her in the gown. He'd never bought clothes for a woman before. And now he wanted to see if his hard work had paid off. "You'd better hurry. You don't want to be late for the ball."

"But what about the note?"

He frowned. Maybe she needed a dose of reality. "You know how you accused your father of being all caught up in the past?" When she nodded, he added, "Well, you're getting just as caught up in this note. It's not healthy."

Her gaze narrowed. "You don't understand—"

"I do understand. Just remember who has stood by you through all of this. I want you to know the truth, but I also want you to realize that there's more to life than that note, than the past. Tonight we go to the ball. And tomorrow we will work on solving the message. Agreed?"

She didn't say anything.

"Annabelle?"

"Fine. Agreed."

Knock. Knock.

When Annabelle opened the door, Mrs. Chambers stood there. Her silver hair was twisted and pinned up. Her expression was vacant, not allowing anyone to see her thoughts about finding Annabelle in Grayson's room. Not that he cared what anyone thought.

The woman said, "Ma'am, I came to help you dress for the ball."

"I'll be right there."

"Yes, Ma'am. I'll wait for you in your room." The woman turned and walked away.

Annabelle waited a moment before she said, "Do you think she overheard us talking about the note?"

He had absolutely no idea, but he knew that Annabelle was already stressed. "I don't think we were loud enough for her to hear us through the door." He moved to her side and brushed his fingers over her cheek. "Just give me tonight and I'll give you my undivided attention tomorrow."

She stepped closer. "Does that mean no laptop?"

He readily nodded, which was quite odd for him. Normally he felt most at ease when his fingers were flying over the keyboard typing code or answering emails. His hands wrapped around Annabelle's waist. But tonight, his hands felt much better right here.

"No laptop." He leaned forward and pressed a quick kiss to her lips.

When he pulled back, her eyes were still closed. They fluttered open. The confusion about why he'd pulled away so quickly was reflected in them.

"There will be more of that later." He had no doubts. "But first you need to change. It wouldn't do for Cinderella to be late to the ball."

"When you put it that way, you have a deal." She lifted up on her tiptoes and pressed a kiss to his lips.

Before he could pull her close again, she stepped out of his reach. A naughty smile lit up her face. "We have a ball to attend."

He sighed. Suddenly the ball didn't sound like that great an idea, but Annabelle was already out the door. He shook his head. This evening was going to be far more complicated than he ever imagined. Because there was more to those kisses than either of them was willing to admit.

And yet this evening was going to be a once-in-a-lifetime experience. A ball attended by a king and a duke. And Grayson would have the most beautiful woman in his arms...all night long.

The answer could wait.

Now that the moment of truth was almost here, Annabelle wasn't so sure she was doing the right thing. What if she learned something bad about her mother?

Annabelle's stomach quivered with nerves. What exactly had her mother gotten herself mixed up in? Did her father secretly know? What if all this time he'd been trying to protect her mother's memory? The thought sent a chill down Annabelle's spine.

She scanned the party guests for her father. At last, she found him talking with one of the village elders. He had come alone to the ball and she knew that he would leave alone too. She did not want to end up like him.

Now wasn't the best time to speak to her father, but she couldn't stand the tug of war going on within herself. She had to know.

She made her way over to him. "Good evening, Poppa."

"Hello, daughter. Shouldn't you be with your date?"

Her stomach churned. She was in no mood to make polite chitchat. The best way to end her agony was just to get it out there. "Do you know why Momma was murdered?"

Instantly the color drained from her father's face. "Annabelle, what's the meaning of this?"

"You said you didn't think she died as a result of a mugging, but do you know what did happen?" And then a thought popped into her mind and she uttered it before her brain could process the implications. "Are you afraid that she did something wrong and it got her killed?"

The color came rushing back to her father's face. His voice came out in hushed tones but there was no mistaking the fury behind each word. "Annabelle, I will not stand for you speaking to me like this. I've done nothing to warrant such hostility and suspicion."

He was right. She'd let her imagination get the best of her. "I'm sorry, Poppa. It's the not knowing. I can't take it anymore."

"Do you honestly think your mother would have done anything to hurt our family? She loved us with every fiber of her being." His eyes glistened with unshed tears. "I miss her so much."

"I miss her too."

"She would have been proud of the young woman you've grown into."

"Thank you."

"For what?"

"Talking about Momma. You never want to talk of her and it hurts because I miss her too. And talking about her keeps those memories alive for me."

Her father cleared his throat. "I'm sorry I failed you in that regard. I will try to do better."

"And I'm sorry my questions hurt you."

They hugged and Annabelle accepted that was the best she could hope for from her father tonight. She decided to go in search of her dashing escort. She didn't care how many balls she attended, they were all magical. But this evening was extra special thanks to Grayson.

Tonight, she would laugh, forget about her problems and kick up her heels. Grayson would make sure of it. And tomorrow, her feet would land back in reality. But tomorrow was a long way off.

Her gaze sought out Grayson, who looked so handsome in his black tux. She was in absolutely no hurry for the sun to rise on a new day because she had a gut feeling that tomorrow would bring her those long-sought-after answers. And she had absolutely no idea if those answers would be good or bad.

"Here you go." Grayson stepped up to her and held out a glass of bubbly. When she accepted it, he held up his glass to make a toast. "Here's to the most beautiful woman at the ball."

Heat rushed to her cheeks as she smiled. The truth of the matter was that she felt a bit overdone. The king had sent along a tiara for her to wear. As far as tiaras went, at least it wasn't big and showy, but it just felt like too much.

"Thank you for the kind words."

"They aren't just words. I mean them." He leaned forward and planted a quick kiss on her lips.

He pulled back before she was ready for him to go. A dreamy sigh passed her lips. If only…

Thoughts of her gown and tiara slipped to the back of her mind. Her heart tap-danced in her chest as Grayson smiled at her. How had she gotten so lucky?

The evening took on a life of its own. She sipped at the bubbly. She talked with the guests. And then Grayson held out his hand to escort her onto the dance floor.

In his very capable arms, she glided around like she was on a cloud. She wasn't even sure if her feet ever touched the ground. And her cheeks grew sore from all of the smiling. But she couldn't stop. This was the most amazing evening and she didn't want it to end…not ever.

Grayson stopped moving.

Annabelle sent him a worried look. "What's the matter?"

"Look up."

She tilted her chin upward. "I don't see anything but darkness."

"And…"

"And a star." She smiled. "Are you making a wish upon that star?"

"Perhaps."

Well, he wasn't going to be the only one to make a wish. She closed her eyes and Grayson's image filled her mind. There was something about him that she couldn't resist. She wished…she wished…

And then his lips pressed to hers. Oh, yes, that's what she wished.

CHAPTER SEVENTEEN

THE FAIRYTALE WAS winding to a close.

The ball was over, but Annabelle was not ready to lose all of her glittery goodness and turn back into a pumpkin. With Grayson by her side, the magic would continue long after the last song finished and the twinkle lights dimmed.

"What are you smiling about?" Grayson's voice broke into her thoughts as they paused outside her bedroom.

"Nothing." Annabelle continued to smile as she had all evening. She couldn't help it. She couldn't remember the last time she was this happy. And she didn't have any intention of letting this evening end.

Grayson's mouth lifted ever so slightly at the corners. "Oh, you have something on your mind."

"How do you know? Do you read minds now?"

"No. But your eyes give you away."

He was right. She did have something on her mind. And as delicious as the thought was, she wasn't sure she should follow her desires. But then again, what was holding her back now?

The deal for the South Shore had been signed. If she didn't act now, it'd be too late. Grayson would be leaving for California and she'd be left with nothing but regrets.

Her heart pounded in her chest. Tonight the moonlight and the sweet bubbly had cast a spell over her. She was falling for Grayson in a great big way.

But if she were honest with herself, this thing—these feelings—had started when he'd played her hero and saved her mother's journal from the would-be thief. There had been something special about Grayson from the very start.

And now she was ready to take the next step—one that she didn't take lightly. She'd never outright asked a man to spend the night. She wasn't even sure what to say. But tonight she was feeling a little bit naughty, uncharacteristically bold, and a whole lot reckless.

She opened the door.

"Well, I'll see you in the morning." Grayson turned to walk away.

Oh, no. She wasn't letting him get away. She needed to do something quick, but what? "Grayson, wait."

He turned back. "What is it?"

"I need your help." Without any further explanation, she took his hand to lead him into the bedroom.

But he didn't move. "Annabelle, I don't think this is a good idea."

She turned to him, not about to let logic rain on their magical night. "Why Grayson, what do you think I'm going to do?" Her voice lowered to a sultry level. "Take advantage of you?"

He didn't say anything at first. "The thought had crossed my mind."

"Tsk. Tsk." She gave his hand another pull. "Come on. I promise to keep my hands to myself…unless you'd rather I didn't. And besides, you did agree to stay with me until we solve the mystery of the note."

Grayson groaned. And she grinned like a Cheshire cat. Without a word, he followed her into the darkened room. Something told her that his capitulation was out of pure curiosity and the fact that no matter how much he wanted to deny this thing between them, he simply could not.

"You might want to close the door," she suggested without making any effort whatsoever to turn on the light.

"Annabelle—"

"Trust me." She moved toward the bed.

He groaned again and inwardly she laughed. Who knew Grayson could be so much fun? Or maybe the fun was in her being bold and sassy. Her smile broadened.

When the door snicked shut, she could hear Grayson's soft footsteps behind her. He wanted this night as much as she did. He hadn't been with anyone since his girlfriend, which was understandable and even a bit admirable, but it was time he moved on. It was time that she spread her wings with a man who wasn't intimidated by her father or her security team. And a man who took her opinions seriously.

"Can you unzip me?" She wished she could see the look on his face right now.

"I... I shouldn't be doing this."

"If you don't, I'll have to sleep in this beautiful gown," she said as innocently as she could muster. "Mrs. Chambers already went to bed. She never goes to the ball. And I can't reach the zipper."

He stepped closer. In the next moment, his fingers were touching the bare skin of her upper back, sending shivers of excitement tingling down her spine. He sucked in an unsteady breath. Millimeter by millimeter the zipper came undone. His fingertips were surprisingly smooth. His touch was being tattooed upon her mind.

This was the sweetest torture she'd ever experienced. And then her gown floated to the ground, landing in a fluffy heap. With nothing but moonlight streaming in through the tall windows to see by, she stood there in her black bustier and organza petticoat.

She didn't move. She could feel his gaze on her. The breath caught in her lungs. What was he thinking? Did he want her as much as she wanted him?

Desire and anticipation mounted within her. This was the most exquisite moment as they stood at the fork in their relationship. No matter which direction they took, after tonight, things would never be the same again.

And then his hands gently caressed her shoulders. His touch was arousing. She imagined turning in his arms and pressing her lips to his mouth, but she didn't. Not yet. She knew what she wanted, but she wasn't sure if he'd overcome the ghosts from his past. For this to work, for this to be right, he had to be all-in too.

His thumbs moved rhythmically over her skin. "Anna-belle, are you sure?"

She blew out the pent-up breath. "I am. Are you?"

His response came in the form of a gentle kiss on her neck. She inhaled swiftly, not expecting such a telling response. Not that she disapproved. Quite the opposite. Most definitely the opposite.

CHAPTER EIGHTEEN

"How long have you been up?"

Grayson's deep, gravelly voice came from the doorway of the library. Annabelle was wide awake, showered and working to find the answer to the clue in the latest note. She glanced up from one of the history books of Mirraccino.

When she saw Grayson, memories of being held in his arms came rushing back to her. Along with the memories came the emotions—powerful emotions that sent her heart racing. Last night had been so much more than she'd ever envisioned.

She was in love with Grayson.

And she had never been so scared.

She'd never been in love before. She'd never wanted to let another man into her life. She already had enough men telling her what to do, why add one more? But Grayson was different. He spoke his opinion, but left room for her response.

The truth of the matter was that she could imagine keeping him around, but never once last night or any time since she'd known him had he mentioned sticking around or inviting her to be a part of his life. He'd warned her in the beginning that he wasn't in this for anything serious. She remembered that moment quite vividly. Why hadn't she listened to him then? Now she'd complicated everything exponentially.

"Annabelle, what's wrong?" Grayson approached her, concern written all over his face.

She held up her hand, maintaining an adequate distance between them. She couldn't bear for him to touch her. And she refused to give in to the tears that were stinging the backs of her eyes. This was her problem to deal with, not his. He hadn't done anything but what she'd asked him to do.

"I… I'm fine."

"You don't look fine. Listen, if this is about last night—"

"It's not. And I'd prefer not talking about it." She couldn't stand the thought of him letting her down gently. She could just imagine him giving her some sort of pep talk.

Grayson raked his fingers through his hair. "I knew that last night was a mistake. I didn't mean to—"

"Stop." Then realizing she'd raised her voice while the door to the hallway was standing wide open, she lowered her voice. "It wasn't a mistake. You have nothing to feel bad about." And she just couldn't talk about it any longer. "And I have to go out. If you need anything just ask the staff."

She started for the door, but Grayson was hot on her heels. She needed to shake him. She needed to get away from absolutely everyone. She needed some time alone in order to think clearly.

The only person she really wanted to talk to was the one person missing from her life—her mother.

Not needing protection while she was within the palace walls, her security detail was out of sight. That left Grayson, who was right behind her. She kept moving with no particular destination in mind.

"Annabelle, you can't just walk away."

"Watch me."

"We need to talk."

"No, we don't." She kept walking, wishing he'd give up. "There's nothing to say."

"I disagree."

He refused to leave the subject alone. What did he want her to do? Say something to make it better? That wasn't possible.

Annabelle went out the back door. When she spotted her little red convertible, she headed straight for it. There wasn't anyone around, thankfully. She jumped inside and was relieved to find the keys waiting. The staff routinely left the keys in a strategic spot so that vehicles could be readily available and moved to the front of the palace for their owners.

After all, the palace was heavily guarded. No one was going to break in and steal a car. Not a chance.

The next thing she knew, Grayson was in the seat next to her. *Just great.*

"You need to get out because I really am leaving."

"I'm not moving. You can't just act like nothing happened last night." He turned to her. "Annabelle, we have to talk."

"So you keep telling me." She put the car in gear. "Well, if you're not getting out, then I guess that means you're coming with me."

Grayson put on his seat belt, crossed his arms and then settled back in his seat. She'd never witnessed him with a more determined look.

"Don't say I didn't warn you." She accelerated toward the front gates.

It was then that she realized she didn't have her security detail following her. She also knew the guards would stop her and ask about her lack of security. She had no clue what to say. When she neared the gate, she found them opening it for a delivery truck. Though the guards waved for her to stop, she kept moving.

"Annabelle, what are you doing?"

"Whatever I want." She knew it was a childish answer, but she wasn't much in the mood for a serious talk.

It wasn't until they were on the main road that Grayson asked, "Would you at least tell me where we're going?"

"You'll find out soon enough."

"Annabelle?" Grayson stared into the passenger side mirror.

"I told you, you'll find out the destination soon."

"No, that isn't it." He tapped on the window. "There's no car behind us. Where's your security detail?"

He stared at her, waiting for this information to sink in. Her face paled as her gaze flicked to her rearview mirror. He knew she hadn't planned this little escapade. It'd been a spur-of-the-moment decision, which led him to believe she had been more upset this morning than she was willing to let on. He figured as much.

The thing was he wanted to talk to her. He wanted to tell her how much last night had meant to him, but she refused to give him a chance.

He'd have sworn by her responses and words that last night had been special for her too. So why had the walls gone up in the light of day? And what had she been doing up so early after such a late night?

That was his problem. He didn't understand women. He never had. Abbi used to tease him about it. But there was nothing funny about this situation—not after that threatening note.

"Annabelle, where's your security?"

"Obviously not here."

"I don't understand. Why would you leave without them?"

"Because…"

"Because what?" He wanted a real answer. What was going on with her? She'd been acting strange all morning.

"Because you wouldn't leave me alone. You kept wanting to talk about last night and I didn't. I didn't plan to leave the palace, at least not at that point and so I didn't tell anyone."

"You ran off?"

"No!" She frowned as her grip on the steering wheel visibly tightened. "I… I just didn't stop to tell anyone."

"Isn't that the same thing?"

She took her eyes off the road for a second to glare at him. "No. It isn't."

Grayson sighed. "Okay. I guess I did push the subject this morning. I'm sorry. I just thought we could talk things out." When she opened her mouth to protest, he continued before she could speak. "But no worries. Just turn around. We'll be back at the palace in no time."

Her lips pressed together. She didn't say anything and the car didn't slow down. Maybe she didn't hear him.

"Annabelle, turn around."

She eased up on the accelerator and the car started to slow down. He breathed easier. She'd turn around and soon they'd be back at the palace. No harm. No foul.

She put on the turn signal. So far so good. He glanced around. "What is this place?"

"It's a historic landmark. It's where our ancestor's fought to maintain our monarchy and traditions."

Any other time Grayson wouldn't have minded stopping and exploring the site, but not today. When Annabelle didn't immediately turn around, he thought she was just looking for a safe place to maneuver the car.

"You can turn here. I don't think there's anyone around to see if you drive off the road."

"I'm not turning around."

"What?"

"This is our destination."

"Annabelle, this isn't funny." A feeling of déjà vu came over him. "Turn around."

"No. We're here and there's something I need to see. It won't take long."

Arguing with her was proving fruitless so he pulled his cell phone from his pocket. He went to dial, but realized he didn't know the phone number of the palace. And that wasn't his only problem. There wasn't a signal out here in the middle of nowhere.

He held up his phone and waved it around. Not even one bar appeared on his phone. This wasn't good. He had a bad feeling about this whole expedition. A very bad feeling.

CHAPTER NINETEEN

THEY'D COME THIS FAR; she wasn't about to back away now.

"Come on." Annabelle got out of the car.

She wasn't so sure Grayson was going to accompany her. He was worried and she couldn't blame him, not after what he went through. But this wasn't her first time without a bodyguard and she highly doubted it would be her last. Sometimes she just needed some privacy and that was tough to do with someone always looking over your shoulder.

She glanced around. Hers was the only car in the parking lot. Everything would be all right. They wouldn't stay long. And contrary to her desires, she wasn't alone.

She started up the path leading to the historic landmark. The cipher had said *PLACARD. TWO. THREE.* Which, if this was the place, had to be just up ahead. She prayed she was right. She just wanted this to be over and to finally have the answers that would hopefully bring her family back together again.

"Annabelle, wait."

She paused and turned to find Grayson striding toward her. He wore a frown on his face that marred his handsomeness just a smidgen. And even if he wasn't happy about being here, she found comfort in his presence. Because maybe she wasn't feeling as brave as she'd like everyone to think. But she refused to be intimidated by that note. She was onto something; she just knew it.

"You're going to do this no matter what I say, aren't you?" His concerned gaze searched hers.

"I am."

He nodded. "Then lead the way."

"Thank you," she said, not expecting a response. But she was grateful that he wasn't going to fight her any longer.

They continued down the windy path that led them to a spot near the cliff that overlooked the sea. Here there was a small park area. There was a sign explaining the historic significance of the spot, but Annabelle wasn't up for a history lesson right now. She needed to see if this was the place with the next clue to her mother's murder and if not, they needed to move on.

"The message said there would be a placard. Do you see one?" Annabelle gazed around the circular patio area. There were a few tables and benches scattered about. But she didn't see a placard.

Grayson was making his way around the circle. "Over here."

He was standing near a rock wall that butted up against a hillside at the back of the park. She rushed over to where he was standing. She looked around and found a bronze placard in the rock wall. It was dedicated to all of the heroes who had defended their homeland in 1714.

"Do you think that's it?" Annabelle's stomach shivered with nerves. Part of her wanted the truth but the other part of her worried about what she might learn. After all of this time, wondering and imagining what might have happened to her mother, she was surprised by her sudden hesitancy.

"Annabelle, what's wrong?" Grayson sent her a concerned look.

"Nothing." She was being silly. They had to find the answers. "Let's do this."

Grayson reached for her hand. "You do realize that this might not be the right place?"

She nodded. "But we won't know until we look."

Together they counted out the rocks, not quite sure where the starting point might be. The first try didn't pan out. The rock in the wall was firmly in there and there was no way they or anyone else was moving it without some serious tools. The second rock they tried had the same results.

"I'm starting to think I got the clues wrong," Annabelle said, feeling silly for taking Grayson on this pointless trip.

"Don't give up just yet. I think this rock is loose." Grayson gripped the stone and wiggled it. "Yes, it's definitely loose."

"This could be it." She moved forward, planning to help.

Before she could move into a position where she could reach the stone, Grayson jiggled it free. Her mouth gaped, but no words would come out. They'd found it. Would they at last have answers or find yet another coded message?

Grayson gestured toward the wall. "Well, don't just stand there, see if you can find anything."

His voice prompted her into action. She felt around inside the hole and grimaced when she realized there were bugs, slime and a whole host of other disgusting things in there. But then in the back of the cavity, her fingers ran across something different. Much different.

"I think there's a plastic bag in here."

"That's good. Can you pull it out?"

It was hung up in some soft dirt, but she easily pulled it free. The bag was covered in muck, forcing Annabelle to swipe it off with her hand if she had any hope of seeing what was inside.

"Is there anything else in there?" Grayson asked.

"Just this. It looks like some sort of thumb drive. An older one."

Grayson returned the rock to its spot and then moved next to her. She handed over the bag. All the while, she wondered what could be so important about a computer file that it cost her mother her life.

"What do you think is on it?" Annabelle asked.

"I don't know, but I'm guessing it's very important."

"It is," a male voice said from behind them. "Now turn around slowly."

Dread inched down Annabelle's spine like icy fingers. When she turned, she gasped. The man standing there holding a gun on them was someone she knew—someone the king knew and trusted. It was one of the palace staff, Mr. Drago.

He was an older man with thinning white hair and the gun he held on them looked to be even older than him. The hand holding the large revolver shook, but she didn't know if it was from nerves or age. Either way, she wasn't feeling so good about his finger resting on the trigger.

"Drop the bag to the ground and kick it over here," he demanded.

Grayson did as he said without any argument.

"And now your keys."

Annabelle had those. She pulled them from her pocket and dropped them to the ground. She gave them a swift kick sending them skidding over the concrete patio.

"Why?" Annabelle hadn't meant to speak—to do anything to provoke him, but the word popped out of her mouth before she could stop it. With the damage already done, she asked, "Why did you kill my mother?"

After the man picked up the plastic bag and the keys, he stuffed them in his pocket. "You don't understand." His eyes filled with emotion. "No one was supposed to get hurt."

The tremors in his hand grew more intense. The gun moved up and down, left and right. And yet his finger remained on the trigger.

"Your mother, she just wouldn't quit interfering. Just like you. I warned you to leave the past alone, but you just couldn't."

"I… I just need to know the truth—to understand." Annabelle couldn't believe she was staring at the man who had killed her mother. Nothing about the man screamed murderer to her and yet, he'd almost come right out and admitted it. "Why did she have to die?"

The man expelled a weary sigh as though he were shouldering the weight of the world. "Since I'm leaving this island—my home—and never coming back, I suppose I can tell you. My wife…she was sick. She needed to be flown to the United States for treatment, but I didn't have that kind of money. And then I got an offer. For some information about the country's defenses, I could get the money necessary to save my wife's life. I'd have done anything for her. She... she was my world."

Annabelle helplessly stared at the man who'd murdered her mother. His hand with the gun continued to shake. And his finger remained on the trigger. Anger and disbelief churned in her gut. And worst yet, she'd dragged Grayson into this mess, risking both of their lives. She deeply regretted her rash decision to rush out here without security.

There had to be a way out of this. Maybe if she kept the man talking a bit longer, a plan would come to mind. "So what went wrong?"

"Your mother caught on to the plan somehow. She said she was going to tell the king, and I just couldn't let her ruin everything."

And then a memory fell into place. "It was you that I saw arguing with her in the South Shore piazza the evening before she died, wasn't it?"

He nodded. "I was trying to find out how much she knew. I needed to know if she suspected me. She wouldn't tell me anything, but then the next day we met again. She said she'd intercepted a note to me—"

"Your name is Cosmo?" For as long as Annabelle had been coming to the palace, she'd only ever heard the man addressed by his surname—Drago.

"Yes, it is." His arm slowly lowered as though he was tired of holding up the gun. In the next breath, he lifted it again. "Your mother said that she was taking it to the king. That's when I pulled out this gun. She reached for it. We struggled and...and it went off. There was nothing I could do for the princess. The shot hit her in the chest. She...she died before she hit the ground."

Annabelle's heart jumped into her throat as she envisioned her mother's final moments. Her mother had been protecting the king and this land that she loved. She was a hero and no one knew until now.

Annabelle swallowed hard. "What…what happened next?"

"My wife…she died before I could get the data to sell."

"And what's on this thumb drive?"

"Instructions on where to deliver the data. And how I'd get my payments."

"So you never met the person behind the espionage?"

"No. There were cryptic messages and a couple of phone calls."

"And they just left you alone after your wife died? Even though they didn't get their information?"

"I was a man with nothing to lose and nothing to gain by then. I told the man on the phone that I'd go to the king and take my punishment before I'd give in to his blackmail."

"Funny how you grew a conscience after my mother died." Annabelle's hands clenched at her sides as she tried to keep her emotions under control. "How could you do that? Do you know how much we loved and needed her?"

The older man's eyes grew shiny with unshed tears and his face creased with worry lines. "I told you I didn't mean for it to happen. It…it was an accident."

"And then what? You made it look like a mugging gone wrong?"

Drago's eyes narrowed. "What choice did I have? I couldn't go to jail. Not with my wife so ill. And it was an accident."

The man didn't even hesitate as he spoke. Annabelle's mouth gaped. The man seemed to think of himself as innocent. No wonder he'd gotten away with it for so many years. Without a guilty conscience to trip him up, it'd been easy.

"What did you do with my mother's jewelry?" Perhaps it was stashed in the palace and could be used as evidence.

"I buried it."

"Where?"

"I… I don't know. It was a long time ago."

"And you just stayed on at the palace, serving the king and acting like nothing ever happened?"

"What else could I do?" A tear splashed onto his weathered cheek. "The king needed me. I couldn't let him down."

But you could kill his sister without batting an eye? Annabelle wanted to tell Mr. Drago about the devastation he'd caused, but she had Grayson's safety to think about. She couldn't agitate this man any further. And there was nothing he could say that would bring her mother back to them.

And that was when she noticed movement behind Mr. Drago.

"What are you planning to do with us?" Grayson asked.

She figured that he must have seen her security team and the police moving into position behind the man. And Grayson was doing his best to distract Drago until they were ready to make their move.

"Do with you?" The man's face broke into a smile. "You think I'm going to kill you too?"

What did one say to that in this very sensitive situation? Annabelle glanced at Grayson, willing him not to upset the man, who was obviously not quite all there.

Grayson shrugged. "I don't know."

"I'm just going to leave you stranded out here. No one ever visits this place. I'm surprised you found it."

"How did you discover we were coming here?"

"It wasn't hard to eavesdrop and do a bit of snooping—"

His words were cut off as the police signaled for Annabelle and Grayson to drop to the ground. Grayson leapt into action shielding Annabelle's body with his own. Seconds felt like minutes as she was trapped between the concrete and Grayson's muscled chest.

"All clear," an officer called out.

Grayson helped her to her feet. "Are you all right?"

Annabelle nodded. With unshed tears blurring her vision, she said, "I'm so, so sorry. I never meant for any of this to happen."

He didn't say anything. In fact, without another word, he turned his back to her. She blinked repeatedly as she watched him walk away. She had a sickening feeling that, although no shots had been fired, there had been a casualty today.

Their relationship.

CHAPTER TWENTY

THE RIDE BACK to the palace was tense and silent.

However, the scene awaiting Annabelle was anything but.

They didn't even make it past the great foyer before her father, followed by the king, confronted her. One glance at Grayson told her that she was in this alone. He wouldn't look at her, much less speak to her. They were acting like she'd planned for all of this to happen. All she'd wanted were some long-overdue answers. Was that so bad?

Speaking of answers, she didn't even get a chance to tell them that she finally had them—she knew what had happened—before her father launched into a heated speech.

"How could you do this?" Her father's face was flushed and his arms gestured as he spoke. "I thought I could trust you. And here you go, sneaking around, risking your safety."

"You don't understand—"

"Oh, I understand." Her father frowned at her before stepping in front of Grayson, who at least had the common sense to stay quiet during this confrontation. "And you, I expected more of you. And yet, you let my daughter go off recklessly without her security—"

"That was not my doing." Grayson's voice rumbled with agitation. "At least it wasn't intentionally. We both got wrapped up in a heated conversation. By the time I realized that Annabelle had forgotten proper protocol, we were almost at the landmark."

Her father's voice echoed throughout the foyer. "How could you not realize you were leaving without any security?"

Grayson and her father glared at each other. Jaws were tight. Hands were clenched.

The king cleared his throat. "We were just really worried about you when your bodyguard reported that you'd slipped off without notifying anyone."

Her father's mouth opened, but before he could utter another angry word, Annabelle said, "And how exactly did you find us if my security wasn't following me?"

Her father paused. He averted his gaze. She knew this reaction. She'd seen it in the past when he'd done something that he knew his family would not approve of.

"Poppa, what is it? What did you do?"

His gaze met hers. "It was for your own good. I knew you were out of control and that things might end badly. I had to protect you."

"Poppa, out with it."

He sighed. "After I learned that you stole your mother's journal—"

"Borrowed."

"Fine. Borrowed. I knew there was a possibility that you'd get caught up in the past and you wouldn't be able to stop yourself—you'd have to follow the clues."

"Of course. How could you expect me not to?"

"Well, I wasn't about to let you go off and get yourself hurt so I installed a tracking device in your purse and your car, as well as a tracking app on your phone. I wasn't taking any chances."

Annabelle checked her phone. "You really did. How could you?"

"What? You're attacking me. My forethought is what saved your life."

Annabelle reached for Grayson's hand, craving his strength and the knowledge that they were in this together. Her fingers brushed over the back of his hand. She was just about to curl her fingers around his when he moved his hand behind his back out of her reach.

When she glanced his way, Grayson was staring straight ahead. She couldn't look into his eyes. She had no way of discovering why he had gone from being so helpful at the landmark to completely shutting down now that they were back at the palace. And the little voice in the back of her mind was warning her this was something different from his confrontation with her father. This thing, whatever it was, had to do with her and her alone.

She turned back to her expectant parent. "Mr. Drago wasn't going to hurt us."

When the king spoke, his voice was hollow as though he were in shock. "Drago, he admitted everything to you?"

Annabelle nodded. "I had to push him a bit, but in the end, it all came out."

"Oh, my." The king's color was sickly white. He stumbled a bit. Grayson and her father rushed to his side and helped him into a chair.

"I'll get help," Annabelle said, afraid this revelation was too much for her uncle.

"No. I'm fine," the king said in an unsteady voice. "I don't believe this. First my wife is murdered and now, my sister— all in the name of the crown." His head sunk into his hands.

Annabelle's heart went out to the man, who had weathered so much during his reign. She'd been so young when her aunt, the queen, was assassinated. The assailant had been aiming for the king but had missed. The whole ordeal had taken a toll on the family, but justice had been carried out. Who'd have imagined a few years later Annabelle's own mother would be killed.

Sometimes she thought being royal was a blessing and other times, she knew that it was a curse. Because the king was right, if not for the crown, both of the women who had meant so much to him—to all of them—would still be here.

"I think that it was an accident," Annabelle said, hoping to lessen the blow for everyone.

"Annabelle, how can you talk like this?" Her father's voice shook with emotion. "He stole your mother from us. Surely you must hate him?"

She shook her head. "No, not hate."

"I don't understand," her father said. "I'm trying, but I just don't get it."

She recalled the time she'd spent with her mother. They hadn't enjoyed many years together but in the time that they'd had, her mother taught her some valuable life lessons. "I don't think Momma would want any of us to hate Mr. Drago. She used to say that hate, and even the word itself, was a more powerful weapon than anything man could ever create. Hate could destroy a man as sure as it could destroy a nation."

Her father's mouth gaped as he tried to absorb his daughter's words. And then he composed himself. "For a moment there, you sounded just like her. I never knew she told you that. I'd almost forgotten that she'd said it. And so you've forgiven this Drago man?"

Annabelle shook her head. "Right now, I'm struggling with the not hating part. Forgiveness, well, it's a long ways off. He stole a very precious person from me—from all of us. And then he nearly destroyed our family by covering it up. He did a lot of damage, but I'm trying to take comfort in knowing he now has to account for his crimes."

"I don't know." Her father rubbed the back of his neck. "I don't think I can be as calm and rational about this as you."

She didn't want to lose her father again to hatred and resentment. Maybe if she explained a little more, it would help. "He said he never meant to hurt her, just scare her. And the gun accidentally fired."

Her father looked at her with disbelief reflected in his eyes. "And you believed him?"

She nodded. "He was leaving the country and never coming back. I'm not even sure that old gun still worked. What do you think, Grayson?"

Instead of answering her, he turned and walked away.

Where was he going? And why wasn't he speaking to her?

She chased after him, following him up the stairs. She couldn't let him get away. Not now. Not after everything that they'd shared. This was the beginning. Not the end.

* * *

Grayson couldn't stand there for one more minute.

It didn't matter what anyone said to Annabelle; she thought that she had done the right thing. He'd only ever been that scared one other time in his life. He'd sworn he would never live through something like it again. And yet just minutes ago he'd been staring down the end of a gun and praying that nothing would happen to Annabelle. And she'd refused to be quiet. She'd kept pushing the man, agitating him.

Grayson's heart pounded just recalling the horrific scene. Why did he think that staying here was a good idea? Why did he think Annabelle would be different?

He strode down the hallway toward his suite of rooms. He needed to get away—to be alone. A headache was pounding in his temples. His neck and shoulders ached. His muscles had been tense since he realized they'd left the palace without her security.

He'd just stepped in his room when he heard Annabelle calling out his name. Couldn't she get the message? He just wanted to be alone.

"Grayson—"

"Not now. Go away." He looked around for his bag. He needed to start packing. He just couldn't stay here any longer.

She didn't say anything for a moment and he was hoping that she'd take the hint and leave. He needed to calm down so he didn't end up saying anything that he would later regret.

"I can't go. I don't understand what's going on." She stepped further into the room.

"You don't understand?" Was she serious?

She sent him a wide-eyed stare. "Why are you so upset?"

"Because of you." At last, he recalled his bag was in the closet. He retrieved it and threw it on the bed. "You're reckless. You think you're invincible. And you don't listen to anyone."

"If this is about earlier, I'm sorry. I was just doing what I thought was best—"

"Best for you. Not best for anyone who cares about you. If that man had shot you…" No, he wasn't going there. He couldn't think about going through that agonizing pain again.

He went to the chest of drawers and retrieved a handful of clothes. The sooner he packed, the sooner he'd be on his way to the airport.

"Grayson, what are you doing?"

"I'm packing. I'm leaving here. I should have left a long time ago."

"But…but what about us?"

He didn't stop moving—he couldn't. He stuffed his clothes haphazardly in the bag. As soon as he was out of here—away from Mirraccino—he'd be able to breathe. The worry, it would cease.

"Grayson?"

He kept packing. In the long run, she'd be better off without him. "There is no us. I can't—I won't—continue this relationship. You take too many needless chances. I can't be a part of your life."

"Seriously?" Anger threaded through her voice. "I did what I had to do. And you know it."

"I know you took a chance with your life—with both of our lives. And it wasn't necessary. The police could have handled it."

Out of the corner of his eye, he spied her pressing her hands to her hips. He didn't dare look at her face. He couldn't stand to see the pain that would be reflected in her eyes—pain he'd put there.

"Don't you understand? The police never would have gotten to the truth. Without it my family would never heal."

Part of him knew she believed the words she uttered. Her entire family was separated with no true hope of coming back together. This discovery would give them a chance to start over.

But he also knew that taking risks and breaking rules was what had cost Abbi her life. He couldn't stick around and wait for Annabelle to take another risk. He couldn't stand the thought of losing her just like he'd lost Abbi.

"Grayson, are you even listening to me?" Annabelle moved to the other side of the bed, trying to gain his attention. "Are you leaving because you never really cared about me?"

It was in that moment he realized he was leaving for the exact opposite reason.

He loved Annabelle.

Normally that revelation would bring someone joy and delight, but it made his blood run cold. He'd cared deeply about Abbi, but he'd never loved her like this.

But with Annabelle, he was head over heels in love. The acknowledgment scared him silly. It didn't matter what she promised, she now had the power to destroy him—to rip his heart to shreds.

"I… I can't do this, Annabelle. I'm sorry." He zipped his bag closed, grabbed his computer case from where he kept it on the desk and headed for the door.

He paused in the doorway. Unable to face her, he kept his back to her. "I know you won't believe this, but I did care. I do care. You're just too reckless. I thought we had a chance but I was wrong. I'm glad you found the truth, but now I have to go."

There was a sniffle behind him, but he couldn't help her now. The best thing he could do for both of them was to start walking and keep going. Because the one thing he'd learned in life was that people let you down, sometimes without even meaning to.

This was for the best.

But it sure didn't feel like it. Not at all.

With each step the ache in his heart increased.

CHAPTER TWENTY-ONE

ALONE.

Not a soul around.

Annabelle made her way along the deserted beach with the bright moonlight guiding her. She had no destination in mind. There was no place she needed to be. And no one who was expecting her.

She should be kicking up her heels and savoring this moment. Or at the very least feeling as though she'd gained something huge—her freedom. There were no longer people looking over her shoulder. There were no reports filed with her father, detailing any of her activities. And that's because the security detail had been officially dismissed not long after Drago was arrested.

Annabelle stopped walking and turned to the water. It wasn't until that moment she realized her freedom was not what she'd been truly craving all of this time. Because if it was then she wouldn't feel so utterly alone and adrift.

Grayson was gone.

For a moment after he'd packed his bags and walked out the door, she'd thought he might change his mind. She'd prayed that he would come back to her. She'd assured herself that he was just having some sort of reaction to the scene at the landmark. Maybe it was shock or fear and it would pass. It didn't.

But how could he just walk away? He did care about her. Didn't he?

There had been lunches and dinners. The chariot race. The gown he'd given her. Their collaboration over the coded messages. And there were so many small moments...a look here or a touch there. Didn't those all add up to mean something special?

Or had she just been fooling herself?

Maybe if she'd been more open, more honest about her

feelings for him instead of keeping it all locked safely inside. Maybe if she'd have taken a chance, he'd still be here.

A breeze off the water rushed over her skin and combed through her hair. She folded her arms over her chest and rubbed her arms with her palms. At last, she realized that freedom wasn't something anyone could give her. Real freedom came from living her life to its fullest and opening her heart to others—something she'd never done with any man—including Grayson.

She missed him so much that her heart ached. There was a gaping hole in it and she didn't know how to stop the pain. By now, he'd be on his way to Italy or California.

How was it that this man had crashed into her life on a city sidewalk and so quickly, so easily snuck past all of her defenses and burrowed so deeply into her heart? And how did she learn to live without his warm smiles, his deep laughs and his gentle touch?

She groaned with frustration. This was a time when a girl really needed her mother. Tears blurred Annabelle's vision and she blinked them away. What would her mother say to her?

Would her mother ask her how she'd fallen so hard? Would she want to know how Annabelle had mucked things up so quickly? And what would she say to her mother? Would she blame it on the severe restrictions her father had unfairly placed upon her? Or would she take responsibility herself for what had happened?

How had she let all of this happen? How had she let herself fall in love only to lose him so quickly?

And then to her horror, she realized her father hadn't put her in a gilded cage, she'd done that all by herself—she'd done it by keeping everyone in her life at arm's length. If she truly wanted to be free, she had to be willing to open her heart…the whole way.

In that moment, alone on the moonlit beach, she knew

what she had to do next. It was time she took that long-thought-about trip to the United States.

But she wouldn't be running away—she'd be running toward something—or rather toward someone.

CHAPTER TWENTY-TWO

AT LAST HE WAS on his way.

Grayson had stood for a very long time outside the gates of the palace waiting for the taxi to pick him up, at least an hour, if not longer. When he'd first called for a ride and given them the address, they'd thought he was joking. They had no idea that joking around was the very last thing on his mind.

It was almost as if fate was giving him time to change his mind—time to calm down. Well, he had calmed down. The panic over how close Annabelle had come to being hurt had passed.

But what hadn't passed was his determination to leave here—leave Annabelle. They didn't belong together. They came from very different worlds and he had no idea how to fit into hers. And she was too reckless for him to even consider sharing something serious with her.

He'd thought that by walking away from Annabelle he would start to feel better. After all, he'd cut things off. He'd protected himself and her.

Now, in a taxi, speeding toward Mirraccino International Airport, Grayson leaned his head back against the seat. He assured himself that he was doing the right thing. So why did he feel so awful?

He sighed. He'd already decided to cancel the rest of his Mediterranean trip. The expansion project would go on, but he'd put someone else in charge. He needed some distance from the sunny shores, blue waters and everything else that reminded him of Annabelle.

She was reckless with her safety. He couldn't be with someone like that. He needed someone in his life who was… what? Cautious? Sedate? Anything that wasn't Annabelle.

And why did he need that?

He didn't want to examine the answer too closely. He

worried about what he might find when he pulled back the layers. Because it wasn't Annabelle who had the problems.

It was him.

As the airport came into sight, Grayson could no longer run from the truth. He had to accept that he was at fault here—not Annabelle. The moment of truth had arrived. He could either take the easy way out or he could do what was right.

The taxi pulled up to the curb outside the terminal. "Sir, we're here."

Grayson didn't respond. Nor did he move.

By flying off into the night, he was doing what he'd accused Annabelle of doing—being reckless.

Not that he was being reckless with his safety, rather he was being reckless with his heart. True love didn't come around all that often and for him to turn his back on it was wrong. Because whether it was convenient, sensible, or for that matter logical, he was in love with the duke's daughter.

"Please take me back to the palace."

Would it be too late?

Would she at least hear him out?

He had to hope so.

CHAPTER TWENTY-THREE

ANNABELLE'S MIND WAS made up.

Now all there was to do was make her flight reservations and pack her bags.

There was no time to waste. Every moment that she knew Grayson was upset with her was torture. She didn't even know if he'd open the door to her, but she had to try. She couldn't live with the what-ifs.

Annabelle trudged through the sand toward the steps that climbed up the cliff behind the palace. As for her father and uncle, she'd have to tell them something, but she didn't know exactly what to say or when to say it—

A movement caught her attention. She glanced up at the top of the steps. She could see the shadowed outline of a person. Who would be coming out here this evening? With her cousins and their families still off on their trips, it didn't leave many people who frequented the beach.

As she studied the figure now moving down the steps at a rapid pace, she made out that it was a man. The breath caught in her throat. Was it possible that it was Grayson? Had he changed his mind? Had he come back for her?

Her heart swelled with hope. A part of her knew that if it was indeed him, then he could have come back for a number of reasons including cancelling his contract for the Fo Shizzle Café.

Please say it isn't so.

Not about to wait, she started up the steps. The closer she got to him, the more certain she was that it was Grayson. This was her chance to fix things. Now she had to pray that she'd find the right words to convince him that they deserved another chance.

She moved up the steps as fast as her legs would allow. Breathless and nervous, she came face-to-face with Grayson on the middle landing. Her gaze met his, but she wasn't able to read his thoughts.

"I'm sorry." They both said in unison.

Had she heard him correctly? She wanted to rush into his arms, but she restrained herself. She had to be sure he wanted the same things as her.

"I never meant to scare you," she said. "When I went to the landmark, I never imagined that anyone would find us there. I'm sorry."

He continued to stare into her eyes. "And I overreacted. I was afraid that something would happen to you. And I just couldn't handle that because…because I love you."

Her heart swelled with joy. "You do?"

He nodded. "I do. I love you too much for you to take unnecessary chances with your safety."

"I promise to be more cautious going forward because I always want to be able to go home to the man I love."

Grayson opened his arms up to her and she rushed into them.

"I love you," she murmured into his ear.

"I love you too."

At last, she had the love she'd always dreamed of.

Life didn't get any better than this.

EPILOGUE

Two months later...

"GRAYSON, WHAT ARE WE doing here?"

Annabelle stood next to the water fountain in the piazza of the South Shore. She was all dressed up as she'd been in business meetings off and on all morning. Grayson knew this because he'd had a horrible time trying to reach her. At one point, he'd feared that his surprise would be ruined. But at last, he'd heard her voice on the other end of the phone and begged her to meet him here.

He smiled at her. "Don't you know what today is?"

"Of course I do. It's Wednesday."

"True. But it's something else. Something very special."

"Aren't you supposed to break ground for your new offices?"

"Done."

She clasped her hands together and smiled. "Great. Is that what you wanted to show me?"

He shook his head. He had fun surprising her and he'd made a point of it over the past two months, from flowers to chocolate to the sweetest kitten. But today, this would be the biggest surprise of all.

She sent him a puzzled look. "Grayson, what are you up to?"

"Do I need to be up to something?"

She studied him for a moment. "You're most definitely up to something." She smiled. "Are you going to tell me? Or do I need to keep guessing?"

This was the moment. He dropped down on one knee. "Lady Annabelle, you captured my heart the first time we stood next to this fountain. You've led me on an amazing journey. You've taught me how to love. And you've made me the happiest man in the world."

Annabelle gasped and pressed a shaky hand to her gaping mouth. Her eyes glistened with unshed tears of joy. All around them a crowd of curious onlookers was gathering, but it didn't faze him. All that mattered now was Annabelle.

He pulled a little black box from his pocket. He opened it and held it up to her. "Annabelle, I love you. Will you be my best friend, my partner, my lover, forever?"

The tears streamed onto her cheeks as she nodded and smiled.

He placed the ring on her finger before he swept her into his arms and kissed her. He would never tire of holding her close.

When she pulled back, she gazed up at him. "You really want to do this? Get married?"

He nodded. "Definitely. I'm thinking we'll have a grand wedding. We could have it right here, if you like."

"Here in the piazza?" She didn't look so sure. "How about we think it over? After all, I don't want to rush this. I plan to be engaged only once and I want a chance to savor it."

"Then how would you feel about the grandest engagement party?"

Her face lit up. "I love it! But the size of the party doesn't matter as long as all of the men in my life are there."

"Then it's a plan. I love you."

"I love you too."

* * * * *

FALLING
FOR THE REBEL
PRINCESS

ELLIE DARKINS

For Mike and Matilda

CHAPTER ONE

'NOT YET!' CHARLIE GASPED, willing herself to be dragged back under.

In her dream her skin was hot and damp, on fire from his touch.

Awake, her tongue felt furry.

In her dream her body hummed, desperate for the feel of him.

Awake, her eyes stung as she peeled them open.

In her dream she begged for more, and got everything she didn't even know she needed.

Awake, she needed to pee.

She admitted defeat and stretched herself properly alive, wincing at the harsh Nevada sunlight assaulting her in the hotel room. As her toes encountered skin she flinched back, realising that she did have this one, small reminder of her dream. The man who'd taken the starring role was beside her on the mattress, his face turned away from her, his arms and legs sprawled and caught in the sheets. She looked away. She couldn't think about him. Not yet.

Easing herself out of bed, she willed him not to wake. And worked her thumb into her waistband, rubbing at her skin where her jeans had left a tight red line. The T-shirt she'd slept in was twisted and creased, and she glanced around the room, wondering whether her luggage had been transferred when the hotel had upgraded them to a luxury suite. She shuddered when she caught sight of herself in the mirror and tried to pull her hair up into some sort of order.

It had started out backcombed and messy, and her eyeliner had never been subtle in her life—but a couple of hours' sleep had taken the look from grunge to tragic. She wiped under her eyes with a finger, and the tacky drag of her skin made her shudder. And desperate to shower.

A glint of gold caught her eye and stopped her dead.

No. That had been the dream. It had to be.

She went over her memories, rooted to the spot, staring at the ring, trying to pull apart what was dream and what was real. After eighteen hours travelling and many more without sleep, the past twenty-four hours barely felt real, images and memories played through her mind as if they had happened to somebody else.

The thrumming, heaving energy of the gig last night. That was real. The music capturing her senses, hijacking her emotions and pumping her full of adrenaline. Real.

Hot and sweaty caresses just before dawn. Dream.

Dancing with Joe in the club, trying to talk business, shouting in his ear. Moving so closely with him that they felt like one body. Feeling the music play between them like a language only they spoke. Maybe that was real.

The slide of his bare skin against hers. So, so dreamy.

Him talking softly as they lay on the bed, trading playlists on their phones, sharing a pair of headphones, until one and then both of them fell asleep. God, she wished she knew.

But as she raised her left hand and examined the demure gold band on her third finger, she was certain of one thing.

Vegas chapel wedding. Real.

She banged her head back against the wall. Why did she always do this? She was losing count of the number of times she'd looked over the wreckage of her life after one stupid, impulsive move after another and wished that she could turn back time. If she had the balls to go home and tell her parents that she didn't want their royal way of life and everything that came with it, maybe she'd stop hitting the self-destruct button. But starting that conversation would lead to questions that she'd never be prepared to answer.

Thinking back to the night before, she tried to remember what had triggered her reaction. And then she caught sight of the newspaper, abandoned beside the bed. The slip of the paper under her fingertips made her shiver with the memory of being handed one like it backstage in the club last night, and she let out a low groan. It had been the headline on the front page: Duke Philippe bragging about his forthcoming engagement to Princess Caroline Mary Beatrice of Afland, otherwise known as Charlie. It was the sort of match her parents had been not so subtly pushing on her for years, the one she was hoping that would go away if she ignored it for long enough. She knew unequivocally that she would never marry, and especially not someone like Duke Philippe.

She'd left the cold, rocky, North Sea island of Afland nearly ten years ago, when she'd headed to London determined to make her own way in the music business. Her parents had given her ten years to pursue her rebellion—as they put it. But they all knew what was expected after that: a return to Afland, official royal duties, and a practical and sensible engagement to a practical, sensible aristocrat.

So there was nothing but disappointment in store for her family, and for her.

She shrank into the bathroom and hid the newspaper as she heard stirring from the bed. Perhaps if she hid for long enough it just wouldn't be true—Joe Kavanagh and their marriage would fade away as the figment of her imagination that she knew they must be.

Marriage. She scoffed. This wasn't a marriage. It was a mistake.

But it seemed as if her body didn't care which bits of last night were real and which were imagined. The hair on her arms was standing on end, her heart had started to race, and she felt a yearning deep in her stomach that seemed somehow familiar.

'Morning,' she heard Joe call from the bedroom, and she wondered if he'd guessed that she was hiding out in there. 'I know you're in there.'

The sound of his voice sent another shiver of recognition. British, and educated. But there was also a burr of something rugged about it, part of his northern upbringing that felt exotically 'authentic', when compared to the marble halls and polished accents of her childhood.

She risked peeking round the bathroom door and mumbled a good morning, wondering why she hadn't just left the minute that she'd woken up—running had always worked for her before. She'd been running from one catastrophe to another for as long as she could remember. Because this was her suite, she reminded herself. They'd been upgraded when the manager of the hotel had heard about their impromptu wedding, and realised that he had royalty and music royalty spending their wedding night in his hotel.

The only constant in her life since she'd left the palace in Afland had been her job. She'd worked from the bottom of the career ladder up to her position as an A&R executive, signing bands for an independent record label, Avalon. And that was the reason she had to get herself out of this room and face her new husband. Because not only was he a veritable rock god, he was also the artist that she'd been flown out here to charm, persuade and impress with her consummate professionalism in a last-ditch bid to get him to sign with her company.

She held her head high as she walked back into the bedroom, determined not to show him her feelings. The sun was coming in strong through the windows, and the backlighting meant that she couldn't quite see his expression.

'How's the head?' he asked, his expression changing to concerned.

She wondered whether she should tell him that she'd only had a couple of beers at most last night. That her recklessness hadn't come from alcohol, it had been fuelled by adrenaline and something more dangerous—the destructive path she found herself on all too often whenever marriage and family and the future entered the conversation.

Had Joe been drunk last night? She didn't think so. He'd seemed high when he'd come off stage, but she had been at enough gigs to know the difference between adrenaline and something less legal. She remembered him necking a beer, but that was it. So he didn't have that excuse either.

Why in God's name had this ever seemed like a good idea—to either of them?

'I've felt better,' she admitted, crossing the room to perch on the edge of the bed.

Up close, she decided that it really wasn't fair that he looked like this. His hair was artfully mussed by the pillows, his shirt was rumpled, and his tiny hint of eyeliner had smudged, but the whole look was so unforgivably sexy she almost forgot that whatever had happened the night before had been a huge mistake.

But sexy wasn't why she'd married him. Or maybe it was. When she went into reckless self-destruction mode, who was to say why she did anything?

Even in this oasis in the middle of the desert, she hadn't been able to escape the baggage that came with being a member of the royal family. The media obsession with royal women marrying and reproducing. Someone had raised a toast when they had seen her, to her impending marriage, asked her if she was up the duff and handed her a bottle of champagne. She'd been tempted to down the whole thing without taking a breath, determined to silence the voices in her head.

'So,' she said. 'I guess we're in trouble.'

Trouble? She was right about that. Everything about this woman said trouble. He had known it the minute that he had set eyes on her, all attitude and eyeliner.

He had known it for sure when they'd started dancing, her body moving in time with his. So at what point last night had trouble seemed like such a good idea?

When they'd left the dance floor, in that last club, their bodies hot and sticky. When she'd been trying to talk business but he'd been distracted by the humming of his skin and the sparks that leapt from his body to hers whenever she was near. When Ricky, the drummer in his band, had joked that he needed to show some real rock-star behaviour if they were going to sell the new album, and Joe had dropped to one knee and proposed.

He hadn't thought for a second that she would go along with it.

But Charlie had stopped for a moment as their eyes had met, and as everyone had laughed around them he had been able to see that she wasn't laughing, and neither was he. The club had stilled and quietened, or maybe it was just his mind that had, but suddenly there had been just the two of them, connected through something bigger than either of their bodies could contain. Something he couldn't pretend to comprehend, but that he knew meant that they understood each other.

And then she had nodded, thrown back her head and laughed along with everyone else, and they had been carried on a wave of adrenaline, bonhomie and contagious intoxication into a cab and up the steps of the courthouse. Somehow, still high from their performance and bewitched by the Princess, he hadn't stepped out of their fantasy and broken the spell.

They'd been cocooned in that buzz, carrying them straight through the ceremony. Such a laugh as they'd toppled out of the chapel. Right up until that kiss. Then it had all felt very real.

Did she remember that feeling as they had kissed for the first time? He knew in his bones that he could never forget it, as they were pronounced husband and wife.

'Are you going to hide in there all morning?' he asked.

In the daylight, she didn't look like a princess any more than she had the night before. Maybe that was how he'd found himself here. He'd expected to be on edge around her, but as soon as he had met her... Not that he was relaxed—no, there was too much going on, too much churning and yearning and *desire* to call it relaxed. But he'd been... He wasn't sure of the word. Her boss had sent her out here to convince him that their label was a good fit—and he'd been right. They had... Maybe fit was the right world. They'd just understood each other. She understood the music. Understood him. And when they had started dancing, there had been no question in his mind that this was important. He didn't know what it was, but he knew that he wanted more.

And marrying her—it had been a good move for the band. You couldn't buy publicity like that. He must have been thinking about that, must have calculated this as a business move. It was the only thing that made sense.

But was she expecting a marriage?

Because she came with a hell of a lot of baggage. Oh, he knew which fork to use, and how to spot the nasty ones in a room of over-privileged Henrys. He'd learned that much at his exclusive public school, where his music scholarship had taken him fee-free. But the most important part of his education had been the invaluable lesson he'd got in his last year—everyone was out to get something, so you'd better work out what you wanted in return.

The only place he felt relaxed these days was on the road, with his band. They moved from city to city, sometimes settling for a few weeks if they could hire some studio space, otherwise going from gig to gig, and woman to woman, without looking back. Everyone knowing exactly what they wanted, and taking what was on offer with no strings attached.

'Come on,' he said, reaching for her hand. As his fingertips touched hers he had another flash of that feeling from last night. The electric current that had joined them together as they had danced; that had woven such a spell around them that even a visit to a courthouse hadn't broken it.

'I can't believe we got married. This was your fault. Your idea.'

Was she for real? He shrugged and reminded her of the details. 'No one forced you. You seemed to think it was a great idea last night.'

So why was she looking at her ring as if it were burning her?

'Wh…?'

He waited to see which question was burning uppermost in her mind.

'Why? Why in God's name did I think it was a great idea?'

'How am I supposed to know if you don't? Maybe

you were thinking it would be good publicity for the album.'

He looked at her carefully. Yes, that was why they had done it. But also…no. There was more to it. He couldn't believe that she was such a stranger this morning. When they'd laughed about this last night, it hadn't just been a publicity stunt—that sounded too cold. It had been a joke, a deal, between friends. A publicity stunt was business, but last night, as they'd laughed together on the way to the courthouse, it had been more than that.

And maybe that was where he had gone wrong, because he knew how this worked. He knew that all relationships were deals, with each partner out to get what they wanted. He had no reason to be offended that she was acting like that this morning.

'I'm not sure why you're mad at me. You thought it was a great idea last night.'

'I hadn't slept for thirty-six hours, Joe. I think we can say that I wasn't doing my best reasoning. We have to undo this. What are my parents going to say?'

Her parents, the Queen of Afland and her husband. He groaned inwardly.

'Last night you said, and I quote, "They're going to go mental." As far as I could work out, that was a point in the plan's favour.'

In the cold light of morning—not such a good idea. Bad, in fact. Very bad.

He had married a princess—an actual blue-blooded, heir-to-the-throne, her-mother's-a-queen *princess*.

He was royally screwed.

'Look,' Joe said. 'I'm hungry, too hungry to talk

about this now. How about we go out for breakfast
and discuss this with coffee and as much protein as
they can cram on a plate?'

CHAPTER TWO

CHARLIE GAZED INTO her black coffee, hoping that it would supply answers. Her memories had started to filter back in as she'd sipped her first cup; shame had started creeping in with her second. She hoped that this cup, her third, would be the one that made her feel human again.

'So how do we undo this?' she said bluntly. 'This is Vegas. They must annul almost as many marriages as they make here. Do we need to go back to the courthouse?'

She looked up and met Joe's eye. He was watching her intently as he took a bite of another slice of toast. 'We could,' he said. 'If we want an annulment, I guess that's how we go about it.'

'If?' She nearly spat out her coffee. 'I don't think you understand, Joe. We got *married*.'

'I know: I was there.'

'Am I missing something? The way I see things, we were joking around, we thought it would be hil*ar*ious to have a Vegas wedding, and we've woken up this morning to a major disaster. Aren't you interested in damage limitation?'

'Of course I am, but, unlike you, I think the reasons we got married were sound. Not necessarily the *best* reasons to enter into a legally binding personal commitment, but sound nonetheless.'

She raised her eyebrows. 'Remind me.'

'Okay, obvious ones first. Publicity. The band needs it. The album is almost finished, we're looking for a new label, and there is no such thing as bad publicity, right?'

'Mercenary much?'

'Look, this isn't my fault. You were good with mercenary last night.'

She snorted. 'Fine, publicity is one reason. Give me another.'

'It shows you're serious about the band.'

She crossed her arms and sat back in her seat, fixing him with a glare. 'I've signed plenty of bands before without marrying the lead singer. They signed with me because they trust that I'm bloody good at my job. Are you seriously telling me that whether or not I would marry you was going to be a deal-breaker?'

He leaned forward, not put off by her death stare. In fact, his eyes softened as he reached for her hand, pulling her back towards him. She went with it, not wanting to look childish by batting him away.

'Of course it wasn't,' he said gently. 'But breaking the marriage now? I'm not sure how that's going to play out. I'm not sure what our working relationship could look like with that all over the papers.'

She shook her head, looking back into the depths of her coffee, still begging it for answers.

'All of which I have to weigh against the heartbreak of my family if we don't bury this right now.'

She avoided eye contact as she tried to stop the

tears from escaping. But she took a deep breath and when she looked up they were gone. 'Do you think anyone knows already? The press?'

'We weren't exactly discreet,' he said, with a sympathetic smile. 'I'd think it's likely.'

'And that can't be undone, annulment or not.'

He leaned back and took a long drink of his orange juice. 'So let's control the narrative.'

'What do you mean?'

'What story would hurt your family more—a whirlwind romance and hasty Vegas marriage, or a drunken publicity stunt to further your career? Because that's how the tabloids are going to want to spin it.'

'What's your point, Joe?' She'd taken her hand back and crossed her arms again, sure that this conversation was taking a turn that she wasn't going to like.

'All I'm saying is that we can't go back in time. We can't get unmarried, whether we get an annulment or not. So we either dissolve the marriage today and deal with the fallout to our reputations...'

'Or...?'

'Or we stay married.'

Her breathing caught as just for a second she considered what that might mean, to be this man's wife.

'But we're not in love. Anyone's going to be able to see that.'

He scrutinised her from under his lashes, which were truly longer and thicker than any man's had a right to be. 'So we're going to have to work hard to convince them. You can't deny that it's a better story.'

'And you can't deny that it means lying to my family. Ruining all the plans they were making for my life.

I don't know what your relationship with your family is like, but I'm not sure that I can pull it off. I'm not sure that I want to. Things are diffi—'

She stopped before she revealed too much. Joe raised an eyebrow, obviously curious about why she had cut herself off, but he didn't push her on it.

'Would you rather they knew the truth?'

Of course not. She had been hiding the truth from them for years, ever since she'd found out that she could never be the daughter or the Princess that they needed her to be.

'Are we seriously having this conversation? You want to stay married? You do know that you're a rock star, right? If you were that desperate for publicity you could have found a hundred girls who actually *wanted* to be your wife.'

'Wow, you're quite something for a guy's ego. For the record, this isn't some elaborate ruse to get myself a woman. I don't have any problems on that score. All I'm doing is making the best of a situation. That's all.'

Charlie took a big bite of pie, hoping that the sugar would succeed where the coffee hadn't. 'Well, I'm glad to hear that you're not remotely interested in me as a woman.'

He fixed her with a meaningful stare, the intensity of his expression making it impossible for her to look away.

'I never said that.'

Heat rose in her belly as he held the eye contact, leaving her in no doubt about how he thought of her. She shook her head as he finally broke the contact. 'I can't believe that I'm even considering this. You're crazy. There's no way we can keep this up. What happens if we slip? What happens when someone finds out it's not for real? What happens when one of us meets someone and this marriage of convenience isn't so convenient any more?'

He reached for her hand across the table, and once again there was that crackle, that spark that she remembered from the night before. She saw him in the chapel, eyes creased in laughter, as he leaned in to kiss her. Those eyes were still in front of her, concerned now though, rather than amused.

'It doesn't have to be for ever. Just long enough that it doesn't look like a stunt when we split. You weren't planning on marrying someone else any time soon, were you?'

'Never.' Her coffee cup rattled onto the saucer with a clash, liquid spilling over the top.

'Wow—that really was a no.'

She locked her gaze on his—he had to understand this if they were going to go on. 'I mean it, Joe. I didn't want to get married. Ever. I'm not wife material.'

'And yet here I am, married to you.'

He held her gaze and there was something familiar there. Something that made her stomach tighten in a knot and her skin prickle in awareness. With all the unexpected drama of finding themselves married, it seemed as if they'd both temporarily forgotten that they had also found themselves in bed together that morning.

Perhaps he was remembering something similar, because all of a sudden there was a new fire in his eyes, a new heat in the way that he was looking at her.

Her memory might be a bit ropey, but between the caffeine and the sugar her brain had been pretty much put back together, and there was one image of the night before that she couldn't get from her mind.

You may now kiss the bride.

They'd all burst out laughing, finding the whole thing hilarious. But as soon as Joe's hand had brushed against her cheek, cupping her jaw to turn her face up to him, the laughs had died in her throat. He'd been looking down at her as if he were only just seeing her for the first time, as if she had been made to look different by their marriage. His lush eyelashes had swept shut as he'd leaned towards her, and she'd had just a second to catch her breath before his lips had touched hers. They had been impossibly soft, and to start with had just pressed dry and chaste against hers. She'd reached up as he had and touched his cheek, just a gentle, friendly caress of her finger against his stubbled skin. But it had seemed to snap something within him; a gasp had escaped his lips, been swallowed by hers. His mouth had parted, and heat had flared between them.

She'd closed her eyes, understood that she was giving herself up to something more powerful than the simple actions of two individuals. As her eyes had shut her mouth had opened and her body had bowed towards her husband. Her hips had met his, and instantly sparks had crackled. His hands had left her face to lock around her waist, dragging her in tight and holding her against him. His tongue had been hot and hungry in her mouth; her hands frenzied, exploring the contours of his chest, his back, his butt.

And then the applause of their audience had broken into her consciousness, and she'd remembered where they were. What they were doing.

Blood had rushed to her cheeks and she could feel them glow as she'd broken away from Joe, acknowledging the whoops with an ironic wave.

'All right, all right,' she'd said, a sip of champagne helping with the brazen nonchalance; she'd hoped that she was successfully hiding the shake in her voice. 'Hope you enjoyed the show, people.'

She'd looked up at Joe to see whether she had imagined the connection between them, whether he'd still felt it buzzing and humming and trying to pull their bodies back together. By the heated, haunted look in his eyes, she wasn't alone in this.

He was worried, and he should be, because this marriage of convenience had just got a whole lot more complicated, for both of them. It had been a laugh, a joke, until their lips had met and they had both realised, simultaneously, that the flirting and banter that had provided an edge of excitement to their dancing that night would be a dangerous force unless they got a lid on it.

In the cold light of the morning after, she knew that they needed to face the problem head-on. She broke her gaze away from him, trying to cover what they had both clearly been remembering.

'Ground rules,' she said firmly, distracting herself by taking another bite of pie. 'If we do this, there have to be ground rules to stop it getting complicated.' He nodded in agreement, and she kept talking. 'First of all, we keep this strictly business. We both need to keep our heads and be able to walk away when the time is right. Let's acknowledge that there is chemistry between us, but if we let that lead us, we're not going to be objective and make smart decisions. And I think we both agree that we need to be smart.'

'People will talk if we don't make this look good. It has to be convincing.'

'Well, duh.' She waved to the waitress for a coffee refill. 'You're really trying to teach me how to handle the press? Obviously, in public we behave as if we're so madly in love that we couldn't wait a single minute longer to get married. We sell the hell out of it and make sure that no one has a choice *but* to believe us. But that's in public. In private, we're respectful colleagues.'

He snorted. 'Colleagues? You think we can do that? You were there, weren't you, last night? You do remember?'

Did she remember the kiss? The shivers? The way that she could still feel the imprint of his mouth on hers, as if the touch of skin on skin had permanently altered the cells? Yeah, she remembered, but that wasn't what was important here.

'And that's why we need the rules, Joe. If you want to stay married to me, you'd better listen up and pay attention.'

'Oh, I'm listening, and you're very clear. In public, I'm madly in love with you. Behind closed doors I'm at arm's length. Got it. So what are your other rules?'

She resurrected the death stare. 'No cheating. Ever. If we're going to make people believe this, they have to really believe it. We can't risk the story being hijacked. Doesn't matter how discreet you think you're being, it's never enough.'

'I get it. You don't share. Goes without saying.'

She dropped her cup back onto her saucer a little

heavier than she had planned, and the hot, bitter liquid slopped over the side again. 'This isn't about me, Joe. Don't pretend to know me. This is about appearances. I've already told you, this isn't personal.'

'Fine, well, if you're all done then I've got a rule of my own.'

'Go on, then.' She raised an eyebrow in anticipation.

'You move in with me.'

This time, the whole cup went over, coffee sloshing over the side of the table and onto her faded black jeans. At least she'd managed to miss her white shirt, she thought, thanking whoever was responsible for small mercies. She mopped hastily with a handful of napkins, buying her precious moments to regain her composure and think about what he had said. Of course she understood deep down that they would have to live together. But somehow, until he'd said it out loud, she hadn't believed it.

They would be alone together. *Living* alone together. No one to chaperone or keep them to their 'this is just business' word. Watching him across a diner table this morning, it wasn't exactly easy to keep her hands off him, so how were they meant to do that living alone together?

But she knew better than anyone that they had to make this look good. If her parents knew that she'd only done this to get out of the marriage to Philippe they would be so disappointed, and she didn't know that she could take doing that to them again.

Separate flats weren't going to cut it. By the time she looked back up, she knew that she seemed calm, regardless of what was going on underneath.

'Of course, that makes sense. Are you going to insist on your place rather than mine?'

'I'll need my recording studio.'

She nodded. 'Fine. So that's it, then? Three ground rules and we're just going to do this?'

'Well, if you're going to chicken out, you need to do it now.'

'I'm not eight years old, Joe. I'm not going to go through with this because you call me chicken.'

'Fine, why *are* you going to do it?' Nice use of psychology there, she thought. Act as though I've already agreed. He really did want this publicity. But it didn't matter, because she'd already made up her mind.

'I'm doing it because I don't want to hurt my family any more than I have to, and because I think it'll be good for my career.' And because it would save her from being talked into a real marriage, one which she knew she could never deserve.

'As long as you're doing it, your reasons are your own business,' Joe replied. She felt a little sting at that, like a brush of nettles against bare skin. Her own business. Damn right it was, but the way he said it, as if there really were nothing more than that between them… It didn't make sense. She didn't want it to make sense. She just knew that she didn't want it to hurt.

'So what are we going to tell people?' she asked after a long, awkward silence. 'I guess we need to get our stories straight.'

He nodded, and sipped at his coffee. 'We just keep it simple. We were swept away when we met each other yesterday, knew right away that it was love and decided we needed to be married. The guys in the band will go along with it. You don't have to worry about that.' Somehow she'd forgotten that they'd been there, egging them on, bundling them in the cab to the courthouse. When she thought back to last night, she remembered watching Joe on stage, sweat dripping from his forehead as he sang and rocked around the stage. Him grabbing her hand and pulling her to the dance floor when they'd gone on to a club after the gig, when he hadn't wanted to talk business.

She remembered the touch of his mouth on hers, as they were pronounced husband and wife.

But of course there had been witnesses, people who knew as well as she did that this was all a sham.

'What if they say something? They could go to the press.'

'They won't. Anyway, to everyone else it was just a laugh. And if anyone did say something, it'd be up to us to look so convincingly in love that no one could possibly believe them.'

'Ah, easy as that, huh.'

As they sat in the diner she realised how little thought they'd actually given this. She didn't even know when she would see him again. Her flight was booked back to London that night. She'd only been in Vegas to take this meeting. Her boss had sent her on a flying visit, instructed to try anything to get him to sign. She'd given her word that she wouldn't leave without the deal done. Would he see through them when they got back? Would he realise how far she had gone to keep to her promise?

'I'm flying home tonight,' she said.

He raised an eyebrow. 'You were pretty sure you'd

get me to sign, then. Didn't think you'd have to stick around to convince me?'

'I thought you'd be on the move, actually. I was told that you were only in Vegas for one night.' She knew that the band were renowned for their work ethic and their packed tour schedule, moving from city to city and gig to gig night after night. This had been her only chance for a meeting, her boss had told her as he'd instructed her to book a flight.

If he was always on the move like that, perhaps this would be easier than she thought. It could be weeks, months, before they actually had to live together. And by then, maybe… Maybe what. Maybe things would be different? There was no point pretending to be married at all if she thought that they would have changed their minds in a few weeks. They had to stick it out longer than that. If they were going to do this, they had to do it properly.

'I am, as it happens. I'm flying back to London tonight too.'

Why had he said that? They were meant to be in the States for two more weeks. Their manager had booked them into a retreat so that he could finish writing the new album. It should have been just a case of putting the finishing touches to a few songs, but he had an uneasy feeling about it this morning. He needed to go back and look at it again. There were a few decent tracks there, he was sure. But a niggling voice in his head was telling him that he still hadn't got the big hitters. The singles that would propel the album up the streaming charts and across the radio waves.

There was studio space booked for them in London in two weeks' time and it had to be fixed before then.

Their manager was going to kill him when he told him he wouldn't be showing up.

He could write in London; he had written the last album in London. It had nothing to do with Charlie. Nothing to do with her feelings, anyway. As she kept saying, this was just business. But it would look better for them to arrive home together.

Nothing to do with their feelings. Right. He would make her believe that today. Because her memory might be fuzzy but he could remember everything. Including the moment that they'd been on the dance floor, him still buzzing from the adrenaline of being on stage, her from the dancing and the music and the day and a half without sleep.

They'd moved together as the music had coursed through him, the bass vibrating his skin. She'd been trying to talk business, shouting in his ear. Contracts and terms, and commitment. But he hadn't been able to see past her. To feel anything more than the skin of her shoulder under his hand as he'd leaned in to speak in her ear. The soft slide of her hair as he'd brushed it off her face. 'Let's do this,' she'd said. 'We'd be a great team. I know that we can create something amazing together.'

She'd reached up then, making sure she had his attention—as if it would ever be anywhere but on her again. And then Ricky had said those idiotic words, the ones that no judge could take back this morning.

She'd laughed, at first, when he had proposed, assuming that he was joking. It had had nothing to do with the way she'd felt when his arm was around her. The way that that had made him feel. As if he wanted to protect her and challenge her and be challenged by her all at once.

He could never let her know how he had felt last night.

It was much better, much safer that they kept this as business. He knew what happened when you went into a relationship without any calculation. When you jumped in with your heart on the line and no defences. He wouldn't be doing it again.

And then there were the differences between them. Sure, it hadn't seemed to matter in that moment that he'd asked her to marry him, or when they were dancing and laughing and joking together, but a gig and a nightclub and beer were great levellers. When you were having to scream above the music then your accent didn't matter. But in the diner this morning there was no hiding her carefully Londonised RP that one could only acquire with decades of very expensive schooling, and learning to speak in the echoey ballrooms of city palaces and country piles.

He'd learnt that when he'd joined one of those expensive schools at the age of eleven, courtesy of his music scholarship free ride. His Bolton accent had been smoothed slightly by years away from home, first at school, and then on the road, but it would always be there. And he knew that, like the difference in their backgrounds, it would eventually come between them.

His experiences at school had made it clear that he didn't belong there.

And when he'd returned home to his parents, and

their comfy semi-detached in the suburbs, he had realised that he didn't belong there any more either. He was caught between two worlds, not able to settle in either. So the last thing that he needed was to be paraded in front of the royal family, no doubt coming into contact with the Ruperts and Sebastians and Hugos from his school days.

And what about his family? Was Charlie going to come round for a Sunday roast? Make small talk with his mum with Radio 2 playing in the background? He couldn't picture it.

But he would have to, he realised. Because it didn't matter what they were doing in private. It didn't matter that he had told himself that he absolutely had to get these feelings under control, their worlds were about to collide.

It wasn't permanent. That was what he had to remind himself. It wasn't for ever. They were going to end this once a decent amount of time had passed, and in the meantime they would just have to fit into each other's lives as best they could.

Just think of the publicity. A whirlwind romance was a good story. No doubt a better one than a drunken mistake. But since when had he allowed the papers to rule on what was and wasn't a good idea for him? No, there was more to it than that. Something about waking up beside her in bed that he wasn't ready to let go of yet.

'I have an album launch party to go to first, though,' he said at last. 'What do you say to making our first appearance as husband and wife?'

CHAPTER THREE

CHARLIE ADJUSTED THE strap on her spike heels and straightened the seam of her leather leggings. As soon as the car door opened, she knew there would be a tsunami of flashes from the assembled press hordes. She was considered fair game at the best of times, and if news of the wedding had got out by now, the scrum would be worse than usual.

These shots needed to be perfect. She wasn't having her big moment hijacked by a red circle of shame.

It was funny, she thought, that neither she nor Joe had called his manager, or her boss yet, and told them about what had happened. Not the best start to a publicity campaign, which was, after all, what they had agreed this marriage was. It was more natural, this way, she thought. If there was a big announcement, it would look too fake. Much better for them to let the story grow organically.

As the limo pulled up outside the club she realised that no announcement was necessary anyway. Word had obviously got around. The hotel had arranged for them to be picked up from a discreet back door, an old habit, so she hadn't been sure whether there had been photographers waiting for her there. If there had, they'd taken a shortcut to beat them here. There were definitely more press here than a simple album launch warranted. The story was out, then.

Without thinking, she slipped her hand into Joe's, sliding her fingers between his. The sight of so many photographers still made her nervous. It didn't matter how many times she had faced them. It reminded her of those times in her childhood when she'd been pulled from the protective privacy of her family home and paraded in front of the world's press, all looking for that perfect picture of the perfect Princess. As a child she had smiled until her cheeks had ached, dressed in her prettiest pink dress, turning this way and that as her name was shouted. It had been a small price to pay, her parents had explained, to make sure that the rest of their lives were private. But as she'd got older she'd resented those days more and more, and her childish rictus grin had turned into a sullen teen grimace.

And then, when she was nineteen, and had realised that she would never be the Princess that her family and her country wanted her to be, she'd stopped smiling altogether. She remembered sitting in the doctor's office as he explained what he'd found: inflammation, scar tissue, her ovaries affected. Possible problems conceiving.

She might never have a baby, no chubby little princes or princesses to parade in front of an adoring public, and no hope of making the sort of dynastic match that would make her parents happy.

Her most important duty as a royal female was to continue her family's line. It had been drummed into her from school history lessons to formal state occasions from as far back as she could remember. Queens who had done their duty and provided little princes and princesses to continue the family line.

And things hadn't changed as much as we would all like to think, she knew. The country had liked her mother when she was a shining twenty-something. But it was when she'd given the country three beautiful royal children that they'd really fallen in love with her, when she had won their loyalty. And that was something that Charlie might never be able to do. She might never feel the delicious weight of her child in her arms. Never breathe in the smell of a new baby knowing that it was all hers.

What if she never made her parents grandparents, and saw the pride and love in their eyes that she knew they were reserving for that occasion?

And as soon as she'd realised that, she had realised that she could never make them truly proud of her, somehow the weight of responsibility had fallen from her shoulders and she'd decided that she was never going back. If she wanted to roll out of a nightclub drunk—okay. If she wanted to disappear for three days, without letting anyone know where she was going—fine. If she wanted to skip a family event to go and listen to a new band—who cared?

Her mother insisted on a security detail, and Charlie had given up arguing that one. Her only demand was that they were invisible—she never looked for the smartly dressed man she knew must be on the row behind her on the plane, and so she never saw him. And the officers didn't report back to her mother. If she thought for a second that they would, she would have pulled the plug on the whole arrangement. That was why they'd not intervened last night: they knew she had a zero-tolerance approach to them interfering with anything that didn't affect her physical safety.

She was never going to be the perfect Princess, so why build her family's hopes up? She could let them down now, get it out of the way, in her own way, and not have to worry with blindsiding them with disappointment later.

Except it hurt to disappoint them, and it didn't seem to matter how many times that she did it. Every time, the look on their faces was as bad as the time before.

What would they say this time, she wondered, when they realised that she had married someone she had just met—so obviously to scupper the sensible match that they were trying to make for her? And she had married a rock star at that, someone who couldn't be further from the nice reliable boys that they enjoyed steering her towards at private family functions. What was the point of going along with that? she'd always thought. Entertaining the Lord Sebastians and Duc Philippes and Count Henris who were probably distant cousins, and who all—to a man—would run a mile as soon as they found out that they might not be needing that place at Eton or Charterhouse, or wherever they'd put their future son's name down for school before they had even bagged the ultimate trophy wife.

Joe leaned past her to look out of the window, and then gave her a pointed look. 'I guess our happy news is out.'

'Looks that way,' she said, with a hesitant smile. 'Ready to face the hordes?'

'As I'll ever be.' He looked confident, though, and relaxed. As if he'd been born to a life in front of the cameras, whereas she, who had attended her first photo call at a little under a day old, still came out in a sweat at the sight of a paparazzo.

But she stuck on what she'd come to think of as her Princess Scowl, in the style of a London supermodel, and pressed her knees and ankles together. It was second nature, after so many hours of etiquette lessons. Even in skin-tight leather, where there was no chance of an accidental underwear flash. She ran a hand through her hair, messing up the backcombed waves and dragging it over to one side in her trademark style. A glance in the rear-view mirror told her that her red lip stain was still good to go, managing to look just bitten and just kissed. She took a deep breath and reached for the door handle.

Joe stopped her with the touch of his fingertips on her knee. 'Wait.'

It was as if the leather melted away and those fingertips were burning straight into her skin. Wait? For ever, if she had to.

But before she could say, or do, anything, they were gone, as was Joe. Out of the door and into the bear pit. Then her door was wrenched open and his hand was there, waiting to pull her out into the bright desert sunshine. She gripped his hand as he helped her from the car, and the flashbulbs were going off before she was even on her feet.

Shouts reached her from every direction.

'When was the wedding?'

'Was Elvis there?'

'Were you drunk?'

And then there it was, the question that she'd never

anticipated but that she realised now had been inevitable from the first.

'Are you pregnant?'

She stumbled, and it was only Joe's arm clamping round her waist and pulling her tight that stopped her falling on her face in front of the world's press. And then she was falling anyway, because Joe's lips were on hers, and her heart was racing and her legs were jelly and her lips…her lips were on fire. One of his hands had bunched in her hair, and she realised that this, this look, this feeling, was what she'd been cultivating in front of the mirror for more years than she cared to think about. Just been kissed, just been ravished. Just had Joe's tongue in her mouth and hands on her body. Just had images of hot and sweaty and naked racing through her mind. He broke away and gave her a conspiratorial smile. She bit her lip, her mouth still just an inch from his, wondering how she was meant to resist going back for more.

And then the shouts broke back into her consciousness. 'Go on—one more, Charlie!'

And the spell was broken. She wasn't going to give them what they wanted. She turned to them, scowl back in place, though there was a glow now in the middle of her chest, something that they couldn't see, something that they couldn't try and own, to sell for profit.

She grabbed Joe's hand and pulled him towards the door of the venue, ignoring the shouts from the photographers.

She dragged him through the door and into a quiet corner.

'So I guess we survived our first photo call.'

She had hoped the relative seclusion of this dark corner would give her a chance to settle her nerves, for her heartbeat to slow and her hands to stop shaking. But as Joe took another step closer to her and blocked everything else from her vision, she felt anything but relaxed.

'Are you okay? You look kind of flushed,' he asked.

'I'm fine. I just hate...never mind.' Her voice dropped away as her gaze fixed on his lips and she couldn't break it away. This wasn't the time to think about what she hated, not when she was so fixed on what she loved, what she couldn't get enough of. Like the feeling of his lips on hers.

'Joe, I thought I saw you come in. And the new missus!'

Ricky, the drummer from Joe's band, Charlie recognised with a jolt.

More flashbacks of the night before: the band laughing with them in the taxi cab to the courthouse, joking about how they were going to have to sign with her now she'd done this. She had to convince them that they'd been mistaken last night. That she'd married Joe for love at first sight, before they started talking to journalists. If it wasn't already too late.

She reached for Joe's hand and gripped it tightly in hers, hoping that it communicated everything that she needed it to.

'Hi, Ricky,' she said, plastering on a smile that she hoped broadcast newly wedded bliss and contentment.

'So your first day as husband and wife, eh. How's it working out for you?'

She tried to read into his smile what he was really saying. If only she could fake a blush, or a morning-after glow. But in the absence of that, she'd have to go on the offensive.

'Pretty bloody amazingly, actually,' she said, leaning into Joe and hoping that he'd run with this, with her.

'Really?'

Ricky gave Joe a pointed look, and it told Charlie everything that she needed to know. He had thought last night that this was all a publicity stunt, and nothing that he had seen yet had changed his mind.

'Well, I'm just glad that you both decided to take one for the team.' He grinned. 'It was a brilliant idea. I wish I'd thought of it first.'

She opened her mouth to speak, but Joe got there first.

'I'm not sure what you mean, Ricky. We're not doing this for the team. I admit it was a bit hasty, but we really meant it last night. We wanted to get married.'

'Because you're both so madly in love?'

She felt Joe's hand twitch in hers and tried not to read too much into it.

'Because it was the only thing we *could* do,' he said. 'I don't care what we call it. Love at first sight. Or lust. Whatever. I just knew that once I had Charlie in my arms there was no way I was going to let her go. And if that meant marriage, then that's what I wanted.'

Bloody hell, maybe he should have been an actor rather than a singer. He certainly gave that little speech more than a little authenticity. She leaned into him again, and this time he dropped her hand and wrapped his arm around her shoulders. She looked up at him, and there was something about the expression in his face that forced her up onto her tiptoes to kiss him gently on the lips.

'Wow, okay,' Ricky said as she broke away. 'I guess I missed something last night. So, someone wants to chat with us about the new album, if you've got a minute.'

'Okay,' Joe replied, 'but you do remember what we decided last night. We're going to say yes to Charlie's label. I'm not going back on my word.'

'A bit early in the marriage for those sorts of ructions, is it?' Ricky looked at them carefully, and Charlie knew that they hadn't dispelled all of his doubts, regardless of how good an actor Joe was. 'Either way, we still need to speak to them. Until this deal is signed, we schmooze everyone, as far as I'm concerned. I know the others feel the same.'

She *had* to call her boss. She couldn't think why she hadn't done it before now. She'd do it on the way to the plane. She glanced at her watch. They couldn't stay long if they were going to make the flight. For a second she thought wistfully of her family's private plane, and how much easier life had been when she'd been happy to go along with that lifestyle, to take what she didn't feel she had earned. But it had got to the point where she simply couldn't do it any more. If she was never going to be able to pay her parents back with the one thing that everyone wanted from her, she couldn't use their money or their privilege any more.

She had some money left to her by her grandparents—despite her protestations, the lawyers had told her that it belonged to her and there was nothing that she could do about it—and her salary from the record label.

'I'm sorry, do you mind if I talk to them?' Joe asked, turning to her.

'Of course not.' She forced a smile, trying to live in the moment and forget all of the very good reasons she should be freaking out right now. 'Go on.'

But Joe turned to Ricky. 'You go ahead,' he said. 'I'll be there in a second.'

'You all right?' he asked, when they were alone. 'Still happy with everything? Because if you're going to change your mind, now's the time…'

She drew away from him and folded her arms. 'Why would I have changed my mind?'

She didn't understand what had happened to cause this change in mood. His shoulders were tense, she could see that.

Was it because he'd just reminded Ricky of their deal to sign with her the night before? The thought made her feel slightly sick, reminded her that whatever they might say to his band, whatever story they might spin for the papers, when it came down to it, this really *was* just a publicity stunt, or a business arrangement or…whatever. Whatever it was, she knew what it wasn't. It hadn't been love at first sight. It wasn't a grand romance. It wasn't a fairy tale, and there was going to be no happy ending for her. Well, fine, it wasn't like she deserved one anyway.

But now that they were married, they had to make it work. They had to appear to be intoxicated with one another. Luckily, intoxicated was one of her fortes. She forced herself to unfold her arms and smile. 'Of course I'm all right.'

Taking a deep breath, she stepped towards him, and with a questioning look in her eye snaked her arms around those tense shoulders. She placed another chaste peck on his lips, and smiled as she drew away. 'See? Picture perfect. Everything's as we agreed. Let's go say hi to everyone.'

Under the pressure of her arms, she felt his shoulders relax and his face melted into a smile. 'Well, we could give them something to talk about first.'

His arms wrapped around her waist, and she was reminded of the rush of adrenaline and hormones that she had felt outside when he had kissed her in front of the cameras. Her breath caught as her body softened into his hold. This time when his lips met hers, there was nothing chaste about it. Her arms tightened around him as he lifted her just ever so slightly, rubbing her hips against his as she slid up his body. His arms wrapped her completely, so that her ribs were bracketed with muscular forearms, and his hands met the indents of her waist. She was surrounded by him. Overwhelmed by the dominance of his body over hers.

His mouth dominated her too, demanding everything that she could give, and it was only with the touch of his tongue that she remembered where they were. She pushed both hands on his chest, forcing him to give her space, to unwind his arms from around her waist.

She smiled as she looked at him, both of them still dazed from the effect of the kiss. 'Do you think they bought it?' she asked, remembering that just a few moments ago they had been discussing the fact that this relationship was just a business deal—that the purpose of the kiss had been to keep up appearances. But Joe's face fell, and she knew that she had said the wrong thing.

'I think they bought it fine,' he said. 'It was a winning performance.'

Through the bite of his teeth, she knew that it wasn't a compliment.

She shook her head, then reached up and pecked him one last time on the cheek. 'Whatever it was, it blew my mind.' She met his eyes, and she knew that he saw that she was genuine. Whatever else might be going on, there was no denying the chemistry between them. It would be stupid to even try.

But beyond that, beyond the crazy hormones that made her body ache to be near his, was there something else too? A reason that the disappointment in his eyes made some part of her body hurt? She slipped her fingers between his and they walked over to where Ricky was holding court with a woman that she recognised from another record label, her competition, and a music journalist.

'So here's the happy couple,' the hack said with a smile, raising her glass to toast them. Charlie spotted a waiter passing with a tray of champagne and grabbed a flute for herself and one for Joe. She saw off half the glass with her first sip, until she felt she could stare down the journalist with impunity.

She watched Joe as they chatted, her hand trapped within his, and tried not to think about whether the warm glow of possessiveness she felt was because she'd bagged him as an artist, or a husband.

As they walked through Arrivals at Heathrow Airport, Joe felt suddenly hesitant at the thought of taking Charlie back to his apartment, definitely not something he was used to. It wasn't as if he were a stranger to taking girls home. Though in fairness home was more usually a hotel room or their place. But now that he and Charlie were back on British soil, he realised how little they'd talked about how this was going to work.

'So we said we'd stay at my place,' he reminded her as they headed towards the end of another endlessly long corridor.

'We did,' she agreed, and he looked at her closely, trying to see if there was more he could glean from these two words. But he had forgotten that his new wife was a pro at hiding her feelings—she'd had a lifetime of practice. Charlie offered nothing else, so he pushed, wanting the matter settled before they had to face the press, who were no doubt waiting for them again at the exit of the airport. Airport security did what they could to push them back, but couldn't keep them away completely. Not that he should want that, he reminded himself. They wanted the publicity. It was good for the band. It was the whole reason they were still married.

But even good publicity wasn't as important as finishing a new album would be—that thought hadn't been far from his mind the last few days. He couldn't understand how he had thought that it was nearly finished. He'd played the demo tracks over and over on the plane, and somehow the songs that he'd fine-tuned and polished so carefully no longer worked when he listened to them. They didn't make him *feel*. They had a veneer of artifice that seemed to get worse, rather than better, the more that he heard them.

His first album had come from the heart. He shuddered inwardly at the cliché. It was years' worth of pent-up emotion and truths not said, filtered through his guitar and piano. It was honest. It was him. This latest attempt… It was okay. A half-dozen of the tracks he would happily listen to in the background of a bar. But it was clean and safe and careful, and lacking the winners. The grandstanding, show-stopping singles that took an album from good to legendary.

He was still writing. Still trying. But he was out of material and out of inspiration. His adolescent experiences, his adult life of running from them had fed his imagination and his muse for one bestselling album. But he couldn't mine the same stuff for a second. It needed something new. So what was he meant to write about—how ten years on the road made relationships impossible? How his parents kept up with his news by reading whatever the tabloids had made up that week? That his only good friends had spent most of that time trapped with him in some mode of transport or another for the last decade? It was hardly rousing stuff.

'Do you want to go back there now, then?' he asked Charlie.

How was this so difficult? Was she making it that way on purpose?

She looked down at her carry-on bag. 'This is all I have with me.'

'We can send someone for your stuff.'

'No.' She didn't want anyone riffling through her things. Occasionally she missed the discreet staff from her childhood home in the private apartments of the palace, who had disappeared the dirty clothes from her bedroom floor before it had had a chance to become a proper teenage dive, but she loved the freedom of her home being truly private. That the leather jacket that she dropped by the door when she got home would still be right there when she was heading out the next morning.

She stopped walking and looked up at him. 'Okay, so we go back to yours tonight. Tomorrow we go to my place and pack some stuff. Does that work for you? Or I could go back to my place tonight. Sleep there, if we don't want to rush into—'

'You sleep with me.'

He couldn't explain the shot of old-fashioned possessiveness that he had felt when she suggested that they sleep apart. Except… The bed share of the previous night. That was a one-off, wasn't it? He supposed they'd find out later, when she realised that his apartment's second bedroom had been converted to a recording studio. Leaving them with one king-sized bed and one very stylish but supremely uncomfortable couch to fight over. He was many things, but chivalrous about sleeping arrangements wasn't one of them. He couldn't remember the last time that he had slept eight hours in a bed that wasn't hurtling along a motorway or through the clouds. So he could promise her a chivalrous pillow barrier if she absolutely insisted, but there was no way he was forgoing his bed. Not even for her.

'For appearances' sake,' he added to his earlier comment. 'What would it look like if we spent our first night back apart?'

CHAPTER FOUR

'WHEN ARE WE going to tell our families?' Joe asked as the driver slid the car away from the kerb, and the throng of photographers who had been waiting for them grew distant in the rear window.

He was probably just hoping to fill the awkward silence, Charlie thought, rather than trying to bait her. But the niggle of guilt that had been eating away at her turned into a full-on stab. She really should have called her parents before she had left the States, but she had just kept thinking about how disappointed they were going to be in her—again—and she couldn't bring herself to do it.

But now they had another load of morning editions of the tabloids to worry about, full of their red-carpet kisses from the night before. Or was it two nights? Losing a day to the time difference when they were in the air hadn't helped her jet lag, or her sense of dislocation from the world. Whenever it was that those kisses had taken place, somehow, she didn't think that they were going to help matters.

'When we get home,' she said, cracking open a bottle of mineral water and leaning back against the leather headrest. In theory she had just had a eleven-hour flight with nothing to do but catch up on missed sleep. And it wasn't even as if she and Joe had spent the time chatting and getting to know one another. He had pulled out noise-cancelling headphones as soon as he was on board and she'd barely heard a word from him after that.

She'd shut her eyes too, pulled on a sleep mask and tried to drift off. But sleep had been impossible. First her mind had run round in circles with recriminations and criticisms; then slowly, something else had crept in. The scent of Joe's aftershave, the drumming of his fingers on the armrest as he got into whatever he was listening to. Her body remembered how she had felt that morning waking up next to him, after her dream filled with hot, sticky caresses. Before her memory returned and she remembered the idiotic thing that they had done. When he was just a hot guy in her head and not the man she had married in a fit of self-sabotage. Lust, pure and simple.

Things were anything but simple now. Attraction could be simple. A marriage of convenience could be simple too, she supposed. She was the product of generations of them. But she and Joe had gone and mixed the two, and now they were paying the price. As Joe shifted on the seat beside her she opened her eyes and watched him for a few moments.

Their late night followed by a long, sleepless flight had left him with a shadow on his jaw that was more midnight than five o'clock. She could almost feel the scratch of it against her cheek if she shut her eyes again and concentrated. She snapped herself out of it. Too dangerous. *Far* too dangerous to be having those sorts of feelings about this man. They had made this arrangement complicated enough as it was. Attraction made it more complicated still. Acting on that attraction anywhere but in the safety of the public gaze was complete madness. No, they were just going to have to get really, really good at self-restraint. She was so looking forward to shutting her bedroom door on Joe and the rest of the world and finally being able to relax and sleep off the jet lag.

Their driver hauled their bags up the stairs to his first-floor warehouse conversion, and Charlie breathed a sigh of relief when they shut the door on him. Home and private at last, all she wanted to do was sleep.

'Do you mind if I just crash?' she asked Joe. 'Which is my room?'

He looked suddenly uncomfortable. 'About that, there's actually only one bedroom.'

Determined not to lose her cool in front of him, she forced the words to come out calmly. 'What do you mean there's only one?'

She crossed the huge open living space and stood on the threshold of Joe's bedroom, her mouth gaping at what he had just told her. He was the one who had suggested they live at his apartment. He couldn't have mentioned he didn't have a guest room?

'You can't think that I'm going to sleep with you.'

'As if, Princess. You're not that irresistible, you know.' Way to kill an ego. Not that she cared right now. All she wanted was to sleep. No, she corrected herself. She needed privacy to call her parents and let them know that she'd messed up—again. And then she needed to sleep. Probably for about three days straight.

'Look, Charlie. I'm tired, I'm grouchy. I have to go call my mum and explain why I decided to get married without her there, and then I'm sleeping. The mattress is big enough for us both to starfish without getting tangled. So you do what you like, but I'm going to bed.

He was tired? *He* was grouchy?

She stood for a moment in the doorway, and could almost feel the delicious relief of slamming it shut with her on the inside. Instead, she pulled herself up to her full five feet ten inches, turned on the spot and stalked off with a grace that her deportment coach had spent months all but beating into her.

Charlie plopped down onto the couch with significantly less grace—no way was she contorting on there to sleep—and pulled out her mobile. She dialled her mum's private number, and heard her voice after a single ring. She could picture so clearly the way the Queen would be working at her desk with her phone beside her blotter, just waiting for her to call.

'Caroline.'

So much said in just one word. She'd been worried about disapproval, disappointment. But the heartfelt, unreserved concern in her mother's voice was the killer.

'Hi, Mum.'

'Charlie, are you okay?'

She dropped her forehead into her hands and wished for the first time that she had gone to do this in person. Surely it was the least her mother deserved. But—like so many of her other mistakes—it was done now, and couldn't be undone.

'I'm fine, Mum. I'm sorry, I know I should have called earlier...' Her voice tailed off and she held her breath, waiting for forgiveness.

'I'm just glad to hear from you. Are you going to tell me what happened?'

She wanted to tell the truth. To confess and tell her that she had messed up again. Her mum would forgive her…eventually. But that wouldn't stop her being disappointed. Nothing could do that. So she steeled herself to lie, to trying to cover up just how stupid she had been this time.

'I met a guy, Mum, and I don't know what happened, but we just clicked. It was love at first sight, and we wanted to get married right away.'

The long pause told her everything she needed to know about how much her mum believed that story.

'If you've made a— I mean if you've changed your mind, Charlie, we can take care of this, you know.'

It was the air of resignation that did it—the knowledge that her mother had been anticipating yet another catastrophe that strengthened her resolve.

'It wasn't a mistake, Mum. It's what I wanted. What we both wanted.' Another long pause, followed by the inevitable.

'So when do we get to meet this young man and his family?'

Her heart kicked into a higher gear as she worried what her mother was expecting—how formal and official was this going to get?

'I was thinking family dinner this weekend. Fly in and stay Friday night—how long you stay is up to you. I've already told your brother and sister. My secretary will ring with the details.'

Charlie couldn't speak. So this was real. She was going to bring Joe to meet her family, pretend that they were crazy in love. She nodded, then realised what she was doing. 'Okay, Mum, we'll be there.' Because when your mum was the Queen it was hard to say no, even more so when you had just done something you knew must have bruised her heart, if not broken it completely.

'I can't wait, darling.' The truth she could hear in her mum's voice broke her own heart in return.

She hung up and for a second let the tears that had been threatening fall onto her cheeks. Just three. Then she drew a deep breath, wiped her eyes and set her shoulders. She had, once again, got herself into an unholy mess and—once again—she would dig herself out of it. There was one other call that she knew she had to make—to her boss, Rich. But she had just disappointed one person whose approval she actually cared about. She didn't have it in her to do the double. She'd need at least a couple of hours' sleep before she could think about that.

She scrubbed under her eyes with a finger, determined to show no signs of weakness to her new husband. This was a professional arrangement and she had no business forgetting that.

As she opened the bedroom door she squared her shoulders. For just a few more hours it was just her and Joe, before the lawyers and managers and accountants wanted to start formalising everything at work. Damned right she was going to enjoy the calm before the storm.

The door opened and she looked over to the bed. *Holy cra—*

She was never going to be able to sleep again. At least not while she was pretending to be married to this man. He hadn't been lying when he'd said that there was room for the two of them to sleep side by side. It was an enormous bed. But the man she had decided to marry had chosen to starfish across it diagonally. There was barely room for a sardine either side of him, never mind anyone else.

And space wasn't the only issue. She'd assumed no naked sleeping, but maybe this was worse. The white T-shirt he must have pulled on before climbing between the sheets hugged tight around his biceps, revealing tattoos that swirled and snaked beneath the fabric, tempting her to follow their lines up his arms. The hem of the shirt had ridden up, showcasing a strip of flawlessly tanned skin across his toned back. And, just to torture her, the sheets had been kicked down to below his tight black boxers—the stretch of the fabric leaving nothing to the imagination. For half a second she thought about sleeping on that back-breaking couch. Or even calling a cab back to her own flat. But the lure of a feather mattress topper was more than she could resist. She kicked off her jeans, noting that her black boy shorts underwear was more than a little similar to her husband's. Luckily *her* white shirt covered her butt.

She crawled onto the mattress beside Joe, trying to keep her movements contained and controlled. Waking him would open the door to a host of possibilities that she didn't want to—couldn't—contemplate right now. Lying on her side on the edge of the bed, she tried to ignore the gentle rhythm of Joe's breathing beside her. She balanced on her hip, the edge of the bed just a couple of inches in front of her. So much for a deep, relaxing sleep. There was no way that was going to happen with her frightened of hitting the floor on one side or Joe on the other. No, she had to start as she meant to go on, and there was no way she was enduring marriage to a man who thought she would perch on the edge of the bed.

She snuck out an experimental toe and aimed at the vicinity of Joe's legs. When her skin met taut, toned muscle, she wasn't prepared for the flash of warmth that came with it. For the memory of the night that flashed back with it. Of her and Joe heading for the bed in their suite, high from champagne, the roulette wheel and the new and exciting gleam on the third fingers of their left hands.

She'd jumped back onto the mattress, the bemused bellboy still standing watching them from the doorway. As Joe had approached her, the look in his eyes like a panther stalking its prey, the bellboy had withdrawn. Her eyes had locked on Joe's, then, and her breath had caught at the intensity in his gaze. And then he had tripped on the rug and fallen towards the bed headfirst, breaking the spell. She'd collapsed back in a fit of giggles, and as her eyes had closed she had been overtaken by a yawn.

She'd fallen asleep so easily the night before. Maybe she could kick him out completely. That might be the only way she was going to get to relax enough to fall asleep. She remembered the look on his face, though, when he'd told her he wasn't giving up his bed for her. She didn't think he'd take crashing to the floor well. And, really, they had enough troubles at the moment without him being any more annoyed with her. She braced herself for the heat that she knew now would come and pushed at his leg again. Success. He shifted behind her and she shuffled back a few inches on the bed. She could hear Joe still moving, but she lay stiff and still, determined not to give up her hard-won territory.

With a great roll Joe turned over, and their safe, back-to-back stand-off was broken. His breath tickled at the back of her neck, setting off a chain reaction of goosebumps from her nape to the bottom of her spine. Maybe she had been better off on the edge of the bed, because her body was starting to hum with anticipation. Her brain—unhelpful as ever—was reminding her of how good it felt to kiss him. How her body had thrummed and softened in his arms. She reached down for the duvet and tucked it tightly around her, though she didn't really need its warmth. But with her body trapped tight beneath it she felt a little more secure. As a final defence, she shoved in her earphones and found something soothing to block out the subtle sounds of a shared bed, and shut her eyes tight.

Joe stood in the bedroom doorway, surveying the scene in front of him. A pair of black skinny jeans had been abandoned by the bed, and silver jewellery was scattered on the bedside table. Dark brown hair was strewn across the pillow and one long, lean calf had snaked out from beneath the duvet. Along with the jeans on the floor, it answered a question that he'd been tempted but too much of a gentleman to find out for himself.

His wife. He had to shake his head in wonderment of how that had happened. A simple kiss from her did things to his body that he had never experienced before. He'd woken with his arms aching to pull her close and give her a proper good morning. And she was the one woman he absolutely couldn't, shouldn't fall for. They had gone into this marriage with ground rules for a good reason. They couldn't risk their careers by giving in to some stupid chemical attraction, or, worse still, by getting emotionally involved.

He'd made the mistake before of giving his heart to someone who was only out to get what she wanted. He'd learnt his lesson, and he wouldn't be making the same mistake again. And of all the women he could have married, it had to be her, didn't it? One who would throw him back into that world of privilege and wealth.

He'd spent just about every day since he was eleven years old feeling like the outsider. And now he had gone and hitched himself to the ultimate in exclusive circles. Once he and Charlie were married, there was no way of getting away from them. But he had learned how to deal with it a long time ago. Keep his distance, keep himself apart, to prevent the sting of rejection when he tried to fit in. The same rule had to apply to Charlie. It didn't matter what she had told her parents, how real they were going to make this thing look— he couldn't let himself forget that it was all for show.

He placed a cup of coffee down among her earrings and bracelets, and from this vantage point he could see the chaos emerging from her suitcase, where more shirts were spilling from the sides.

Charlie jerked suddenly upright, knocking his arm and sending the coffee hurtling to the floor.

'Crap!'

He jumped back as the scalding liquid headed for his shins. Charlie was scrambling out of bed, and grabbed her jeans from the floor to start mopping up the coffee from the floorboards. 'What the hell?' she asked, crouching over the abandoned coffee.

'I thought I'd bring you a cup of coffee in bed, you ungrateful brat.' She sat back at the insult and crossed her arms across her chest. 'I suppose I ought to expect the spoilt little princess routine,' he continued, and they both flinched at the harsh tone in his voice. 'Sorry. Look, you wait there. I'll grab a towel.'

He retreated to the kitchen and took a deep breath, both hands braced palms-down on the worktop; then grabbed some kitchen roll and headed back to the bedroom. Charlie was crouched like a toddler, feet flat on the floor, attacking the coffee with a hand towel from the bathroom. She took a slurp from the cup as she worked, swishing the towel around ineffectually, and chasing streams of coffee along the waxed floorboards and under the bed.

'Here,' he said, taking the sopping towel from her and holding out a hand to pull her up. 'I'll finish up. You drink your coffee.'

'Thanks,' she said, relinquishing the towel with a look of relief. 'And for the coffee. Sorry, I was just a bit disorientated.'

'Forgot you picked yourself up a husband in Vegas?'

'Something like that.' She grabbed her watch from the bedside table and shook off the coffee, leaving flecks of brown on the snowy white duvet cover.

'Ugh. I've got to be at work in an hour.'

She walked over to the bathroom, and he directed his gaze pointedly away from the endlessly long legs emerging from beneath that butt-skimming shirt. He had no desire to make this arrangement any more difficult than it undoubtedly was. Keeping it strictly business was the only way that it was going to work. She eyed her suitcase uncertainly. 'I've got more jeans, but I'm all out of clean tops. Can I raid your wardrobe?'

'Go for it. I'm jumping in the shower. We'll need to leave at quarter to if we're going to walk.'

She stopped riffling through the rails in his dressing room for a second.

'We?'

'I think I'd better come talk to Rich. There's a lot to go through before we can sign anything.'

Of course she hadn't forgotten that Rich had sent her out to Vegas with a job to do. So why wasn't she exactly thrilled about the prospect of going in and seeing him this morning? Because this hadn't been what he'd meant, she knew. It hadn't been what she'd wanted either. If this was a casting-couch situation she wasn't sure which of them had been lying back and thinking of the job, but she knew that she was good at what she did. She knew that she could have bagged this signing without bringing her personal life or family into the picture. But who was going to believe that now?

Her face fell, and somehow he knew exactly what she was thinking.

'You think he's going to be pissed at you?'

'Why would he be? He sent me out there to close this deal. Job done, mission complete. He's going to be thrilled.'

'Really? So why don't you look happy about it?'

'It's nothing.'

'It's clearly something.'

He sat on the edge of the bed as she turned back to

the wardrobe and started looking through his shirts again. Sliding them across the rail without paying much attention.

'I'm just not sure how he's going to react to…this.' She waved a hand between them so he understood exactly what 'this' was. His hackles rose.

'You told me you weren't involved with anyone. Are you telling me you and he are…a thing? Because that would be a major problem. I can't believe you'd—'

'It's nothing like that.' She grabbed hold of a shirt and pulled it from the hanger. 'God, why does everyone assume that any professional relationship I have is based on sex?' He lifted one eyebrow as he took in her half-dressed form and the unmade bed.

'Oh, get lost, Joe. This is nothing to do with sex. This was *your* idea. I'd have got you to sign anyway.'

'Really? Why did you say yes, then?' She had been starting off to the bathroom, but she stopped halfway across the room, his shirt screwed up and crumpled in her hand.

'Oh, why does a party girl do anything, Joe?' Her smile was all public, showing nothing of the real woman he had spent the last couple of days with. 'I'm an idiot. I was drunk. It was a laugh.' It was what everyone would assume, there was no doubt about that—but what was most shocking to him was that she didn't believe that any of those statements were true. So if it hadn't been just for a laugh, and it wasn't about her job either, then why had she done it?

He waited for the water to shut off and for Charlie to emerge from the bathroom before he grabbed his wash bag from his suitcase. She kept her back to him as she emerged and headed straight into the dressing room. Respecting her obvious need for privacy, and reluctant to continue their argument, he went straight into the bathroom and locked the door.

So what was the deal with her boss if she wasn't sleeping with him? Why was she so bothered about what he would think about their marriage? Their reasons for staying together were still good. The papers had been full of stories about the two of them, and there had been talk about the anticipation of their new album. It was exactly the sort of coverage that you couldn't buy. Her boss would be able to see that. He should be pleased that she'd got the job done and with a publicity angle to boot.

He stepped under the spray of the shower and let the water massage his shoulders. Maybe he should let her go and deal with her boss on her own. But he was keen to get this contract signed. He had meant what he had said. He'd been impressed with what the label had pitched to him—he would have signed even without Charlie turning up in Las Vegas.

He followed in her footsteps to the dressing room and wasn't sure whether to be disappointed or relieved that the towel had been discarded on the floor and she was fully dressed. One of his shirts was cinched in at the waist with a wide belt of studded black leather. A pair of black leather leggings ended in spike-heeled boots and she was currently grimacing into the mirror as she applied a feline ring of heavy black eyeliner.

'Walk of shame chic,' she said as she met his eye in the mirror. 'What do you think?'

'I think that now you're a married woman we can't call it the walk of shame. This is home. If you want it to be.' He leaned back against the wall as she paused with a tube of something shiny and gold in her hand. His eyes met hers in the mirror, and he gave a small smile. Relaxing in that moment, he enjoyed their connection—the first since they had woken up that morning. And he remembered again that feeling when he had first met her. When he had glanced across the stage and seen her in the wings, watching him. How they had danced and felt so in tune, so together, that the idea of marriage had seemed inevitable, rather than idiotic.

He laughed as she broke their eye contact to apply a coat of mascara, complete with wide open mouth.

'Come on,' he said, heading to the kitchen. 'I'll make another coffee.'

She glanced at her watch, returning his smile.

'We might have to drink on the go.'

He couldn't deny that he was startled. Princess Caroline all worried about being late for work the morning after bagging the biggest signing of her career. She was just full of surprises.

In the kitchen he set the coffee machine going and grabbed his only travel mug from a cabinet. 'Okay, but we're sharing, then,' he shouted back to her as he added frothy steamed milk.

By the door, he grabbed wallet and keys from the tray on the console where he'd dropped them the night before. Waiting for Charlie, he had an unimpeded view of her kicking her coffee-stained jeans towards her suitcase, and swiping some of the jewellery from the bedside table, but knocking the rest of it under the bed. Spot the girl who'd grown up with staff, he thought again to himself. They were going to have to talk about this at some point, he realised. He wasn't going to pick up after her like some sort of valet.

Was that how she saw him, he wondered—on a par with the staff? Barely visible in a room? She swept past him and out of the door; then drew up short in the corridor, clearly surprised that he wasn't just following in her wake.

'Are you coming?' she asked over her shoulder.

Slowly, Joe turned his key in the lock and then walked towards her. He took a long sip of coffee from the travel mug and then met her eye.

'You're not a princess here, sweetheart,' he told her gently. 'Home means you do your own fetching and carrying.'

Her brows drew together and he knew he'd pissed her off. 'I'll start by carrying this, then, shall I?' She took the coffee from him and walked into the lift, letting the door close in his face behind her.

Charlie swiped them into the office with her key card and waved at the receptionist on her way past. Avalon Records was based in a rundown old Regency villa on a once fashionable square. The grandeur of the high ceilings and sweeping staircases was in stark contrast to the workaday contents. Laminate wood desks had been packed into every corner of the building, and tattered swivel chairs fought for space with stacks of paper and laser printers.

She headed to her desk with eyes forward, intent on not letting anyone—especially Joe—see how nervous she was. Not that she needed to worry about that. She had been so keen to get into the office early that the place was practically deserted. She reached her desk and stashed her bag in a drawer, making herself busy for just a few more moments, turning on the computer and getting everything straight in her head so that the minute Rich arrived she could sell the hell out of this situation.

This was a good day, and there was no way she was leaving Rich's office until he agreed with her. Not only had she closed the deal that Rich had sent her out there to do, she had tied Joe and The Red Kites to their future in the closest way possible. Rich should— and he would—be eternally grateful. This was a massive coup for their indie label, tempting the hottest band of the year away from the big multinationals. She grabbed a couple of files and a notebook from under a pile of papers and then turned back to Joe.

He was staring at her desk with a mixture of shock and despair.

'What?' she asked, alarmed by his expression.

'Oh, my God. You're a slob.' He laughed as he spoke, his eyes wide. She leaned back against her desk and crossed her arms across her chest.

'I am so not.'

'You totally are. I thought maybe back at my place it was because we were both still living out of our cases. I need to clear you some space in the war...' His voice drifted and a shadow crossed his expression before he shook it off and got back to the point. 'But this proves it. I mean...how do you find anything?'

She waved the files in her hand at him.

'Because they're exactly where I left them.'

He shook his head again. 'But wouldn't they also be exactly where you left them if they were...say... filed neatly in a drawer?'

She raised her brows. 'You wouldn't by any chance be interfering, would you, Joe? Because this is my desk, and my office, and my job, and you don't get to boss me around here.'

He snorted out a breath. 'Oh, right, because at home you're so biddable and accommodating.' He laughed again, taking a step closer until she was trapped between him and the desk. She could smell his shower gel, the same one that she'd borrowed that morning, knowing even as she'd done it that she was going to be haunted by this reminder of him all day. She looked up at him, enjoying the novelty of a man who was still a smidge taller than her, even when she was in heels.

'I'm not interfering. I'm just getting to know you. We can talk about this more at home.' He took another half-step closer and she hitched a butt cheek onto her desk, looking for just a little more space, a little more safety. Breathing space for sensible, professional decision-making.

Then Joe lifted his hand and even without knowing where it was heading—hair, cheek, lips—she knew it would be more than her self-control could stand. She grabbed his hand mid-air, but that didn't help. It just pulled him closer as their linked hands landed on the desk by her hip. The front of his thighs pressed against hers, long and lean and matched so perfectly to her body he could have been made for her. She could feel the gentle pressure of his breath on her lips, and her eyes locked on his mouth as she remembered the times that they had pressed against hers. Her brain was desperately trying to catch up with the demands of her body. Remember the agreements they had made. They were meant to be madly in love in public. They were business associates when they were home. But what were they to each other here? In this public place, but with no one there to see them.

She dragged her gaze away for a moment, over Joe's shoulder to the still-deserted office. She had wanted to be in early. To show Rich that she was still as committed—as professional—as ever. But it had left her and Joe dangerously secluded.

His fingers untangled from hers, and she was hit with syncopated waves of regret then relief. But neither lasted long as his hand completed its original journey and landed this time on her cheek. His palm cupped her face as he tilted her head just a fraction. The sight of his tongue sneaking out to moisten his lips set off a chain reaction from the tight, hard knot low in her pelvis to the winding of her arms around his shoulders to the low sigh that escaped her throat as she closed her eyes and leaned in, waiting for the touch of his mouth.

A door slammed behind her and she jumped back, whacking her thighs against her desk in the process. She pushed at Joe's chest, knowing even before she turned to look at Rich's office what she was going to find.

Her boss was standing in front of the closed door to his office, leaning back against it with his arms crossed. Proof that the slam had been entirely for effect. Bloody drama queen, Charlie cursed him under her breath.

'The lovebirds return,' Rich said, leaning forwards and extending his arm to shake Joe's hand. 'It's good to see you again, Joe. We weren't expecting you. Are you just seeing the wife to work, or…?'

'Actually, Rich, we have good news.' Charlie

watched her boss's face closely, trying to judge his reaction. 'Joe and the rest of the guys are all in agreement. They want to sign with us. Joe wanted to come and give the good news in person this morning.'

Rich's professional smile didn't give anything away, but she knew him well enough to see the slight hint of tightness around his eyes that told her that this wasn't unmitigated pleasure.

'That is great news,' he said, clapping Joe on the back. 'I guess this is a pretty good week for us all, then. Congratulations to you both. Married? Love at first sight, the papers are saying. I have to admit, I was surprised not to hear it from the horse's mouth.' He gave Charlie a pointed look and she pulled herself up to her full height, determined not to act like a chastised teenager. She had every right to do just what she wanted. She didn't need Rich's permission, or his approval, to marry whomever she chose.

'You know how it is, Rich. The papers knew what was happening almost before we did. We didn't have a chance to tell people ourselves.'

'Funny how that happens, isn't it?' Rich said with a quirk of his eyebrow. So he definitely wasn't going to buy 'love at first sight' then. Time for Plan B.

Joe looked from her to Rich, and must have picked up on the atmosphere between them.

'Look, we just wanted to give you *this* news in person,' Joe said. 'I know that there's loads to work out with the lawyers and stuff so just let me know when you want to start.' He leaned forward to shake Rich's hand again before turning back to Charlie. She waited to hear Rich go back into his office, but the click of the door handle didn't come. Was this a test? Was he trying to see if this was all for show?

She didn't have time to worry about it as Joe's lips descended on hers. His hands framed her face, his fingertips just teasing at her hairline. His lips were warm and soft as they pressed against her mouth, full of promise and desire. But then his hands dropped to her shoulders as he broke away, and when she opened her eyes she was met by a twinkling expression in his. 'See you at home, love.'

He swept out of the office with a final wave at Rich, and she fought the urge to lean back against her desk to catch her breath.

Instead her hands found the files that she'd grabbed before Rich had arrived, and she stalked into his office with her head held high.

'Are you ready to get started? We've got a lot to cover.'

Rich stood in the doorway, not joining her at the table as she pulled out a chair and sat. Then shook his head as he took in her determined glare. 'I'll be with you in a second.'

Five minutes later he returned with two cups of coffee and a look of determination that matched her own.

She was reading through a boilerplate contract, making notes in the margin with a red pen, and Rich waited for her to finish scribbling before he sat.

'Here, have a caffeinated peace offering. Have you slept at all since you left for the airport? I'm betting your body has no idea what time zone it's in right now.'

'Thanks.' She took the coffee and realised that he was right. She should be exhausted, but she wasn't.

Something to do with having a brand-new husband she wasn't sure if she was meant to be keeping her hands off or not, she supposed.

'So are you going to tell me what happened?'

'I thought you said you already knew.'

'I told you I'd read the papers. I want the real story. From you, preferably. I think I deserve that. This affects us all. This is work. When I sent you out there to seal the deal, I didn't mean do *any*thing. I thought maybe… I don't know. The Princess thing: sometimes it works. I never expected you to… Just… What happened, Charlie?'

She looked him in the eye, still trying to work out her angle. How much she should share. How much she should hide. But Rich was right. This went beyond her personal life. She and Joe had made a calculated business decision—he couldn't expect her to keep it from the head of the business.

'We got carried away. Vegas, you know.' She gestured vaguely with her hands. 'We'd had too much to drink. We thought it would be funny. And that, you know, the publicity wouldn't be a bad thing for the band.'

'So it wasn't…' He hesitated, and Charlie just knew he was trying to find the right words. The ones that would annoy her the least. She prayed he wasn't about to ask the question she knew deep down was coming. 'It wasn't a quid pro quo deal. Nothing to do with the contract.'

She bristled, even though she'd been expecting it.

'What are you implying, Rich? Because if you think that I would do that—that I would need to… There's nothing I can say to that.'

Rich held out his hands for peace.

'I'm just trying to understand here, Charlie. I wasn't implying anything. So you thought it was a laugh, to celebrate the deal, and the publicity wouldn't exactly harm the band. But…now? What's going on now? You're living together?'

'We thought it would look better if it was love at first sight rather than a Vegas mistake. We're both committed to keeping up the pretence until the publicity won't be as harmful.'

'And it's all for show?' Rich asked. She nodded. 'So that little moment I walked in on earlier?'

'All part of the act.'

Rich sighed, non-committal. 'Okay, all of that aside, this is an amazing opportunity for us. Great job on getting the signing. I knew that I could trust you to take care of it.'

Charlie straightened the papers in front of her, enjoying the warm glow of Rich's praise for her work. She'd survived the first meeting: it could only get better from here.

'So how did it go with your boss after I left?' Joe asked when she arrived home that evening. 'It looked like things were about to get heated between you.'

She crossed to the fridge and surveyed the contents as she thought about it.

'It was a bit hairy at first,' she admitted as she grabbed a couple of beers and waved one in Joe's direction. He took them both from her and reached behind him into a drawer to find a bottle opener.

'Does he always get so involved in his staff's personal lives?'

'Only when they go around marrying potential clients.'

He raised his eyebrows in a 'fair enough' expression, pulling out the bar stool next to him at the kitchen island.

'Why do you care so much what he thinks anyway? If you're so adamant that there's nothing going on between you.'

'Jealous again, darling?' She threw him some serious shade while taking a sip of her beer and resting her hip on the stool. The hardness of his gaze drew her up short. 'Don't be an idiot, Joe. I'm not impressed or in the least turned on by the jealousy thing. Drop it.'

'Okay,' he conceded. 'So there's nothing romantic going on between you. Tell me what that weird vibe was, then. Why were you afraid of disappointing him?'

'He's my boss. I'd quite like to not get fired. Are you so much of a celeb these days that you don't remember what it's like to hold down a job?'

'Said the Princess.'

'You wanted to know why I don't want to disappoint Rich? Because he's the only one who doesn't call me Princess. Even when others aren't doing it to my face, they still treat me differently, and it drives me crazy. Rich is the only person who doesn't make exceptions or allowances. He's the one person who treats me like a normal goddamn human being and expects me to act like one. If I stepped out of line he'd fire me in a heartbeat.'

'And you'd walk straight into another job.'

She resisted the urge to throw her beer at him. 'Maybe I would. But not one that I deserve. Not one that I could do as well as the one I have now. Rich has made me work my arse off for every achievement. Every signing. Every bloody paycheque has been in exchange for my blood, sweat and tears. He's the only one who could see that I can do it. I work hard, I earn my keep. When I let him down, I'm proving them right. All the people who just expect the world to fall into my lap.'

Which was why there was no way that she was walking away from the life that she'd built for herself, just because she'd promised her parents she'd come home at some fixed point in time.

'I'm sorry, I didn't mean to.'

'It's a sore point, okay. Because I have let him down. This whole thing is stupid. It's beneath me. I messed up, and I don't like having it pointed out to me by the people whose opinion I value.'

He gave her a long, assessing look. 'We never talked about how it went with your parents, did we?'

She knocked back another long glug of beer.

'They want to meet you.'

'Mine too.'

She caught his eye, and managed a tentative smile. 'How do you reckon that's going to go?'

'My mum asked if she needed to wear a hat.'

Frothy beer hit her nose as she snorted with laughter.

'What did you tell her?'

'That I had no idea. I have no idea how this works.' The laughter died in his eyes and he looked suddenly solemn.

'Are you freaked out by it? The royalty thing? Because I thought you went to Northbridge School. My cousins are there. And you didn't seem all that impressed when I arrived in Vegas.'

He hesitated; the last thing that he wanted was to talk about his school days. He'd been awkward enough there, the scholarship kid from up north. And that was before the school's very own Princess—she didn't need the royal blood to call herself that—had used and humiliated him. 'Yeah, I knew your cousins at school,' Joe said, 'but we weren't friends. I didn't exactly click with my classmates.'

'School can be a cruel place.'

'I guess.' He took another swig of his beer and thought back. It had been a long time since he'd really thought about that part of his life. After he'd been ignominiously dumped in front of half his school year, he'd taken the lesson, moved on, and tried to forget about the humiliation. 'There wasn't any bullying or anything like that. The masters would never have stood for it. It's just, I didn't fit in, you know.' There was no need to tell her the whole ugly story. It had been embarrassing enough the first time around.

'And you're worried it's going to be like that with my family?' Charlie leaned forward and rested her elbow on the bar and her chin on her hand as she asked the question. 'They're really nice, you know,' she said earnestly. 'Well, my brother's an idiot, but every family has one of those.'

'I'm sure they are nice, Charlie. But they're different. We're different. And that's not something that we can change.' The last time that he'd been around people who moved in royal circles, the fact that he was different had become a currency in a market that he hadn't understood. Luckily, he was older and wiser now. He knew to look out for what people wanted from him, and to make sure he was getting a good deal out of it too. He also knew that no one was ever going to see their match as a marriage of equals.

'It's a good job that this is just all for show, then,' she added. 'So my family won't be making you uncomfortable for long.'

A look of pain flashed across her face, and he wondered what had caused it. It was too deep, too old to have been caused by this argument.

'It doesn't matter,' she said after a long pause, turning away from him almost imperceptibly. 'I'm never going to marry, so you don't have to worry about some future husband being trapped in that world.'

'I hate to break it to you, but it's a bit late for never.' He leaned in closer, nudging the footrest of her stool, trying to bridge the gulf that had suddenly appeared between them.

'Well, except this isn't real, is it?' she said.

He nodded, trying to hide his wince at the unexpected pain her statement had caused. Time for a change of subject, he thought. 'So why are you never getting married? Well, getting married again.'

'It's just not for me.' She shuffled to the back of her stool, reinstating the distance that he had tried to breach.

'Wow. That's enlightening.' She was hiding something from him, he knew it. Something big. And while she could keep her secrets if she wanted—it worried him. Because how was he meant to know how to handle this situation if he didn't have all the information? With all the women that had come before her, he knew exactly what they wanted, and they knew what he wanted in return.

With Charlie, despite their best efforts to keep this businesslike, he knew that everything she said carried shades of meaning that he didn't understand. It made him nervous, knowing that he was making calculations without all of the information he needed.

'Look, what does it matter, Joe? I wouldn't make a good wife, it wouldn't be fair for me to get married—not to someone who actually wanted to be my husband. But you'll have a chance to see them all for yourself. When I spoke to my mother yesterday she invited us over for dinner with the family on Friday. We'll need to stay. It's too far to fly there and back in an evening.'

'Yeah, great,' he said, though he knew that his lack of enthusiasm was more than clear.

'Anyway, I don't want to talk about this any more. How about we go out? I'm not sure what's going on with the jet lag, but I'm not sleeping any time soon. We could go get a drink—I know a place not far from here.'

'Like a date?' he asked, uncertainly. Had she suddenly decided that that was what she wanted?

'Like a chance for the press to see us as loved-up and glowing newly-weds.'

He nodded, trying to work out whether he was relieved or disappointed that it was all part of the act. 'Wouldn't newly-weds be more interested in staying home and getting to know one another?'

She spoke under her breath so quietly he could barely hear her reply: 'All the more reason to go out.'

CHAPTER FIVE

SHE PULLED THE front door closed behind them while she smudged on a bright red lip crayon. The bar was a ten-minute walk away. She'd been to their open mic night a few times, looking out for artists that she'd seen online but wanted to check out playing live before she decided if she was interested. As they turned the corner by the bar, though, she realised that this wasn't going to be one of those nights where she struck professional gold. And when they walked in and saw the screens showing lyrics, her worst fears were confirmed. It was no-holds-barred, no-talent-required, hen-parties-welcome karaoke. A trio of drunk students were belting out a rock classic, spilling pints of beer with their enthusiasm. Well, at least their taste in music couldn't be faulted, Charlie thought, boosting the roots of her hair with her fingers in honour of her spirit sister.

'Well, they're certainly going for it,' Joe said with a grin that slipped slightly as they hit a particularly painful note. 'This your usual kind of place?'

She looked around. The place itself was great: a shiny polished wood bar, real-ale pumps gleaming and—importantly—well stocked with decent beer.

Plus there was plenty of gin on the shelves, and good vodka on ice for later in the evening. But most importantly of all, the manager, Ruby, had her number and would call with any hot tips for new acts she might be interested in.

'Charlie!' Ruby greeted her with a smile. 'Don't usually see you here on a Tuesday. Don't tell me this is your honeymoon. That would be too tragic.'

Charlie forced a laugh at this reminder of her newly married status.

'I wish. No time for a honeymoon. But Joe—or we, now, I guess—live just round the corner and we fancied a quiet drink. I'd say you'd be seeing more of me, but…' She looked over at the singing students.

'Wanted to try something new. Don't worry, I won't be repeating the experiment.'

They all watched the tone-deaf trio with similar expressions of amusement.

'Sorry,' Charlie added, realising that she hadn't introduced Joe. 'Joe, this is Ruby, she runs this place. Ruby, this is Joe, my…er…'

'Her husband,' Joe filled in, sliding one arm around her waist and with the other leaning over the bar to shake Ruby's hand.

'I read about your news. Congrats! Vegas, huh. You guys have a wild time?'

'"Wild" is one word for it.'

'The best.'

Charlie, remembering her part, relaxed into Joe's arms. Ruby was watching them carefully, and Charlie wondered what she was thinking. Was she trying to judge whether they were for real? Were they going to face this scrutiny from everyone they met? She might not count Ruby as quite a friend, but Charlie would normally have at least considered her an ally. Well, they would just have to convince her, she decided. Because they were going to make this pretence of a marriage work. The alternative was to disappoint her family even more than she already had.

She just had to remember that it was all make-believe. She didn't get to be the glowing newly-wed in real life. Being a wife, like being a princess, came with certain responsibilities, certain expectations that she knew she couldn't fill. There was no point letting herself fall for a guy only to have him up and leave when he found out that she might not be a complete woman.

Charlie ordered a couple of beers and led Joe over to one of the booths in the back of the bar. It was comfy and private, upholstered in a deep red leather, and just the sort of spot that a loved-up couple would choose, she thought.

'They're really going for it, huh,' Joe said, indicating the girls on the karaoke, who had moved on from rock to an operatic power ballad. He took a swig of the ale, and Charlie watched as his throat moved. His head was thrown back, so he couldn't see her watching him. From inside the sleeve of his tight white T-shirt she could see half a tattoo, weaving and winding around his arm. She was concentrating so hard on trying to trace the pattern that she didn't notice at first that his eyes had dropped and she'd been totally busted.

'Looking at something you like?' It could have sounded cheesy. It *should* have sounded cheesy. But somehow the sincerity in his gaze saved it. 'You wanna see the rest of it?'

Okay, so that was definitely flirtatious. She looked around quickly to see if anyone was eavesdropping. Surely if they were already hitched she should know what his tats looked like.

Ruby was serving at the bar, the drunk girls were still singing enthusiastically, and most of the other customers had been scared off.

She slipped off her bench and darted round the table, sliding in beside Joe until her thigh was pressed against his.

'All yours,' he said, lifting his arm. Her fingertips brushed at the edge of the cotton T-shirt, which was warm and soft from contact with his skin. She traced the band that wound around his bicep, looking up and meeting his eye when he flinched away from her touch as she reached the sensitive skin near his underarm.

'Ticklish?'

'Maybe.' One side of his mouth quirked up in a half-smile, and she filed that information away, just in case she should ever need it.

She shouldn't ever need it, she reminded herself.

This was just an arrangement, and she had no business forgetting it. No business exploring his body, even something as seemingly innocent as an arm. Her body remembered being in bed with him. It remembered those kisses. The way that she had arched into him, desperate to be closer. She shot off the bench, diving for safety on the other side of the table.

'It's nice. I like it.' She tried to keep her voice level, to prevent it giving away how hard she was finding it to be indifferent to him.

'Well, there's plenty more. But maybe we should keep those under wraps for now.' She nodded. Not trusting herself to reply to that statement. She took a sip of beer, hoping the chilled amber liquid would cool her blazing face.

'So the open mic here's usually good?' Joe asked, and she jumped on the change of subject gratefully.

'It is,' she said. 'Very different from tonight. It's normally pretty professional. I've found a couple of great artists here.'

'You like to find them when they're still raw?'

'Of course. I mean a fully formed band with a track record is pretty great too.' She inclined her head towards him and he smiled. 'But there's something about finding raw talent and helping it to develop. It's… It's what gets me to work on a Monday morning when sometimes I'd rather drag the duvet over my head.'

'Must be tough to stay motivated when you don't really have to work.'

She dropped her bottle on the table a little harder than was strictly necessary. 'And why do you think I don't have to work?'

'Oh, I don't know, royal families are all taxpayer-funded, right?'

She placed both palms face down on the table, forcing herself to appear calm, not to slam them in a temper. 'The *working* royals are taxpayer-funded. Yes. And the key word there is "working". Do you know what the royal family is worth to my country's economy in terms of tourism alone? Not that it matters, because I opted out. I don't do official engagements and I don't take a penny.'

'Come on, though. You've never had to struggle.'

'Oh, because a wealthy family solves all problems. We all know that.'

She wished it were true. She had asked the doctor when she had first got her diagnosis whether there was anything that could be done, and the answer was a very equivocal 'maybe'.

Maybe if she threw enough money at the problem, there might be something they could do to give her a chance of conceiving. But it wouldn't take just money. It would take money and time and invasive procedures. Fertility drugs in the fridge and needles in her thighs. It could mean every chance of the world discovering she was a failure on the most basic level, and absolutely no guarantee that it would even work. No, it was simpler to accept now that marriage and a family weren't on the cards for her and move on.

'Where did you pick up this chip on your shoulder, anyway?' Charlie asked. 'I thought your education was every bit as expensive as mine.'

He looked her in the eye, and for a moment she could see vulnerability behind his rock-star cool.

'I had a full scholarship,' he said with a shrug.

'Impressive.' Charlie sat back against the padding of the bench. 'Northbridge don't just hand those out like sweeties. Was it for music?'

She was offended by his expression of surprise. What, did he expect her to recoil at the thought that he didn't pay his own school fees? God, he really did think that she was a snob. Well, it was high time she straightened that one out. Finishing her beer in one long gulp, she slid out of the booth and held out her hand to pull Joe up.

'Somehow,' she said, when he hesitated to follow

her, 'you seem to have got totally the wrong idea about what sort of princess I am. We're going to fix that. Now.'

His expression still showing his reluctance, he allowed her to pull him to standing, but leaned back against the table, arms folded over his chest.

'How exactly do you plan to do that?'

'We, darling husband, are going to sing.'

He eyed the karaoke screens with trepidation.

'Here?'

'Where else?' But he still didn't look convinced.

'Are you any good?'

'I'm no music scholar, but I hold my own. Now, are you going to choose something or am I?'

She grabbed the tablet with song choices from Ruby at the bar, who looked eternally grateful that someone would be breaking the students' residency.

'Are you going to help choose? Because I'm strongly considering something from the musical theatre oeuvre.'

That cracked his serious expression and he grinned, grabbing the back pocket of her jeans and pulling her back against the table with him, so they could look at the tablet side by side.

'As if you'd choose something that wasn't achingly cool.'

She swiped through the pages in demonstration.

'Hate to break it to you, but there's a distinct lack of "achingly cool". The only answer is to go as far as possible in the other direction. We go for maximum cheese.'

'I was so afraid you were going to say that.'

'Come on.' She swiped through another couple of

choices until she landed on a classic pop duet. 'It's got to be this one.' She hit the button that cued up the song and bought another round at the bar to tempt the drunk girls away from their microphones. With another couple of beers for her and Joe in hand, she stepped up onto the little stage.

She glanced around the bar—the girls had done a good job of emptying the place, but a few tables had stuck it out, like her and Joe, and now had all eyes on her. She could see the cogs whirring as they tried to place her face. Obviously not expecting to see a princess at the karaoke night. Even one with her reputation.

'It's a duet!' she shouted to him from the stage. 'Don't you dare leave me hanging!'

She held out her hand to him again and this time he grabbed it enthusiastically, pulled himself up to the stage beside her and planted a heavy kiss on her lips.

The surprise of it stole her reason for a moment, as her breath stopped and her world was reduced to the sensation of him on her. She lifted her hands to his arms, bracing herself against him, feeling unsteady on the little stage as one arm slid around her waist and his hand pressed firmly on the small of her back, pulling her in close.

Her fingers teased up his bicep; though her eyes were closed, her fingers traced the pattern of his tattoo from memory, nudging at the hem of his sleeve as they had earlier, keen to continue their exploration.

A wolf whistle from the crowd broke into their little reverie, and Charlie looked up, only to be greeted with the cameras of several phones pointing in her direction. Well, they'd be in the papers again. She shrugged mentally and reminded herself that that was the whole idea of this marriage.

That was why he'd kissed her.

It took a few moments for reality to break through. For her to remember that of course he'd only kissed her because they had an audience. This wasn't real— they just had to make it look that way. And just as her confidence wavered, and she wondered why that thought hurt so much, the music kicked in and Joe passed her a microphone.

'Come on then, love. Show me what you've got.'

She pulled her hair to one side, puckered up her finest pout and prepared to rock out.

They made it through the first verse without making eye contact, never mind anything more physical, but as they reached the chorus Joe reached around her waist and pulled her back, so her body was pressed against him from spike earrings to spike heels. She faltered on the lyrics, barely able to remember how to breathe, never mind sing.

She looked round at Joe to see if it had had the same effect on him, but when she saw his face she knew that he wasn't feeling what she was feeling. He was just feeling the music: every note of it. His throaty, husky voice giving the pop song a cool credibility it had never had before.

She pulled away to see him better, and though she picked up the words and joined in, it was only a token effort. Backing vocals to his masterful performance. This was why she'd agreed to marry him. The man Joe became on stage was impossible to refuse. She had kicked herself every minute since she'd woken up with a Vegas husband she no longer wanted, asking how she could have been so stupid.

But she hadn't been stupid, she realised now. It was just that they had been so magnetically drawn to one another because of his passion for music—any music—that it would have been pointless even trying to resist. Joe's eyes opened as the song slowed, and their gazes met, freezing them in the moment.

Does he feel it too? she wondered. Or had he just been so high on the adrenaline of performance that he would have agreed to marry anyone who had crossed his path?

She could see his adrenaline kicking up a notch now. His gestures growing more expansive, his grin wider, his eyes wilder.

She sang along, trying to keep pace with his enthusiasm, but whatever performance gene he'd been born with, she was clearly lacking.

The song finished with an air-guitar solo from Joe, and a roar of applause from the bar. She'd been so intent on watching him that she hadn't noticed the place fill up. From the many smartphones still clutched in hands, she guessed that they were about to go viral.

Joe grabbed her around the waist, and before she could stop him, before she could even think about whether she wanted to, his mouth was on hers, burning into her body, her mind, her soul, with his intensity. His hands were everywhere: on her butt, in her hair, gently traipsing up her upper arm. His lips were insistent against hers, demanding that she gave herself to him with equal passion. And his tongue caressed hers with such intimacy that it nearly broke her. Soft and hard, gentle and rough, he surprised her with every touch.

When, finally, he pulled away, they both gasped for air, and she was grateful his arms were still clamped around her waist, keeping her upright. And that she'd turned so that her back was to the bar, so no one would be able to see her flaming red cheeks or the confusion in her eyes.

'Uh-oh. Looks like we've got an audience,' Joe said, and Charlie registered that the surprise in his voice seemed genuine. Had he really not noticed that they were being watched? Because if not, that kiss needed an explanation. The knowledge that it was all for show had been the only thing keeping her from losing her mind. He couldn't go and change the rules now.

'Are you up for another?' Joe asked.

Another song? Another drink? Another kiss? None of the options seemed particularly safe after that performance.

'I think my singing days are done,' she said with a smile, jumping down from the stage and heading back to the relative safety of their booth.

'Where did they all come from?' Joe asked, drinking the beer he'd abandoned when he'd gone into performance mode.

'Happened quickly, huh.'

'So fast I didn't even notice.'

Then why did you kiss me? The question hung, loud and unspoken, in the air.

'So what's your family like?' Charlie asked, suddenly desperate for a change of subject. 'You're from up north, right?'

Joe nodded, and named a town near Manchester. Of course she already knew where he'd grown up from her research into the band, but small talk seemed the safest option open to them at the moment. 'They must have been proud of you. For the scholarship. For everything since.'

'Of course. They were chuffed when I got into the school. It was their idea, actually. My mum was a gifted pianist but never had the opportunity for a career in music. They wanted me to have the best.'

'Sounds like a lot of pressure.' If there was one thing she understood it was the heavy weight of family expectation. But Joe shrugged, non-committal.

'Their motives were good. Still are.'

'But you weren't happy?'

'It was an amazing opportunity.'

'That's not what I asked.'

He sighed and held up his palms. 'I don't like to sound ungrateful. I have no reason to complain. The school funded me. My parents made sacrifices.'

'You remember who you're talking to, right? I do understand that having the best of everything doesn't always make you happy. It doesn't make you a bad person to acknowledge that. It makes you human.'

He was quiet for a beat. 'So what's making you unhappy, Princess Caroline?'

'Oh, no. You are so not changing the subject like that. Come on. Mum and Dad. What are they like? How did they react to…' she searched for the words to describe what they were doing together '…to Vegas?'

He grimaced; she cringed. 'That bad?'

'They weren't best pleased that we did it without them there. They're hurt, but happy for me. I don't know, but I think that made me feel worse.' He was silent for a moment, fiddling with the label of his beer bottle. 'They want to meet you.'

And she was every bit as terrified of that as he was about meeting her family. She knew that she had a reputation that was about as far as you could get from ideal daughter-in-law. 'I could ask my mother to invite them this weekend? Face everyone at the same time?'

He choked on his beer, caught in a laugh.

'That's sweet, Charlie, but how about we start with introducing them to one royal and go from there. Not everyone is as super cool as me when it comes to meeting you and yours.'

'Oh, right,' she laughed. 'Because you were so ice-cool you practically dropped to one knee the night that we met.'

She wondered whether her tease had gone too far, but his mouth curved in a smile. 'What can I say? You give a whole new meaning to irresistible.'

She could feel herself blushing like a schoolgirl and incapable of stopping it. 'So we see my parents Friday night. Do you want to see yours this weekend too? If you wanted to go sooner I guess I could talk to Rich. Work remotely or something.'

He shook his head. 'Don't worry. I think this weekend will be plenty soon enough. We can fly into Manchester on Saturday. Be back home by Sunday night. No need to miss work.'

'Actually, I could do with stopping by a festival on Sunday, if you fancy it. There's a band I'd like to see perform, and try and catch them for a chat.'

He nodded, and then Charlie glanced at her watch, realising with surprise that over an hour had passed since they had left the stage. The bar had thinned out a little again, leaving the atmosphere verging dangerously on intimate.

'Speaking of work, I've a fair bit to catch up on. I need to be in the office early tomorrow. Mind if we call it a night?'

He swigged the last of his drink and stood, reaching for her hand as she slipped off the bench. 'I like that you're tall,' he said as they left the bar with a wave to Ruby. 'As tall as me in those shoes.'

'Random comment, but thanks,' she replied, trying to work out if there was a hidden message in there that she wasn't getting. 'Are you just thinking out loud? Is this going to be a list?'

'I'm just… I don't understand. You're right. I didn't play it cool, that night. I didn't play it cool on stage just now. I'm just trying to figure this out. Maybe it is the royal thing, but I didn't struggle not to kiss your cousins when I was at school with them.'

'So you think it's because I'm tall?' Really thinking: What are you saying? Are you saying you like me? That this is real for you?

'I'm thinking about everything. I just figure that if I can work out what it is…you know…that makes us crazy like that, we can avoid it. Stop it happening again. Keep things simple.'

Her ego deflated rapidly. So it didn't matter what he was feeling, because all he wanted was a way of not feeling it any more. After their madness on stage, they were back on earth with a crash, and she had the whiplash to prove it.

'Well, I'm sorry, darling, but I'm not losing the heels.'

'God, no. Don't,' he said with so much feeling it broke the tension between them. 'I love the heels.'

Which was meant to be a bad thing, she tried to remind herself, but the matching grins on their faces proved it would be a lie.

'Or maybe it's the hair,' he came up with as they walked back to his flat, their fingers still twined. 'There's so much of it. It's wild.'

She tried to laugh it off. 'So we've established you have a thing for tall women with messy hair. I guess I was just lucky I fit the bill.' She turned serious as they reached the front door of the warehouse and stepped into the privacy of the foyer. 'Are your parents going to hate me?'

'Why would they hate you?'

'Notorious party girl seduces lovely northern lad into hasty Vegas marriage. Am I not the girl that mothers have nightmares about?'

'Is that how you see what happened? You seduced me? Because I remember things differently...'

'It's not about what I remember. It's about what your mum will think.'

'My mum will think you're great.' But his tone told her that she wasn't the only one with reservations about the big introduction. 'You'll mainly be busy with dodging hints about grandchildren.'

Her stomach fell and she leaned back against the wall for support while the rushing in her ears stopped.

'She won't seriously be expecting that, will she?'

'She's been bugging me for years about settling down and giving her grandkids. Isn't that what all mums do?'

Apparently they did—that was why she made a point of seeing hers as little as possible.

She drew herself up to her full height again, not wanting Joe to see that there was anything wrong.

'Well, we'll just have to tell her that we don't have any plans.'

Joe was looking at her closely, and she wondered how much he had seen. Whether he had realised that she had just had a minor panic attack.

'It's fine; we'll fend her off together. Are you sure you're okay?'

So he had noticed. She pasted on a smile and pushed her shoulders back, determined to give him no reason to suspect what was on her mind. 'Of course. Just tired. That jet lag must be catching up with me after all.'

It wasn't until she reached his front door that she remembered the whole bed situation. How was she meant to sleep beside him after a kiss like that? After he'd all but told her that he was finding it as hard to resist her as she was to resist him.

She dived into the bathroom as soon as they got into the apartment, determined to be the first ready for bed, and to have her eyes closed and be pretending to sleep by the time that Joe came in. Or better still, actually *be* asleep, and not even know that he was there. She pulled a T-shirt over her head, still warm from the dryer, and gave herself a stern talking-to. She couldn't react like that every time someone mentioned babies or pregnancy. There were bound to be questions after the hasty way that they had got married, and she was going to have to learn to deal with them.

CHAPTER SIX

THERE WAS DEFINITELY something that she wasn't telling him. Something to do with the way that she'd reacted just now when he'd warned her that his mum would probably be hinting about grandchildren.

What, did she already have an illegitimate kid stashed away somewhere? No. It couldn't be that. There was no way that she'd be able to keep it out of the papers. What if she was already pregnant? That could be it. After all, she had accepted a completely idiotic proposal of marriage from a man that she barely knew. Was she looking for a baby daddy, as well as a husband?

And how would he feel if she was? That one was easy enough to answer: as if he was being used. Well, there was nothing new in that. He'd learnt at the age of eighteen, when it transpired that the girl he had been madly in love with at school was only with him for the thrill of sleeping with the poor northern scholarship kid, and bringing him home to upset her parents in front of all their friends, that women wanted him for *what* he was, not who.

And after years on the road, meeting women in every city, every country that he had visited, he knew that it was true. None of them wanted him. The real him. They wanted the singer, or the writer, or the rock star, or the rich guy.

Or—on one memorable occasion—they wanted the story to sell to the tabloids.

Not a single one of them knew who he really was. Not a single one of them had come home to meet his parents. And that was fine with him. Because he knew what he wanted now too. And more importantly he knew that relationships only worked if both of you knew what you wanted—and didn't let emotions in the way of getting it.

But it didn't mean anything, he told himself, Charlie coming home with him at the weekend. Like all the others, she was just using him. He provided a nice boost to her career, and a new way of causing friction with her family, though he couldn't pretend to know why she wanted that. And he was using her to get exposure for his band, and sales for his new album. If he ever finished it.

He tidied up the bedroom while he waited for her to finish in the bathroom, chucking dirty clothes in the laundry hamper and retrieving the rest of Charlie's jewellery from under the bed. They would have to pick up the rest of her stuff from her flat at some point. He'd clear her a space in the wardrobe. Of all the things that he'd thought about that night that they got married, how to manage living with a slob hadn't been one of them. He surveyed the carnage in his apartment, and shrugged. Lucky his housekeeper was going to be in tomorrow. He'd leave a note asking her to clear some space in the drawers and wardrobe.

The thought of it was oddly intimate. Strange,

when they were already having to share a bed. Sharing hanging space should have been the least of their worries. But there was something decidedly permanent, committed, about the thought of her clothes hanging alongside his.

It wasn't permanent.

They'd both known and agreed from the start that this wasn't real, and it wasn't going to last. They just had to ride out the next year or so. Let the press do their thing, and then decide how they were going to end things in a way that worked out for both of them. It was as simple as that.

Joe waited outside Charlie's office, wondering whether she'd be pleased or not if he went in. Somehow, over the past three days they'd barely seen each other. That night after the karaoke she'd been asleep by the time that he'd got out of the bathroom, lying on her side on the far side of the bed, so far away that they didn't even need a pillow barrier as a nod to decency. Then she'd been up before him the next morning, though she had said that she had a lot to catch up on. The pattern had stayed the same ever since. She was in the office before he'd had his breakfast every morning, and came home late, clutching bags and suitcases from her flat.

The only sign that they were living together at all was the increasing chaos in his apartment. His housekeeper did her best in the daytime, but once Charlie was home she was like a whirlwind, depositing clothes and hair grips and jewellery on every surface. Leaving crumbs and coffee rings all over the kitchen and the coffee table. He wasn't even mad: he was amused.

How had the prim and proper royal family produced such a slob?

It wasn't as if she were lazy. The woman never stopped. He knew that of her reputation at work. That she worked hard to find her artists, and then even harder to support them once they were signed. She was on the phone to lawyers, accountants, artists all day long, and then out at gigs in the evening, always looking for more talent, more opportunities.

Perhaps that was it, he thought. Why waste time picking up your dirty clothes when there was new music to be found?

The pavements started to fill with knackered-looking workers as the clock ticked towards six. As East London's hipster types exited office buildings and headed for the craft-beer-stocked pubs as if pulled by a magnet.

She'd told him she'd arranged for a car to collect her from work and swing by the apartment to pick him up, but as the hours after lunch had crawled by he'd realised that sitting and waiting for her was absolutely not his style.

He strode into the building, mind made up, and smiled at the receptionist.

'Hey, Vanessa. I'm Charlie's husband. Okay if I go straight through?' There. He made sure he sounded humble enough not to assume that she'd know who he was—though he would hope that the receptionist at his own label would recognise him—but confident enough to be assured that he wouldn't be stopped. He breezed past her, wondering why he felt so nervous. All right, he hadn't even visited Afland before, never mind the private apartments at the royal palace, but he had met a fair few royals, between his posh school and attending galas and stuff since his career took off. Deep down, he knew it wasn't who her family was that was making him nervous. It was the fact that he was meeting them at all.

He'd not been home to meet the family for a long time. Not since the disaster with Arabella.

That weekend when he was eighteen, he'd thought he had it made. His gorgeous girlfriend, one of the most popular girls in school, had invited him and a load of their friends to a weekend party at her parents' country house. For the first time since he had started at the school he had felt as if he had belonged. And more importantly had thought it meant that Arabella was as serious about him as he was about her. He'd been on the verge of telling her that he loved her. But as soon as he'd arrived, he'd realised that there was something wrong. She'd introduced him to her parents with a glint in her eye that he knew meant trouble, and had stropped off when they'd welcomed him with warm smiles and handshakes.

Turned out, he wasn't the ogre she'd been expecting them to see. And if he wasn't pissing off her parents, he was no use to her at all. So she'd broken it off, publicly and humiliatingly, in front of half the school and their parents.

Was Charlie doing the same thing? Perhaps marrying him was just one more way for her to stick her middle finger up at her family. Another way to distance herself from her royal blood. But instinctively he felt that wasn't true. Whenever they'd discussed her family, she'd made it clear that she didn't want to upset them. That had been the main thing on her mind that first morning in Vegas. But she hadn't been so concerned about it that she hadn't married him in the first place.

He showed himself through the office, over to where he remembered Charlie's desk was. She couldn't see him approach, her back to him, concentrating on her computer. Her hair was pulled into a knot on the top of her head, an up-do that could almost be described as sophisticated, and a delicate tattoo curled at the nape of her neck. He'd never noticed it before—and that knowledge sent a shudder of desire through him. How many inches of her body were a mystery to him? How many secrets could he uncover if they were to do the utterly stupid thing and give in to this mutual attraction?

They couldn't be that stupid. *He* wouldn't be so stupid. Opening up to a woman, especially a woman like Charlie, was like asking to get hurt.

By the time that he reached her desk, she still hadn't looked up. He couldn't resist that tattoo a moment longer. He could feel the eyes of her co-workers on him, and knew that they were watching, knew that they had read the gossip sites. It was all the excuse he needed, the reminder that he had a part to play.

He bent and pressed his lips to the black swirl of ink below her hairline.

The second that he met her skin a shot of pain seared through his nose and he jumped back, both hands pressed to his face.

'What the h—?'
'What the h—?'
They both cried out in unison.
'Joe?' Charlie said, one hand on the back of her

head as she spun round on her chair. 'What were you *thinking*?'

He gave her a loaded look. 'I was thinking that I wanted to kiss my wife. What I'm thinking now is that we might need a trip to A&E.' She looked up then, clocked the many pairs of eyes on them, and stood, remembering she needed to play her part too.

'Oh, my goodness, I'm sorry, darling.' She reached up and gently took hold of his hands, moving them away from his nose. 'Does it still hurt?'

She turned his head one way and then the other, examining him closely as she did so.

'Not so much now,' he admitted, finally making eye contact with her. It was the truth. With her hands gently cupping his face like that, he could barely feel his nose. Barely think about any part of his body that didn't have her soft skin against it.

'No blood anyway,' she added.

He smiled. 'Can't meet the in-laws with a bloody nose and a black eye,' he said. 'Not really the best first impression.'

'They'll love you whatever,' she said, returning his grin, but he suspected it was more for their audience than for him.

She was wearing a black dress, structured and tight, giving the illusion of curves that her tall, athletic figure usually hid. Was this what her parents wanted of her? he wondered. For her to tone herself down and wear something ladylike?

Her phone buzzed on the desk behind her, breaking the spell between them. 'That'll be the car,' she said, gathering up her stuff and shutting down her computer. As she grabbed her purse off the desk she sent a glass of water flying, soaking a stack of scrawled notes.

'Argh,' she groaned, reaching into a drawer for a roll of paper towels. 'Last thing we need.'

'It's fine,' he said, grabbing a handful of the towels. 'Here.' He mopped up the puddle heading towards the edge of the desk and spread out the soggy papers. 'They'll be dry before we're back on Monday. No harm done.'

She blotted at them some more with the paper, glancing at her phone, which was buzzing again on the desk.

'Is it time we were going?'

'Mmm,' she said, non-committal, silencing it. 'It's okay, we've got time.' She started straightening up another stack of papers, and throwing pens in a cup at the back of the desk.

'Wait a minute. Are you tidying?'

She shrugged. 'It's happened before, you know.'

'Maybe, but right now you're stalling, aren't you?'

She stopped what she was doing and looked him straight in the eye, leaning back against the desk with her arms crossing her chest. 'Says who?'

'Well, you just as good as admitted it, actually. What's going on? Ashamed to introduce me to your family?'

She started with surprise. 'Why would I be ashamed?'

'Because you're nervous. Why else would you be?'

'Maybe I'm desperate for them to fall in love with you.'

'Maybe.' He watched her with a wry smile. 'I guess we're going to find out. Are you ready?'

She sighed as she pulled on her jacket and swung her bag over her shoulders. 'Ready.'

As the car pulled through the gates at the back of the palace a few hours later, Joe took a deep breath. He might have been all blasé with Charlie, but now that he was here at the palace, with its two hundred and fifty bedrooms and uniformed guards and a million windows, perhaps he was feeling a little intimidated. Regardless of what he'd thought earlier, his brief brushes with royalty before he had met Charlie hadn't left him at all prepared for this.

Throughout the short flight to the island, he'd been making a determined effort not to feel nervous—forcing his pulse to be even and his palms dry.

And now, as they stepped out of the car and through the doors of the palace, perhaps if he closed his eyes, shut out the scale of the entrance gates, the uniformed staff in attendance, and the police officer stationed at the door, he could almost imagine that this was just any other dinner.

Eventually, following Charlie into the building and through a warren of corridors, he had to admit to himself that there was no escaping it. 'The private apartments are just up there,' Charlie told him as they rounded yet another corner.

He nodded, not sure what the appropriate response was when your wife was giving you the guided tour of the palace she had grown up in. In fact, he'd barely spoken a word, he realised, since the car had pulled through the gates.

The uniformed man who had met them at the door faded away as the policeman ahead of them opened the door. He nodded to them both as Charlie greeted him by name, and Joe followed her through the door. Unlike the corridors they'd followed so far, the interior of the private rooms was simple. Plush red carpets, gilt and chandeliers had fallen away, leaving smart, bright walls, soft wood flooring and recessed lighting.

'It's like another world in here,' Charlie said with a smile. 'My parents had it renovated when we were small. They were doing big repair work across the whole palace, so they took the opportunity to modernise a bit.'

'No chandeliers, then?'

'Not really my mother's style. They keep them in the state rooms for the visiting dignitaries and the tourists. But my parents have always preferred things simpler.'

He followed her down the corridor, and she paused in front of a closed door. 'Ready?' she asked.

He took her hand in his and squeezed. 'Let's do it.'

She opened the door into a light-flooded room.

Her parents were seated on a sofa to one side of a fireplace, what looked like gin and tonics on the coffee table in front of them.

'Oh, you caught us!' said Queen Adelaide, Charlie's mother. 'We started without you. I know, we're terrible.' She stood and kissed Charlie on the cheek.

Joe just had time to register the stiffness in Charlie's shoulders before her mother, Her Majesty Queen Adelaide of Afland, was stepping around her and holding out her hand.

He held his own out in return, but couldn't find his feet to step towards her. Was it because she was the head of state or the head of Charlie's family that was making him nervous?

'You must be Joe,' Queen Adelaide said, smiling and filling the silence that was threatening awkwardness. 'How do you do?'

Charlie's father stepped forward and shook his hand too, but he wasn't as skilled as his wife at hiding his feelings, he noted. And in his case, his feelings appeared to be decidedly frosty.

'Joe. How do you do?'

He wasn't the only frosty one, Joe realised, watching Charlie as they took a seat on the sofa opposite her parents. Her shoulders were as stiff as he had ever seen them, and her back was ramrod straight. She reached for one of the drinks that had appeared on the coffee table while they were getting the formalities out of the way.

They sipped their drinks as silence fell around them, definitely into awkward territory now. And still a distinct lack of congratulations. Perhaps they were waiting for the others to arrive.

Just as he was taking a deep breath, preparing to dive into small talk, he heard a door open, and the apartment filled with the noise of rambunctious children.

'Grandma! Grandpa!'

The kids barrelled into the room with squeals of excitement. The tense atmosphere was broken, and Queen Adelaide and Prince Gerald beamed with proud smiles and stood to scoop up their grandchildren. But Charlie stayed seated; though she smiled, the expression seemed forced.

Three adults followed the kids into the room. Joe recognised Charlie's sister and brother-in-law, and a second woman who he guessed must be the nanny.

She drifted out of the room after seeing the children settled with book and toys, and Joe shook hands with his new in-laws.

'So, Vegas!' Charlie's brother-in-law said as they all sat down. 'Wish we could have done that. Would have given anything to avoid the circus that we had to endure.'

'Endure?' Charlie's sister, Verity, slapped her husband's leg playfully. 'If that was a circus, I don't know how you'd describe our life now, chasing after these two.' But she smiled indulgently as she said it. Charlie leaned forward and helped herself to her sister's drink, uncharacteristically quiet.

'It was definitely low-key,' Joe said. 'Just us and a couple of friends.' He took hold of Charlie's hand, wondering whether she was planning on checking back in to this conversation again at any point. He withheld the details of the kitschy chapel they had chosen: it had seemed so funny at the time, but less so now that they were facing the consequences of their actions. He looked across at Charlie, and saw the tension in her expression that revealed how uncomfortable she was.

Isn't that what I'm meant to be feeling? he thought. You're back in the bosom of your family. This is meant to be your home, so why are you so uncomfortable?

He was so distracted by wondering what was preoccupying her that he forgot that he had been nervous about meeting the family. Her family were half of the reason he was so sure that this relationship wouldn't work so if it wasn't her family causing the problems, then where did that leave them?

Using one another—that was it. And he knew that

he had to keep his head if he was going to stay ahead of the game, make sure that she was never in a position to hurt him.

His thoughts were interrupted by the arrival of Charlie's brother, Miles, who bowled into the room wearing an air of privilege that outshone his exquisitely tailored suit. He greeted Charlie's brother-in-law with hearty slaps on the back—they'd been friends at school, Joe seemed to remember—and then doled out kisses on the cheek to his female relatives.

'So you're the guy who seduced my sister,' he said when he reached Joe.

He gave Miles a shrewd look. Was he trying to get a rise out of him? Well, he'd have to try harder than that.

'I'm Joe,' he said, standing to shake his hand. 'It's good to meet you.'

Charlie had risen beside him and he wrapped an arm around her waist. She seemed calmer with her brother than with her sister. Interesting, Joe thought. Because so far, her brother seemed like a bit of an ass. But families were strange, he knew. Maybe she'd always been closer to her brother. He tried to push it from his mind as they all sat down again. The nanny came back in, then, and the room was suddenly in chaos as toys were put away, negotiations for 'just five more minutes' were shut down and a pair of desultory kids doled out goodnight kisses.

When they got to Charlie, that stiffness came back to her shoulders, and she straightened her spine, sitting beside Joe on the sofa as if she were in a job interview. She sat deadly still as the children climbed up onto the couch, still offering kisses and messing around.

In contrast to all of the other adults in the room, who were joining in with the kids' silliness, Charlie pretty much just patted them on the head and dodged their kisses.

What was her issue with the kids?

There was no getting away from the fact that there *was* something going on. Joe looked over at Charlie's mum and sister to see if they had noticed—looking for any clues to what was going on—but their attention was completely on the children. Joe's earlier suspicion came back to him. Could she be pregnant? Did that even fit with what he was witnessing?

It did if she was in denial, he supposed. If she was pregnant and didn't want to be. Or didn't want to be found out.

Finally, the kids were bundled out of the room by the nanny, and a member of staff appeared with a silver tray bearing champagne flutes and an ice bucket.

'Ah, perfect timing,' Adelaide declared as the glasses were handed round and champagne poured.

The tone of her voice shifted ever so subtly, from relaxed and convivial to something more formal. Maybe more rehearsed. Charlie was close by Joe's side still, and this time it was she who took his hand, and ducked her head under his arm as she wrapped it around her shoulders and turned in towards him, until she was almost surrounded by his body. He tried to meet her eyes, but she evaded him. He couldn't be sure with her avoiding eye contact, but if he didn't know better he'd say that she wanted him to protect her. From her own family? Who seemed—to his surprise—a bunch of genuinely nice people who cared about one another. Her slightly annoying brother aside. It just didn't make

any sense. Not unless she was keeping all of them—
him included—in the dark about something.

'Joe and Charlie,' Adelaide began, 'I'm so pleased
that we are all together this evening. While we can't
say that we weren't surprised by your news…' her
raised eyebrows spoke volumes about how restrained
she felt she was being '…your father and I are delighted you have found someone you want to spend
your life with. Now we didn't get to do this on your
wedding day, so I'm going to propose the traditional
toast. If you could all charge your glasses to the bride
and groom. To Charlie and Joe.'

Queen Adelaide took a ladylike sip, while Charlie polished off half her glass and pulled Joe's arm
tighter around her.

'Joe, we're absolutely delighted to meet the man
who wants to take on, not only our wonderfully wild
Caroline, but also her family, with everything that en-
tails. We're always so happy to see our family grow,
and, who knows, perhaps over the next few years it
might be growing even further.'

From the corner of his eye he saw Charlie flinch,
and he knew exactly how she had taken that comment
of her mother's, whether it had been meant as a jibe
about grandchildren or not. He sipped at his champagne, having smiled and nodded in the right places
during Queen Adelaide's speech.

'Are you okay?' he whispered in Charlie's ear when
the toasts were done and attention had drifted away
from them.

She nodded stiffly, telling him louder than words
that she absolutely wasn't.

'Want to try and make a break for it?'

She cracked half a smile. 'We'd better stay. I'd never hear the end of it.'

He wondered if that were true. Charlie's parents looked delighted to have her home. But were they really the types to nag and criticise if she left? They'd welcomed him with good grace in trying circumstances. Perhaps they deserved more credit than Charlie was giving them.

But there was no getting around the fact that she was still on edge, even after all the introductions were out of the way and they were all getting on fine. Which meant there was more to this than just her worrying whether they were going to buy their story.

What if he was right? What if she was pregnant, and was using him? Would he walk away from her? From their agreement? How would that look to the press…?

He suspected there was nothing worse as far as the tabloids were concerned than walking away from a pregnant royal wife.

He still had his arm around Charlie's waist, but he could feel a killer grip closing around him, making it hard to breathe. He'd thought that he'd gone into this with his eyes open. He'd thought he'd known what she wanted from him. Had he been duped again? Was he being used again, without him realising it?

'So, Joe, you were at school with Hugo and Seb, is that right? At Northbridge?' Charlie's brother had come to sit beside them, dragging his thoughts away from his wife.

'Yeah, they were a year or two ahead of me though. You know what it's like at school. A different year could be a different planet.'

'They remembered you, though.'

He heard Charlie move beside him, and, when he glanced across at her, she looked interested in the conversation for the first time since they'd arrived.

'What did they tell you?' she asked, a glint in her eye. 'You have to share. Don't you dare hold out on me, big brother.'

'Oh, you know, the usual. Ex-girlfriends and kiss-and-tells. God, you've let your standards slip, getting yourself hitched to this one.'

'Standards? Really? Who did he date at school?'

'You really want to know?' Miles laughed and rolled his eyes. 'Masochist. Fine, it was Arabella Barclay,' Miles said.

He watched Charlie's reaction from the corner of his eye. It was clear that she knew her, or knew of her.

'Wow. Miles is right, Joe. Blonde, skinny, horsey. If you've got a type, I'm definitely not it.'

Her brother laughed, and Joe resisted the urge to use his fists to shut his mouth.

'Thank God I came to my senses and left all that schoolboy rubbish behind,' he said. Trying not to think of that leggy, horsey girl. Or maybe he *should* be thinking about her. Really, looking back, he owed Arabella a big thank you. She'd done him a favour, teaching him about how relationships *really* worked, rather than the schoolboy idealism he'd had at eighteen.

'Trust me,' Joe said, dropping his arm from Charlie's shoulders to her waist, 'you were everything I didn't know I was looking for.' He closed his eyes and leaned in for a kiss, thinking that a peck on the lips would finish off their picture of newly wedded romance nicely. And banish bitter memories of Arabella into the bargain.

How could he have forgotten? Perhaps his brain erased it on purpose, in an attempt to protect him? The second his lips met Charlie's a rush of desire flooded his blood, and he clenched his fists, trying to control it. To control himself. Was this normal? This overwhelming passion from the most innocent of kisses? He pulled away as Charlie's lips pouted, knowing that another second would lead them to more trouble than he could reasonably be expected to deal with.

Her eyes were still closed, and for the first time since they'd arrived at the palace her features were relaxed. A hint of a smile curved one corner of her lips, and the urge to press just one more kiss there was almost overwhelming.

'Okay, you've proved your point.' Miles laughed. 'I will never mention Arabella again. Or the fact that she's still single and still smoking hot.'

Charlie opened her eyes to roll them at her brother.

'Do you think we can stop trying to set my husband up with his ex?'

Miles held up his hands. 'You're the newly-weds. Your marriage is your own business. I was just providing the facts,'

'Well, as helpful as that is, darling,' Charlie's mother interjected, 'I think we can leave gossip about school friends for another time.'

Joe glanced at Adelaide, and as she met his eye he realised that he had an unexpected ally. He smiled back, curious. Charlie had been so worried about how her parents were going to react that it had never occurred to him that they'd actually be pleased to meet him.

They sat down for dinner in one of the semi-state-rooms, and Joe looked around him in awe. Away from the modest private apartments, it struck him for the first time that this really was Charlie's life. She'd grown up here, in this home within a palace. Her life had been crystal and champagne, gilt and marble and staff and state apartments. Carriages and press calls, church at Christmas and official photographs on her birthdays. And she'd walked away from all of that.

She'd chosen a warehouse apartment in East London. A job that demanded she work hard. A 'floor-drobe' rather than a maid. A real life with normal responsibilities. It occurred to him that he'd never asked her why. He'd mocked the privileges that she'd been born with, but he'd never asked her about the choices that she'd made.

As the wine flowed and they settled in to what to Joe seemed like a banquet of never-ending courses, Charlie relaxed more. He watched her banter with her brother and sister, and marvelled at the change in her since they had first arrived. When her hand landed on his thigh, he knew that it was all for show. Part of appearing like the loved-up new couple they were meant to be. But that didn't stop the heat radiating from the palm of her hand, or the awareness of every movement of her body beside him.

It didn't stop his imagination, the tumble of images that fell through his mind, the endless possibilities, if this thing weren't so damned complicated.

He wanted her. Could he have her? Could they go to bed, and wake up the next morning and *not* turn the whole thing into a string of complications? Could they both just demand what they wanted, take it, and then agree when it needed to be over?

They shouldn't risk it. He looked down at her hand again and caught sight of the gold of her wedding ring. It would never be that simple between them. They were married. They worked together. There was unbelievable chemistry between them, but that didn't mean that a simple night in bed together could ever be on the cards. They'd acted impulsively once, when they'd decided to get married, and that meant that the stakes were too high for any further slips on the self-control front.

Work. That was what he should be concentrating on. Like the fact that he still hadn't managed to write anything new for the album. He'd told Charlie and her boss that it was practically finished when he'd agreed to sign the contract. It *had* been finished. It still was, he supposed, if he was prepared to release it knowing that it wasn't his best work. What he really needed was to lock himself in his studio for a month with no distractions. Unfortunately, the biggest distraction in his life right now was living with him. And then there was the fact that if he was holed up in his studio, then where was the inspiration supposed to come from? What he'd end up with was an album about staring at the same four walls. What he needed was a muse. A reason to write.

Taking Charlie to bed would give him all the material he needed. He was sure of that. But at too high a cost.

They left the drawing room that night and headed to bed with handshakes and kisses from Charlie's family. Charlie stiffly accepted the kisses from her mother, and she climbed the stairs stiff and formal with him.

Joe watched her carefully as she led them down corridor after corridor, low lit with bulbs that wouldn't damage the artworks. He was vaguely aware of passing masterpieces on his left and right, but his attention was all on Charlie.

'Did you have a good time?' he asked. 'I thought it went pretty well; I liked your family.'

She nodded, staring straight ahead instead of at him. 'They liked you. Even Miles.'

'That's how he acts when he likes someone?'

She huffed an affectionate laugh, and turned to face him. 'I know. He's an idiot. We keep hoping he'll grow out of it.'

'Do you think they bought our story?' he asked. Her eyes seemed to turn darker as she looked ahead again. The sparsely spaced lights strobed her expressions, yellow and dark, yellow, dark.

'I'm not sure,' she admitted. 'But I don't think they're going to call us out on it. My mum already—'

She stopped herself, but he needed to know. 'What?' he asked.

'When I first called and told her what we'd done, she told me that she'd take care of it. If we wanted this marriage to go away.'

'And you didn't take her up on it?'

'We'd already talked about why that would be a bad idea. We made an agreement and I'm sticking to it.'

Her face was still a mystery. She was hiding something else. He knew that she was. Something that meant she was happy with their lie of a marriage rather than the real thing. Maybe he'd shock it out of her with some brutal home truths.

'Charlie, I want you. I know we said that sleeping together would be a disaster. But what if it wasn't?'

She turned to him properly now, her eyes wide with surprise. 'And where the hell did that come from?'

'It needed saying. Or the question needed asking. Maybe it could work. Maybe we could give it a go. I mean, we're acting out this whole relationship, so why not make it that bit more believable?'

'Why not? Do you really need me to list the million reasons it's a horrendous idea? As if our lives weren't complicated enough—you want to add sex to the mix?'

'But that's what I'm saying. Maybe it doesn't have to complicate things. Maybe it would simplify them. We're living together. We're married. We're making everyone believe that we're a couple. I mean, how would sex make any of that more complicated?'

'Because you forgot the most important thing— we're pretending. Yes, we had a wedding, but this isn't a marriage. We're not a couple. We're doing this for a limited time only, and mixing sex in with that would just be crazy.'

'So you don't want to. Fine, I just thought I'd ask the question. Clear the air.'

'Whether I want to or not isn't the issue, Joe.'

'So you do.'

'Urgh.' She threw her head back in frustration. '*Totally* not the point. And to be honest I'm surprised you're asking, because we both know that there's some crazy chemistry between us. We've talked about it before. And at no point has either of us thought that doing something about it was in any way a good idea. I don't know why we can't just drop it.'

'Maybe I don't want to.'

They stopped outside a door and Charlie hesitated with her hand on the doorknob, a frosty silence growing between them. Joe decided to take a punt, knowing that he could be about to set a bomb under their little arrangement. But if she wasn't going to volunteer all the facts, he had to get them out of her somehow. A pregnancy wasn't the sort of thing you could ignore for ever.

'How are you planning on passing me off as your baby daddy, then, if we're not sleeping together?'

Charlie took in a gasp of breath, and as he watched her straighten her spine he realised that he'd been right about one thing—this was going to be explosive. But a shiver ran through him as Charlie walked into the room and he wondered whether he had just made an enormous mistake.

CHAPTER SEVEN

CHARLIE KEPT WALKING, calm and controlled, past the four-poster bed, trying to cover the typhoon of emotions roiling through her. She stopped when she reached the bathroom, an island of cool white marble after the richness of the bedroom.

'What are you talking about, Joe?'

Her teeth were practically grinding against one another, and she didn't seem to be able to unclench her fists.

'You're pregnant, aren't you?' His voice faded towards the end of the sentence, as if he were already regretting asking. But she didn't care about that, because the grief and pain that she had been holding at bay all night, seeing her sister's happiness with her children, her easy contentment, broke through the dam and flooded her. Winded, as if she'd been punched in the gut, she turned. She retched into the sink, as a week of new pain caught up with her. This had been building since she'd seen the newspaper headline announcing her own imminent engagement. She'd held it at bay, distracted herself with her stupid Vegas wedding and then burying herself in her work. But with Joe's crazy, heartless words—his absolutely baseless accusation—the pain had gripped her and wouldn't let her go.

Joe caught up with her and leaned against the bathroom door frame as she retched, hoping that she wasn't going to get a second look at her dinner.

'Are you okay?'

She threw him the dirtiest look that she could muster before hanging her head over the sink.

'Is it morning sickness?'

It took every ounce of self-control she possessed not to howl like a dog and collapse in a heap on the floor. Instead she forced herself upright, regaining control over her body.

'I. Am. Not. Pregnant.'

She forced the words out as evenly as she could, determined not to give him the satisfaction of seeing how he was hurting her, driving the knife deeper and twisting it with everything that he said.

'Are you sure? Because—'

She broke.

'I'm infertile, Joe. Is that sure enough for you?'

Her spine sagged and her legs turned to jelly as she spoke the words that she'd buried for so many years. She didn't even put out her hands to break her fall. There was no point—what could hurt more than this?

But instead of hitting cold marble, she landed on soft cotton, hard muscle. Joe's arms surrounded her, and her vision was clouded by snowy white shirt. She pushed away, not wanting him here, wanting no witnesses to her despair. But his arms were clamped around her, his lips were on her temple and his voice was soft in her ear.

'God, Charlie, I'm so sorry. I never would have said that if… I didn't know. I'm sorry.'

More murmurs followed, but she'd stopped listening. The tears had arrived. The ones that she'd kept at bay since she was a teenager. That she'd forced down somewhere deep inside her.

They tipped off the mascaraed ends of her lashes, streaking her cheeks, painting tracks down Joe's shirt as he held her tight and refused to let go, even as she struggled against him. Eventually, she stopped fighting, and accepted the tight clamp of his arms around her and the weight of his head resting against hers. She listened to the pulse at the base of his throat, heard it racing in time with her own. And then, as her heaving sobs petered out to cries, and then sniffs, she heard it slow. A gentle, rhythmic thud that pulled her towards calm. They'd slumped back against the claw-footed bath, her legs dragged across Joe's when he'd pulled her close and she'd fought to get free. The shoulder of his shirt was damp, and no doubt ruined by her charcoaled tears.

'You know,' he said eventually, 'we'd be more comfortable in the other room.' Their conversation in the corridor, when he'd oh-so-casually asked if she wanted to sleep with him, felt like a lifetime ago. Surely he couldn't be suggesting…

But he was right. The floor was unforgiving against her butt, and as comfortable as the bath probably was once you were in it, it didn't make for a great back rest.

She stood, pulling her dress straight and attempting something close to dignity.

'Let's just forget this whole conversation. Please,'

she added, when he stood behind her and met her gaze in the mirror.

He crossed his arms.

'I'm not sure that I can.'

'Well, I'm sure that if I can manage not to think about it, you can too.' She didn't care that he'd just been gentle and caring with her. Spiky was all she had right now, so that was what he was going to get. She walked through to the bedroom, her arms crossed across her chest and her hands rubbing at her biceps. She was cold, suddenly. Something to do with sitting on a marble floor perhaps. She climbed under the crisply ironed sheets and heavy embroidered eiderdown, pulling it up around her shoulders in a search for warmth. She figured she didn't need to worry about Joe's suggestion about sleeping together. There was no way that he was going to be interested in her now, with her messed-up mascara and malfunctioning uterus. When she looked up he was still standing in the doorway of the bathroom, watching her. She pulled the sheets a little tighter and sank back against the padded headboard, wondering if he was going to drop the subject.

'So how's that going for you?' he asked eventually. 'Not thinking about it, I mean.'

She shut her eyes tight, trying to block him out. She didn't need him judging her on top of everything else. But he wasn't done yet. 'Because it looks to me like burying your feelings isn't exactly working.'

Throwing the sheets down, she sat up, and met Joe's interested gaze with an angry stare. 'Just because you catch the one time in goodness knows how many years that I let myself think about it and get upset—all of a sudden you're a bloody expert on my feelings.'

'You might not think about it, but that doesn't mean that it's not hurting you.' His voice was infuriatingly calm, just highlighting how hard she was finding it to keep something remotely close to cool. If she didn't get a handle on her feelings, she was heading for another breakdown, and that little scene in the bathroom did not bear repeating.

'God, Joe. Stop talking as if you know me. You know *nothing* about this.'

He came to sit beside her on the bed, and his fingertips found the back of her hand, playing, tracing the length of her fingers, turning them over to find the lines of her palm. 'I know that it's getting between you and your family,' he said at last. 'I know that it hurts you every time you see your niece and nephew. Every time your mother casually mentions grandchildren.'

She looked up from their joined hands to meet his eye. He'd seen all that? 'You think you're so insightful, but an hour ago you thought that I was pregnant,' she reminded him.

He boosted himself up on the bed, and with a huff she scooched over, making room between her and the edge of the bed. He picked up her hand again, and focussed intently on it as he spoke. 'So I misinterpreted the reason you were acting funny. That doesn't mean I didn't see it. That I don't understand.'

'You don't. How could you?' She tipped her head back against the headboard and closed her eyes, wishing that he would just drop this. It wasn't as if it really affected him. He had no vested interest in whether she could procreate. It wasn't fair that he was pushing this when she so obviously didn't want to talk about it.

But if she could admit it to herself, perhaps talking felt almost…good. She realised that there had been a heavy weight in her stomach, sitting there so long that she'd forgotten how hard it had been to carry at first. Over time, she had got so used to the pain that she had lost sight of how it had felt not to have it there.

'I know that you let it push you into doing stuff that you regret. What happened that night in Vegas. Was it something to do with this?'

'I was just letting off steam. Having fun.'

'I don't believe you. I've not known you long, Charlie, but I can see straight through you. If I'd known you better that night I'd never have gone through with it. If I'd been able to see how you were hurting.'

'Hurting? I was enjoying myself. I got carried away.'

'For God's sake. Can you still not be honest with me, even now? I'm trying to tell you that you don't have to bury this any more. That if you want, we can talk about it. But you're trying to tell me you don't even care and I know that that isn't true. This is why you said you never wanted to get married, isn't it?'

She rolled her eyes, and tried to fake a snort of laughter. 'As if I even have to worry about that. Who would marry me if they knew?'

'Is that really what you think?' Pulling back, he put some distance between them so he could look her in the eye.

'It doesn't matter, Joe. I came to terms with it a long time ago. But yes, it's what I think. What would be the point of getting married?'

'I don't know. Speaking hypothetically here…isn't it usually something to do with spending your life with someone that you love?'

She snorted. 'Who knew you were such a romantic? But in a real marriage, sooner or later, kids always come up. Everyone's expecting it. Everyone's waiting for it. When you come from my family, especially.'

'And you're going to let that dictate what you do—who you date. What the great unwashed masses expect of you?'

'It's not just them, though. You don't understand. You don't understand my family. It only exists to perpetuate itself. To provide the next generation.'

'And that's the sort of person you'd want to marry, is it? The sort of person who sees you as a vessel for the next generation? If someone's looking at you like that, Charlie, you need to run, as fast as you can, and find someone who deserves you.'

The fire in his voice and in his expression was disconcerting, so much so that she found that she didn't have a counter argument. Because how could she argue with that? Of course she wanted someone who saw her as more than just a royal baby maker, but that didn't mean that he existed.

Joe's arm came around her shoulders, and she turned in to him, accepting comfort from the one person who could truly offer it. The one person who knew what she was going through—even if he couldn't really understand.

Listening to the rhythmic in–out of his breathing, she gradually felt her muscles start to relax. First her shoulders dropped away from her ears as her own breaths deepened to match Joe's. Then her fingers unclenched from their fists, her back gave out as she let Joe's side take her weight, and then her legs, bent at the knee and pulled up to her chest, tipped into Joe's lap, and were secured by the presence of his hand tucked in behind her knee.

With everything that had been said and revealed in the course of a night, there was no danger of things turning sexy. Charlie could feel that her eyes were swollen, and her skin felt red and tight from tear tracks. She felt anything but desirable. Burying her face in Joe's shirt, she tried to decide what she *did* feel.

Secure.

Anchored.

Not that long ago, an emotional night like this one would have seen her out on the town, running from her problems, looking for a distraction. But tonight, with Joe's solid presence beside her, she was exhausted. And where had running got her over the years anyway? Right back here in the palace, with her problems exactly where she'd left them.

She took a deep breath in, and as she let it go she released the remaining tension in her arms and legs, concentrating on loosening her fingers and toes. Her eyelids started to droop, and she knew that there was no point fighting it. She was going under, and she didn't want to go alone.

CHAPTER EIGHT

CHARLIE SNORED.

As in she was a serious snorer.

As in it sounded as if he were sharing a bed with a blowing exhaust pipe.

It seemed there was no end to the ways that this woman kept on surprising him.

Not that the snoring was bothering him, particularly. After all, there was no way that he was ever going to be able to get back to sleep. Not with the way that she had turned her back to him and scooted in, tucked inside the circle of his arms, and pressing back against him. Every time that he moved away, she scooted again, fidgeting and squirming in a way that was just…too good. So he'd stopped fighting it and pulled her in close, where at least she kept still, and his self-control had half a chance of winning out over his libido.

When they had fallen asleep last night they had been sitting against the headboard, one of his arms draped loosely around her shoulders. She had been curled up and guarded. Forcing herself into the relaxed state that she couldn't find naturally. He'd felt protective. As if he wanted his arms to keep out all the hurts that seemed to be circling her, waiting to strike. And he'd wanted to get into her head, to show her that the way she saw herself wasn't the way the rest of the world saw her. He certainly didn't see her as damaged goods. As being less than a woman whose insides happened to work differently. But he knew she wouldn't believe him if he told her that.

And more to the point, he didn't want her to think that he had some vested interest in the matter. He'd crossed a line yesterday by suggesting that they sleep together, and, now that he knew how narrow a tightrope she was walking, he felt like kicking himself for adding more uncertainty and confusion into the mix. They weren't going to sleep together. She had been right—it would make an impossibly complicated situation even worse. He didn't want to lead her on. This was a limited-time deal, and it would end when they thought the timing was right for both of their careers. He wasn't getting involved emotionally—he had known all his adult life that relationships worked best when both parties knew exactly where the boundaries were, exactly what they wanted to get out of it. They would be crazy to go back on those agreements now.

He just had to remind himself that she didn't want that either. She wanted this marriage for what it could do for her career. For the ructions it would cause with her family. And, in light of recent revelations, perhaps she wanted it as a hide-out. An excuse not to meet some suitable guy who might have marriage and babies on his mind.

But that was last night. This morning, 'protective' had well and truly taken a back seat. There were more pressing things on his mind, like the way that her legs fitted so perfectly against his: from ankle to hip they were perfectly matched. Or the way that his arm fitted into the indent of her waist.

Or the fact that if she were to wake up this minute, she'd know exactly how turned on he was, just by sharing a bed fully clothed.

How had his life got so complicated? In bed with a woman he wanted desperately—whom he had already married—but whom he knew he absolutely couldn't have. He cursed quietly, trying to pull his arm out from under her. If he wasn't getting back to sleep, he could be doing something useful, like taking a cold shower and then trying to write.

They were due to fly back to the UK and be up at his parents' house by tea time—they'd made no plans for the rest of the day, and he wondered whether he might be able to find some time alone to work. Last night, Charlie had promised to show him the music room, and the urge to feel the keys of a beautiful grand piano beneath the pads of his fingers had been niggling him since he'd woken. But every time he'd tried to make his escape, Charlie had pressed back against him again and he'd thought…not yet. Just another few minutes.

When she settled, he went for it again, this time pulling his arm out firm and fast, determined not to be seduced into laziness another time. His arm was free at last, and Charlie rolled onto her front, a frown on her face as she turned her head on the pillow first one way and then the other. He felt bad, seeing her restless like that. She had had too little sleep since her overnight stop in Las Vegas, and he knew that for once the black rings under her eyes had nothing to do with eyeliner. He stood watching her for a moment, reminded of that first morning, another night where they had collapsed into bed fully clothed.

He pulled off his T-shirt as he headed for the bathroom, and turned on the shower. He let it run cool before he climbed underneath, concentrating on the sensation of the water hitting his head and shoulders, trying not to think of the beautiful woman lying in his bed.

He wished that they could get out of their second trip this weekend. He wasn't sure that there was a good time to introduce your parents to your fake wife, but he guessed that the morning after a huge row and a heartfelt confession was pretty low on the list. Would Charlie be funny with him this morning? He tried to guess how she would act—whether she'd want to talk more, or pretend that it had never happened and she had never said anything—but had to admit to himself that he didn't even know her well enough to predict that.

By the time that he got out of the shower, she was sitting on the edge of the bed, rubbing at her eyes. So much for some alone time. He secured his towel firmly around his waist before he called out to her.

'Morning.'

Really, was that the best he could come up with? he asked himself.

'Hey,' she said back, tying up her hair and stretching her arms up overhead. 'Have you been up long?'

'Just long enough to shower. I was going to take you up on the offer to play in the music room. Have you got stuff you need to do this morning?'

She frowned, and he realised how that had come

across. But was it really so unreasonable of him to tell her that he needed some space? She had no problem with staying at the office late when she didn't want to see him—this was practically the same thing.

'I was just going to chill. Maybe hang out with Miles for a bit. I've not had a chance to do that since we got back.'

He nodded, trying not to show how claustrophobic he was starting to feel. Was this a normal part of newly married life? he wondered. This discomfort with sharing your personal space?

He crossed to the bureau, where he'd discovered their clothes had been unpacked, and pulled on a T-shirt and a pair of jeans. He'd wondered when he first woke up that morning whether she'd be uncomfortable with him today, he'd not expected when he'd been lying next to her that he would be the one trying to put space between them.

But it wasn't about her, or even about him. It was about feeling inspired to write for the first time all week, and wanting to make the most of it before the motivation deserted him again.

'You don't mind, do you, if I go?'

He was already halfway out of the door as he asked the rhetorical question, hoping that he remembered how to find his way back to the room she'd pointed out to him the day before.

When he eventually saw the piano in front of him, he let out a long sigh of relief. Then sat on the stool and let his fingertips gently caress the keys, pressing first one, then another, and listening to the beautiful tone of the instrument. One to one with a beauty like this, he could forget that he had a wife somewhere in this maze of a palace. Forget all of the complications that she had brought into his life.

He ran up and down a few scales, warming up his hands and fingers, trusting muscle memory to conjure up the long-memorised patterns. He'd been no more than a baby the first time he'd played the piano, he knew. Remembering family photos with him perched on his mother's knee as they picked out a nursery rhyme together.

These scales and arpeggios had taken him through recitals and grade exams. From his perfectly average primary school to the most influential and exclusive private school in the country.

They never changed, and he never faltered when he played them. From the final note of a simple arpeggio, his fingers automatically tipped into a Beethoven piece. His mother's favourite. The one that he'd practised and practised until his hands were so sore they could barely move, and he could see the notes dancing before his eyes as he tried to get to sleep. It was the piece that he'd perfected for his scholarship interview. The one that had opened up a new world of possibilities in his career—and had eventually taught him the truth about human relationships. Okay, so he wasn't writing any new material. Not yet. He let the thought go; saw it carried away by the music. Because this was important too, these building blocks of his art and his craft.

He let his hands pick through a few more pieces, and he stretched his fingers, feeling the suppleness and strength in them now that they were warmed up. He placed his tablet on the music stand, flicked through folders, looking for where he'd jotted down ideas for new lyrics and melodies, stored away for future development.

There'd been nothing new added for a while. Lately, when he'd been working on songs for the album, he'd been much further down the line than this. It was ages since he'd been at square one with a song.

He listened to a few snippets of audio that he'd recorded. A few odd words and phrases that had struck him. None of it was working. He'd been right the first time around when he'd chosen other ideas over these. He shut off his tablet and returned his fingers to the keys. It was only since he'd met Charlie that he'd been so dissatisfied with the songs that he'd written before. Why should that be? He tried to reason it out logically. Because maybe if he could work out why he suddenly hated those songs, he could work out how to write something better. He let his fingers lead, picking out individual notes, and then chords, moving tentatively across the keyboard as he experimented with a few riffs.

A combination of chords caught his ear, and he played them back, listening, seeing where his fingers wanted to trip to next. Maybe that was something…it was something for now, at least. He grabbed a guitar from beside the piano and tried out the same chords. Then picked a melody around them. He turned on the recorder on his iPad. He wasn't in a position to risk losing anything that might be any good. He turned back to the piano and tried the melody again, tried transposing it down an octave, shifting it into another key. He crashed his fingers onto the keyboard harder. There was something there, he knew it. Some potential. He just couldn't crack it. He needed to get through to the nub of the idea to find out what made it good. How to work with it to make it great.

He'd just picked up his guitar again, determined to at least make a start on something good, when the door opened behind him. He spun round on the stool and threw an automatic glare at the door.

Charlie drew up short on the threshold.

'S-sorry,' she stammered, and he knew his annoyance at being disturbed must have shown on his face. 'I brought you a coffee.'

He noticed the tray in her hands and thought twice about his initial instinct to kick her straight out. Maybe he could do with the caffeine, something to get his brain in gear.

'Thanks,' he said grudgingly. 'You can come in—you don't have to stay in the doorway.'

He set the guitar down and turned back to the piano, hoping that she would get the hint, but, instead of hearing the door shut behind him, he was being not so gently nudged to the side of his stool while Charlie held two cups of coffee precariously over the keyboard.

'That sounded interesting,' she said. 'What was it?'

He fidgeted beside her, wishing she'd just go and leave him to it.

'It's nothing. Just playing around with a few ideas. Trying to generate some inspiration.'

She plonked herself down beside him and he held a breath as the hot dark liquid sloshed dangerously close to the piano. Somehow, miraculously, the coffee didn't spill. 'What for?' she asked. 'I thought the songs for the album were all done.'

He shrugged. He really didn't want to go into this now. 'They were.'

'Were?' She finally placed the drinks down on the top of the piano and turned towards him, trying to catch his eye. 'Are they not any more? What happened to them?'

He kept his eyes on the keyboard, his fingers tracing soundless patterns in black and ivory. 'Nothing happened to them. I'm just not sure that I want to include all of them. There's one or two I'm looking at rotating out.' He kept his voice casual, trying not to show the fear and concern behind this simple statement. It didn't work. Charlie's back was suddenly ramrod straight.

'And you're telling me this now? How long have you been thinking this?'

'Are you asking as my wife or as a representative of Avalon?'

'I thought they were the same thing.' The monosyllables were spoken with a false calm, giving them a staccato rhythm. But then she softened, leaned forward and sipped at her coffee, looking unusually thoughtful before she spoke.

'What can I do to help?'

His first instinct was to tell her to leave him in peace—that was the best thing she could do for him. But the timing of this creative crisis suggested that she was in some way to blame for his current dissatisfaction with his work. So maybe she could be the solution too. 'What about a co-writer? I can call a couple of people. Maybe someone to bounce ideas off.'

'I'm not sure,' he said eventually. 'I was happy with

everything before we went to Vegas. I didn't feel like
I had to do anything more to it.'

'And now?'

'I don't know. I listened to the demo when we were
on the plane. I reckon half the tracks need to go.'

She visibly paled. But to her credit she clearly tem-
pered her response. Regardless of the fact that losing
half the tracks would throw a complete spanner into
the plan that she and Rich had been working on for
recording and releasing the album.

'Can we listen together?' she asked. 'You can talk
me through what you're worried about.'

He hesitated. No one outside the band had heard the
new tracks. The record companies that had been so
keen to fight over them had taken their history of big
sellers, and not insisted on listening to the new material. Letting his songs loose on the world was hard
enough when he was happy with his work. Letting
someone listen to something he knew wasn't right…
It was like revealing the ugliest part of his body for
close inspection.

But this was what Charlie did. He knew her reputation. He knew the artists and albums that she had
worked on. She got results, and her artists trusted her.
Maybe he should as well. He'd spent the last week with
his head buried in the sand, trying to ignore the problem. It was time to try something different.

He reached for the tablet, ready to cue up the demo,
but Charlie stopped him with a hand on his arm.

'Why don't you play?' she asked, nodding at the
piano keyboard in front of them. 'One-man show.'

He shrugged. It didn't make much difference to

him. The songs weren't good enough, and it wouldn't matter how she heard them.

He rattled through the first bars of a track he picked at random. Trying to show her with his clumsy hands on the keys how far from good the song was.

She didn't say a word as he played, but her knee jigged in time with the music, and as he reached the middle eight her head nodded too.

He reached the end and looked over at her—ready for the verdict. 'I don't hate it,' she said equivocally. 'Are there lyrics?'

'The chorus maybe. The verses are definitely going.'

She nodded thoughtfully.

'Well, let's hear it before we do anything drastic.'

He returned his hands to the keys and took a deep breath, straightening his back until his posture rivalled hers. He'd been taught to sing classically at school, and there was a lot to be said for getting the basics right.

It had been a long time since he'd sung to someone one-to-one, with just a piano for company. In fact, he couldn't remember ever sitting like this with someone. With so much intimacy.

A lump lodged itself in his throat. Was he really nervous? He'd sung to her the first night that he'd met her. Spotted her on the side of the stage halfway through the gig and made eye contact. Had that been it? The moment that everything had changed for them?

There had been thousands in the audience that night. He'd played at festivals where the audience stretched further than he could see. Just a couple of days ago he'd sung with her in front of a growing crowd of Londoners. It hadn't occurred to him that day to be nervous.

But the thought of singing with her sitting beside him at the piano was bringing him out in a sweat.

She waited, letting the silence grow. Waiting for him to fill it. He pressed a couple of keys experimentally then worked his way into the intro.

Her thigh was pressed against his leg; he felt the pressure of it as he worked the piano pedal. He closed his eyes, hoping that banishing her from at least one of his senses would get his focus back where it needed to be.

He took a deep breath and half sang the first words of the verse. His hands moved without hesitation and he felt his voice grow stronger as he moved from verse to chorus and back again. He winced as he sang the second verse, aware that the lyrics were trite and clichéd.

He'd written about love. Or what he thought love might feel like as a thirty-something. The more he thought about the only time he'd thought he'd been in love, the more uncertain he was that that was what he had really felt for Arabella. Sure, it had been intense at the time. There were songs that he'd written then that still tugged at the heart strings. But something told him that love was meant to be…bigger than that. The connection he felt with Charlie right this second, for example. That was big. In fact, he couldn't quite decide if it was warm and enveloping big, or heavy and suffocating big. All he knew was that it was scary big. And a million miles from what he had felt for Arabella when he was eighteen.

And of course all that was seriously bad news—

because big scary feelings did not make for a happy marriage of convenience. He tackled the middle eight with energy, abandoning his original lyrics, and just singing what came into his head. Trying to lose himself in the notes and not overthink.

He sang the last chorus as if there were no one else listening, new lyrics streaming through him as if he were a vessel for something greater than him.

He let his hands rest on the keyboard when he finished, and kept his eyes locked on them as well. He couldn't let her see. It was too dangerous. Too risky to the arrangement that they had both agreed to. He waited until he could be sure his expression was neutral before he picked up his mug from the table beside the piano and took a sip.

'So?' he asked, not sure that he wanted to know what she thought of it.

'Please, please tell me that's not on the cull list.'

He took a second to really look at her. Her eyes were wide, almost surprised. Her bottom lip was redder and fuller than the top, as if she had been biting on it and had only just let it go. He imagined that if he looked hard enough he would be able to see the shadowed indentation of her top teeth still there. That if he leaned down and brushed his own lips against it it would be hot and welcoming.

'I'm not sure about the first half,' she went on at last, 'but the lyrics in the second? The bridge? That last chorus. That's winning stuff, Joe. That's straight to number one and stay there. That's break the internet stuff. I can't believe you were going to toss that.'

'The first half though.'

'The first half we can fix. Anyone who can write the second half can fix the first, I promise you that.'

He stayed quiet for a long moment. He could ask himself what had just happened, but the truth was that he already knew. She had happened. She was what was different about his writing. He finally had the inspiration that he needed.

He had no doubt that he still had a lot of work to do, but maybe working with Charlie would be a good thing. It had certainly helped with these lyrics; they'd worked their way into his brain as he was singing, reaching his lips as if he were channelling them, not writing them.

He launched into the opening chords of another song. One he was more sure of. He tweaked the words as he sang, reaching for more unusual choices, to pinpoint emotions he'd only been able to sketch before.

He glanced across at Charlie and she was smiling. A weight of pressure lifted slightly; a measure of dread fell away. They could fix this. Together.

More than anything, this was what really brought it home to him what they'd done. They had tied themselves together in every possible way. His career and his personal life were indivisible now.

For so long 'personal life' had been synonymous with 'sex life'. When Charlie had stipulated *no cheating* he'd known that it was a no brainer. Of course he wouldn't sleep with anyone else. But had he really thought it through? He'd voluntarily signed up for months of celibacy. Maybe years. Perhaps he had assumed unconsciously that 'no cheating' and celibacy weren't necessarily the same thing.

Everything seemed to keep coming back to that

question—even though they had agreed right from the start that that wasn't going to happen. And now he had acknowledged that his feelings for her were so much more serious than he had originally thought. Had he really thought the word 'love' earlier?

He finished the song on autopilot and knew from Charlie's expression that she could feel the difference. Her smile was more polite and that sparkle had gone from her eyes.

'Lots of potential in that one,' she said diplomatically. 'Definitely one we can work on.' She glanced at her watch and had a final sip of her coffee.

'I should let you work. Are you sure I've packed the right stuff for your parents' house? Because I can go out and pick something up if I need to.'

'Well, you probably can leave your tiara here,' he said with a smile, so she knew it wasn't a dig. 'Just something for dinner tonight. Doesn't need to be as fancy as at your place.'

Had he really just referred to the palace they were sitting in as 'your place'? Perhaps he was getting more used to this royal thing than he had thought. Getting used to her.

It was getting harder and harder to remember they were only in this to forward both of their careers. The lines between business and personal were blurring to the point that he couldn't see them any more. And that was dangerous, because the further they moved away from that simple transactional relationship, the more at risk his heart and his feelings would be.

'And make sure you've got something you don't

mind getting dirty if we're going to that festival. I'm not going to spend the whole time in VIP.'

She rolled her eyes.

'You so don't need to worry about that.'

CHAPTER NINE

CHARLIE CRAWLED UNDER the duvet and across the tiny double bed until she was almost pressed against the wall. Really, the sleeping arrangements in this marriage kept going from bad to worse.

'Do you think they liked me?' she whispered as Joe unbuttoned his shirt and pulled it back over his shoulders, revealing those tattoos she was still getting to know. He pulled a T-shirt from his bag, and then they were covered again. She almost spoke up and asked him not to, but stopped herself. Cosy sleeping arrangements or not, she had no rights over his body. No authority to ask for a few more minutes to look at his skin.

'They loved you,' he replied, sitting on the side of the bed and pulling off his jeans. 'Of course they did. What did you expect?'

'You know what I expected,' she said, tucking her hand under her pillow and turning on her side to face him. He slid between the sheets and lay beside her, mirroring her posture until they were almost nose to nose in the bed.

'And I told you that you didn't have to worry,' he said, though she didn't quite remember it that way.

Why should she care anyway? In a few months these would be her ex in-laws. She wouldn't ever see them again.

He wondered whether his parents had suspected that there was something off about their relationship. But they had been so distracted by Charlie, and protocol and the whole Princess thing that they hadn't seemed to notice anything.

He could feel the warmth of her under the cool sheets, and for a second was flooded by the memory of waking up with her that morning, with her legs fitting so closely to his. Did she even know what she had done?

'Did you know you're an aggressive spooner?' The question just slipped out of him. She looked shocked for a second, but then had to stifle a laugh.

'What's that meant to mean?'

'It means you were grinding into me like a horny teenager this morning. I didn't know where to put my hands.'

Her mouth fell open. 'I did not.'

He couldn't resist smiling. 'You so did. Forced me out of bed.'

Not strictly the truth, of course. He'd lain there so much longer than was a good idea, just soaking up the feel of her.

'A gentleman would have moved away,' she said.

'A lady wouldn't have reversed straight back in again every time I did.'

She kicked out at his leg. 'You're totally making this up.'

'Why would I do that?' he asked.

'I don't know. Maybe you want me to do it again.'

'Would you?' The very air around them seemed to be heavy with anticipation as he waited for her to answer.

'I asked first,' she said at last, deliberately not answering his question.

Was she serious? Were they really talking about this as if it might happen? She looked as if she wanted it. Her eyes were wide, her lips moist and slightly parted. One hand was tucked under her cheek and the other below her pillow. He didn't dare look any further down. He'd seen her pull on a pyjama top and shorts earlier, and he knew that gravity would be making the view south of her throat way too distracting. Too tempting.

'Maybe,' he replied at last.

Such a simple word. Tonight, such a dangerous one.

She turned her back to him but didn't make any effort to come closer. Was she testing him? Seeing if she came halfway whether he would come forward the other half.

With her back to him it was safe at last to look down. From where she'd tied her hair in a messy knot, the ink at the nape of her neck, down the length of her long, elegant spine. The tapering of her waist disappeared into the shadows under the sheets.

If he reached for her, would that be the point of no return?

Would the touch of his hand on her waist be the same as telling her that he wanted a relationship? That he loved her?

Were those statements true?

He wanted her. He knew that. That was the easy question. But how many times did he have to tell him-

self that having sex with the woman pretending to be
his wife was a bad idea? That it could never be just
sex, because it was already so much more than that.

What would she want from him in return? More
than sex meant thinking with his heart, rather than
his head, and that had got him badly hurt—and embarrassed—before.

He had tried his hardest to learn his lesson after
Arabella, but even that humiliation hadn't been
enough for him to spot the woman who was only with
him so she could sell his secrets to the highest bidder.

Could Charlie really want him for who he was,
rather than what he could do for her?

He couldn't remember ever being more turned on,
more tempted than he was right now, but he had to be
smarter than that.

Taking what he wanted came with a price tag. But
tonight he couldn't be certain what the price was, or
whether he would be willing to pay. And so as much
as it killed him to do it, he turned over, pulled the
duvet high on his chest and squeezed his eyes shut.

He heard a rustle behind him and tried not to imagine Charlie lifting her head from the pillow and looking over at him, wondering what had happened. He
didn't want to see her confusion as he cut dead their
flirtation. Her head hit the pillow hard, and the duvet
pulled across to her side of the bed.

'Night, then,' she said, nicking territory and duvet
as she spread out her limbs.

He was so tempted to retaliate. Almost as tempted
as he had been to kiss her. To be pulled back into their
banter. But he kept silent and still, feigning sleep.

* * *

Had she imagined it, last night? she wondered, trying to decide if she should be blaming Joe or her over-active imagination for what had happened. Why, oh, why had she had to be so insistent that they didn't have sex? Because that was where this relationship had been heading, before they were so stupid as to get married.

If they'd done the sensible thing and had a one-night stand that first night, like any self-respecting party girl meeting a rock star, they could be thou-sands of miles apart and a week into forgetting it all by now. Instead she had been shacked up at her new in-laws', trapped in the world's smallest double bed and ready to explode from frustration.

Surely her imagination wasn't good enough to have imagined that flirtation last night. Joe was the one who had brought up the subject of spooning, and when she'd decided she was so goddamned turned on that she didn't care any more whether it was a good idea or not, and all but wiggled her arse at him, he'd literally turned his back on her—the body-language equivalent of 'thanks, but no thanks'. Only less polite.

So when she'd woken first this morning, there was no way she was going to hang around for him to wake up and rehash the whole thing. One rejection was plenty, thanks. She'd known as soon as she told him about her infertility that she was taking herself well and truly off the market as far as he was concerned. It had been stupid to expect any other reaction to her advances than the one that she had got.

So she'd got up and found Joe's mum already in the kitchen, and before she quite knew what was happen-

ing there was a cup of strong tea in front of her and
the smell of bacon coming from the stove.

'Did you sleep well, then, love? Oh, I shouldn't
ask that really, should I? Not to a newly-wed. And
that bed in there's so small. Not even a proper double.
Hardly room to—'

'Shall I put the kettle on?'

Charlie breathed a deep sigh of relief—not the emotion she'd expected to feel when setting eyes on Joe
that morning. He leaned in the kitchen doorway, colour high on his cheeks as he crossed his arms and
gave his mum a look.

'No need, love.' His mum bustled round, pouring
another cup from the pot and setting it on the table
for Joe.

'I was just saying to Charlie—you are sure it's okay
for me to call you Charlie?' She didn't stop for an answer. 'I was just saying that the bed in your room.
It's hardly big enough for you on your own, never
mind for the two of you great tall things. We'll have
to do something about that. Maybe you should have
our room.'

Joe kissed his mum on the cheek and extracted the
tongs from her clasped fist.

'You're babbling, Mum. Sit down and drink your
tea.'

His mum sat and he shot a glance over her head to
Charlie, who smiled conspiratorially in return.

'You sure you don't want to come with us today,
Mum?' Joe asked as he served up the bacon sarnies.

'Me in all that mud? You must be mad, love.'

'Mud? It's twenty-five degrees outside. Not every
festival is Glastonbury in the rain, you know.'

'I've seen these things on the telly, love. Maybe if you were playing, but I'll give it a miss. You two love birds don't want me and your father there playing gooseberry anyway.'

Joe rolled his eyes as he picked up a sandwich, 'Mum, there'll be thousands of people there. It's not like we're expecting to be alone.'

'Don't be obtuse, Joe. You know full well it's not the same.'

'I feel awful shooting off like this,' Charlie said. They'd sat down to dinner barely an hour after they had arrived last night, and she'd been so beat after four courses and dessert wine that they'd retreated to bed long before midnight.

'Don't be daft, love. You young people are so busy, and Joe's already told me how hard you work.' Interesting…when had he told her that? 'It's been lovely that you made it up here with everything that you've both got going on. Don't go and spoil it by overstaying your welcome.'

Charlie smiled, surprised by how at home she felt with Joe's parents already. As if she really were becoming part of the family. Probably best that they were leaving this afternoon, then. Before this became another reminder of how hard it was becoming to keep reality and pretence straight in her head.

They climbed into Joe's car, chased by kisses and offers of baked goods for the journey. The festival was out in the countryside, about half an hour from his parents' house. Thank God it was no further, Charlie thought, twenty minutes of isolated confinement later. There was a limit to the tension that her body could take, and she was rapidly approaching it.

They were going to have to talk about what had happened last night. She'd hoped that maybe they could just ignore it—forget it had happened. And then his mum had been so funny with her babbling that she'd thought that they'd taken a shortcut and moved past it. But after breakfast they had been back in Joe's tiny bedroom, trying to pack their bags without touching. Moving around each other as if they were magnets with poles pointing towards one another. And she knew it would take next to nothing for those poles to flip and they would be back where they had been last night, drawn together, with only their self-control and better judgement fighting against the inevitability of the laws of nature.

She rested her chin on her hand; her elbow propped on the door as she gazed out of the window. They had barely spoken a word since they'd climbed into the car.

'Have you played here?' Charlie asked, needing the tension broken—before it broke them. The question counted as work. Talking about the band and work was safe. It was the only safe zone they had.

'Two years ago,' Joe replied, his eyes still locked on the road. They hadn't left it for a second since they'd left his parents' driveway. 'Were you here?' he asked.

'Yeah, with one of my artists. I didn't see you.'

'I wonder how many times that's happened,' he said, and for the first time he glanced over at her.

She furrowed her brow. 'That what's happened?'

'That our paths have crossed and we've not seen each other.' His eyes were back on the road now, but he looked different somehow, as if he was having to work harder to keep them there.

She tried to keep her voice casual, not wanting to

acknowledge the way the tension had just ratcheted up another notch. 'I don't know. Must be loads if you think about it.'

'I can't believe it,' he said.

She looked over at him again, to find him watching her. They'd pulled up at a junction, but his attention was all on her, rather than looking for a gap in the traffic crossing their path.

'Why?'

'Because…*this*. Because of the atmosphere in this car for the last twenty minutes. Because of how it felt in Vegas, knowing that you were watching me. I just can't imagine being in a room with you and not feeling that you were there.'

How *what* had felt in Vegas? She thought back to that moment when she was watching him from the side of the stage and their eyes had met. He had felt that too?

He reached for her hand. She considered for a split second whether she should pull away. It was what he'd done last night. She'd reached out to him, and he'd known it was too dangerous. A bad idea.

Could she be as strong as he had been?

His hand cupped her cheek, and she knew she could. She could be strong and resist, as he had. But maybe she could be a different kind of strong. Maybe looking at all the reasons this was a bad idea, all the reasons it was a terrifying choice, and *still* choosing it, maybe that was strong too.

She leaned forward across the centre console, sliding her hands into his hair and bringing their mouths together.

Her body sighed in relief and desire as his tongue

met hers, simultaneously relaxed and energised by this feeling of…perfection. This was it. This sense of fitting together.

A horn blared behind them and she sprang back, reeling from her realisation.

He grimaced as he slid the car into gear and pulled away, with just a slight lurch as the clutch found its biting point. This was what she'd been waiting for; and it was what she'd been dreading. She'd been running from it her whole adult life. She didn't want to be completed. She didn't want to belong with someone. Her one-off dates and casual boyfriends—she never had to tell them she was infertile. Never had to spell out the future that they would never have. Never had to explain that if she shacked up with someone long-term and the babies didn't come that they'd be hounded by the press and his virility would be called into question. Their bins would be searched and their doctors harassed. Her body had been public property since before she was born. Anyone who wanted to spend their life with her would be volunteering for the same deal—who in their right mind would do that?

Ten more minutes. She had to survive just ten more minutes in this space with a man she was finding it impossible to remember to resist. They showed their passes at the gate and, in silence, Joe directed the car through the gates and down a rucked track towards the VIP parking, waved along by marshals. When they arrived, Joe pulled on the handbrake and opened the door, while she gathered her things from the footwell. Her door opened, and Joe was there, holding out his hand like a cartoon prince.

'Very gallant,' she said lightly, knowing that her

confusion was causing a line to appear between her eyebrows.

He handed her down from the car, and as her feet reached the ground he pressed her back against the rear door, one of his knees nudging between hers. His hand caught at the ends of her hair and he pulled gently, bringing a gasp of pleasure and anticipation to her lips. She tilted her head to one side as she met his eyes, and saw passion and desire. Another inch closer and she was trapped. Car behind, hard body in front, and still that hand in her hair, pulling to one side now, exposing the pulse of her throat. She licked her lips in anticipation and closed her eyes as Joe moved closer. First cool lips descended and then a flicker of warm tongue in a spot that made her shudder. The butterfly caresses of his mouth traced up the side of her neck, then suddenly down to her shoulder, where her shirt had slipped, exposing her collarbone. The sharp clamp of his teeth on her sensitive skin made her gasp in shock. But the noise was lost as his lips were suddenly on her mouth, and his tongue was tangling with hers.

She wound her fingers in his hair, levering herself a little higher, desperate to bring their bodies in line. Cursing her decision to wear flat biker boots instead of her usual heels. Who cared about practicalities when there was a man like this to kiss?

Joe pressed into her with an urgency she'd not felt from him before. An urgency that made her wonder how spacious the back of his car was, and how much faith they wanted to put in the tinted windows.

It was as his lips left hers, to dip again to her neck, that she heard it.

Click.

Her eyes snapped open and she pushed at Joe's chest. She didn't have to look far over his shoulder to see the photographer. She took a second, breathing heavily and trying to remember that she was meant to be pleased about the press involvement in her life for once, before she spoke.

'You knew he was there?' she asked quietly, her lips touching Joe's ear. Her calves burned as she stretched up on tiptoes, but she wasn't ready to back down, back away, just yet.

'Spotted him as I got out of the car,' Joe whispered back.

Which explained the little display he'd just put on, then. Thank God she hadn't suggested taking the party back into the car.

'You okay?' he asked, and she forced a smile, pushing slightly on his chest and trying to regain her equilibrium. Desperate for a balance between trying to convince the photographer that that kiss had rocked her world, and not letting Joe see the truth of it.

'I'm fine.'

Their encounter with photographers at the airport seemed a long time ago and a long way away. She'd barely noticed over the past week that they hadn't been harassed by the paparazzi as much as she'd thought they might be—perhaps her mother had had a discreet hand in that. But there was no way that even her mother could keep them away here. The reality of the situation struck her—something she'd not counted on when she and Joe had been making plans for seeing family and work: they were going to be on display, all day. They couldn't afford to slip up. She closed her eyes and kissed Joe lightly on the mouth, telling herself it was just her way of warming up for the performance she knew that they had to nail.

'Want to go listen to some music?' she asked.

'No,' he said with a smile. 'I want to stay here and kiss you.'

She couldn't help grinning in return, not even trying to work out if it was for real or for show. Leaning back against this car in the sunshine, kissing a superhot guy—that sounded pretty good to her too. But the moment was gone, and she couldn't lose the photographer from the corner of her eye.

'You're so going to get me fired,' she said. 'I'm meant to be working.'

'Well, then, jump to it, slacker. I'm not going to be one of those husbands who expects you to stay home and play house. Get out there and earn your keep.' He took a step back from her, and she slid her hands behind her butt. She knew real life was waiting for them, but what was just a few more minutes?

'I'd make a lousy housewife.'

'Oh, I don't know,' he said with a laugh. 'Some people like the hovel look. I hear it's big this year.'

She poked him in the ribs and laughed back.

'I'm not that bad.'

'You're worse.' He turned and stood beside her, draping a casual arm around her shoulder and pressing a kiss to her temple.

It would be too easy to take this little scene at face value, she knew. A week ago she'd be giving herself a stern talking-to. That all this was for the benefit of the photographers and the eager public. But today... today the line was more blurred. Her first thought had been that Joe was just putting on a show, but they had been moving so much closer for the last few days that she knew that some part of it was real. Their performance, it didn't feel like some random invention— it was more... Maybe it was what their relationship might have been if their lives were simpler. If she weren't a princess with a wonky reproductive system. If he formed actual emotional relationships rather than using women to get what he needed. Would it work? she couldn't help but wonder. If they had been two ordinary people, with ordinary lives, would they have been happy together?

'Come on, then,' she said at last, pushing herself away from the car, trying to shake the thought from her mind. It didn't matter if it would work that way, because they weren't those people, and never could be. Joe moved with her, his arm still around her shoulders as they made their way into the festival.

As Joe had promised, they were in the VIP zone for no more than half an hour before she was dragging him through a dusty field of festivalgoers, littered with abandoned plastic cups. She refused to watch the band from the side of the stage—she wanted the full experience, to see what she would be working with if she ever got this band to agree to sign with her.

The Sunday afternoon vibe was chilled and relaxed, with families dancing to the music, kids on shoulders, or eating on picnic rugs on the ground. Groups of people sat on the floor, passing round cigarettes and bottles of drink.

The sun was hot on her back, and she was pleased she'd pulled on one of Joe's long-sleeved shirts with her denim shorts, protecting her shoulders from burning.

For a while they just wandered, soaking up the atmosphere of a group of people united by a passion for music. Joe's fingers were loosely wound between hers, keeping her anchored to him. To their story. The impression of that kiss was still on her lips, and had been refreshed every now and again with a brief re-enactment. They couldn't just keep an eye out for cameras and people watching. For the first time since they had arrived back in the UK, they were truly having to live out their fake marriage in full view of the public.

And the weirdest part…it wasn't weird at all. In fact, it felt completely natural to be walking round with her hand in his. The way he threw an arm over her shoulders if they stopped to talk to someone. For once, she decided she actually liked being in flat shoes. Liked that his extra height meant that she was tucked into his body when he pulled her to him. It felt good—warm, safe, protected. Everything she'd been telling herself she didn't want to be.

'Want to find something to eat?' Joe asked when the band they had been watching finished.

'Dirty burger?' she asked, with a quirk of her brow.

'Whatever turns you on.'

You know what turns me on. The response was right there on the tip of her tongue, but she held it back, not trusting where it might lead them.

'Come on,' she said, pulling him towards a van selling virtuous-looking flatbreads and falafel. 'These look amazing. I'm having a healthy lunch, then I'm going in search of cider.'

With lunches in hand, they picked their way across to another stage, where Casual Glory, the band Charlie wanted to see, were just warming up at the start of their set.

'I saw these guys in a pub last year,' she told Joe. 'I wanted to sign them then and there. But then all the suits got involved and… I don't know, maybe they got spooked but somehow it didn't come off. I don't want to let them out of my grasp again.'

'They're still not signed?' Joe asked.

She dropped to the floor and sat cross-legged, watching the band while she ate.

'Free spirits. Didn't like the corporate stuff. And I'm not sure what I do about that, to be honest, because the music business doesn't really get much more laid-back than with Avalon.'

'You think you can get them to change their minds?'

Charlie nodded. 'I'm going to. I'm just not sure how yet.'

'You're not going to marry him, right?'

She laughed under her breath.

'One husband's already too many, thanks.'

He wound an arm around her neck, pulling her close and planting a kiss on her shoulder.

'You're right: they're good,' Joe said after they finished another song. 'Loads of potential. You should bag them.'

'Yeah, well, try telling them that,' she joked.

'I will, if you want. Are we going to say hi when they're done?'

'That's the plan.'

She leaned against his shoulder, soaking up the sun warming the white cotton of her shirt. Her head fell to rest against Joe's and she shut her eyes so she could appreciate the music more.

'Tired?' Joe asked in her ear, and she 'mmm'ed in response. She couldn't remember the last time she'd had a properly restful night's sleep. Turned out being married was more likely to give you black bags than a newly-wed glow.

'Come here, then.'

Joe pushed her away for a moment, then slung his leg around until she was sitting between his thighs, her back pulled in against his front. She relaxed into him, shutting out all thoughts of whether this was a good idea or not. Just letting the music wash through her. Soak into her skin and her brain.

'Comfortable?' Joe whispered in her ear.

'Too comfortable.'

She felt more than heard him chuckle behind her as his arms tightened. A press of lips behind her ear. A kiss on the side of her neck. A tingle and a clench low in her abdomen: a silent request for more and a warning of danger ahead.

Instead of heeding it, she let her head fall to one side, just as she had done by his car. They were in public, she reasoned with herself. There was only so far this could go. It was all a part of their performance.

'How about now?' he asked, pulling her hair over to her other shoulder. 'Feeling sleepy still?'

God, he was driving her insane.

'Like I could drop off at any moment.'

He growled behind her and she smiled, revelling in the way she was learning to push the boundaries of his self-control. His hand in her hair was tough and uncompromising now, and she let out a gasp as he pulled her back slowly, steadily, never so hard that it hurt. Making her choose to come with him rather than forcing. She opened her mouth to him without question. The hand still round her waist flattened on her belly, pressing her closer still.

She let out a low sigh of desire and her arm lifted to wind round his neck, opening her body. Was Joe controlling her without her realising? She didn't remember meaning to do it. Then his hand dropped from her hair and cupped her jaw: the kiss gentler now, sweeter.

She opened her eyes and smiled back at him, and she knew her eyes must look glazed, dopey. 'All right, I'm not likely to sleep in the next year. Is that what you wanted?'

'I'll take it,' he said with a smug smile. She leaned back into him again, languor and desire fighting to control her limbs.

CHAPTER TEN

'I WISH WE didn't have to go back tonight,' Joe said, stretching out his legs and leaning back on his elbows. Maybe it was the sun making him lazy, making him feel that he never wanted to leave this place. Charlie moved so she was lying to one side of him, her head propped on her hand.

'I thought you'd be dying to get back in your studio,' she said. 'You seemed all…inspired and stuff yesterday.'

'I am. I do want to write.' He'd had ideas swirling round his brain for two days; when they'd been at his parents' house he'd been desperate for a bit of space and time to try and get them down on paper, or recorded on his phone. But since they had arrived at the festival, since that kiss, everything felt different. 'I can't remember the last time that I was relaxed like this. The last time I felt still. I like it.'

'You can be still in London,' Charlie said.

He shrugged—or as best he could with his body weight resting on his elbows. 'I don't know if I can. Or maybe it's that I know that I won't.'

She sat up and gave him a serious look. 'Not every day can be Sunday afternoon at a festival. Real life is still out there, you know.' Of course he knew, but somehow he was managing not to care.

'I do know. But it feels that it can't get us here.'

'What are you worried about "getting us"?' she asked.

Why did they have to think about that now? Why couldn't they just enjoy this? He wished he knew. He'd just told her he felt still—what he'd wanted to say was that he felt happy. Content. He'd wanted to say that he'd stopped trying to work out if what she was saying was loaded. A way to get something more than they'd agreed from their arrangement.

Here at the festival, life was simpler. He could kiss and touch her. Laugh with her. Treat her as the woman he was in love with. No holding back.

Was that really it? Was that what was making him feel so…serene? Because he didn't have to pretend not to love her?

His phone chirped and he fished it out of his pocket, grateful for the distraction from his own thoughts.

'Amazing, they're here. Some friends of mine have stopped by,' he told Charlie. 'Want to say hi after you've done your work stuff?'

'Sure, why not? Who are they?'

'Owen's band supported us at a couple of gigs a few years ago. We hung out a bit. His wife's lovely too. You'll like them.'

He stood and pulled her up as Casual Glory finished their final number. His arm fell round her shoulders in that way that felt so completely natural. Perhaps it was just their height, he thought. He'd told her that he'd liked that she was so tall, but her flat biker boots today meant that he was a few inches taller than her. Or maybe it was something else—something to do with escaping their real lives and real pressures. They were meant to be putting on a show to the public today—but in reality it had given them permission to stop pretending for the first time since they had woken up married.

They passed through security to the VIP area, and Charlie headed straight for the lead singer of Casual Glory and gave him a hug. Joe hung back a little, watching her work, impressed. She didn't just schmooze—though she did compliment them on their awesome set. She also challenged them, asked them about their goals and their hopes for the future. Showed them subtly that she would be their ally if they wanted to make that a reality. And she made sure that each member of the band left with her business card in their pocket and some serious thinking to do.

Charlie cut the conversation short before they outstayed their welcome, and they headed over towards the bar. He surveyed the room once he had a jar of craft cider in hand—it was full of people resting their feet, snatching glasses of free champagne, and trying to get a sneaky snap of the VVIP whose hen do was in full drunken flow in the corner.

He tapped the side of his glass, wondering whether he had missed his friend, and whether they should commandeer one of the golf buggies to go in search of him when he recognised Owen's shaggy, shoulder-length hair and waved at him from across the crowd, squeezing Charlie's hand at the same time. He wondered for a split second whether he had done the right thing in looking Owen up, but it was too late to back out now. Owen turned and saw him, waving from across the tent.

'Hey,' Joe called out, making a move towards his friend.

Charlie followed the direction of Joe's wave and saw Owen—she recognised him from a gig she'd been to last year. And then a blonde woman—polished and beautiful—stepped from behind him, a chubby baby settled on her hip. Charlie's stomach lurched and she felt bile rise in her throat. Joe should have warned her.

He was the one who had called her out on how uncomfortable she had been acting around her sister and her kids. He had to know just how hard this would be for her. Especially with the way that talking about everything had been tearing open old wounds recently.

She realised that she'd come to a halt, and only Joe's hold on her hand pulled her forwards.

'Owen, hey, man. Alice, you look gorgeous.' Joe shook his friend's hand and kissed Alice's cheek. 'Guys, this is Charlie.' He'd pulled her to him and wrapped his arm around her waist. He was putting her through this and he didn't even care—didn't even think to try and understand how much this was hurting her.

Alice leaned in and kissed her cheek and Owen shook her hand.

'Congratulations, you two!' Alice said with a friendly smile. 'I can't believe someone's tied this guy down. You deserve a medal, Charlie. I can't wait to hear all the details.'

Charlie tried to return her smile, but felt her facial muscles stiffen into a grimace.

'And who's this?' Joe asked, chucking the baby's cheek and being rewarded by a belly laugh. 'Looks like we should be the ones saying congrats.' Charlie sensed something slightly forced in his cheerful tone. What was he up to?

'This is Lucy,' Alice said, and shifted the baby to hold her out to Joe. 'Want to hold her?'

'Are you sure?' He took the baby awkwardly and held her up to his face, pulling funny faces. Joe with a baby. Charlie watched him closely, trying to work out what he was feeling. His smile was open and straight-forward, and she envied him for it. She wished she could enjoy the sweet, heavy weight of a baby in her arms without being haunted by the inevitable regret and sadness.

'That must have moved quickly, then,' Joe was saying. She struggled to follow the conversation—feeling as if she had missed some vital part. 'The last time I saw you, you were still mired in bureaucracy trying to bring this one home.'

'Our social worker was awesome,' Alice replied. She turned to Lucy with another megawatt smile. 'We've adopted Lucy,' she said.

And the bottom fell out of Charlie's stomach. She stumbled, and the only thing to grab hold of to stop her falling was Joe. Again, goddamn him.

Had he planned this? Manipulated her into meeting this gorgeous family, with their beautiful baby?

Of course he had—that was what she'd heard in his voice. He'd been planning this behind her back. So after everything he had said about her being enough for any man just as she was, and it didn't matter if she could have children or not, here was the proof that he felt otherwise. She'd always known that it was always going to be true in the end.

It was as if he'd not listened to a word she'd said since they'd met. As if he didn't know her.

'L-lovely to meet you,' Charlie managed to stammer, and then she turned and started walking. She didn't even care where she was going. She just had to get out of there. Away from Alice and her gorgeous baby. Away from Joe and his lies and manipulations.

She reached sunshine and fresh air but kept walking, wanting as much distance as she could get between her and Joe. She couldn't remember where the car was so she just walked out. Out as far as she could. Tears threatened at the edges of her eyeliner, but she knew that she must not let them fall. Even now, they had to make this deception work, or what had been the point of any of it? She spotted the VIP car park and headed towards Joe's car. She just wanted to not be here.

The keys. Damn it. Well, maybe there would be someone else leaving and she could hitch a ride—

'Charlie!'

She recognised Joe's voice, her body responded to it—to him—immediately, but she fought it and kept walking. He couldn't possibly have anything to say to her that she would want to hear.

'Charlie, stop. Please!'

Ahead of her, someone was staring at them. She wanted so much not to care. To be a nobody—unrecognisable in a crowd. Someone no one knew or cared about. But she stopped, because she wasn't that person. She could never be that person.

Joe caught up with her, rested his forearms on her

shoulders. God, if he asked her what was wrong, that was it. She was running and crying and she didn't care who saw.

'I'm sorry,' he said. 'I should have warned you that they have a baby.'

She shrugged his arms off her shoulders. He was trying, but he still didn't get it. 'I'm not angry about the baby, Joe. Babies don't make me mad. I'm angry because you tried to manipulate me.'

'Manipulate you? How?'

He'd raised his voice, but then looked around. Remembered where they were.

'Maybe we should talk about this in the car.'

She narrowed her eyes. Right—they needed to protect their secret. He climbed into the car and she sat on the passenger seat, looking straight out ahead, not able to face looking at him properly.

'I should have warned you about the baby,' he said again. 'But I thought I was doing something good. I thought seeing how happy they are to have her would help. That they're a family, even if not by conventional means.'

'So what are you telling me—you want to adopt a kid? Is that your next big idea? Your next publicity campaign? It doesn't matter that I'm damaged goods, because you can always stick a plaster on that?'

'Don't be ridiculous, Charlie. This isn't about me and you know it.'

'Oh, of course, because all this is just for show. It's all about your career.'

'Yours too,' he bit back. 'You make me out to be mercenary, but don't pretend that you're not using me every bit as much as I'm using you.'

He was using her.

Of course he was, she had known that from the start. But to hear him say it like that—no sugar coating—it winded her. And he thought that she was just as bad as him. That she had made a cold, calculated decision to use him. Well, she couldn't let him go on believing that. She wasn't that much of a bitch.

'My career? You know that that wasn't why I married you. Unlike you, I'm not that mercenary. I saw a headline in the news, that night. My parents trying to marry me off to one of those suitable husbands who'd be waiting for his heir and spare. I married you because my family were trying to force me into being the happy wife that I knew I never could be. When I have reminders of my infertility thrust in my face, Joe, I have been known to go a little crazy and act out. I could see the life I had built for myself slipping away and I was so heartbroken I couldn't think straight. That doesn't make us the same.'

CHAPTER ELEVEN

'You were still using me,' Joe said. Charlie rolled her eyes at him, but he was still reeling.

'Oh, because you're such a goddamn expert, are you?' she said. 'Is it all women that you know so well, or is it just me? Because I've been on your telly and in your newspapers my whole life you think you know what I'm feeling.'

'I never said I think I know you—but I think I know something about women. About relationships. I do have some experience of this.'

'Oh, so we're finally going to get to the bottom of this. Good. It was Arabella, I assume, who broke your heart.'

'Nobody said my heart was broken.'

'You scream it without saying a word, Joe. You with your trust issues and fear of commitment. You've already seen every article of my dirty laundry. Are you going to tell me what went on to make you such a cynical son of a b—? Or are we going to carry on trying to work out what's going on with us while having to avoid stepping on the elephant in the room?'

He slapped the steering wheel. Why was she so determined to make this about him—to make him the bad guy? He had been trying to help, and now she wanted to drag up his past as if that had anything to do with what they were arguing about. 'There is no elephant. Arabella and me—it wasn't a big deal. I wasn't heartbroken. If anything I'm grateful to her. She taught me a lot.'

'Like what?'

'Like how relationships actually work—and I don't mean the hearts and flowers rubbish. I'm talking about real adult relationships where both partners are upfront and honest about what they expect.'

'And let me guess, what Arabella expected wasn't just to enjoy your company. What else did she want?'

He tried to wave her off, but he knew that she wasn't going to let this drop. The fastest way out of this argument was just going to be to tell her the truth. Then she'd see that Arabella had nothing to do with any of this.

'She wanted to piss off her parents. She thought that taking me home to meet them would do that.'

Charlie raised her brows. 'And when did you find this out?'

'When we turned up at her house for the weekend. They were perfectly nice to me and Arabella was furious. I think that she thought that one whiff of my accent and they'd be threatening to disinherit her. She'd read too much D H Lawrence.'

'And before that… Were you in love with her?'

He shrugged, because what did it matter how he had felt when he was a naïve eighteen-year-old?

'Before that, I thought things were as simple as being in love with someone. I know better now.'

'That's a pretty cynical way to go through life.'

'Is it? Are you telling me that if you meet a guy you love you'll just marry him—no thinking about real life, your family, your career? Children?'

'I married you, didn't I?'

He didn't know what he could say to that. She had just told him that she hadn't been thinking straight. Surely she couldn't be saying that she loved him. But she didn't deny it either. He shook his head—he had to try and make Charlie understand how Arabella had helped him. That he was happy with his life as it was. Or he had been, until he had met her.

'All I know is that since Arabella, I've not been hurt,' he said. 'Someone tried. Pretended that she wanted me, when all she wanted was something she could sell to the papers. If I'd not learnt my lesson after Arabella, maybe that would have affected my heart too. But I'm a quick study.'

Charlie reached for his hand and absent-mindedly traced the lines of the bones beneath the skin. He tried not to notice, tried not to feel that caress in the pit of his stomach. She was still looking out of the window, and he was cowardly grateful that she wasn't making him do this eye to eye.

'And is that what you want from life?' she asked. 'From the women in your life—just to not get hurt? Or, one day, are you going to want more than that? Are you going to want to risk going all-in? Risk your heart, and see what you get back.'

He let his head fall back against the head rest, and let out a long, slow breath. 'I don't know, Charlie. What could be worth that?'

She turned to face him, and he knew that she was not going to put up with his evasion any more. That all pretence that they were not talking about them now was flying out of the window.

'Are you serious?' she said, her eyes blazing. 'Don't you think that this could be worth it? That *I* could be?'

Her expression was wide open—she was holding nothing back, now. No more secrets. Nowhere left to hide.

'This was meant to be all for show,' he said.

'And yet here we are. We both know we didn't go in to this for the right reasons, Joe. But the more time we spend together, the more I feel this…this pull between us that I've never felt before. And I don't know what to call it. I'm scared to call it love, but nothing else seems to fit.'

'But what do you *want*, Charlie?'

'For God's sake. Why do I have to want anything, Joe, other than you? Why can't you believe that that's enough? I want what we had last night, whispering and laughing in bed together. I want yesterday, at the piano, feeling like I can see into your soul when you play and sing just for me. I want this afternoon, sitting in the sun with my eyes closed and your arms around me, not able to imagine feeling more complete. But what about you? Do you want a string of girls who will give you what you ask for and nothing more, or do you want a relationship? A connection. Something *real*.'

He opened his mouth to speak, but she held up a hand to stop him. He wanted to tell her that of course he wanted all that, but how was he meant to know if that was what she really wanted too? That laying his heart out there in the open felt like asking to have someone come and smash it until there was nothing left.

'I don't want your knee-jerk reaction,' she told him. 'Whatever the answer is going to be, I need to know that you've thought about it. That you mean it.'

They sat in silence for a long minute.

'I think we both need some time,' he said eventually. 'And some space. I don't think you should come back to London,' Joe said. 'Not yet.'

Her face dropped instantly, and he knew that he had hurt her. He reached out to her and softened his expression. 'Go back to your mum. Tell her what you've told me, and make your peace with her. Make your peace with what your parents want for you, and decide, with all your cards on the table, whether it's what you want too. If it is, we'll find a way to get it for you. I'll disappear from your life if that's what you need from me.

'But if you don't…even if, with no secrets, you still want to be married to me? Come home to me, Charlie.'

CHAPTER TWELVE

CHARLIE SAT IN silence as the car sped along the roads that were so familiar to her from her childhood. She had spoken to her mother as soon as she had set off for the airport, and sensed that she wasn't entirely surprised that she was on her way back already.

She still hadn't decided what she wanted to say to her. How she would explain that she loved her parents, all her family, but that she didn't want the life that they had decided on for her.

Now the heat of the argument had faded, she could see that Joe hadn't been cruel to introduce her to his friends. The opposite, in fact. He'd shown her what she should have seen all along. Her ability to bear children or not had never been the problem—if she couldn't have kids naturally that was something that might be sad, and difficult for her and a husband to overcome. But it didn't mean that she could never have a family on her own, and it definitely wasn't a reason not to marry at all.

No, her reason for not marrying the men that her parents had introduced to her was much simpler—she didn't want them.

She didn't want the men, or the families, or the life that they represented.

She didn't want to give up her home in London, or her job, or the pride that she had built in herself and her abilities since she had left home.

She didn't want to go back to Afland just because of a promise she had made when she was eighteen and wanting to leave. Didn't want the life that she had made for herself to be over just because the date on the calendar ticked over and she was twenty-eight years old instead of twenty-seven.

Charlie bit at a nail as the car pulled through the gates of the palace and her hand barely moved from her mouth until she was in her mother's study, sitting on the other side of her expansive desk, feeling more like a job candidate than a daughter. And then she remembered that she was the one who had stalked in here and sat, leaving her mother standing on the other side of the desk, arms raised in greeting.

'So, was there something in particular you needed to talk about, sweetheart?' Adelaide asked, drawing her chair around the desk to sit beside her daughter.

Charlie felt her spine stiffen as she thought about all the things that she'd not said to her mother over the past ten years, not knowing where to start.

'I don't want to come back, Mother. After my birthday. I know I promised I would—'

'That was a long time ago,' her mother interrupted gently. 'I'd hoped that you would want to come back to live here, that your father and I might see a little more of you. But I'm not going to force you. I don't think I could if I wanted to. Now, are you going to tell me what this is really about? Is it Joe? Because we never really had a chance to talk properly before. I thought when you called after the wedding, maybe you had done something that you regretted, but then when you were here...honestly, darling, the atmosphere between you.'

Charlie couldn't help but smile when she thought of him.

'So I'm right,' her mother continued. 'You two are crazy about each other.'

'It's complicated,' Charlie said with a sigh.

'Well, I think it often is.' Her mother gave her an encouraging smile. 'Maybe if you tell me everything, it would help.'

'I wish it would, Mum. But the thing is...' She couldn't believe that she was about to volunteer the information that she'd held secret for so long, that she'd had nightmares about her mother finding out. What if she did react as she had in her dreams? Pushing her out of the family, banishing her from the island of Afland for ever? But wasn't that what Charlie had done to herself? She'd all but cut herself off from her family—her mother couldn't do any worse than that. She took a deep breath, squeezed her fingernails into her palms and spoke.

'The thing is, I might not be able to have children.' The words tumbled from her mouth in a hurry, and she kept her gaze locked on the surface of the desk, unable to meet her mother's eye.

Adelaide reached for her hand, and held it softly in her lap. 'I'm so sorry, darling. That must be terribly hard for you. And is having children important to Joe?'

'No.' She shook her head, and finally lifted her

gaze to meet her mum's eyes. The gentle kindness and love on her face made a sob rise in her throat, but she forced it down, wanting to finish what she'd started. Wanting, more than anything, her mum's advice. 'He says… It doesn't matter, does it? It's not about Joe. It's about me, it's about the fact that I'm never going to be who you want me to be.'

'I just want you to be *you*, darling. And more than that, I just want you to be happy.'

But that was crap, because she'd seen for herself what her mum wanted for her. A suitable husband, marriage, babies. 'Then what was all that with Philippe?' she asked, an edge to her voice. 'Why was he talking about engagements and moving to Afland with your blessing? Why did I have to read about it in the paper?'

'Honestly, Charlie, after all this time how can you believe anything that you read? Philippe came for dinner with his parents and he asked if you were still single. You know that he'd always had a soft spot for you. Then his father asked if you were planning on moving back to Afland. I don't know where he got the rest of it from. If I know his father as well as I think I do, the story probably came directly from him. I'm sorry that the press team weren't able to keep his mouth under control. I'm not going to lie and say that I haven't thought that you might be happier if you moved home and made a good match. It's kept your father and I happy for thirty-odd years, and your sister fairly blissful for the last seven. But we were never going to force you. Did you really think that we would?'

Yes, she had. She'd thought that there was only

one way that she could make her parents happy and proud of her, but she could see from her mum's face that she'd got it wrong.

'No, I don't think you'd force me, Mum.' She stayed silent for a moment. 'I'm sorry that I've not been home much.' Her mum wrapped an arm around her shoulders. 'But seeing Verity, and the children…'

'That must have been hard.'

'I just knew that that might never happen for me, and if it doesn't then where do I fit in this family?'

Adelaide squeezed her shoulders and reached for a tissue from the silver dispenser on her desk. 'You're my little girl, Charlie. That's where you fit. Where you'll always fit. But maybe things aren't as bad as they seem. Have you seen a doctor about it?'

'Not since I first found out. I didn't want to talk about it, didn't want the press getting hold of anything.'

'Well,' Adelaide said. 'How about I set up an appointment with my personal doctor, and you can have some tests? At least then you might know where you stand. If you knew the secrets that man had kept for me…well, let's just say I know that he can be discreet.'

'And if I definitely can't have children?' Charlie asked, a shake in her voice.

'Then it won't change the way I feel about you even a tiny bit, Charlie. Surely you know that. I just want you to be happy. Is Joe making you happy?'

'He's trying. I'm trying.'

'That's good. Keep trying, both of you.'

Charlie looked up and smiled at her mum, and could see from her expression that they weren't finished yet.

'What, Mum? I know there's something else you want to say.'

'I just… I'd like to see you at home more, darling. I know that you want to stay in London. I know how important your career is. But it doesn't have to be all or nothing. You could come back to visit more. We'd love to see you. And maybe you could do a few official engagements. I can't tell you how much I've missed you.'

Charlie plugged in her headphones as she climbed into the car and cued up the tracks that Joe had sent her. They had only been apart for a night—nothing in the grand scheme of things—but the already so familiar resonance and tone of his voice managed to relax her muscles in a way she didn't know was possible. She closed her eyes as the car crept along the London streets from the airport, drumming her fingers in time to the music in her ears, remembering the morning they'd been in the music room, sitting at the piano where she'd taken lessons as a girl, next to a man who made her skin sing.

Was it pathetic that she'd broken into a smile as soon as she'd seen his name on her phone?

She tapped at the screen to bring the message up again.

Call me when you get in.

Did he mean it? Or was it just a pleasantry? Like, *Call me when you get in, but obviously not if it's late, or inconvenient. Maybe just leave it till morning.*

Ugh. She was irritating herself, sounding like one

of those pink glitter princesses she'd tried all her life not to be.

She shot off a text, the traditional middle ground between calling and not calling, telling him she'd landed and was heading back to her place. It was too much to just turn up on his doorstep, especially when she wasn't even sure that he wanted her there.

The car twisted through the darkened streets of the city, over brightly lit dual carriageways, past the twisted metal of the helter-skelter sculpture in Stratford, and on towards her flat.

Her stomach sank at the thought of another night sleeping without Joe. She told herself that a month ago she'd been perfectly happy barely aware that he existed. But that had all changed the minute that she had set eyes on him, and they couldn't change that now. Somehow, she knew that without him her flat would feel empty, even though he'd never set foot there before.

As the car approached the stuccoed, pillared front of her apartment building, she spotted a dark shadow on the front steps and her stomach lurched. She glanced back through the windshield, checking that the police officers she knew should be on her tail were there, and breathed a sigh of relief when she saw one of the officers speaking into a radio.

Just as the driver asked her over the intercom whether she wanted him to drive on, the headlights illuminated the steps, throwing light onto Joe's face, and shadows into the space behind him. She let out the breath she had been holding, and told the driver that it was fine, he could stop. She took a moment before she opened the door to gather herself, prepare for what might come with Joe.

Had he come to tell her that he wanted her? That he wanted to make this a real marriage, or that he wanted out?

'Hi,' she said as she stepped out of the car and up the steps.

'Hey,' Joe replied, giving nothing away.

She grabbed her bag from the driver and stepped past Joe, unlocking the door and pushing it open.

She reached down to grab the mail and then dumped it on the hallway table, glancing round and trying to remember what state she'd left the place in. She didn't normally care about the condition of the flat, as long as it was warm and watertight. She had spent her whole childhood and adolescence looking forward to the freedom of space that was entirely her own. But there was something selfish and lonely about that, about the fact that she didn't have to consider a single person's feelings except her own. Maybe that was why she felt irrationally pleased that the worst of the mess had been bundled into bags and carted over to Joe's place. Her flat was usually her sanctuary but today it felt cold and unloved, and for a second she thought about the warm exposed brick and softly waxed wood of Joe's warehouse and felt a pull of something like homesickness.

She shook herself as she crossed to the windows and pulled back the curtains and blinds and opened a window. It was just feeling a bit neglected in here, because she hadn't been home for a few days, she reasoned. It was nothing a bit of fresh air and the warm light of a few lamps wouldn't fix.

'Want a drink?' she called out to Joe—anything

to stall actual, meaningful conversation. She grabbed them both a beer from the fridge and handed one to him.

'Nice place,' Joe said. Small talk. Good—she could handle small talk. She had plenty of formal training. Or maybe it had been bred into her. Either way, she grabbed his opening gambit and held onto it like a raft.

She chatted about the flat. How she'd chosen it for the big south-facing windows. The French doors out into the shared garden. The view of the park and lack of traffic noise from the front. She sounded like a desperate estate agent trying to close a sale.

Opening the French doors, she took her beer out to the patio, dropping onto one of the chairs and propping her knees against the edge of the little bistro table. The fairy lights her upstairs neighbour had threaded through the boughs of the trees twinkled at them, creating a scene she could have found in a fairy tale.

Shivering, she wished she'd grabbed her jacket, but she was too bone-tired to move.

'You're right, it's quiet out here,' Joe said, following her. 'Peaceful, and pretty. I can see why you like it so much.'

She looked up and met his eye, trying to judge if he was being sarcastic. But he looked genuine. He sat in the seat beside her, his thighs spread wide as he leaned back and let out a sigh.

'Long trip back,' he commented. 'For both of us.'

She 'hmm-ed' in agreement.

'Lots of time to think,' he added.

She looked up at him, wondering if this was it. When all their tiptoeing finally stopped and they decided if they wanted to run from the relationship they'd both been fighting from the first.

'Come to any conclusions?' she asked.

She wasn't sure she even wanted to know, because, whatever the answer, she knew that they still had a lot of work to do. He could declare his undying love for her this minute and that wouldn't remove a single one of the obstacles in their way. Still, even the thought of it made the hairs on her arms stand up.

'You're cold,' Joe said, stripping off his jacket and handing it to her. She draped it round her shoulders, refusing to acknowledge how delicious it felt to be wrapped in the warm, supple leather that smelt of him.

'I care about you, Charlie. I think you know that I do. But it's not as simple as that, is it?'

'I don't think that it ever is.'

'Honestly, after Arabella, and then the kiss and tell, when I'd picked myself up and convinced myself it hadn't been that bad, I thought I'd cracked it. That I'd finally figured out how these things work. And I've had no reason to doubt that I was right. What I was doing—it was working for me. Honestly, I've had no complaints.'

'So that's what—'

'Please, let me finish,' he said with a gentle smile. 'It was great, until I saw you watching me from the side of the stage in Las Vegas, and I felt something so overwhelming I still don't have the words to describe it. And I told myself that getting married was a great joke, or a killer career move or… I don't know. I told myself it was about anything except falling in love with you before I'd even said hello.'

Her heart pounded. She was desperate to say something, to ask if that was what he felt now—love. But he'd asked her for space to talk, and he deserved that.

'But I was kidding myself. I love you, Charlie. I think you knew that before I did.'

She let out the breath she had been holding, her thoughts whizzing by so fast it was impossible to concentrate on just one of them.

He sat watching her for a moment, and then grinned. 'That's it. I'm done,' he said. 'Twenty-four hours' thinking and that's all I've worked out. Say anything you like.

'Did you speak to your mum?' he asked eventually, his face falling when she couldn't think of what to say in response.

She nodded, still searching for the words. 'It was good,' she said eventually. 'I think… I think I got a lot of things wrong.'

'About me?'

She smiled, tempted to call him out on his self-centredness that only a rock star could get away with.

'About family, about children, about myself.' She looked up and met his eye. 'Yes, probably a few things wrong about you too.' She sighed, knowing that she was going to have to dig deeper than that. For so long, she'd kept as much as she could get away with to herself, but Joe deserved more than that from her.

'I'm not going back, to Afland. Well, not properly. I told my mum I'd take on some official duties, but my life will be here, Joe. I'm staying in London. And I hope to God that it's with you, because I've missed you like… I don't know. Like I suddenly lost my hearing and there was no music in the world.'

Now it was her turn to squirm, looking into her

man's eyes as she waited for him to reply. 'Is that what you want, Joe?'

'I want you, Charlie. Any way I can have you. Is that enough?'

She leaned forwards and pressed a hard kiss against his lips, gasping with pleasure as his hands wound around her waist under the warm leather of his jacket. 'It's enough,' she managed to whisper between kisses. 'We can make it enough—if we both want it.' His arms pulled tighter around her waist and she moved away from him for just a split second, and then she was sitting on top of him, her legs straddled around him and the chair. He leaned back, meeting her eyes as she settled on top of him. 'We're doing this?' he asked.

She answered him with a kiss.

EPILOGUE

'YOU KNOW, YOU HAVEN'T said it,' Joe said sleepily, brushing a strand of her hair back from her shoulder. He pulled the duvet up around them and Charlie in close, settling her in the crook of his arm as he laid his head on the pillow.

'Said what?'

Her eyes were shut, her body loose and languid, and her voice so sleepy she barely formed words.

'You know what.'

She opened her eyes and looked up at him, a teasing smile on her lips. 'I can't say it now that you've asked.'

Joe pressed a kiss into her hair. 'I don't need you to. But, you know, tomorrow, if you happened to feel the urge…'

'I predict lots of urges, tomorrow.' She smiled wickedly. 'It's a long, long list. But if that's the one that you want to put at the top…'

If he'd had any energy left, he would have rolled on top of her and taken care of a few of those urges right now. But instead he pinched her waist. 'Give me an hour's sleep and I'll put myself entirely in your hands.'

'Good. Exactly where I want you. Later,' she said,

with another kiss against his chest. 'I think there's something we need to talk about first.'

He sighed sleepily. 'I thought we were done talking.'

She shuffled away from him on the bed, pulling up the sheets to try and find some modesty.

'It's important, Joe,' she said, and he opened his eyes properly at the serious tone of her voice. 'There's a lot we didn't talk about. Children for one. It's not a fun conversation, but we have to have it. I'm going to see my mum's doctor, but there are no guarantees. What if it never happens for us?'

He rubbed his face and sat up. 'If it comes to that, Charlie, we'll deal with it. Together. There are other ways to have a family.'

'Is it what you want?' she asked, a wobble in her voice. 'Because I don't know if adoption is something that I could take on. With my family, the succession, it's complicated.'

He kissed her on the forehead, smoothing a hand down her spine. 'I know that. But no, it doesn't matter to me. You're what matters to me.'

'But I might never have a family, Joe. And there's no point taking this any further if that's not something that you can live with. If you're always going to want more.'

He stopped her with a kiss on the lips. 'The only thing I want in my future is you,' he said, between kisses. 'We're going to travel the world. We're going to make beautiful music. We're going to party until we can't take any more. If children come along, the more the merrier. But nothing, *nothing* is going to make me a happier man than knowing that you will come home with me every night, and wake up with me every morning.'

'I love you,' she whispered, and he smiled as he squeezed her tight and pressed a kiss against her hair. She ran her hands over his chest, and he stretched, bringing their bodies into contact from where she had propped herself on his chest right down to their toes.

'And I love you too. Now, are we making a start on that list of yours?'

* * * * *

COMING SOON!

We really hope you enjoyed reading this book. If you're looking for more romance, be sure to head to the shops when new books are available on

Thursday 4th April

To see which titles are coming soon, please visit

millsandboon.co.uk/nextmonth

LET'S TALK
Romance

For exclusive extracts, competitions
and special offers, find us online:

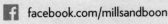